The Lost Garden

London-reared of Irish parents, Kate Kerrigan worked in London before moving to Ireland in 1990. Her books have been widely acclaimed – *Recipes for a Perfect Marriage* was shortlisted for the Romantic Novelist of the Year Award and *Ellis Island* was a TV Book Club Summer Read. She is now a full-time writer and lives in County Mayo with her husband and sons.

Praise for Kate Kerrigan

'This story is written with so much heart'   Cecelia Ahern

'A feel-good story about love, freedom, belonging and the meaning of home'   *Stylist*

'An enjoyable romantic tale that you'll want to devour in one sitting'   *She*

'This book is one to keep. Anyone who reads it will return to it, time and again, either for the story or to seek out one of the many old recipes'   *Ireland on Sunday*

'Both wholesome and satisfying'   *Heat*

Also by Kate Kerrigan

Recipes for a Perfect Marriage
The Miracle of Grace
Ellis Island
City of Hope
Land of Dreams

The
Lost
Garden

KATE KERRIGAN

MACMILLAN

First published 2014 by Macmillan
an imprint of Pan Macmillan, a division of Macmillan Publishers Limited
Pan Macmillan, 20 New Wharf Road, London N1 9RR
Basingstoke and Oxford
Associated companies throughout the world
www.panmacmillan.com

ISBN 978-1-4472-1080-1

1 3 5 7 9 8 6 4 2

A CIP catalogue record for this book is available from the British Library.

Typeset by Ellipsis Digital Limited, Glasgow
Printed and bound by CPI Group (UK) Ltd, Croydon, CR0 4YY

Visit **www.panmacmillan.com** to read more about all our books
and to buy them. You will also find features, author interviews and
news of any author events, and you can sign up for e-newsletters
so that you're always first to hear about our new releases.

For Johnny Ferguson,
1963–2013

'There are only two ways to live your life.
One is as though nothing is a miracle.
The other is as though everything is a miracle.'

—ALBERT EINSTEIN

Prologue

Spring 1942

It was a quiet day at sea. Jimmy Walsh allowed the boat to float a little across the shallow bay and then called for his cousin Tom to anchor her there. On either side of them, wide purple mountains stretched up to the clear blue sky, and in front of them was a small beach whose narrow shoreline was hemmed with a glittering chain of sharp sunlight. Usually when the weather was glorious like this the sea itself could be unsettled, seeming to bounce with small, excited waves. Today, however, the sea was eerily still, like gliding on glass.

The boat, a Galway hooker, belonged to Jimmy's cousin, and they were taking it for a spin round the coast. Tom didn't know the islands like Jimmy did: the eager young fisherman had spent most of his nineteen years weaving in and out of these large rocks and small shorelines catching mackerel with his father. Yet even Jimmy did not recognize the white-rimmed beach ahead of them, or the imposing purple mountains either side of it. The speedy hooker had carried them further down the coast than he had ever been before and he wasn't entirely certain of where they were. Mayo, in all probability, though the scattering of smaller islands they had just passed suggested they could be even further south on the edges of Galway. In any case, this was as good a place as any to bob around while they put down the sails. They'd stop here for an hour and have some lunch before heading back up the coast to Aghabeg.

His mother had packed a hunk of bread and some smoked fish for them. She'd also filled two porter bottles with tea – although Jimmy smiled as he opened the basket and found that his father, Sean, had sneaked in two bottles of real porter as well.

The older man would have justified slipping the lads a beer by telling himself this was a celebration of sorts. His brother's eldest son, Tom, had been living and working in Galway for the past five years and already had a third share in this fine commercial fishing vessel. A far cry from the small, shallow currachs that had served his family of fishermen well enough on the islands – a Galway hooker would put them into an entirely different league altogether. Sean Walsh and Tom's father, Joe, were close to having raised enough money between them to buy in. A boat like this working the Donegal coastline could transform not only the lives of their own family, but of all four families on their small island.

Jimmy drained the last mouthful of the bitter black beer. Looking upwards, he thought that, despite the stillness, the sky looked uncertain today. A couple of dark clouds that seemed to threaten rain began to move towards the shoreline. Driven across by a gust of wind, they miraculously parted, allowing a shaft of sunshine to burn down onto the beach. He noticed something odd to one side of the strand, a strange movement – like a fire. It was too far away to see, but he was curious, so he picked up his telescope and adjusted it towards the beach. He trained the instrument past the small waves foaming along the shoreline, some rocks and a pecking gull until it reached the confusing movement. The red mass was lost in a blast of sunlight and he screwed up his eyes to try and see what it was. Not flames – darker. A spray of seaweed stuck to something perhaps? As the clouds moved behind the mountain, the picture sharpened and revealed the frantic flickering of a girl's long auburn hair blowing in the wind. A hand drew up and slid the snaking strands back from her pale young face.

Jimmy's breath stopped. She was the most beautiful thing he had ever seen.

Chapter One

Aileen crumbled her final handful of good soil over the tomato plants. She had just finished planting them in the wide raised bed that her brother Martin had made for her that morning. She had asked him to put it to the side of their cottage that faced the mountain so that her vegetables might benefit from its shelter. Although it was spring, the sea wind that blew across from the west side of the island could still rear up: last year, she had lost a full bed of lettuces when a bruising spit of salt from a short summer storm had battered across them. She looked down at the fledgling seedlings, gently pulling her fingers up the feathered stalks. She held her hands to her face; she could already smell the fruit in these tiny fragile plants. Barely there, as slender as blades of grass, as flimsy as the red hairs on her head and yet already somewhere inside them these delicate plants she had grown from seed were making good on their promise to produce huge globes of heavy fruit.

'Would you look at them tomatoes,' her father would say, slicing through them with his own sharp knife at the teatime table. 'Is there another man on this earth whose daughter could produce the likes of that for the table?'

Aileen was glad when she made her father happy, and she enjoyed seeing her mother cook her vegetables and her brothers tucking noisily into platefuls of her spuds, but what Aileen enjoyed most about gardening was simply watching things come to life.

The summers were so long with her father and brothers away in Scotland picking potatoes to earn enough money to see them through the long winter on this rocky outpost off the Irish coast. With Aileen and her mother left at home in their remote cottage without their men, growing vegetables and flowers gave Aileen something to do when her monthly supply of books from the mobile library ran out.

It also gave her somewhere to go when she needed to escape her mother's moods. Anne Doherty was often sad when the men were away, and when her mother grew mournful, Aileen felt a shadow fall over her very soul. Then if something went wrong, like Anne broke a cup or cut her finger while peeling an onion, she would often shout out, 'Why must your father go away like this? I need him here!' and Aileen would go outside for a while until her mother's temper had passed. Sometimes she would pick a bunch of clambering hedgerow roses and put them in a jar on the kitchen windowsill, knowing that their scent would bring some sweetness back into their home.

The bed her brother Martin had built was too wide and too deep for the tomatoes and he had thrown in lumps of terrible stony clay. Aileen had done her best to crumble some life into the heavy soil, breaking it up with sand, but she was still worried for her tiny strips of green. Their roots would be overwhelmed, she thought as she poked the translucent threads into the hard, sandy soil. Their hold on life was too tenuous; they needed something to help them along. Something strong and sturdy to hold them in place and fill them with the nourishment they needed to survive.

Seaweed.

Aileen called out to her parents and ran down to the beach, ten minutes at a fast run across the fields and bog towards the back of the dunes. She came to the narrow path between the two highest dunes and paused for a minute, as she always did, to close her eyes. She liked to relish the moment when the sea became visible, opening up in front of her, filling her nose with the scent of possibility. The sea was Aileen's window on the world; beyond it was where her life was waiting for her. She opened her eyes, drank in the view, then walked through the white, powdery sand towards the rocks at the shoreline. It was a still day, so the seaweed would be easy to harvest from the shallow rock pools at the water's edge.

Every day Aileen walked down to this beach and stood here gazing out across the vast Atlantic, thinking about the day when she might leave the island. Would she learn to drive a car? Travel to America? Work in a factory? She would surely fall in love like the heroines of the books she read. Who would be the man of her dreams then? Would he be an angry Englishman like Heathcliff or a distinguished American writer like Ernest Hemingway?

As she idly dreamed of her future, Aileen gathered armfuls of the rubbery brown kelp into a pile on the sand. Then, as she leaned down to tie them into a bundle to carry home on her back, she noticed a pile of seed pods sitting on the stone next to them. They were peculiar-looking things, long and brown, the length and width of her thumb and like nothing she had seen before. As she popped them in her pocket, she had the strangest feeling that she was being watched. Aileen stood up to look around, but as she did, she felt a gust of wind flicker across her hair and so she closed her eyes and threw back her head, shaking the hair from her face and allowing the air to catch every strand.

'Aileen? Aileen! Come back! What till you hear . . .'

It was her brother Martin.

He would be leaving for Scotland with her father and Paddy
Junior any day now and she would not see them for three long
months; what was she doing down here on the beach mooching
and dreaming when she should be relishing every last minute of
her time with them?

She ran towards Martin, but he kept his stout, sturdy legs
one pace ahead of her, laughing and refusing to tell her what
the 'news' was. When they reached the cottage, her father, Paddy,
and eldest brother, Paddy Junior, were standing with their arms
crossed over their broad chests, looking at her, smiling.

'Come out, Anne.' Her father turned his head slightly on its
thick, solid neck and called for her mother.

Anne came out, wiping her hands on her apron and not looking
nearly as happy as the men.

Aileen had some idea of what was coming, but she was afraid
even to dream such a thing.

'Who'll tell her, Da?' said Martin.

'I dunno,' said her father. 'Will you tell her, Paddy Junior?'

'Maybe I will,' his elder son said then, picking up on the joke,
'and maybe I won't.'

Patrick Doherty turned, his face full of mischief, from one
son to the other and said, 'Should we tell her at all, do you
think, lads, or leave the surprise for another day again?'

Aileen loved it when they teased her like this. She felt like
Queen of the World when her father and brothers made her the
centre of attention.

'Will you tell the child, for God's sake?' shouted Anne. 'I have
the tea on.'

'We're leaving for Scotland tomorrow,' said Paddy Junior.

Then his younger brother added, 'And we're taking you with
us.'

Chapter Two

Jimmy knew that red-haired women were bad luck for fish-ermen.

If you passed a red-haired woman on the road before heading out for the day, you might as well pack up your nets and go home. Ditto a red-haired man, or a child in fact – all red hair was a no-no. Jimmy's grandmother had told him that a red-haired infant had once been born to an otherwise entirely black-haired family. The whole lot of them, three generations of islanders, left Aghabeg before the child was six days old and moved to the mainland, never to be seen or heard of again. Jimmy's grandmother believed them all surely dead at the hands of the fairies, or otherwise that they had drowned the baby and then escaped to England, which amounted to the same thing. Red hair was a curse, whichever way you looked at it. Jimmy knew that, but he didn't believe it. He might have thought there was some truth to it if it was the only thing people on his island were suspicious of – except that red hair was only the tip of it. The men wouldn't like any class of woman near them when they were mending their nets. The eldest woman of the house, no matter what her age or how harsh the elements, had to throw a hot coal from her home fire directly after the boats when they were leaving land. Indeed, they could only leave when the sun was set a certain way in the sky so that you would be facing it but not too directly. There were so many things that could bring bad luck on a fisherman that if you believed it all, it would surely be the most dangerous job in the world.

It was a line of thinking with which Jimmy frequently tortured his father, Sean. 'If you ever let on that you think that in front of your grandmother,' Sean would say, because big man and all that he was, he was still afeard of his mother, 'so help me but I'll throw you overboard myself for the sharks and the gulls!'

'Ah – but I'll be swum ashore before they can get me, Da.'

Then his father would raise a mock fist at his incorrigible son, and if he could catch him, hold his head in a lock and make the pup confess he was not 'invincible'.

Invincible Jim.

That was the nickname his carefree son had earned himself at the age of eleven, when he had been caught teaching himself to swim.

No one on the island swam. Swimming was the worst thing a fisherman could learn to do, because if the sea wanted to take you, it would. There was no escape in being able to swim – you were just prolonging the inevitable. The fishermen of Aghabeg respected the might of the sea alongside the might of God Himself. They worked in tandem. To try and save a drowning man, even a member of your own beloved crew, was an act of treason against both.

Yet, knowing all of this, on the summer he turned eleven years old, Jimmy Walsh had, without giving warning or notice of any kind, jumped into the deep, clear water at the edge of the rocky path down to where the men kept their currachs; then, using his arms and legs to propel himself upwards, he had pushed his head through the wall of freezing water and held himself there, kicking his legs and screaming with delight. As family and neighbours stood open-mouthed in a mixture of shock and awe at the immediacy with which this young boy had conquered the water, Jimmy splashed around laughing and feeling on top of the world while his father roared at him to get out.

'Perhaps he's special,' his mother had said that night, when his father complained about his son's insubordination.

'Perhaps he's a fool that'll get us all killed,' Sean mumbled, although nobody had said anything against the child, and that was Sean's main concern.

Secretly Sean wondered sometimes if the talk and superstitious nature of the island women wasn't worse in itself than the dangers they constantly predicted, that the fears they inspired were worse than the fate itself could ever be. On a still summer's day fishing near the shoreline, he would surely prefer a son who could find his way back into the boat with the strength of his arms and legs rather than surrender to the depths, sinking slowly out of sight while men watched on, helpless – bereft. Sean suspected that believing was the undoing of his fishing community, that it stopped them from doing all that could be done to protect themselves, and perhaps also from being all they could be. However, Sean kept his reservations to himself. The island was small and there was no value in upsetting people.

So his rebellious son became Invincible Jim, an exception to the no-swimming rule – a sort of lucky charm for the island's fishermen. He was too young and too likeable for anyone to think badly of him, so his defiance of the sea simply proved to the islanders that young Jimmy Walsh was blessed with good luck.

So when Jimmy saw the beautiful girl flicking her long red hair on the beach, he saw no reason not to steer the hooker in a bit closer to land, at least far enough so that he might swim in.

He put this to his cousin Tom, who was having none of it.

'Are you mad in the head, Jimmy? I have to get this baby back into port by teatime or I'll be skinned. We're cutting it fine for getting you back home as it is, and anyway, I can't see anyone out there.'

Jimmy held up the telescope again. She was gone. Curse and damn his stupid cousin for distracting him. He shouldn't have taken his eyes off her for a second. What direction had she gone in? She can't have gone too far, anyway. He started to unbutton his shirt.

'Don't you even think about it.' Tom was considerably more suspicious by nature and sceptical about Jimmy's 'lucky' status. 'We have no idea what the pull is like on the water around here. This coastline is full of shoals and sandspits – you wouldn't know what's happening under the water.'

'I'll be fine,' Jimmy said, so impatient with the buttons he was already pulling the shirt off over his head.

'Oh no, you don't.' Larger and a good deal stronger than his wiry young cousin, Tom grabbed him and held the struggling teenager down on the bench. 'I'm not going back to your father to explain how I lost you to a mirage of a woman,' and as the shirtless youth struggled wildly against him, he added, 'happy and all as I'd be to see you drown . . . Jesus!'

Jimmy had bit his arm and in one swift movement set himself free and dived overboard.

It took longer than usual for Jimmy's face to surface, especially as he had barely remembered to draw breath properly before diving in. He spat out a mouthful of saltwater and, grimacing, checked the shoreline ahead of him. There was still no sign of her. No matter. He'd find her – and he began to swim. He had not taken six strokes when he felt what seemed like hands pulling him down under the water, except that he knew it wasn't hands; it was a whirlpool gathering around his legs. The waters around Aghabeg were predictable. When they were still on the surface, they were still beneath. This was different. He'd move free, though – it was only wat—

As he was pulled beneath the surface with an almighty tug, he heard his cousin cry, 'Grab this, Jimmy. Grab it . . .'

Flailing around – down, down, down – drowning, Jimmy – don't breathe in – don't drown, Jimmy – something hard and sharp hit the side of his head and he reached up and grabbed it as his cousin pulled him up, up, up, bringing Invincible Jim to the surface of the water and over to the boat. Every bone in Jimmy's body wanted to let go of the anvil and try to swim ashore again, but he was woozy from the hit to the side of the head, and he wasn't sure if it was worth risking his life again – for a girl? And a red-haired one at that?

As Tom dragged him up the side of the hooker, roaring at his stupid cousin for his foolhardiness, Jimmy smiled as broad and bold a smile as his face had seen in nineteen years.

Ah, but yes. She would have been worth it surely.

Chapter Three

Aileen patted the last of the seaweed down on top of the compost where she had planted the seeds from the pods that she had found on the beach. Then she carefully placed the shallow tray between the vegetable bed and the low stone wall where it would get maximum shelter. What would happen to these strange seeds in the next three months? What would they grow into, and how would *she* have altered when she came back to claim them?

Aileen felt that she had been waiting for this moment all her life; at sixteen, she was finally leaving Illaunmor.

Although they would all be coming back in three months' time, the young girl knew her first trip away from the island would change everything. Her oldest brother, Paddy Junior, had left for his first summer in Scotland as a boy of fourteen and come back a man with hair on his arms and a voice as deep as a holy well. As the youngest, and the only girl, everyone in the house had always treated Aileen like a child. By working in the world and earning money, she would be making the transition from girl to young woman.

That night, Aileen went into the bedroom and crawled in between her two brothers' warm bodies. Familiar with the rigours of the journey they were facing the next day, Paddy Junior and

Martin were already asleep, but Aileen was too excited to close her eyes.

She looked up at the soot-blackened ceiling as clouds of her brothers' warm breath wafted past her in the chilly spring night and thought how tomorrow she would be leaving for somewhere else, somewhere beyond Illaunmor – to enter a world so thrilling it was beyond her imagination.

The young woman lay awake for all of the night, her stomach twisting with excitement, her toes curling, waiting until it was time to get up, dressed and spend the day doing her chores before she and the Doherty men left for the night train at dusk.

The family spent the day leaving the house in good order for her mother – doing the heavy work that needed to be done before they left. The men dug out the vegetable field, stacked the turf in neat piles by the back door and cleared out the chimney, while Aileen swept and scrubbed the stone floors, washed and hung out the sheets to dry – jobs done willingly because she knew the repetitive boredom of this household drudgery would soon be behind her.

Now that this reality was upon her, Aileen suddenly had a pang of fear. This house and the patch of land that ran down to the road were all she knew. What would happen to her vegetable patch while she was away? Would her mother remember to keep the herbs trimmed back? Would she bother to plant out the carrots to be ready for the end of summer when they got back? Aileen put childish worries about her precious garden out of her mind and looked around the cottage. Although she knew she would be back in a few months, she was anxious that she had never eaten a meal, or lit a fire, or swept a floor in any place other than this house. It was all so familiar; she knew every inch, every detail. The long wooden table with a dip in the centre where it had been scrubbed down by generations of

Doherty women; the dresser against the corner wall with the good blue and white china jug and teapot they were never allowed to touch; the picture of the Sacred Heart above the fire mantel – his forlorn face streaked with turf dust – and the pot oven where Aileen had burned her first loaf of bread aged ten. On the hook by the fire was the grey and green pinafore her mother had ingeniously made for her from an old woollen blanket three years ago. She loved that pinafore and wore it doing all her chores. Aileen washed it every month, scrubbing it extra hard on the washboard and using a cupful of the expensive soapsuds her mother had hidden under the sink, instead of the cheaper bar of carbolic they used for everything else. The wool was thin and soft as silk now, and Aileen had planned to bring it with her, but last night, her father had said it would be too bulky to carry: 'We must travel light, Aileen, and besides, picking potatoes is warm work – you'll be roasted alive in that thing.'

Aileen resigned herself to leaving her apron behind, even though she sensed her mother wanted her to bring it to Scotland – perhaps as a talisman. The fact that Aileen was going meant that her mother would be left alone on the island for three long months. Aileen felt guilty about that, especially as she felt, more and more with each passing year, less inclined towards her mother's company.

Their neighbour John Joe was waiting outside to bring them down to the bridge to meet the rest of the squad. From there they would walk to the station to catch the overnight train to Dublin Port, then the boat the following morning.

With the sun low in the sky and the air cooled, the moment had come to leave. Her father was calling for her to get into the cart, her brothers complaining John Joe's horse was getting antsy (John Joe was too quiet a man to complain for himself), but Aileen had begun to feel giddy and faint. She had not eaten a spoonful of food all day – despite her mother putting the last of the sugar on her oatmeal for her – and her excitement had turned into a kind of sickness.

'Did you pack your rosary?' Aileen's mother was fussing over her, but the young islander was too excited to care. 'Here they are.' Anne picked her pink glass beads up from the dresser where they were always left and put them round her daughter's neck, tucking them inside her geansaí and buttoning up her coat for her. 'There now, child,' she said, and kissed her. 'Small wonder you look so pale and wanting leaving these behind.'

In that moment Aileen felt so tired that she just wanted to lie down on the settle and have her mother put a woollen blanket over her and sing her to sleep.

'Pray to her every morning and night, Aileen, and the Blessed Virgin will keep you safe.'

'For the love of God, woman, hurry up!' Paddy was anxious to get going.

Both women turned towards the doorway. The house faced east to the Atlantic, and as the sun was lowering in the sky, it suddenly sent a shaft of deep orange light piercing through the open door that was so strong it seemed to trap them inside with its warm intensity. It appeared to Aileen, in her overtired state, that the outside world was on fire.

'I've changed my mind. I want to stay here.'

Anne took her daughter's face in both her hands, and using her thumbs to stroke back some strands of auburn that had escaped from her side plaits, she smiled gently and said, 'Whist, my girl, you'll be fine – and back before you know it. Now go.'

Then she prodded her gently out through the door. Aileen held out her hands for Martin to pull her up onto the cart, and even as her feet left the ground, steadying themselves on the wooden step, she felt the excitement of the past few days returning.

They trundled down along the stony boreen towards the road and Aileen looked back at her family home. Her mother was standing by the door waving them off. They would be home in three months, when the summer that was just about to start was all but ended. One season, yet it seemed like a lifetime.

Chapter Four

One season tattie-hoking in Scotland would guarantee the Walshes enough money to buy into Tom's Galway hooker and young Jimmy desperately wanted in on that boat.

One day out in it was all he had needed. The speed of it! The sturdiness! On a good day, the currach would take you a mile out to sea. If God was kind and the nets were good, you'd come straight back in. If not, you could be drifting around in small helpless circles and return empty-handed. The hooker would take you as far out as you could go – until you found the fish yourself – then hold you there until you carried in such a haul you'd have to go to Galway itself to find a trader big enough to buy it from you. 'You'd never have a bad day's fishing in a hooker,' he told his father. If you wanted, she could carry you as far as Dublin. Jimmy, invincible as he was, thought perhaps he could drive the beauty all the way to England and back again. America maybe! There was even a cabin with a bed on board. It was like a house! A man could live in a boat like that and adventure all round the world. He didn't say that to his father, but nonetheless Sean had not taken much convincing that the hooker was the way forward for them as a family of fishermen. 'I can handle it easy, and we could fish the whole coastline, Da. We'd never be short a load again.'

Jimmy was restless. Sean could see that his feisty son was not going to be content with life as a small currach fisherman. It was a miracle he was still here with them at nineteen, that he had not gone to England seeking adventure. A new boat would mean his son could be off down along the coast catching and selling fish in Galway and Cork even. He could find a wife and bring her home. A bigger boat was the only way to keep their status quo and ensure Jimmy a happy future.

Sean's wife, Morag, wasn't so sure.

'What do we need another boat for?' she said, when Sean told her his plans to go back to Scotland with Jimmy for a season. 'Aren't we good enough as we are? A family can only eat so much food, and we've enough meat cured and enough fish smoked to see us through the winter and the season's barely begun!'

'A bigger boat will change things. A bigger boat could make things better for the whole island. It's progress.'

'My eye,' his wife said, wiping one of his filleting knives on her apron.

If his mother didn't approve, his father wouldn't go. Jimmy would have to let his father argue it out himself. He knew enough to keep his mouth shut when it came to his mother.

Morag Moffat wasn't an islander. His father had met her in Scotland when he was working there as a young man and had lured her back to the small Irish island. The slight girl had been raised an orphan in the slums of Glasgow and at sixteen had acquired her first job as housemaid and cook to a small tomato farmer for whom Sean was also working. The boss had not been impressed when he caught Sean canoodling with his housemaid and cook. He fired them both and Sean carried the young girl back to his island, took up his father's currach and had felt neither the inclination nor the need for migrant work after that.

A fact he repeated to his wayward son every time Jimmy talked about going away.

'There is nothing out there you can't get right here on this island, son. Trust me – I know it.' Then he would tell him again the story of his mother and himself. About how his own mother and sisters had welcomed Morag as if she had been one of their own. How they had taken a while to familiarize themselves with her strange foreign accent, but had been instantly in awe of her beauty and the skills she had acquired at such a young age. Morag could read and write, like a proper scholar. The island women had taken to her right away and had showered her with the love she had missed out on as a parentless child. Jimmy's mother would sit by the fire knitting, pretending not to listen or care, but a small smile would play on her lips as his father once again told the simple story of how he had come to realize his travelling days were over.

'And we were back from Scotland not six weeks and I came in from the devil of a day at sea. We came back in with no fish and lucky with our lives. It had been so bad that for a moment I forgot myself that I was married and I came in and found this wee Glasgow girl piling the fire and in an instant my spirits were lifted. She didn't hear me, and her hair dragged up at the back of her neck and I went over and I kissed her, like this –' then Sean would go to wherever his wife was and kiss her with a big, comical mouth on him until she shooed him away, laughing '– and I said to myself, Sean, the only reason you ever went away in the first place was to find yourself this fine young woman. You'll stay where you are now and luck will find you. And thank God it has. There was no man made as rich or lived as content a life as Sean Walsh of Aghabeg from the day he met this woman.'

If his love for Morag was the reason Sean was content to stay on Aghabeg, she was not happy at the news that he was prepared to go back over to Scotland to work for the sake of a bigger boat to pay for a life they neither needed nor wanted.

'You just want to be the biggest man with the biggest boat on Aghabeg, Sean Walsh, because you think it makes you more important than everyone else.'

'And sure aren't I already the most important man on the island with the biggest prize of them all,' he said, grabbing her from behind, 'and all the other men jealous of me and my fine wee Scottish wifey?'

She ignored him. 'And who will cut the turf, would you mind telling me, if you head off now for the whole summer?'

'I'll have it cut before I go.'

'Is that so?'

'And I'll have flour and sugar and tea stored up dry in the sheds for you, and praties dug and washed if you need them, and we'll be back before you know it.'

'One season?' she asked.

'One. I promise. That's all it will take.'

'That's all I'll take of you being away. One season is all I will put up with. Do you hear me?'

'You're the best wife any man ever had,' Sean said, and embraced her.

Over his shoulder, the wiry Scottish woman's eyes were trained on her incorrigible son, Jimmy. She knew this was his doing.

Chapter Five

There was one road through Illaunmor, which ran from the bridge to the top of the island. Then another, smaller one – little more than a dirt track – ran round its edge. The main road, like the island, was five miles long, and the pub and the church were at the bottom of the island next to the bridge.

After an hour on John Joe's cart, they reached the part of the road where the rhododendron bushes were so overgrown it appeared they closed off the path, and then at the bend they opened to reveal the short, wide stretch leading directly to the bridge. Aileen felt her stomach tighten with excitement. She had been off the island a few times before today, but only on short trips across to visit the 'big' shop with her mother. These were the occasions when the travelling shop that came to their part of the island once a month let them down. Although Illaunmor wasn't five hundred yards from the mainland, and there had been a bridge there since 1910, many of the islanders treated it like another country.

Island people were suspicious of everyone except their own and Aileen thought sometimes that was why her mother, a 'blow-in' from the mainland, seemed unhappy living there.

Sometimes Aileen thought that her father didn't just leave

every summer to earn money, but was trying to escape the island itself.

Whatever the case, it didn't matter now, because this summer, this glorious summer, she was going with him.

The gang was at the far side of the bridge already. Aileen had quizzed her brother on the journey and knew everyone in any case. The island was small and even if you lived in the remotest corner, as they did, and spoke to few people, as they did, news of the comings and goings of their fellow islanders seemed to carry on the very wind.

'Carmel Kelly. Are you sure she is going, Paddy? Carmel is as sour as rhubarb – she's hated me since school.'

'She'll like you well enough now that she's sweet on your brother,' Martin butted in.

'Shut up, you with your big mouth,' Paddy Junior, the elder of the two, roared, and gave his brother a belt on the arm, although, Aileen noticed, he was smiling a bit.

'Michael Kelly was a fine thing in school too, as I remember,' Aileen said. 'He'll be going as well, I suppose?' She had no interest in Michael Kelly, only in keeping her brothers' and father's attention on herself.

'We'll have no more talk like that,' her father said.

'If that dirty scut Michael Kelly as much as looks at my sister, I swear I'll flatten him stone to the ground,' Martin growled.

Michael and Carmel Kelly were both there with their father, who was the gaffer of the Illaunmor group. Mick Kelly was the man who took on all dealings with the Scottish farmers. He was responsible for the management of the Irish workers – their wages, their food and accommodation. Although he was technically the foreman, Mick was more friend to everyone than boss, elected to be in charge by the group themselves as the most senior and experienced among them. They would be with each other every day and night over the following months, so it was important that the group got along. Aside from Carmel Kelly, there were three other girls that Aileen knew from school, all not too far off her own age, although she could not call any of them a friend. There was Attracta Collins, a quiet girl with blondish curls, with her father, Tom, and two brothers, Kevin and Noel; then Claire Murphy, Carmel's cousin. She was noisy but plain and had a twin brother, Iggy, who was as crazy as his sister – though wiry and a little more attractive. Also there were brother and sister Noreen and James Flaherty – who Aileen barely knew. In the whole group there were more men than women, but Aileen hoped that between the four girls there, she would find a friend. Apart from the group stood one older woman, Biddy O'Callaghan – a spinster in her fifties who Aileen gathered would be the cook – or fore graipe – of the party.

Paddy was embarrassed to see that they were the last to arrive – especially given that most of the others had walked and not travelled by cart – so he hopped straight off to square things with Mick, whose son, Michael Kelly, in the meantime made a beeline for Aileen to help her off the cart.

Aileen thought Michael was a fine thing – large and square and handsome like her brothers – but by the time they reached the train station, Aileen was already fed up with him. She was anxious that she should get talking to the other girls. Not having sisters or female neighbours meant Aileen was uncertain of herself with women other than her mother. She was happiest of all in the company of her brothers, but they had made it clear that she was not to be hanging around them all summer. Paddy Junior and Martin had told her that while they would look out for her, she had to carve out her own place in the crew independent of them. Her mother, too, had instructed her to establish cordial relations with the other women straight away or she might have a difficult few weeks ahead: 'Make sure you get in with the women early on,' Anne had warned. 'Girls can be poisonous, especially if you're pretty. You're better having them for than against you.'

'What will I talk to them about?' Aileen asked.

Her mother got flustered then. Anne herself had no friends that Aileen knew of, aside from her sister, who lived on the mainland. 'Oh, I don't know – dresses, boys?'

Aileen knew nothing about either. 'Books?'

Although Aileen had left school at twelve, she had been schooled by her mother since then. Now, at sixteen, she had read every book in the travelling library ten times over. However, for all that she would get lost in the dark jungles of H. Rider Haggard or delight in the prim and petty machinations of Louisa May Alcott's *Little Women*, when she laid the book down on her lap, she would still be there in the dark kitchen looking across at her mother's sad face staring into the fire and wishing for their men to come home. Oh, there were days on the beach when her brothers came back and would chase her across the golden sand. Tall and grown as the Dohertys were, they would throw great fistfuls of surf at each other and tease and shout and run like they all were still small children. But such days were gems in the chain of drudgery Aileen felt her life becoming. The same routines day after day, year after year: clearing the grate, setting the fire, baking the bread, putting on a pot for the dinner, stacking turf, whitewashing the walls, washing the same mugs and dishes, churning the same sheets and petticoats in the same worn buckets over and over again. The monotony broken only by her books and ticking off the days until the men came home, when the work would get greater, and the washing more diverse, but at least she would have their company.

Every year since she was ten and deemed old enough to be

of use about the place, Aileen had begged her father to take her with them to Scotland. Every year he had said no. She was to stay and finish school. Aileen would not leave school until she was fully literate. Her mother had lost her two boys to the land, but she would not have her daughter left wanting for an education. When she finished school, she then found she had to stay at home and keep her mother company. How could she tell her father that her mother was no company without him, that she spent the summers mourning and moping like a widow?

So, every Sunday from the age of twelve, Aileen Doherty walked the four miles to and from Mass barefoot, carrying her pampooties in her pocket, so that God might reward her penance by allowing her to leave with her father and brothers.

Now her dream had finally come true and her mother had conceded to let her go. The last winter had been harsh and killed off their best cow and several of their hens. The extra couple of shillings Aileen could earn for the family could replace both.

Aileen loved stories and would read any kind of fiction she could find. Besides the novels she read, Aileen had been made to read the Holy Bible and *The Home of Today*, a modern English tome that had been gifted to her by her mother. As well as being an education in household management and cooking, *The Home of Today* also contained thrilling photographs of houses in England and America where everything ran on electricity and they even had machines that would suck dust up off the floor. In England, they needed them because there were carpets everywhere. Aileen wondered if there would be carpets on all the floors in Scotland. If there were, she would be happy to sleep on the floor.

'I doubt any of them can even read,' Anne had said haughtily of the other women in the group. 'An educated woman is a rare thing – you remember that.'

So on the one hand, Anne wanted her to make friends with the women, and on the other, she was to look down her nose at them. Aileen knew this was why her mother did not have any friends. While the other women and their daughters stood around talking after Mass on a Sunday morning, she and her mother never joined them. Aileen knew that her mother courted her own loneliness and she worried that if she did not find a way of getting along with these girls, she might do the same. Although, in all honesty, she did not know where to begin.

For the entire walk to the station Michael Kelly, the big hefty lug, had plodded alongside her, creating a wall between Aileen and the other girls, who were chatting and laughing away with each other. She could not get past him as he gabbled nervously about this and that: farming and milking and mastitis. He was trying to impress her with talk of a motorized tractor belonging to his cousin who had a 'fine big farm in Louth'. The stupid eejit. On the one occasion Aileen managed to look beyond his bulk, she saw Carmel and the other girls talking behind their hands and pointing. She clearly heard Noreen say, 'The dowdy cut of that jacket!' and although she dearly hoped they weren't talking about her long, brown coat, she knew that they probably were.

The train was already waiting for them in the station, steam firing out from its underbelly. The station house was packed with families saying goodbye and others tripping over each other to get onto the platform. This was the start of the season and it seemed that everyone on the island was leaving for the farms of Yorkshire and Scotland.

Aileen pushed herself away from Michael and searched for her brother Martin, who had been just in front of her a moment ago. She had lost sight of him when a rich-looking town woman in a smart coat had walked between them. Panic began to well up in her at the thought of becoming separated from her father and brothers. The woman bent to pick up her case and at that moment Aileen saw her brother's face turn as he called out her name. How could she have thought they would leave her behind? She almost knocked the woman down in her hurry to get to him, but as she grabbed her brother's arm, he pulled it sharply away. He was still mad at her for not walking alongside them.

'You'll bring bad luck on us,' he said. 'I bet you didn't even think of that, and you flirting with Michael Kelly like a prostitute – I've half a mind to throw you to the big amadaun.'

'Don't talk like that, Martin – can I sit with you on the train?' She looked up at him and deliberately softened her eyes. She could always get round Martin: he was sensitive and he hated to see her cry. 'I've never been on a train before.' She squeezed both her hands into his folded elbows, which lay firmly across his chest, and coaxed her own slim arms into the gap. 'I'm afraid. Please, Martin . . .'

They both knew she was playing him, but Martin was excited for his sister to be on a train for the first time and she knew that.

'Come on, then,' he said, and he hauled himself up onto the high step, taking her bag with him, and pulled her after him with his two hands.

They turned down a narrow corridor and her father poked his head out of a side carriage and waved them in. The carriage was small, with dark wooden panels and cushions built into the seats themselves. There was room for six – three on opposite sides. Seated opposite her father and their older brother, Paddy Junior, was the gaffer, Mick Kelly, and next to him was his daughter, Carmel. Attracta, the plain-looking girl with a large rear, was there too. Aileen had noticed that the pair of girls had stuck together on the walk down.

'Carmel, push up there and let Aileen sit in next to you,' Mick Kelly told his daughter.

Carmel was sitting opposite Paddy Junior, and from the way she was gazing across at her brother Aileen observed that she wanted to be sitting next to him. The handsome young man was looking intently out of the window, even though the train was still stationary.

'Leave the girls where they are. Paddy, you get up and let your sister sit down.'

Paddy Junior couldn't get out of the carriage fast enough, and, followed by his younger brother, went and sat in another carriage with the rest of the crew. By the look that Carmel gave her as Aileen sat in her handsome brother's seat, she could guess why. Paddy Junior was tall and broad and a younger version of his father, with a face that seemed chiselled by God out of smooth rock. Even his sister could see he was a head-turner. Poor Carmel had limp mousy hair that hung down the sides of her flat, mournful face like a pauper's shroud.

Almost immediately after he had left, a determined Carmel said, 'I'd better go and find Michael,' and started to move from her seat.

'You'll do no such thing,' her father said. 'Sit back down. We've ten hours ahead of us and I won't lose that seat.'

Carmel plonked back down next to Attracta, who looked equally horrified on her friend's behalf that her beau had fled. Aileen thought that the two of them resembled stunned fish and she could not help but smile a little. She hoped the two girls wouldn't notice, but was certain, as she turned her face towards the window, that they had.

The train started with a jolt and a hiss.

'We're off,' Paddy said.

Aileen gazed out in wonder as the world sped by, the edge of the fields turning to a blurred line of midnight blue, the faint glitter of fires from inside houses dotted around the vast purple shadows of the Mayo hills.

They saw the silhouette of a man standing out against a moonlit patch, watching the train pass, his face lit up with embers from his pipe.

'There's the Progressive Farmer,' Paddy said.

'How do you mean?' Mick said, smiling already for the punch-line.

'A man out standing in his own field.'

'Well, that's a good one, Paddy,' Mick said. 'That's as good a one as ever I heard.'

Aileen wasn't entirely sure what it meant, but she laughed anyway – from happiness perhaps. As the train rocked her body from side to side, she closed her eyes and leaned her cheek against the rough wool of her father's coat. The musty smell of stale sweat and woodsmoke made her feel safe, as if she was at once away having this strange adventure but also still at home. Carmel and her catty looks didn't matter. She was with her father and brothers, and that was all that mattered. In moments she was asleep.

Chapter Six

At Dublin Port, the crowd for the Glasgow boat was arranging itself into some sort of order before making its way down to the steerage part of the ship. Aileen was nervous of this stretch of the journey. Her brothers had warned her that this was the hardest part and, unlike at the train station, were in no hurry to get themselves on board. The third-class compartments were crowded, with no seating, and were next to the stalls transporting cattle to Scotland.

'I slept next to a bullock last year,' Martin told her. 'I swear to God I thought he was going to eat me.'

'Or worse,' said Paddy Junior, laughing, although Aileen wasn't sure what could be worse than being eaten by a bull.

Martin landed him a wallop on the arm. 'Still, it was better than bunking down with your brother and him getting sick all over his shoes.'

'I did not!'

'Did so, you big alp!'

As her two idiot brothers locked themselves in an angry clinch, Aileen wandered away from them. There was a wind coming up, and although the steamer seemed like a large, solid vessel, she was not relishing spending the next twelve hours aboard it. She walked towards the edge of the dock and stood peering down into the narrow gap between the vast flat edge of the boat and the low sea wall. That was the sea down there. That deep, dirty expanse like a massive bog hole. In Illaunmor, the sea looked so different at its edge. On a still day, small simpering waves bubbled white and nibbled the sand. When God's anger was up, the waves tore at the rocks and peeled back across them with an angry hiss.

The engines on the steamer were firing up, making a huge racket. A gust of steamy wind blew up through the dark, water-floored tunnel and Aileen leaned into it, pushing her hair back from her face to catch the breeze on her neck.

'You are the most beautiful girl I have ever seen!'

She had not noticed the boy creeping up behind her and his loud words gave her such a fright that she almost fell into the water. She would have, in fact, if the wiry young man had not caught her arm and pulled her away from the edge just in time.

She turned and, even though he had been the cause of her almost falling in, even though she had got a fright, in the moment that she saw this stranger's face she felt something peculiar happen inside her. It was as if her heart, which had kicked with the shock of almost falling in the water, had taken a second to turn itself to one side, as if about to ask a question.

Aileen noticed how close her feet were to the edge and her heart started thumping again. What had she been doing leaning towards the dark water like that?

The nearness of her fall hit her and she shouted, 'What the hell are you doing?' at the idiot who had shouted and nearly caused her to fall. Who was this boy who had sneaked up on her? She looked at him but found his searing blue eyes unsettling and had to look away again.

'Saving your life,' he said in a northern Irish accent.

'By nearly killing me!' she replied, incredulous at his stupidity.

She held on to the feeling of being annoyed. She was afraid if she let it go, she might drown. Not in the water but some other way.

'You shouldn't have been standing so close to the edge.'

'I wasn't expecting somebody to *shout in my ear*!' she screamed at him. The steamer was very loud.

'I had to shout so you would hear me tell you that you are the most beautiful girl I have ever seen!' he shouted in return.

She began to walk quickly back towards where her father and brothers were, but the boy stuck to her side.

'You can't have seen many girls, so . . .'

'Maybe not,' he said.

Aileen was cross to find herself feeling strangely disappointed at his concession, until he added, 'Although I've seen enough to know you are one in a million.'

'You're stone mad,' she said, although inwardly she felt weakened by the compliment. Nobody had ever spoken to her in that way before.

'Were you going to jump in?' he asked.

'No, don't be stupid. Why would I do that?' she said.

'If you had, I would have jumped in and saved you – I can swim.'

This boy was a worse fool than Michael Kelly! What kind of a soft idiot was she, having these silly warm feelings towards him? He would not shut up either, asking questions without giving her the chance to answer him: 'What's your name? Where are you from? No, wait – I bet you're from Mayo?'

As she moved into the queue with her family, the boy was still there, badgering her. 'You can go now,' Aileen said, annoyed, with herself for the nagging notion in her stupid, stupid heart, but mostly that he had put her in the position of having to dismiss him in front of her father and brothers. 'Please go away.'

'Jimmy Walsh,' the boy said, ignoring her request and holding his hand out to Paddy. 'I assume you are father to the most beautiful girl in Ireland?'

Paddy looked at the wiry young man as if he had two heads, and Martin was already moving in. His fists curling, he snarled, 'You heard my sister. She said, "Go away."'

Jimmy ignored him and kept his blazing eyes firmly fixed on Paddy's face, his hand outstretched and shaking somewhat with nervous energy. Aileen's father could see from this Jimmy's demeanour that he was smitten with his daughter. He also knew himself how immediately these things could happen, and as much as his big son Martin thought he could trash any man, lean lads could be as deadly to deal with – especially where affairs of the heart were concerned – and the last thing they needed before their long, arduous boat journey was a fight.

'Paddy Doherty,' he said, holding out his hand to the young man, who grabbed it gratefully and shook it a bit too vigor-ously, 'and this is my younger son, Martin.' Jimmy had a flash in his eyes that Paddy could not help but like, although it made him nervous. There was a kind of magic in the boy.

'And this is my daughter, Aileen.'

'Ignore him, Da – he's not right in the head,' said Aileen.

'You got that right enough,' said a round-faced, rather jolly-looking man who put his hands squarely on Jimmy's shoulders. He in turn held his hand out to Paddy. 'Sean Walsh from Aghabeg. This troublesome scallywag is my son, Jimmy.'

'Paddy Doherty from—'

'Illaunmor. Sure I would know you anywhere from your father's face. He was a legend. My own da was out fishing with him many the time, and I along with them as a child.'

Paddy smiled weakly. He looked vulnerable and Aileen could

see he was not quite sure what to make of this ebullient stranger having known his own father.

'Ah yes – Donegal. He went there sometimes surely.'

'He was a fine fisherman and he could handle himself in any weather, but then the sea only takes the very best for herself.'

There was an awkward pause before Paddy asked, 'Are there many of you in it?'

'Just the two of us,' he said. 'Aghabeg is small and few of us leave. Only me and the lad here are looking for a few extra shillings this year. We're hoping to tag on to a crew at the other end – find one that's short maybe. Otherwise, sure we'll just head for Glasgow and take it from there. To be honest, Paddy, it's been a long time since I did this. I'm not sure how it works anymore. I'd be grateful for any ideas.'

Paddy's shoulders straightened with the challenge of being in charge. 'I'll introduce you to the foreman of our crew,' he said. 'Maybe we'll squeeze two more in – your son looks like a fine worker, anyhow.'

'You're a gentleman, and you can tell him there's a bit of graft left in this aul' dog too,' he jibed. 'I'm not as old as I look.'

As Paddy walked away with Sean, Aileen turned to Jimmy and said, 'Are you not going with them?'

'No,' he said. His arms folded as he stood in front of her.

'Go on. Off you go,' she insisted, waving her hand at him.

'I am staying right here,' he said. 'By your side, Aileen. Forever.'

Then he closed his eyes and threw his head back and sang, starting quietly and getting louder, 'Aileen, Aileen, my angel Aileen,' to no tune in particular.

Martin, more embarrassed than disgusted, walked off. 'He's madder than a bag of cats.'

Aileen told Jimmy to be quiet, but he wouldn't shut up. On and on he went singing out her name until a few of the people gathered about formed a circle round him and started clapping and whooping, encouraging him until the foolish boy fell down onto his knees in front of her and carried on. 'Aileeeen! Aileen. I'm in love with an angel called Aileeeeen!'

She said, 'Get up, you eejit – you're making a show of me,' but he would not stop and continued pleading and singing to her until, for all his silliness, Aileen found that she was laughing so hard she was breathless, and everything inside her filled suddenly with light.

Chapter Seven

The boat journey was as long and as terrible as promised.

Jimmy didn't care. He had found the love of his life.

When he had seen Aileen standing by the side of the ship, her hair caught back from her face in a gust of wind, he thought he must be seeing things. It could not be the same girl from the island, but, impulsive as he was, he barely stopped to consider that fact before he had put himself by her side. When he discovered that she was not a vision but a real girl, he lost himself altogether. Jimmy knew he was making an eejit out of himself. Even as he was sneaking up and shouting, 'You are the most beautiful girl I have ever seen!' like a foghorn and nearly sending her sideways into the water, he knew it was a stupid thing to do. Sticking to her side like a limpet, introducing himself to her father in the abrupt way he did, singing to her in front of the whole crowd on the boarding ramp – in his rational mind Jimmy knew that none of these things was the way to a girl's heart, but in truth the young fisherman was already beyond all of that. From the moment he had set eyes on her again, Jimmy knew for certain that this red-haired angel belonged to him. She had been sent to him by the gods – the powerful force of the sea, the same thing that took the lives of so many good men, yet had allowed him to swim, had turned this creature from a mirage of fire on a distant beach into a real woman for him alone. No matter how she rebuffed him, no matter how idiotic she thought he was, no matter how her brothers threatened and fussed and his own father might laugh at him and call him 'mad in the head', Jimmy knew that they were meant to be together. Aileen Doherty belonged to him and he belonged to her – and that was all there was to it. All he had to do now was not move one inch from her side until she loved him back. Which she would. Soon.

'Will you get away from me?' she said. 'You are getting on my nerves. Da, will you tell him . . .?'

It turned out that the Illaunmor crew were almost last to get on the boat and the third-class cabins were packed. Even if Jimmy had wanted to leave, there were precious few places he could have moved away to.

Paddy Doherty laughed before looking out on the large cabin in front of them. 'Holy God, the place is jammed. I swear it gets worse every year,' he said, shaking his head and tutting as he looked out on the heaving mass of standing bodies.

The crowd comprised all adults, men and women of similar build in dull-coloured heavy outdoor clothes – wearing them to save on luggage. There were none too old and none too young – tall and lean, small and stocky. All had strong working bodies, all seeking out a space to settle themselves into for the next twelve hours.

'Like matches in a box.' Sean, Jimmy's father, seemed quite shocked at the number of people.

Jimmy had slipped out of the currach last summer and swum underwater through a huge shoal of mackerel. This reminded him of that.

'Wouldn't you think the shipping company would cop themselves on and give us a bit of comfort?' Sean said.

'No need,' Paddy assured him. 'No matter how bad the sailing, it gets more packed every year – and only set to get worse. With the war on, sure there's not an Englishman left in the country to pick up a spade, so they'll be paying "the poor Irish" to do their dirty work till they've had their fill of Hitler.'

'You've got to love the aul' Germans,' Sean agreed. 'There's nothing as good for an Irish farmer as the English at war.'

'Provided it's not against us,' said Paddy.

'Oh, I don't know,' Sean said. 'We ran them the last time.'

'After a fashion,' Paddy agreed, 'although it took us long enough.'

Mick was paying them no heed; the gaffer's face was all business as he scanned the cabin for their next move. 'Come on, you men, and follow me.'

Quickly, before she thought to object, Jimmy grabbed on to Aileen's hand and held it tight. Leading her, he followed their broad-chested gaffer through the crowd as Mick assertively shouldered his charges through the bustling bodies. Jimmy held his true love, turning often to check she was still there. He would have liked to have carried her in his arms to protect her and had an ambitious vision that one day she might let him.

At the opposite end of the room, the path began to clear and they reached 'their spot' near the back wall. Carmel and the other women from the group were already there. They had boarded first and were now settled comfortably on makeshift seats made from their cases and a few crates that were scattered around the edges of the vast packed room. Jimmy noted there were one or two windows, but they were too high up to look out of. Over in the corner was another doorway with steep steps that he presumed led up to a deck.

'Surely to God it's like a coffin ship,' said Sean, surveying people like themselves who had arrived hoping to find a crate to sit on but had instead to drop down on their haunches to the grimy floor.

'Except, Sean, my friend, you might feel dead by the time we get there,' said Mick, 'but you'd better not be, as there's a savage body of work waiting for us at the other end. It's a good idea to find yourself a corner to bed down in.'

Aileen had not let go of Jimmy's hand. Jimmy brushed aside the glad feeling he had about that when he noticed she was the only woman still standing. The other girls had gone on without her and he was feeling guilty that she had nowhere to sit.

It was his fault the women had left her behind. He had held her back from them, and however much he didn't want to, he would have to hand her back to them now. The island women stuck together – that's the way it was on Aghabeg with his mother and her cronies. Always in each other's kitchens, weaving and sewing and cooking each other boxty pancakes and talking, talking, talking while using up all the tea and sugar so there wasn't a bit left for the men and them coming in from a hard day at sea. That was how his father saw it, anyway, and as Jimmy got older, he came to see that his father wasn't far wrong.

'Women are different from us, Jimmy,' Sean had told him. 'They are a law unto themselves – never forget that, son. Just keep your head down and out of their way most of the time. Never contradict a woman, and never approach one when they are in a group. That's my advice, and if you ever cross one, you'll learn why.'

His father loved his mother, but he was afraid of her, which Jimmy could never understand. However, standing in front of this group of women, Jimmy himself felt a little afraid – a feeling he was so unfamiliar with he could barely name it.

The women were sitting comfortably enough, their shoulders supported by the arched walls, many of them with their knitting and sewing already on their laps. They were settled, not looking up, as if they had lived there all their lives in that way that women had of making a home in the most unlikely of places, while a man could stand at his own hearth and look like a stranger warming his behind on another man's fire.

One of them, a plain-looking creature, looked up and said, 'Here she comes with her shadow.'

Jimmy didn't really know what that meant, so he took a deep breath and said, 'Sorry for keeping Aileen from you, ladies.'

One or two of them looked up as he spoke, but then looked aside again as if whatever he had to say was of no interest to them. He did not understand women, but at the same time he felt there was something amiss. None of them had moved aside to make room for Aileen. The plain one sucked her teeth and said something like, 'You can keep her.' Jimmy smiled nervously, and having barely heard what she had said but being glad that she had said something, he considered asking her to repeat herself. However, just as he was about to, he noticed her nudge the girl sitting next to her in a conspiratorial way that made him feel sick in his stomach. Jimmy shifted on his feet. He was unsure what to do next. He felt uneasy leaving Aileen there, and he knew that whatever nasty game they were playing, his love was feeling it, because she had not yet let go of his hand.

'Would you like to go up deck and have a look around, Aileen?'

Jimmy looked at her and nodded his head to one side as if inviting her out to take the floor at a dance. He realized in that moment that this was the first time he had looked at Aileen directly. He had been too afraid to before now. God, but she was so beautiful he had to force out the words for fear of his heart stopping. It was as if a statue of the Blessed Virgin herself had come to life and was staring him in the face – her beauty was that mysterious, that powerful to him. Her skin was as pale as the whitest beach pebble, and sad and afeard though she was, her eyes were still dancing with life. Were they green or blue? He could not look at them long enough to discern their precise colour.

'Yes,' she said. 'That would be lovely.'

Jimmy raised his eyes to heaven and thanked God Himself for the mean, cold hearts he had put in the Illaunmor women that had gifted him exclusive rights to his own true love this day.

Truly, he was the luckiest man alive.

Chapter Eight

The sky was drizzling, and the sea below them was flat and still. The whole world seemed shrouded in grey. Aileen's journey into the wide world had barely begun, yet already she was torn. On the one hand, she was glad that Jimmy had been there to stand up for her and take her away from the cruel girls, but on the other, she was annoyed with him because perhaps he had made the situation worse.

Aileen was not a fool. She could see that Carmel was dead set against her and had turned the other women that way. This was exactly how her mother had warned her it would happen – which made the fact she had failed with the women even more upsetting for her.

'You can keep her,' Carmel had said.

Aileen didn't want to be on deck with this strange boy, and she didn't want to be downstairs with the women. She was thoroughly miserable and wanted to be back home with her mother, supping warm milk in their kitchen and waiting for the men: at least when she had felt sorry for herself on Illaunmor, she had known where she was.

Now, she wanted only to be in the company of her brothers and father, but they had made it clear that she had to make her own way. Her father had all but thrown her at this boy Jimmy, and the women had been supposed to look after her as 'the new girl', but they had been so mean. Carmel was as spiteful as she had been at school. She had spread it around then that Aileen was cursed on account of her red hair. This whole thing had been a mistake – she wanted to go home. She blinked at the flat, grey sea and a tear rolled down her cheek.

'What's ailing you, my love?'

How was it possible for a man to elicit such feelings of warmth in her stomach and yet be so . . . annoying?!

'What's "ailing" me? Are you Shakespeare? Who talks like that?'

Jimmy had reached over to wipe the tear from her eye and she swatted his hand away like a fly.

'Lay a hand on me and I swear I will send you flying!'

'You're upset,' he said, pointlessly, infuriatingly.

'Yes, I'm upset,' she said, her words amplified by the empty deck and the expanse of sea, as if the whole wide world were supporting her in her annoyance. 'Because you won't leave me alone and you have spoilt my friendship with the other women. Everything was going perfectly fine before you came along.'

As she said it, Aileen thought that while it was not strictly true, Jimmy's presence was complicating things. If he hadn't turned up, the women would have had to have been nicer to her.

'Go away, why don't you?'

Although it was not her intention, Aileen saw that her words had hurt him as truly as if she had planted a slap on his face. His open-eyed upset infuriated her even more.

'Oh, why don't you just go away and leave me alone?' she shouted at him.

He stood looking at her, hurt but incredulous also.

This Jimmy was a strange-looking boy, and despite that instant attraction she had had towards him, she could not quite decide if he was handsome or not. He was not as obviously fine-looking as her brothers and father – certainly not as square-shouldered or broad. At just a little taller than herself, he was of slim build, although he was physically strong – she could sense that more than see it. His features were pointed in a way that was full of character but also somewhat devilish. He had large blue eyes that spangled with life and mischief, and were rimmed with long, dark lashes – like a girl. These were matched in character with a strong Roman nose and a broad mouth that seemed to take up his whole face when he smiled, which he did every time she gave him the slightest encouragement.

Jimmy was not the type of man she had always imagined she would fall in love with. Aileen was a fan of the brooding, troubled Heathcliff – dark and mysterious and strikingly handsome. Heathcliff never smiled, but was full of a bleak, unstoppable passion for his true love. Aileen had read *Wuthering Heights* a dozen times or more, imagining herself to be on the other end of such dark passions. Her rugged island was as similar to the Yorkshire Moors as one could imagine and the landscape had helped fuel a small fantasy. Aileen knew her hero was the figment of a writer's imagination and that such a man probably did not exist in real life, and even if he did, he did not, in all likelihood, reside on Illaunmor. But Aileen had not yet known enough men to be entirely certain. The evidence so far pointed to Michael Kelly boasting of his Louth cousin, and while Jimmy's dramatic opening of saving her life and his demonstrative singing on the quayside put him somewhat above Michael's promise of a relation with a motorized tractor, they were both still a far cry from her Brontë idol.

'Maybe I will go,' he said, and turned – although he was

moving slowly enough for her to see he had very little intention of actually leaving her there.

The fool.

'Go on,' she said. 'Off you go.'

He took a step forward towards the steep metal stairwell down to the cabins, then looked back at her with an expression of yearning that she found intolerably irritating.

She stared at him accusingly, then waved him on his way before abruptly turning her back on him and facing out to sea again.

What an annoying man he was, and how much better off she would be without her 'shadow'. In the very moment that she thought that, Aileen looked around her and suddenly felt afraid. Alone on the empty deck, with its cold metal hull, the vast expanse of water stretched ahead, and beyond it was a world full of strangers. A feeling of bleakness and emptiness washed over her.

She turned and shouted, 'Jimmy,' and he came bounding back up the stairs towards her.

'We'll wait until the boat takes off, anyway.'

His face filled up with a smile, and although she pushed it aside, she could not help feeling glad.

For the next twelve hours Jimmy did not leave her side – not once.

Shortly after he came back up the steps, the engines started and the two of them hung over the railing as the large boat ploughed through the water, creating vast troughs of white on either side.

'I should like to be down there,' said Jimmy. 'There will be some action underwater surely.'

'You're an awful eejit – you know that?' said Aileen. 'You'd be killed stone dead if you were down there.'

'Not me,' he said. 'I'm invincible.'

She could not help but smile, and when she did, he smiled too. With the wind in her hair and the cold spray from the water misting her face, Aileen knew her suitor was thinking how beautiful she was but was too afraid to say it in case she bit his head off and sent him away again. Despite herself, Aileen realized that she no longer cared so much about her troubles with the women because she had this boy by her side.

After a short while, the waves grew and the boat began to plunge and skip across the water, and with the engines directly below them, Aileen began to feel sick. She quickly moved and put her head over the side of the boat but swallowed back the bile for shame of being sick in front of Jimmy.

He put his arms around her and helped her back down the stairwell to find somewhere to settle herself in the cabin, but the place held no comfort. Every inch where you might sit down was already taken, and as they reached the bottom step, there was a man being sick into a bag. Aileen almost retched, but Jimmy kept his arms around her and led her gently through the cabin to another large door off the main corridor. He looked about before opening it quickly and sneaking them in. The cabin was large and comprised what Aileen could clearly see were cattle stalls, with the smell of hay and cow dung in the air. At the far end, a calf was in one of the stalls; the rest were empty.

'On the way in, I saw a man bring in that little lad down there. All the cattle came over on the boat last night save this one wee lad who they squeezed on today. When I saw them drive him in, I knew the cattle cabin would be all but empty.'

He reached over to a pile of hay just inside the first stall and dragged out a bag.

'How did you know the boat would be full?'

'Did you see the crowds?' he said. 'Sure I've never been on a boat before, but I could see from the amount waiting on the quay that it would be jammed. Anyway, my da worked in Scotland before he got married. He told me the boat journey was terrible back then and the only hope you had was to bed down on a bit of hay and sleep it off. I think he thought it'd be better now.'

He stood looking at her nervously as if he may have said or done something out of turn. Aileen was struck dumb with his ingenuity – his sheer cleverness. Jimmy shuffled from foot to foot and added, 'The train across was fantastic – we couldn't get over it. It had toilets and everything.'

The boat lurched forward and Aileen clutched at her stomach – Jimmy gave her a bucket quickly and left her alone while she brought up her meagre breakfast.

'Will I go and get one of your brothers?' Jimmy asked.

'No,' she said quickly. 'They'll only be mad at us sneaking off.' In any case, she was happy with the company she had, although she could not help but add, 'And anyway, they will kill you stone dead for annoying their sister.' As punishment for her teasing, the boat lumbered forward, then sank back and Aileen got sick again.

When she was finished, she turned and saw that Jimmy had made her a mattress, fashioning a raised pillow out of the soft yellow straw and laying his own coat on top of it. Tired and sick, she took his hand and let him settle her, arranging her skirts over her woollen-stockinged legs and loosening the laces of her good boots to allow her more comfort. Then he closed the wooden gate of the stall and sat down on the hard floor to guard her while she slept.

The awareness that she was alone, in this place, with this boy filled her with an excitement that she dared not name.

Aileen felt so tired she could hardly speak, but still she asked him, 'Are you not lying down yourself?'

'No,' he said.

She knew it would be the height of impropriety, but every inch of her wished he would lie down by her side close enough that she might feel his breath on her face and see what would happen next.

Chapter Nine

'Jimmy?'

Jimmy felt himself jerk awake.

He was still sitting, his arms folded over his chest, and Aileen was calling him.

'We've arrived.'

Damn – he must have dropped off. She was pushing his arm, waking him up, which was all wrong, because he should be the one waking her.

Jimmy had watched over Aileen for most of the journey. Although he knew it was foolish, Jimmy still feared that Aileen might flee him again – disappear as she had done on the beach.

He watched her sleeping, her white skin almost glowing in the faint daylight coming through the cabin window, the soft lids of her large eyes as smooth as pebbles – translucent and flickering with thoughts he did not dare imagine.

Every now and again her pink mouth opened and closed as if she were speaking in her dreams. He would wonder then if she was dreaming of him, then hurt himself by dismissing the notion as foolish and premature. He longed to touch her, to place his hands gently on her cheeks and touch the soft plump-ness of her mouth with his fingers – to dare to kiss her. To even be thinking such a thing was wrong, but Jimmy could not help himself. What else was a man like himself to think about the woman he loved? However, Jimmy knew that any impropriety would surely chase her away and that he must wait. So as Aileen slept, Jimmy sat with his hands locked firmly under his armpits, lest tiredness should lead them to wander without reason. He thought how lucky a man he was to have found his own true love and how he should prove himself by staying awake and watching over her. When his body became so tired he could not even stand and he feared the swell of the boat might simply cause him to fall down next to her, Jimmy would take a deep breath, summon the gods to help him and glower at his true love's face, willing her to wake up and distract him. When she did, Jimmy would then cheerfully feed her from the bag of bread and cold bottled tea that his mother had packed for him, gratefully remembering her last words to him on the sea steps at Aghabeg.

'Do not touch the food in this bag until you are at sea, because you'll think the journey is all but over, but let me tell you, it will have only just begun.'

In the twenty-odd years she had been married to Sean Walsh, Morag had never been back to Scotland, the place of her birth.

'What would I want to go back there for?' she snapped at Jimmy when he once asked her if she ever had the yen to return. 'Haven't I everything I need here and more besides?'

Jimmy had been reared by his parents – his mother in particular – to believe that he had everything he could ever need and he knew that to be true. His family had health, good land, a decent boat and kind neighbours – more than any man deserved. The new boat was a wild ambition, but Jimmy was a dreamer and God had big plans for him. Hadn't He sent him this red-haired nymph to take as a wife? He knew that this trip to Scotland with his father heralded the beginning of his own independent life. Not one away from the island – there was no need to leave Aghabeg or his family and friends. He had no desire to go and live in England or America, like so many of the people from the mainland had to do. People who did not have the gift of his father in divining where the good fish could be found, whose land was all bog or all rock and not the balance of turf and grass that allowed his family to both farm and heat their home all year round. His father had earmarked him land for his own home and had half the materials salvaged and saved in a shed out the back to build it.

Now he had found the woman he wanted to share all this good fortune with, although they would adventure together first. While Aileen was asleep, Jimmy planned them the longest honeymoon travelling the world together in the new Galway hooker: Liverpool, Paris, New York maybe. Aileen on the bow of the boat in a long green velvet coat, her hair being pushed back in soft wisps from her face, looking over her shoulder at him, smiling broadly as he steered them into some exotic port. After they had had their fill of rich food and spices, and handled monkeys and ridden elephants, and seen all that they could see, they would return to his island and live out their days in a low white house with the thickest thatch in all of Ireland – fishing and farming and making babies by the dozen.

Although, for the time being, he decided to keep his plans to himself. He simply watched as Aileen nibbled silently but gratefully on the dry bread before lying back down and allowing him to cover her again in his coat. They barely spoke a word to each other the whole trip, but Jimmy felt a closeness in their silence – as if they had been together forever and there was nothing now left to say.

'We'd better get a move on,' she said, 'or they might sail back to Ireland with us still on board.'

As Aileen laced her boots, Jimmy felt a little sadness that his tenure as her guard and keeper was over. She was excited to be here, in Scotland, which was understandable, except that he was mostly just excited to be with her. He had no inkling of how Aileen felt about him, but he knew he was not going to blow it by bearing down on her with unwanted attention. There was too much at stake. Aileen was everything, and if he felt this much, she must feel something too. If she didn't, he prayed she would. He had thought he felt a flicker once or twice, but it was too much to hope for. He would wait; like catching a trout in a moving stream, he would hold steady and watch, then when the right moment came, swoop in and scoop her up into his arms.

Mick had secured a place for Sean and Jimmy with the eighteen-strong crew and the six families plus Biddy got on a train in Glasgow for the final four-hour leg of their journey to their first farm, where they would be working for the next six weeks.

As they were getting on the train, Jimmy saw Aileen's brother Martin stamp up the platform towards them, his thick shoulders ploughing a path through the crowd of other passengers.

'If you've touched my sister, I'll—'

Paddy Junior pulled him back and said firmly, 'We were worried about you, Aileen, when we didn't see you at all on the boat.'

'I was fine.'

Martin nodded at Jimmy.

'Oh, for goodness' sake – he's harmless,' said Aileen, exasperated.

'All the same,' her father said, appearing behind them, 'I think you should travel this part of the journey with us now. I've a carriage saved.'

Aileen grabbed her brother's hand and hopped up on the train without looking back. Jimmy was hurt that she seemed so eager to escape him, but also knew that such a small disappointment would not be enough to deter him.

Jimmy settled in an end corridor and spent the journey smoking and playing cards with some of the Illaunmor men. After all, he needed to get to know them if he was going to marry Aileen. Jimmy was a keen hand at poker and won the promise of a full shilling from Michael Kelly, who – as it turned out – was also the brother of one of the girls Aileen had been having problems with on the boat. Carmel Kelly was sniffing around behind him and Jimmy thought she was giving him something of a measured eye. With that in mind, he let the big fool off the money to ingratiate himself with what he could see was an important family on that island. There was still a way to go on that front with Aileen's family. Her father, Paddy, liked him all right, but Aileen's brothers were by no means impressed that he had spirited their sister away for the whole journey, and although he did not like the way she referred to him as 'harmless', Jimmy told himself she had said it purely to placate them, which it had, but all the same he did not like being described as such. He would certainly never do her any harm, but Aileen had not yet seen the fearless and intrepid side to him, and besides that, Jimmy had always considered himself to be something of a fine-looking young man. He was by far the best-looking man on Aghabeg, although he had to admit the competition was not as fierce as it might have been elsewhere. With a population of under a hundred, many of the families were related, and everyone having known each other all their lives, it was a challenge to judge if one person was as good-looking as the next. Jimmy was not as broad or as tall as Aileen's brothers, nor did he have as calm and rugged a face as the Kelly men did, but he was as powerful, surely, as any man you could name. His arms were strong from swimming and he could beat the very best of them in an arm-wrestle. Added to that, he had 'an elegant Roman profile'. His own mother had christened it such and there was not a biddy on the island who didn't agree with her – they couldn't all be wrong!

Throughout the train journey Jimmy made sure to walk over and back past Aileen's carriage to ensure she was still there. Once or twice he accidentally caught Martin's eye and smiled at him, but Aileen's brother shook his head back in disbelief. Jimmy reassured himself it was better to incur her family's amusement and pity than their protective anger. That way, they would be more inclined towards him marrying their sister.

After four hours and what seemed to Jimmy like an eternity, they pulled into Kiltirnagh Station. Jimmy looked around anxiously for Aileen, but he could not see her – or her family. For a terrible moment he thought she had disappeared – spirited away from him again as punishment for having taken his eyes off her. Sean jostled him onto one of two open carts that were waiting to transport the Irish tattie-hokers off to their farms.

Sean sat himself down next to his son as a dozen more men and women clambered up and took their places on the sack-covered floor.

'I haven't a clue where it is they are taking us, son, but I'll tell you this one thing – I'll be glad to get my feet in under any sort of a table, and I'm praying to the Lord Jesus himself that there'll be some sort of a hot meal at the end of it, and curse your mother to hell for not packing more grub for us on the boat. Jesus, but whatever they're made of out on that Illaunmor Island, well, they can live off very little surely. I swear not one of them ate a scrap the whole journey. They were full of sausages, Paddy said, but, by God, twenty-four hours on a fry alone? I'll tell you what they're hardy.'

Jimmy looked anxiously around, fixing his stare on people

getting onto the cart behind theirs. If Aileen wasn't there, he'd have to go back. He'd have to jump back on the train and find her. If she wasn't there, he would stow away on the boat and get himself back to Dublin, then catch the train up to Galway and steal the hooker from his cousin and retrace the journey they made that day when they took that view of what he now knew was Illaunmor and the island where the ethereal beauty who was the woman he loved lived.

He was about to stand up and take his leave by hopping over the side of the cart when he saw her.

The shock of auburn hair was visible behind the shoulder of one of her brothers, and as he craned his neck to check it really was Aileen and not some heathery mirage, he saw her white face come into view. Her green eyes glistened like emeralds as the light caught them and they searched the crowd – looking for something.

When he met her anxious stare and noticed it soften into the slightest smile, Jimmy lost his breath as he realized that she had been looking for him.

Chapter Ten

They were on the cart for less than an hour, but it felt like the longest part of the journey to Aileen because she was not with Jimmy.

How was it possible that she had become used to this stranger after knowing him for less than a day?

While she had been falling in and out of sleep on the boat, she had felt his presence all around her as if he had somehow imbued the very hay she was sleeping on, the very coat that lay over her, with some of his spirit. He was a strange boy surely – strange-looking, strange-talking – and yet she felt safer under his guardianship than she had with anyone, even her brothers. She should not, perhaps, have called him 'harmless' in the way she did, but she had meant it at face value. She did not feel she could come to any harm when Jimmy was around her. His company itself was armour protecting her from the rigours of the big wide world she felt she had so suddenly entered.

On the cart, she sat between her brothers. Jimmy was in the cart in front of theirs. The night was dark and the air cold and damp, and Aileen was aware of being far from home. Excited but nervous too – of what lay ahead. She curled her hands around her eldest brother Paddy Junior's arms and leaned against his chest, but didn't get the comfort she was seeking. His chest was still and impervious; his hands did not grip hers as they always had done when he had comforted her as a small girl during thunderstorms, or carried her on his shoulders back from the beach, or defended her if she got into a fight with the younger Martin. She looked across at her father and tried to catch his eye, but couldn't. He was busy talking with Mick Kelly, quiet and conspiratorial men's talk – all business. He had no time for her. Perhaps she was not his little girl anymore, but a woman. Could that be why Paddy Junior would not hold her hand? Were they to abandon her now to womanhood? To the savage intentions of Jimmy Walsh? The very idea that he might not be as 'harmless' after all terrified and thrilled her in equal measure.

When they did, finally, stop, Aileen stayed where she was while the others alighted, momentarily disbelieving that they had really reached their destination.

It was dark and they were in the courtyard of what seemed to be a large farm – Aileen made out a few horse stables and the shadows of some farm machinery. To one side were two long, low buildings running at right angles to each other with oil lamps clearly burning at their windows.

Aileen felt a twinge of excitement as she imagined what cosy set-up must be inside; would there be carpets and 'teak sideboards' like the English homes in her mother's housekeeping book? Her brothers started to gather their bags from the cart, and as she went to climb down, Jimmy was there holding out his hand to help her, as she had known he would be. He squeezed her hand as he held it briefly, letting go when he saw Martin's murderous glare.

The two of them walked side by side, then across to the accommodation. Inside, the building was not the furnished home Aileen had imagined. While from the outside the building looked rather large and grand, inside it was basically a shed with no furniture to speak of. There were large shallow crates that were potato-seed boxes and that she later learned had to be laid in lines along the wall to be made up into beds. The other women were already inside, hurriedly stuffing straw into sacking to make mattresses without even taking off their coats – busying themselves to get the place liveable before the oil in the lamps ran out.

Aileen's disappointment did not last for long, however.

'Don't be standing there catching flies in your mouth,' an older woman shouted across. Aileen recognized her from the ship as the centre point of the women's tableau she was excluded from. She was a good deal older than her own mother and squatting next to an old stove. 'There's work to be done! You –' she pointed at Jimmy '– get me in a barrow of coal from the other house, and, girl, you can help me set the stove.'

'I thought I was to set the stove, Biddy,' Carmel said, emerging from the darkness behind the woman, her face as hard and cruel as it had been on the boat. 'That one hasn't the brains to light a match, and her scrawny shadow won't be much good to you either.'

'I'll decide who I'll have working for me,' said the woman, 'and when you're here, you'll call me Mrs O'Callaghan, Carmel Kelly – and I don't care whose daughter you are. Your daddy may be the boss out on the fields, girl, but I'm the fore graipe of this house, so you'll do as you're told. You can make a start by washing that bucket of spuds at the door. We'll go to our beds with full stomachs tonight.'

Aileen did not afford herself a moment of satisfaction in light of Carmel's dressing-down – indeed, this boss-woman might be harder to please than any of them. Instead, she busied herself about the stove. Aileen had a way of building fast, effective fires. She started at the bottom with the paper balls and a handful of crisp straw, placing the few dry clinkers of coal left from the last fire around them, then carefully setting the fresh coals on top before putting a match to it. It went up as smooth and fast as butter melting on toasted bread.

The fore graipe heard the discreet *whoosh*, then looked back and raised her eyebrows, impressed.

'Load that up good and high, girl – thanks be to God we've somebody good for something around here.' Then she turned on the others: 'Are you finished making those mattresses yet, Noreen? And we'll hand out the blankets. For love of the merciful Mother of Jesus, there's no need to put so much straw in a single bed – we are not the Savoy of London, girl.' Then she turned back to Aileen and said, 'Well? What are you still doing in here? Didn't I tell you to go outside and build us a fire for the cooking?'

Aileen did not argue and went straight outside, where the dark, empty yard had no signs of a fireplace. Jimmy took up helping her with gusto. He fetched some large stones that were piled up near the gate and in a flash built them into a three-sided wall on the cobbles between the two buildings. Aileen went about building her fire, and while it was settling, Jimmy magicked up a rusting cattle grid and balanced it over the top. On this he placed a bucket of cold water to heat for the spuds. In moments the whole courtyard was glowing orange as Jimmy and Aileen gathered various buckets and planks of wood and old farm machinery to use as stools and tables and placed them in a wide semicircle round the new fireplace.

When Biddy came out to roar at them to hurry themselves up, she stopped short with surprise.

'My God,' she said, when she saw the water already boiling ready for the potatoes. 'What kind of magic is this at all?' For a moment Aileen thought her senior was going to tear the head off her for being a witch (red-haired women got a raw deal in that respect in some quarters, she knew), but Biddy shook her head and, wiping her forehead with the heat of the roaring fire, exclaimed, 'Well, I'll say this only once, Aileen Doherty –' she knew her name all along '– but your mother should be proud of you.' Then she turned and roared, 'Noreen? Carmel? Are you growing them fecking spuds or peeling them, would you mind telling me?'

The six women and twelve men of the tattie crew sat round the fire and ate heartily. There was no talk as they mashed the floury potatoes into the bowls they had brought with them from Ireland, every now and again one of them leaning across the other to reach for a ladleful of buttermilk from the bucket the host farmer had set aside for them.

'This is rotten sour,' Carmel said, then looking across at Biddy, added cheekily, 'Is there any salt, Fore Graipe?'

Aileen saw Biddy look up over her bowl and hoped she never made her eyes slant with such a cold stare.

'Carmel,' Mick chided her, 'show some respect.' Carmel glowered at him as if unaware of what the word even meant. 'Besides,' Mick said, 'Biddy hasn't had time to get the full kitchen set up as yet.'

The insult reverberated round the silent circle as everyone's eyes reached down to the bottom of their bowls. Biddy's face was as set as stone. Mick coughed, knowing he had said the wrong thing, but pride would not have him take it back, so he looked down as well.

Aileen remembered there was a dish of salt next to the stove inside. As in her home, with the damp sea air and the cooking steam, it was the only place the condiment would stay dry. Biddy must have set it there and yet the old woman did not move from her seat.

Aileen thought she was right not to hop up at every command, but at the same time she wanted everyone to see that Biddy was in control of her domain.

As Aileen got up from her seat to fetch it herself, Carmel said cattily, 'Mind you don't leave your shadow behind or he might run off on you.'

Aileen did not know what made her angrier – the patronizing attitude to Jimmy or her suggestion that he might leave her. She went inside and fetched the salt dish, then scooped up a palmful and tipped it on top of Carmel's spuds.

'What are you doing?' Carmel screamed. 'You've ruined my food, you little bitch!'

Mick, still smarting from his own mistake, stood up in front of his daughter. 'Right, madam,' he said, 'I have had enough of this. You apologize to this good company for using that language and you apologize to Aileen.'

'Ah now, Mick,' Aileen's father, Paddy, said, 'leave the poor girl be – sure we're all tired here tonight. It's been a long journey, and Aileen maybe went a bit heavy with the salt all right.'

However, Aileen knew by the tone of her father's voice he was being disingenuous. Nobody else came to Carmel's defence, and looking around at the group, it seemed that everyone was delighted to see Carmel Kelly get a dressing-down – even her brother, Michael. Everyone, except, Aileen thought, her own brother Paddy Junior.

'No,' Mick said, 'in fairness now, you said it yourself, we're all tired. But look at your young one. It's her first year and she is helping Biddy as if she has been here all her life. She is a credit to you, Paddy. Carmel, you will apologize for being nasty to Aileen.'

'I will not,' said Carmel. 'She deliberately ruined my—'

'Right!' and with that Mick grabbed his daughter by the arm

and marched her away out of the company, presumably to give her a good hiding, which, in their absence, the present company decided she deserved.

'A good round kick up the behind is what she needs.'

'Long overdue.'

'Mick's a fine gaffer, but he has ruined that child.'

'The rest of us working twice as hard to make up for her.'

'Don't get next to her in the field, that's for sure – she'll not do a scrap and will take credit for your load.'

'Wasn't she left behind in the bothy all of last season "helping" Biddy?'

'Sure she didn't as much as wipe a spoon . . .'

Biddy contributed the occasional 'humph' of agreement, but she was the kind of wise old bird who didn't say much, generally communicating disapproval through the movement of her brow.

Mostly it had been the three girls, Noreen, Claire and Attracta, giving out about Carmel. Mick's exit had signalled the end of the meal and most of the men had gone off about the yard smoking or getting settled in their beds before the lamps and the fires went out.

A young man with a round, open face and the slanted eyes of a simpleton who was still sitting with the women blurted out, 'She does be sitting about her bed mooning over Paddy Junior.'

Aileen's eldest brother got up and stormed out of his seat.

One of the girls poked the lad and said, 'You're a stupid eejit, Noel Collins – keep your mouth shut,' but he replied right back, 'You're the same, Claire Murphy – I heard you calling his name in your sleep. "Oh, Paddy, Paddy, kiss me, Paddy Doherty! I love you, Paddy Doherty!"'

They all laughed at his exaggerated impersonation.

'Still,' Claire said, 'you'll all admit Paddy Junior is a fine thing.'

'Keep in with Aileen there and you might have a chance your-self, Claire.'

'What do you say, Aileen – will you fix me up?'

Aileen wasn't sure if she was joking or not.

'Cross her palms with silver, Miss Murphy, and she just might make a match,' Jimmy cut in.

Claire smiled at Jimmy, showing off every tooth in her head, and wriggled her shoulders from side to side, delighting in the banter.

'You're as cheeky as a monkey, Shadow Man.'

'There's no shame in being a shadow,' he said, 'to a woman like this – and I'll follow her to the ends of the earth and back again.'

Aileen didn't like the way they were talking about her as if she wasn't there, but at the same time she wasn't really able to join in all this chatter. She was still afraid of saying or doing the wrong thing.

'Well, if you ever get bored following her around and you want to step out into the limelight . . .'

'Thanks, Claire,' he said. 'I'll keep that in mind.'

Aileen had had enough. She grabbed Jimmy's arm and, tugging him to his feet, said, 'Let's go for a walk.'

As soon as they were out of earshot, over to the side of the women's house, she turned to him, raging, and mimicked, '"Oh, I'll keep that in mind. Thanks, Claire." What was that, Jimmy Walsh? You think you're so fine every woman wants you now? You think I can't speak for myself? You think you have to follow me around everywhere? That I can't look after myself? Well, let me tell you—'

In that moment Jimmy reached down, and gripping the

back of her head in his small hands, he kissed her firmly on the lips.

It seemed then that a door opened on a room inside Aileen that she had not known was there and flooded it with light.

Was this love?

If it was, it felt something like terror, and something like joy, and something like her heart melting into a pool of blood, then opening out and sealing itself into the velvet petals of a freshly opened deep red rose.

Aileen Doherty did not know how it came to pass that this young man, and no other, had taken her first kiss from her. She was not entirely sure she was happy about it, but then Jimmy Walsh the swimming fisherman from Aghabeg took her in his hands and looked down at her with his funny, crazy face and said, quite inappropriately and far too soon, 'I love you.' And in the deepest, truest part of herself, Aileen knew that, forever and ever, that was that.

Chapter Eleven

'Now,' said Sean Walsh, as Jimmy and the rest of the crew climbed into the truck that would take them on the short ten-minute journey back to the bothy, 'there's another honest day's work done.'

It was day twenty of the season and the end of another long session of potato-picking. Five bells sounded from the church tower in the nearby village of Cleggan and the workers trooped over to the long trough at the edge of the field where they threw the last of the day's harvest to be collected, dusted and finally sold to the good people of Scotland.

'Surely,' said Tom Collins.

'Never was a thing more certain,' agreed his son Noel.

'Aye,' added fourteen-year-old Kevin, the younger of the Collins boys, always following the 'big men' in the family with his final affirmation.

Jimmy was starting to really enjoy the company of these men. Aside from Sean and himself, there were ten other men: Aileen's family and the two Kelly men, the three Collins men, Noreen Flaherty's brother, James, and then the hilarious Iggy Murphy, whom Jimmy teased by saying that his twin sister, Claire, was after him.

Iggy was sweet on Noreen Flaherty, and while the others were hard men for the work, Iggy and he enjoyed an unspoken cama-raderie in their wiry, somewhat romantic appearances.

'I'll be off for the morning tomorrow,' said Mick. 'I'm away into town. I'll be relying on you to keep an eye on the younger lads,' he said across to Sean.

'Aye, boss,' Jimmy's father said.

Jimmy believed his father to be the hardest-working man he knew, but he had never seen Sean work for another man before in this way. Everyone on Aghabeg pulled their weight – that was a given if you wanted to survive on an island. However, you chose how and when you worked – there was no one there ringing bells telling you when to start and finish. The fishermen worked as a team, and although that could be said to be true with the tattie-hokers, there was nonetheless a pecking order and Jimmy found this difficult to fathom at times. There was a queue for who got first pick of the hot bacon straight from the pan and the tea still steaming hot at the midday dinner break. As newcomers, Sean made sure that he and Jimmy held back and kept themselves at the end of the line.

It wasn't in Jimmy's nature to be compliant and hang back, but when he complained to his father about this, the older man explained, 'We are not just earning a wage, son; we are earning our right to be here. The Lord gave you luck in being born a fisherman – the island and its waters give us all the fish we can eat and a bit besides to sell. It's a great life surely.' Then his face hardened and he became deadly serious. 'Working for a wage is a different story altogether. You must have humility, keep the head down and work hard for pride as much as money, son. When you work for another man, he gets your respect as a given, but you have to earn his respect back by doing his bidding. It's a challenge for every man, Jimmy, but it's what makes the working man great.'

Their working day started early. At first light, all of them would go straight outside, where the fore graipe already had the fire going and was waiting with a mug of tea and a hunk of lavishly buttered bread to keep them going through the morning. If they dilly-dallied or were last in line, as Sean and Jimmy were, they ate their bread on the truck.

On their first day out, having secured a kiss from Aileen the night before, Jimmy had waited to see where she would sit on the cart into the fields. She had thrilled him beyond belief by cocking her head high in the air past her brothers and sitting next to him on the cart. Paddy, her father, sat directly opposite them and held Jimmy's eye as Aileen, ignoring her father, flirtatiously hooked her arm into his coat and rested her head on the young fisherman's shoulder. Paddy made no move to stop this, which was in itself a sign of approval, but his mere presence nonetheless made it clear that his tolerance was limited to Jimmy behaving with propriety towards his daughter. So Jimmy sat every morning like a statue, smelling the sharp tang of his new lover's breath on his neck, knowing that while he could not kiss her in view of all the company, the wait made the want in him all the sweeter because he looked forward to the moments they would steal together later.

Their days developed a routine. Jimmy and Aileen worked alongside each other for the first few hours. He dug and turned the soil with a shovel as Aileen followed behind. Her slender body bent, her shoulders arched so that her small breasts tucked themselves into her waist – picking the hard muddy orbs and throwing them into her bucket with surprising agility and speed.

'She's like a machine,' Iggy remarked on their first day out, as Jimmy carried his belle's bucket over to the trough for her.

'She's a natural,' Mick said, as he weighed the bucket. 'Some people have the land in them – she's a great asset to the crew.'

'She'll keep you on your toes, anyway,' Iggy added. 'Sure you can hardly dig them as quick as she can pick them.'

The cheeky lad looked as if he was going to say something else, but Jimmy stared at him good and hard and made him think again. Jimmy was a joker, but when it came to people talking about Aileen, the men had learned to hold their tongues with the banter.

'He's got it bad with that Doherty girl surely.'

'Red hair? You'd never have a moment's luck in your life.'

'Skinny wee thing too – not enough meat on her for my liking.'

The men were worse gossips when they got together than the women, but Mick's job was to keep them in line.

'Mind Jimmy doesn't hear you on about her like that. He may be small, but I'd say he'd take an awful lump out of you as soon as look at you if he was riled. And as for the brothers, they'd kill you stone dead.'

By mid-morning Aileen had filled as many buckets as the grown men would do in a full day. By the end of the first week she had been selected by Biddy to be the assistant to the fore graipe. This was a big honour, not only because it took you from hard labour into the more feminine domain of the kitchen, but it also meant you got paid a small stipend for the extra work. So, at 11 a.m. sharp, the truck came to take the two women back to the bothy to prepare the main meal of the day, which would be eaten at midday. Mick would have put money aside from each of their wages to pay for the best of meat – steak, ham – and he always made sure there was plenty. Because Mick had been coming to Scotland for so long, he was friends with the locals and would buy animals direct from a pig farmer; then, for an overall price for the season, he would keep them with Finlay, the butcher in Cleggan, whose wife also provided them with such foods as Biddy did not have the equipment or ingredients to make herself – like butter and jam. Dinner was as good as you would get in any fine restaurant. Not that Jimmy had ever eaten in a fine restaurant, but it was as good as anything his mother had ever served up to him, and privately, he thought this bode very well indeed for Aileen's prospects as his wife. On one or two occasions he had looked over at his father as the two men were pounding gratefully into a plate of fried bacon, cabbage and spuds, and given him a look that clearly said, 'Well? What do you think?'

Sean had just smiled and shaken his head in amusement at his hopelessly infatuated son.

'Will you have some sense, boy, and stop hounding the poor girl? If you hold back, you'll get further.'

'I think she'll be a grand wife,' the incorrigible boy said. 'Will Mam like her?'

'Of course she will – she'll love her.'

Twice a week Biddy and Aileen missed the afternoon shift and stayed behind in the bothy to catch up on the housekeeping. On these occasions Jimmy could barely wait for the day to end. Just those few hours when she was not within his sights made him feel anxious. So he was always first on the truck and hauling the others up onto it trying to hurry them along.

Carmel was the last on, as usual, dragging her heels and complaining. 'My feet hurt,' she'd whine. 'Ow! Don't tug my arm – I've caught my skirts . . .'

Although she was certainly difficult, Jimmy was starting to feel sorry for Carmel. He could see that she was madly in love with Paddy Junior, and he knew what it was like to be so in love with somebody that you were in constant danger of losing yourself. As the weeks had passed, people were starting to distance themselves from Carmel's constant spoilt moaning. Even her father had taken to travelling on the other truck both to and from the fields. He was fearful, Jimmy suspected, of either admonishing his outspoken daughter or incurring the disrespect of his workforce if he was seen not to.

He said as much to Aileen that evening, as she was drying up the food things after supper, although she was not sympathetic.

'Carmel Kelly was a spiteful brat in national school and she's a bitch yet. Small wonder her own father can't stand the sight of her.'

'She's in love with your brother,' Jimmy said.

'She's not a hope in hell with Paddy Junior,' Aileen bit straight back at him. 'She's a face as flat and plain as a bun, and she's malicious too. She is no more in love with him than she is with you, though she'd take a chance on you for the sake of it if I gave her half the chance!'

Aileen was fiery. Jimmy liked that.

'Sure it wouldn't be you giving her the chance,' Jimmy teased her then; 'it'd be me surely.'

Aileen's lips tightened and her eyes flashed wide as she spat, 'If you want to go off with Carmel Kelly, you're welcome, Jimmy Walsh. See if I care a jot if you do.'

Jimmy could see the whites of her knuckles as she gripped the cup so tightly that he thought she might break it and he knew she was jealous.

He smiled and said, 'Don't you know I'd never leave you for another, Aileen. I'm only teasing.'

'You can tease all you like and you can go off and do your worst with that Kelly cow or any other woman of your choosing – if you can find one that would have you, and you would be lucky at that!'

'Ah, don't be cruel, Aileen,' he said – although he was as entered in the game as she was.

'I can be very cruel, and don't you forget that for one instant of your sorry life, Jimmy Walsh, if you carry on teasing me with your stupid talk.'

As she glowered at him defiantly, Jimmy looked at her small, hard hands rubbing away at the porcelain and imagined them scraping with the same angry voracity down the skin of his naked back. He quickly pushed the thought aside, something that he found he had to do often since that first kiss, and the kisses that had followed whenever they got the chance to be alone together.

'There's a picture on in Cleggan tonight,' he said. 'I was thinking we could go.'

'Maybe I'll go with one of the girls,' she said.

Jimmy decided to take his father's advice, for once. Aileen needed a firm hand or she might disappear on him altogether, so without giving himself time to think about it, Jimmy turned his back on her and, walking towards the door, said, 'Suit yourself.'

He closed his eyes and bit his lip but kept walking, and as he reached the door, Aileen suddenly said, 'I'll be ready at seven.'

Without turning round, he added firmly, 'Put on something pretty and I might take you for chips afterwards.'

As he stepped out of the bothy, Jimmy was aware he was beaming like a goon. He had her on her toes all right, and when it came to Aileen Doherty, that was the only way to have her.

Chapter Twelve

There was a world of work to be done before Aileen met Jimmy for the pictures at seven.

The men's sleeping quarters were next to the women's, but the unpredictable Scottish weather had turned chilly in the past few days and some of them had been complaining about the cold at night. Mick wanted his workforce happy, so decided to move the men's beds to an empty barn that contained an open fireplace.

The gaffer was determined to have the men set up in their new sleeping quarters that night and so the moment the supper bowls were washed, everybody got to work moving the twelve potato boxes and mattresses from one barn to the other. Making the beds and moving the effects took no time at all, but clearing the barn first was hard work. The long, narrow space had originally been an outdoor shed and still had an earth floor, although it had been so compacted by sweeping and footsteps that it was as good as a stone floor for dryness. It had been used to store farm equipment, some of which was too heavy to move. Jimmy and two other men tried to move a large barrel of tar from smack bang in the centre of the room and it was comical seeing the strong young men's faces gurn with the effort of moving it two inches.

'Here,' Biddy said, throwing a cloth over the top of it, 'now you have your own table.'

'A bar maybe,' one of them laughed, and then to drive home her point, Biddy produced a teapot and placed it ceremoniously on the cloth, saying, 'There'll be nothing stronger than tea consumed in this room, I can assure you!' and they all laughed.

One wall of the barn was taken up almost entirely by two sliding doors that would only stay shut when padlocked from the outside. In effect, the new 'bedroom' could therefore only really be accessed from the kitchen, which Biddy was not happy about.

'I don't like the idea of big men traipsing in and out of my kitchen.'

'We'll get the doors fixed, Biddy, but in the meantime I'll make sure they all bed down together so as not to be causing you too much disruption.'

The men rigged up a heavy tarpaulin as a temporary wall, sealing it on one side by laying it up against the wall with bags of coal and leaving the other end open as a makeshift entrance. Since the weather had been fine up to that point, Biddy had been cooking outside and had not lit the fire in that room before.

'Stick a brush up there, Aileen, good girl, and check the chimney is clear.'

Aileen hesitated. It was half past six and she had her good dress on ready for the pictures.

The new bedroom was finished, and the men were all outside smoking and talking; the other girls were scattered about the bothy tending to their various grooming routines and romances.

Biddy never stopped working. The extra money she made as fore graipe meant she could never be seen to rest like the others. Aileen instinctively followed her lead but stalled, worrying with the amount of work ahead of her that she wouldn't get out in time for the pictures.

This outing would be their first proper evening together, and while Jimmy was blasé about it, Aileen knew that they had earned this permission from her father for not acting improperly up to now. Even at that she and Jimmy had managed to catch a little time together each day – but with her brothers never far away, sometimes it was just a hastily stolen kiss after supper.

Jimmy was still something of a mystery to her except for the fact that he loved her wildly, although she didn't need to know much more than that. She knew that she loved him too, though she certainly did not feel ready to tell him.

'Say you love me, Aileen,' he said, as she sat back into his chest and felt the sureness of his arms wrapped around her waist in the nook behind the coal shed where they went to hide away from the others after supper.

He wrapped tendrils of red hair round his finger and kissed the tip of her curls.

'It's bad luck, you know,' she said, teasing him as she always did by changing the subject, 'my red hair.'

'Sure I know that and you'll be the death of me, Aileen Doherty,' he said, 'unless I don't get you back to your brothers and they get to me first.'

She pulled him back down and pushed his mouth onto hers and he groaned but pulled away. It was always him who did the right thing.

'I can't upset your family,' he'd say. 'I've the future to think of.'

'Fool,' she said, laughing. 'Come back down and let me kiss you.'

If she told him she loved him in that moment, he would stay

and Lord knows what trouble they might have got into, but the longer she spent in his company, the less she cared about anything or anyone but him.

Still, she wouldn't tell him she loved him. Not yet. Invincible Jim was as weak as a kitten when it came to her affections and that was the way she would keep it, for now.

When she was out in the fields working, Aileen could always feel his eyes on her, sometimes protective, sometimes just admiring her, wanting her, and she would look across at him and they would share a moment when it felt like they were touching, even though they were on opposite sides of the field. Even when he was in the field and she was back at the bothy, Aileen could still feel him around her.

'Well, girl,' Biddy said now, her back turned as she made newspaper balls for kindling, 'where's my fire? Get on with it.'

Aileen bent down and tentatively looked up the chimney. At its base was a film of heavy cobwebs grey with dust – there would be some mess coming down at her if she wasn't careful. Closing her eyes and turning her face away, she shoved the broom handle up as far as she could. There was a small clatter as a blackened bird's nest fell with a firm *plump* into the grate, followed by a cloud of coal dust. Aileen jumped back to avoid it and almost pushed over Biddy.

'Mother of God, child, what is the matter with you?'

'Sorry, Biddy – it's my good dress.'

'Are you going somewhere?'

'Jimmy is taking me to the pictures in Cleggan – that is, if that's all right with you?'

'You should know by now that everything and nothing is all right with me . . .' She looked down into the grate behind Aileen and said, 'Well, that's the worst of it down, I suppose.'

Biddy adjusted her shoulders and took a deep breath, puffing

it out in a dramatic sigh. Biddy was old, more than fifty anyway, and Aileen could see she was tired. For a moment Aileen
thought she was going to ask her to stay and help watch the
fire for the evening. Instead, she looked her carefully up and
down and said, 'That's a pretty dress all right. The green looks
well on you.'

Aileen wondered if perhaps she should cancel the pictures,
stay back and keep Biddy company for the evening. There would
be other nights, and it might be no harm to let Jimmy down
that day. He had given her an awful teasing earlier, pretending
to flirt with Claire Murphy to get a reaction out of her brother,
Iggy. In any case, he had not even bothered to find out what
picture was on. It was probably just some boring John Wayne
cowboy movie – they were all the same.

'I might stay here and keep an eye on the fire with you,' she
said.

Biddy smiled, a rarity, and swiped her with a rolled newspaper. 'Go on out to that eejit of a sweetheart and don't let him
get you into any trouble.'

Aileen flew out the door to find him.

Jimmy, in grand style, had ordered a taxi to take them to the
pictures. Aileen had never actually been in a car before, but she
did not let on. She was familiar with them, of course. She was,
after all, from a big island and they had cars. Well, three that
she knew of, but in the summer, when the tourists came, it was
not unusual to see a bus packed full of holidaymakers. The bus
would take them across to the 'English' hotels that opened season-
ally next to the sandy beaches on the north side of the island.
She guessed that Jimmy's small island didn't even have a proper
road that might carry a car. Yet here he was being Mr Big Stuff
and opening the door of the taxi for her as if he had been at it
all his life. He was a funny boy surely, but nonetheless she felt

a definite thrill sliding along the shiny leather seat and arranging herself in the corner.

Jimmy sat in the front with the driver. When they reached the town hall in Cleggan, Aileen watched as Jimmy paid the driver and shook his hand firmly. She found herself thinking how elegant and gentlemanly he appeared. This was a Jimmy she had not seen before: a man of the world. Quite the catch.

As she stepped out of the car then, she could not believe her eyes. On a billboard outside the entrance was an advertisement for that night's picture: *Wuthering Heights*. 'I am torn with Desire – tortured by hate!' the poster screamed. The devilish eyes of Heathcliff, played by the English actor Laurence Olivier, glimmered from the shadows and bored angrily into the innocent beauty of Merle Oberon's ribboned ringlets. Aileen thought she might fall into a dead faint in excitement right there on the street.

'That is my favourite book!' she said to Jimmy. 'Why didn't you tell me this was on?'

He paused and then said sunnily, 'It was a surprise!'

She knew right away it was no more than a happy accident. In all likelihood he had not even known it was based on a book, let alone the most romantic, passionate, perfect book in the world. In any case, she was thrilled beyond reason.

She let Jimmy buy the tickets and herself a quarter-bag of Iced Caramels because he knew she liked them. However, Aileen was irritated to note that he didn't get any sweets for himself. She knew his favourite were Emeralds, a chocolate-covered toffee, but the crafty lad knew there would be scant kissing opportunity if there were two of them chewing toffees at the same time. Did he think of nothing else besides kissing? A proper man – a man like Heathcliff – would have his mind on higher, more poetic things. When Jimmy tried to manoeuvre her into a row of seats near the back, Aileen marched right down to the front row. There would be no canoodling opportunities down here with them in full view of the audience behind. She would be able to enjoy the film and allow herself to completely sink into the fervent spine-tingling passion of Olivier's Heathcliff without Jimmy's bothersome groping.

'You may as well get yourself a bag of Emeralds,' she said to him when he asked if she was sure she wanted to sit so close to the screen. She almost added, 'Because that'll be all you're chewing on,' but held her tongue because it would have sounded common and already she was starting to feel ladylike and wistful, like Cathy.

However, Aileen did not find the movie as engaging or satisfying as the book. Although Laurence was handsome enough, he was not the swarthy Heathcliff of her dreams. If anything, his dark, pointed features and intense staring eyes made him look a little like Jimmy. Merle Oberon was tolerable as Cathy, but as Aileen had always imagined herself in that role, it was somewhat disconcerting to see her being portrayed as somebody else. All in all, the whole experience was something of a disappointment, and on a number of occasions throughout she wished she could steal a kiss from Jimmy, although he seemed to be enjoying the film, which vaguely surprised and annoyed her too. The best Aileen could say was that Jimmy was so mesmerized that she got to eat half his packet of Emeralds scarcely without him noticing.

Before the curtain was drawn down, she nudged Jimmy, saying, 'You promised me chips – come on now and we'll beat the crowd.'

The chip shop in Cleggan got very busy after the pictures on a Friday and Aileen wasn't in the humour for queuing in the rain.

However, Jimmy didn't move. His jaw was set, his brows furrowed, and his eyes glowered darkly as he sat silently staring at the rolling credits.

'Come on,' she said, as the man at the side of the screen switched the town hall's lights on and pulled across a makeshift red curtain. 'Everyone will be out before us – hurry up.'

Still Jimmy didn't move. She took hold of his arm and then got a fright as he pulled it away from her with a rejecting, angry tug.

'What's the matter, Jimmy?' she said.

The cinema was all but empty. The man who had switched on the lights was gathering the last of the audience out through the door and seemed to have missed these two stragglers at the front.

Jimmy turned to her and his lips curled into a nasty sneer the likes of which she had never seen on his face before.

'You know well what's wrong with me, Aileen Doherty, and don't pretend. It's clear to me now.'

Aileen's stomach twisted into a tight knot. What was the matter with him? What was he talking about?

'You're mad in the head,' she said, bluffing. She felt afraid. She wanted to cry. What was wrong with him at all?

'Now you've said it,' he said, leaping up from his seat and standing in front of her. 'I am mad – mad with love for you. You put a spell on me from that first day I saw you – with your fire and your witchery – and now you have me driven to distraction. I can barely look at you without my heart fit to bursting, and when you're not there, I don't know what to do with myself, Aileen. I'm like yer man in the film – I'm sick with love for you and that's the truth.'

Jimmy was shaking from his outburst, too emotional to even look into her face. Tears formed at the corners of his eyes, and for the first time since this foolish young man had burst into her life, Aileen felt completely overtaken by emotion herself. He loved her – properly, passionately. He loved her like Heathcliff loved Cathy. Compelled out of her seat and into his arms, she put both her hands behind his neck and pulled him down to her for a kiss that was so intense she felt she would never want to emerge from it. He gripped her tightly around the waist and all but lifted her from the ground and laid her down on the dusty wooden floor, where they entwined their limbs, then pressed their bodies so close to one another that they could not be certain which body belonged to whom as they tumbled and turned on the floor.

There was a noise behind them and they fell suddenly still and silent, limbs still wrapped round each other like they were one animal. From under the metal legs of the seats they could see through across to the door, where the manager was checking the hall. Satisfied it was empty, he turned off the lights. Now they were alone together in a dark place, unseen, for as long as they wanted: for as long as they might need. They paused to take in this fact, and the timbre of their lovemaking altered to accommodate it. Jimmy held Aileen's face and kissed her tenderly on the lips, then moving down to the delicate skin of her neck, he unbuttoned her dress to the waist and kissed whatever bare flesh he could find until her hands reached up behind and loosened the clasps of her bra. As his mouth shunted aside the loose fabric and his lips brushed the escaped breasts, Jimmy let out a groan. Then he moved his hand slowly up her leg until she felt his cold fingers on the flesh at the top of her stockings and the thin fabric of her dress being pushed aside. She could feel he was rock hard pressing against the side of her leg. She had some idea of what might happen next – her curiosity about nature had led her to understand these things – and although she wanted it to happen, more than anything, she was also afraid. That was the way of disaster and damnation. She must not give in. They had already gone far enough, further than they should ever have gone, and that was her fault. It was always the woman's fault. Although she could not say she regretted it for one single moment, she knew that she had to draw a halt before things went any further.

'No,' she said, grabbing his wrist as it crept higher up her thigh, although it would take more strength than she could muster to hold it there, never mind move it away.

'No,' she said again, but it sounded even less convincing now.

As her hold on his wrist loosened, Jimmy reached his thumb across and rubbed her gently, rhythmically, so that Aileen thought it was his intention to unravel her until she was completely un-done, which, with a howl of delight, she soon was. He looked down at her and smiled wildly, and she laughed and smiled back.

'That was wrong, Jimmy Walsh,' she said, but they both knew she wasn't one bit sorry.

'You make a man want to do bad things, Aileen Doherty,' he said, which made her want to go again. But before she could suggest anything, Jimmy stood up and, straightening himself, said, 'Now, did you say something about going for chips?'

The chip shop in Cleggan was thronged.

'Fresh fish! No war rationing on chips!' a sign in the window advertised.

Her father and the men had talked about how Scotland was like Ireland in that way. 'You wouldn't know there was a war on,' Paddy had said.

'The Scots are more like the Irish than the English,' Mick agreed.

Both countries had an easy, friendly way of going about things that wasn't a bit like the uptight formality of the English. Plus, the island men all concurred, the English were arrogant warmongers – over-interfering with Germany when they should mind their own bloody business. 'I'd never fight in an Englishman's war.' More agreements, and the more beer they had drunk, the more vehement the nodding would be.

Jimmy went inside to queue and Aileen sat on a low wall on the side of the road to wait for him. Facing out into the town, she saw the lights of hundreds, maybe a thousand houses all clustered together. How many people must live here? she thought. A girl could surely get lost in a place like this. You could lose yourself in the crowd, do as you pleased. The air was fresh and chilly, so she pulled her coat close into her chest, crossed her legs and hunched herself all together. She allowed her body to remember how much Jimmy loved her.

She was out and about in the big wide world, with the security of her father and brothers there to look out for her. Jimmy was, after all, the great love of her life. On top of all of this, there was chips and a half-bag of leftover Emeralds to look forward to.

The chips were heavy with vinegar, just how she liked them, and she and Jimmy ate them in contented silence. There was nothing more they needed to say to each other. Jimmy loved her to the detriment of himself, and she loved him back. He knew that, but she still wouldn't say it yet. She wanted to keep something for herself. Aileen was afraid that, if she let go, she might be in danger of losing herself entirely to him.

When they had finished their chips, Jimmy got down on one knee in front of her and said, pleadingly, 'Will you marry me?'

'Of course, you silly boy,' she said, delighted with herself.

The other couples outside the chipper laughed at him.

'He's as soft as shite,' one of the lads said.

'Sure he doesn't even have a ring,' his girlfriend added.

Aileen didn't care. They didn't know what true love was – nothing was going to ruin this night.

Sean Walsh came to collect the couple in a horse and cart. He'd been allocated the task by the other men, who were all in bed, asleep. Aileen and Jimmy decided not to tell him about their engagement until the next day. On the way back, Aileen lay across the floor of the cart with her head on Jimmy's lap and looked at the stars and counted each one as a blessing on her own life as her sweetheart stroked the side of her cheek with his soft hand.

As she felt the cart turn the bend into the drive of their farm, she heard Sean cry out, 'Mother of God, is that smoke?'

He whipped the carthorse and they lurched forward. Jimmy sat up suddenly, with Aileen after him, as Sean drove them into the heart of the burning bothy.

Chapter Thirteen

As the cart trundled across the cobbled stones of the courtyard, Jimmy's father roared, 'Fire! Fire!' to rouse everyone out of their beds.

'What's all this?' Biddy cried, rushing towards the cart in her night attire. She was followed by Attracta, Claire, Carmel and Noreen, half asleep in their nightgowns. Biddy screamed, 'Holy God!' as she saw the curtain of black smoke licking up the building in long, sooty lines from under the kitchen doorway.

Jimmy felt Aileen grip on to him, but he had no time to comfort her. Lives were in danger. Already his blood was up; he could feel the energy soaring through him, propelling him forward towards the building.

Sean hammered at the padlocked doors to the men's sleeping quarters, remembering, in his panic, that Mick, who was inside, had the keys, but forgetting that the room could be accessed through the kitchen.

'They're trapped inside!' Sean shouted at the women to look for a crowbar, a hammer, something – anything to wrench the sliding doors open.

Jimmy knew that the door next to the sliding ones, the ordinary kitchen door, would be open – although it was concealed by the curtain of black smoke rising up from under it. He would take a chance and fly in there and get the men out that way. There was no time to explain, no time to lose, so saying nothing to anyone, Jimmy opened the kitchen door and rolled under the deadly puff of thick black smoke that came thundering out at him. He heard his father call after him, but it was too late. Without stopping for one moment to consider his own safety, or indeed the common sense of the situation, Jimmy decided he was going to save Iggy and the other lads, Aileen's brothers and her father; he was unstoppable. He was Invincible Jim.

From the outside, it seemed as if the inside of the building would be filled with ferocious flames, so Jimmy was surprised to find that was not the case.

The smoke that had been pouring out seemed to have cleared when he opened the door, and although the place felt eerily silent and still, there was no dangerous fire – only a large ball of smoke above his head, which seemed to be drifting like a black ghoul towards the doorway he had just come through. He looked over at the fire in the grate and was amused to note nothing more than a cluster of dying embers – almost gone out. Jimmy was mystified as to where all of the smoke outside had come from, but he assumed it was gone now, and in any case, he had to get the men out of there.

Jimmy looked around, but there was no sign of anyone. He called out, 'Hello?' but the single word became muffled and faint when it hit the air and nobody answered. They must be all still asleep. The cloud of acrid smoke was moving steadily towards him, and so keeping his head down, Jimmy moved towards the tarpaulin curtain separating the kitchen from the sleeping quarters. As he pulled it back, he noticed that all the men were still in their beds, sleeping. He smiled to himself. Lazy bastards out cold and all the women running about and screaming for them!

In the far corner, there was a small, neat pile of coal burning where it had clearly fallen out of one of the bags of fuel. It didn't seem angry or dangerous and was more like the sort of small cooking fire you might make outdoors. Coal takes an age to set alight, he thought to himself – there's no panic at all, and we'll be all right for a few minutes yet. He was relieved, amused even that the men had not so much as been disturbed and thought of how they would all laugh at the fuss being made on their behalf. Nonetheless, the room was hotter in here and heavy with smoke. In fact, Jimmy's own eyes were smarting and he was starting to feel dizzy. Holding his sweater over his nose, he realized it was pointless calling out to wake them. Firstly because it would bring them into a terrible panic, but also because the smoke was now filling his throat. He had better get a move on. So, crouching down on all fours, he crawled across to the nearest bed to rouse the first man. It was Aileen's brother Paddy Junior. He prodded his chest and shook his arm, but there was no movement. He reached up and gave him a firm pinch on the nose. Just as he did that, he heard his own father's voice call out from behind him, 'Hold on there, lads – I'll have the doors open for you now . . .'

There was a clatter as Sean pulled the doors outwards; then – *whoosh* – burning coals from the small fire in the corner of the room rushed towards him like a dozen cannons, bringing the tarpaulin up in a single sheet of flame. As Jimmy called out, 'No!' there was a loud explosion and a shower of red-hot pain blasted across his face. Then everything went black.

Aileen did not notice that Jimmy had run into the building for some time after it had happened; neither did she fully consider that her father and brothers were in the burning building. She was aware that Sean was shouting for help in opening the doors, and that Biddy was rushing backwards and forwards calling for everyone to get pans and buckets of water. She saw Carmel screaming, her plain features drawn back in a shocking contortion, grabbing and clawing at the doors of the bothy as Sean tried to wrench them apart. She noticed how Biddy's skirts were dragging and drenched at the hem from the puddles left by the buckets she was frantically, pointlessly throwing in the kitchen door. She noticed how the spilt water wormed its way down the gaps between the cobblestones and landed at the tips of her good brown boots, creating a lacy pattern at her feet. She was sitting at the edge of the yard fireplace on a raised bench of bricks. This was where she always sat to eat her supper. She could not move. Everybody was running about; people were shouting at her to help, to move herself, but Aileen could not lift herself up from her seat. She was stuck there as surely as if she had been glued there, or frozen in time. If she did not move, if she stayed exactly where she was, perhaps she would find that this event was not happening after all. Perhaps she would wake, as if from a dream, and find that her brothers and father had gone to the pictures with them that evening, or were still in the other house complaining of the cold and had never moved at all to the burning barn.

She could see that Carmel was screaming and that Biddy was shouting, but she could not hear them.

All she could hear was a sound from the chimney she had been cleaning earlier, one she heard just before the bird's nest had plumped comfortably into the grate. Repeating itself in her head, in her ears over and over and over again, drowning out all other noises, all other thoughts. She was transported back to earlier on in the evening when she had been rushing her task. The muted clatter she had not given a second thought to at the time had been the snap of the flue closing.

Chapter Fourteen

Biddy had long since known that the Scottish people were good: that had certainly been her experience in her years as fore graipe for the Illaunmor tattie-hokers. However, even she could not get over their kindness towards them in the days after the bothy fire.

When the people of Cleggan heard about the terrible tragedy, they raised all the money needed to pay for the bodies to be returned home to Ireland. There were ten men dead in all: Mick Kelly (fifty), Michael Kelly (twenty), James Flaherty (twenty-one), Tom Collins (thirty-seven), Kevin Collins (fourteen), Noel Collins (fifteen), Iggy Murphy (twenty-one), Paddy Doherty (forty-seven), Paddy Doherty Junior (twenty-two) and Martin Doherty (nineteen). The fire had raged for the guts of that night; the barrel of tar had exploded and devastated the inside of the building with ferocious intent. The local Cleggan firemen could not put the fire out with their own pump and needed to call in two other units from large neighbouring towns to help stem the fire and prevent it spreading to the other farm buildings. When they had beaten back the flames, only the stone walls remained. It was a terrible sight that Biddy knew she would never forget. Worse than the death of her parents, worse than the death of her brother; it was an act that shook the devout woman's very faith in God Himself.

The bodies of the ten men sleeping in the barn that night were destroyed. Nothing more than black cadavers, she had heard the firemen describe how their exposed bones were lying flat in the places where their beds had been, as if arranged there by some evil intent. One was even curled on his side like a baby. The coroner concluded afterwards that each of the men had been dead from smoke inhalation long before the doors had been opened and set the fire into a rage. Their positions of repose suggested that each of the men had died in their sleep, so at least they had not suffered, but they did not find this out for a long time afterwards.

However, that was small comfort to the Cleggan firemen, who would be haunted to their own dying days by the sight of the ten 'sleeping' cadavers, along with the pitiful sobs of the women, as they came out shaking their heads. Biddy tried to console the young girls as best she could, while the firemen stood guard at the bothy doorway, four of them keeping the young Irish girls away from the ghoulish sight of the bodies before they were removed to the funeral home. Biddy tried her best, but the girls, wild with grief, clawed at the blackened uniforms begging to be let inside to say goodbye to their men. The Cleggan firemen stood firm and impervious to the women's pleadings, even though their own hearts were breaking. What worse fate was there than to lose a father, a brother? Only to lose a son or a husband – and breaking the news to the mothers and wives back in Ireland was all these women had to look forward to now.

Biddy had not lost anyone directly belonging to her in the fire and, being the elder of the group, had to take charge of the young mourners. She was beyond grateful when complete strangers from the local community, and beyond, stepped in to make all of the arrangements. The firemen from Cleggan called upon their colleagues from as far away as Glasgow and Fife to come out in support of their fellow Celts. Most of the Scottish firemen were themselves volunteer reserves and so were far from inured to the horrors of firefighting. Although it was agreed that the fire was no more than a terrible tragedy – and that in no way could they have saved the lives of the men inside the building – they still felt somewhat responsible for the welfare of these Irish unfortunates and wanted to help them in any way they could.

A fund was set up and enough money was raised to pay for the funerals and recompense the tattie-hokers for the money they had lost – not just in the fire but in earnings for the rest of the season.

News of the tragedy spread through Scotland and Ireland, and consumed two countries already weighed down with the bad news of war so that two days after the fire took place and each of the ten coffins arrived in Glasgow, the streets from the train station to the port were lined with ordinary Scottish people come to pay their respects.

Biddy was astonished to see the coffins being transported in black carriages with plumed horses; then each one was lifted onto the boat by uniformed firemen and passed into the care of the Dublin Garda Síochána, who had travelled over to accompany the bodies back.

However, with the overwhelming grief of these five young women resting on her spinster shoulders, Biddy was very grateful for the practical help given to her by the Cleggan women who travelled with them across to Dublin. The Cleggan branch of the Scottish Women's Rural Institute and St Andrew's Ambulance Association volunteered to travel with the six distraught women and make sure that their nutritional and medical needs were tended to, making their return trip more comfortable than their journey across. A section had been cordoned off for them in the first-class area of the ship as a gift from the shipping company. Delicious food was also made available, with tea and coffee served to them as if they were gentry. There were cushions at their back and beds for them to sleep on, with soft down blankets laid over them with the attentive care of the gentle Scottish women.

At Dublin Port, it seemed as though every soul in the whole of Ireland had travelled to meet them. Biddy and the girls stood at the top of the steps of the boat, three decks up. They were already in awe at being so elevated, but as they looked down, each one gasped in astonishment at the sea of people stretched out in front of them. Their plight had touched the hearts of every newspaper reader and every radio listener in their homeland and Ireland's mourners were out in force; the black of their clothes was woven through the city landscape, making it appear as if a deep hole had been carved through the streets of the capital. Although in Scotland Biddy had been surprised by the number of people who had come to pay their respects, she could see that here in Ireland, a dark shadow had been cast and the country was in mourning. Biddy knew they were not just weeping for the Cleggan tattie-hokers and the frail girls in her care, but for their own husbands and sons gone to England and America, and working to send money home. Some would die in factory accidents or bare-knuckle fights or anonymously of drink on the streets of London, Birmingham or New York; others would get good jobs and write and send money home; but the vast majority would never be seen again. They existed to the families they left behind as photographs on the mantelpiece, next to the Sacred

Heart of Jesus to whom their mothers and wives prayed daily for their safekeeping. By the time their duty was done, and their homes in Ireland paid for and their families secure, they were English or American men.

They found wives and had children who existed only in name to their Irish families. Many more men had simply 'disappeared' because they set up new lives abroad and abandoned their wives in Ireland altogether, and that was worse than a death in itself. Every person who had lost a son, or a husband, or a father in this way came out to mourn them and their own losses that day. The city people walked across town for an early spot at the docks. The country people locked up their cattle and put down their tools and travelled on carts and buses and trains to be there for the women who shuffled pitifully behind the ten coffins in black clothes gifted to them by the Scottish Protestant women.

Biddy was an intelligent woman; she understood why people came out that day and how the tragedy of the five vulnerable, shivering creatures standing on the deck of the ship with her had captured the hearts of the whole country. However, she still wished that they would all go home and mind their own business and let them travel back to Illaunmor in peace.

As they waited for an escort to lead them down the steps through the crowd, Biddy took one last look across at Aileen. The other girls looked dumbfounded, but nonetheless were aware of the fuss. Aileen had not seemed to notice anything since the fire. Not the luxury of the first-class passage, not the kindness of the Cleggan women, not the vast crowds or the pomp of the funeral procession and certainly not the scrappiness of the black clothes that had been lent to her. She wore a shapeless dress with a lace collar and a coat with sleeves that were too long and buttons that were large and awkward to close.

'Why in the name of Christ did you allow yourself to be landed with this get-up?' Biddy had complained that morning as she fiddled with the front of her young charge's coat, although she had not expected an answer.

Aileen Doherty had not spoken a word or, in effect, moved an inch of her own volition since the fire.

She had simply put one foot in front of the other, shuffling dutifully behind the others from bothy to boat.

She had eaten some food, but only through Biddy's persistence. On the morning of their journey, Biddy had cleared the kitchen so she could spoon-feed the young woman a half-bowl of creamy porridge.

All of the women were shocked by what had happened. Biddy herself was not convinced that the whole thing was not simply a bad dream that she had yet to waken from, and young Carmel Kelly had gone half mad. After her initial screaming on that dreadful night, she had convinced herself that her father and brother were not inside the building at all.

'I feel sorry for all of you,' she insisted, over and over again. 'All I can say is thank goodness Daddy and Michael were meeting with Finlay the butcher in Glasgow when it happened. I don't know why they've been delayed this long, but I'm sure they'll be back soon.'

She then told herself they had gone ahead to Illaunmor and would be at home on the island waiting for her. No one contradicted her. The young women barely had the energy to deal with Carmel at the best of times, even Biddy, and with their own grief weighing so heavily, they simply played along with her fantasy. Soon they would be back on the island and Carmel's madness could be dealt with by her own mother.

The same could be said for Aileen, although Biddy had a

special feeling of responsibility for the girl – perhaps because she had been her assistant but more likely for some reason that, as yet, she dared not name. Biddy was as sorry as any person could be for the other girls' losses, but her main concern was looking after Aileen. The other girls had each other, but Aileen was very much out on her own and had withdrawn herself even further from the group.

Her sweetheart, Jimmy, had been so badly injured in the explosion it seemed doubtful that he would survive, although Aileen was in such a daze she had not even asked for him.

When the bodies were cleared from the bothy, Biddy saw Aileen wander in there and she followed her, standing by the door so she wouldn't know she was being watched.

The earth floor of the barn had cracked open and there were broken craters of sand and ashes where the day before it had been a flat surface she herself had swept over in preparation for the men's beds to be made on.

She saw Aileen sit on the ground, and instinctively this child of the land reached down and grabbed a handful of earth. She held it in the palm of her hands and seemed to study it, as if expecting some miracle to rise from the ashes. After a moment, she stood up, still in a trance-like state of grief, but instead of simply letting the earth fall from her hands, she automatically placed her hand in her pocket.

Biddy got a sharp pain in her stomach just looking at the girl pitifully preserving the ashes from her father's and brothers' deathbeds. She felt compelled to protect her, although as she realized that, a terrible thought crept into the honest old woman's conscience. Looking across at the fireplace that had caused all this damage, she thought that perhaps in protecting Aileen, she was trying to protect herself too. However, she put all thoughts of that nature to the back of her mind. It would be a long journey home to Ireland, and she had many long days ahead to contemplate the horrors of what had happened and the conse-quences that lay ahead. For all of them.

Chapter Fifteen

Dublin guards carried each of the coffins off the ship, and the Illaunmor women followed in a sombre procession as the crowd parted to allow them to pass through a path no less than four people deep. The throng of bodies standing in silent respect in the harbour and beyond on the Dublin Quays created a blanket of people around the women, muffling the wind from the sea, surrounding them with humanity. To an observer, the goodwill of thousands of mourners should have overwhelmed the frail female bodies at the centre of the fray, but instead it seemed the other way round. The women linked themselves together, clutching each other's forearms, their bare fingers white and tense like the claws of some dying bird, their young bodies stooped in the staggering gait of the grieving. Following the coffins of their men, they were oblivious to the crowd that surrounded them. The very blindness of their grief wielded them a strange power over the gathered mob. The intensity of the island women's loss caused involuntary sobs and shouts from random mourners. The enormous sadness emanating from the tiny women seemed to fly over the crowd and snatch painful memories from them – the death of a husband, the loss of a child – sucking tears and buried grief like some vampiric demon.

Biddy held on to her girls, although she felt very flustered by the huge crowds. She just wanted to get home; even in the best of circumstances she had no time for the 'Irish' and considered herself an Illaunmor islander in totality, with no connection to the mainland – if she could help it. While the mainland Irish claimed the rugged, romantic islanders as their own – celebrating their traditions and their 'curious' ways and folklore in their museums, art and literature – true islanders like Biddy considered themselves completely apart. Her address ended 'Illaunmor Island' – and she called the country over the bridge 'Ireland'. She had always felt more comfortable in Scotland – 'The Scots showed me more kindness and gave me more work than the Irish ever did' – and thought it typical of the Dublin jackeens to turn up in their hordes to gawk at the 'poor islanders'. People meant well – she knew that in her heart – but she also felt their ghoulish curiosity at witnessing the arrival of the 'Illaunmor Ten', as they had doubtless already been christened. She had seen half a dozen photographers at least, their cameras clicking and flashing in the silence like some demented child set loose during High Mass. This was a shocking carry-on altogether and Biddy couldn't understand where all these people had come from and how the news of their loss had travelled so far so quickly. It felt intrusive to have all of these people here watching their grief, like it was some form of entertainment.

She took Aileen's arm and guided her down the steps of the ship. Biddy and Aileen were the last in the procession behind the coffins. In front of them, Carmel swaggered, a bored expression on her face, still deluded in her belief that it was not her own dead she was following. Aileen was numb. While the young woman's stride was firm and her face set in an expression that could almost be described as calm, Biddy understood that she had not begun to take in what had happened to her. Her already pale skin was as white as the collar of her dress beneath, and the mist had stuck her red curls to the side of her cheeks, giving her an almost ghostly appearance that Biddy found hard to look upon. While the other women wept and comforted each other, Aileen remained apart, not just from them, but, Biddy sensed, from herself as well.

Biddy stayed with her because she was afraid the young woman might descend into the kind of madness where a person could be in so much pain they became estranged from themselves. This affliction had already befallen young Carmel. Although, Biddy knew that Aileen was a very different creature to the spoilt Kelly girl. Despite Aileen's ethereal appearance and the silly romance with the brave young lad who had nearly got himself killed in the fire, Biddy took her to be peculiarly grounded. She was practical enough about the kitchen and a decent enough young cook, but it was when Aileen was tattie-hoking out in the fields that Biddy saw something else at play. Her hands moved with such speed, picking through the earth as if they were small burrowing animals, almost detached from the pale beauty they belonged to. In the twenty years she had been travelling to Scotland doing this work, Biddy had never seen anyone work with such an obvious affinity with the earth. Had Aileen been a young man working with that deftness and speed, she would have been lauded – carried home on the shoulders of the other men. However, because Aileen was a girl, Mick Kelly had made note of how well she worked but not afforded her any great fuss. Biddy knew that there was something different about this girl. Sometimes when she was bent working, she seemed to become invisible, to blend into the earth as if the land itself had gathered around her and made her a part of it.

Sceptics would have simply called the girl a hard worker, but Biddy believed there was something more to Aileen than that. The devout Catholic knew that such magical people existed:

somewhere between sprites and saints. Their special talents marked them out and meant that they never felt that they truly belonged among ordinary humans. Biddy could see that the young girl was dependent on the men in her life: her father and brothers were the anchors that grounded her. Now that she had lost them in this sudden and terrible way, Biddy was afraid her young friend might become lost entirely, in her own mind at least. She was no parent, but the substantially built island spinster took it upon herself to be Aileen's keeper, at least until she was delivered home safely into the arms of her mother.

She gripped Aileen's hand, tucking it in under her own and holding it tightly in place.

Biddy thought they would never get to the train. As they walked through the parting crowds at their slow mourner's pace, the grey drizzle starting to seep through their heavy wool clothes, she felt like shouting out to the guards to hurry them along before they were all soaked through. What was the point of dragging it out like this? The funeral proper wasn't until the following day at least, and while they'd be trudging around for miles then, at least you knew there was an end to it. Goodness knows – were they going to be expected to walk like this all the way to the train station? Biddy felt like they were simply on parade. Once or twice Biddy looked down to check that she was still holding Aileen's hand in her own. The girl was so fragile and moved so seamlessly beside her that it was almost as if she wasn't there at all.

They walked at a snail's pace out of the huge square of the harbour and started down the quays towards the train station. The further they walked, the more protective Biddy became of Aileen and all the other women, and the angrier she got at the Dubliners' expectation that they make a show of their grief. Their tears weren't going to dry up – not that day, or the day after – or for many years after that, if, indeed, any of them ever got over it. So what was the sense in prolonging what was already an arduously long removal of remains with this circus of grief? What were the stupid Irish putting them through this for? They were island people. Let them get back to their island and bury their dead, and the rest of them could mind their own business!

As they reached Kingsbridge Station, Biddy saw there was an army of priests and bishops and important-looking dignitaries in suits and mayoral chains waiting for them in the grand fore-court. One or two of them, including their own parish priest, were raised up on a small podium with a lectern and a micro-phone on it.

'Mother of Divine Jesus,' she muttered under her breath. 'Now they're making theatre out of us.'

While the guards carrying the coffins walked into the station proper and formed a military line along the concourse, Biddy noticed that the girls at the front of their procession baulked at following them into the station.

Aside from their obvious terror at being confronted with such a formal grouping, after an hour's solid walking and crying, the women were hungry and utterly exhausted.

Biddy had had enough. She broke away from the procession, and gently placing Aileen next to the other women, she made her way over to Illaunmor's parish priest, Father Dooley. He was standing next to some class of a robed cleric – a bishop or a monsignor: it was hard to tell, as their official duty robes were somewhat more muted than their opulent High Mass garb – and looked incandescent with pride to be in such elevated company. Biddy took a deep breath. This was not going to be easy. Dooley was a pompous man and not local. Doubtless this was a great day for him, being the centre of attention with all the clerical high-ups out in force, and Biddy was only afraid of what he might come up with if he was called upon to say a few words publicly, which by the cut of him, he looked like he had every intention of doing. Thankfully, his young curate, Father Smyth, was with him – a practical, open-faced local lad of no more than thirty and a distant cousin of Biddy's. She approached him first. An expression of almost immeasurable sadness spread across his innocent features.

'Ah, Biddy, I am so sorry – we all are. The whole island is in mourning.'

'A word, Father,' she said, as he took her hand in both of his in that way nice priests do.

'The girls are exhausted and I can see there's some class of an official ceremony planned here and . . .'

He nodded and patted her hand. 'No need to explain,' he said, and immediately set about gathering the women up and herding them onto the platform, past the waiting line of guards and coffins and onto the Mayo train before Father Dooley and his coterie of bishops and counsellors could object. As the young curate settled them into the carriage appointed to them, Biddy thanked him.

'No problem,' he smiled at her.

Biddy really appreciated his help because she knew that he would probably get into trouble with Father Dooley, the ambitious parish priest, who was doubtless plotting how he could use their public misfortune to gain advantage with the bishop. Biddy watched him leave the platform and then enter into an arm-waving conflab with Dooley before she retreated back to the carriage. Attracta and Noreen were asleep already, their heads on each other's shoulders, and Claire was sharing out a bag of scones given to them by the Scottish women. Biddy looked around the carriage and noticed that her young charge was not there.

'Where is Aileen?'

Attracta and Noreen woke from their slumber, and all four girls looked across at her, puzzled.

'Oh,' Carmel said, 'she didn't get on. I saw her, just now, walking down the platform.'

'What way?' Biddy asked. She could feel the panic rising in her.

'That way,' Carmel said, shrugging and pointing left towards the front of the train. 'Is there any with jam? I can't eat scones without jam . . .'

Biddy went straight back out to the corridor, leaped off the train and ran down the platform. Steam puffed at her skirts: the engines were starting. Let the train go without them; there would be another – as long as Aileen was all right.

Biddy saw her almost straight away, standing at the edge of the platform in front of the train. Her ankles were balancing at the edge of the deadly precipice, and the tips of her toes were dangling directly above it. She was holding her skirts and gazing down into the tracks like she was at the edge of a rock pool looking at crabs and thinking of dipping her toes in.

Biddy froze. 'Aileen.' She mouthed her name silently in terror. Any noise would surely send Aileen tumbling onto the tracks.

'All aboard!' a guard shouted behind her. Biddy flinched, but Aileen seemed to have heard nothing. She was lost to the world around her. Biddy moved forward towards the girl, keeping her eyes set firmly on her feet as if it was her gaze alone holding them on solid ground. More smoke belted out from beneath the train and there was a loud roar as the engines proper started up. Aileen turned round, a questioning look on her face as if suddenly remembering where she was. Biddy was afraid that she was about to lose her balance. She took two long strides, grabbed Aileen by the shoulders and pulled her away from the edge. The girl did not object, or indeed even seem to notice Biddy was there, but allowed herself to be walked back up the platform, where an irritated guard hustled them both up onto the train.

The rest of the journey passed without incident. The women ate and slept, woke and ate some more. Every hour or so either Noreen, Claire or Attracta would break down and call out the name of their brother or father in a heartwrenching sob, then the other women would comfort her as best they could. Each knew there was much keening and wailing waiting for them back on the island, so they did what they could to preserve some energy for that. They distracted each other as much as they could with titbits of food and stories about towns they passed on their journey across the country, but each one of them had a rock of dread painted with their mother's and siblings' faces sitting in the pit of their stomachs.

Aileen remained detached from the group. Her eyes gazed out at the changing landscape, her pale face more distant than the sun. Biddy tucked Aileen's hand into the crook of her own arm and then stroked Aileen's hand for the duration of the journey. The girl was so still in her body it was as if she was dead herself. Biddy wondered if her spirit had deserted her and gone in search of her father and brothers.

At the station, there were no fond goodbyes among the girls. Each of them flew gratefully into the arms of their mothers as if they were glad, finally, to be free of each other's company. Biddy held herself back from approaching the mothers. They were grateful, she knew, for the kindness she would have shown their daughters, and they would say thank you in their own time, but that time was not now. There was nothing for her to say to them. *I'm sorry for your loss.* It did not begin to cover the magnitude of their grief. She would wait until the funeral.

However, when she noted that Anne Doherty had not come

herself to get her daughter but that she was being collected by their neighbour John Joe Morely, even though Biddy lived on the side of the island nearest the bridge, she insisted on going with Aileen in the bachelor farmer's cart.

'I'll see her delivered to her own door,' said Biddy.

She knew John Joe. He was a quiet, respectable man. Well turned out. Never married. Like herself. Although, he had the two small children his feckless brother had left behind. There wasn't much you didn't know about people on this island. They sat quietly, gazing out across the darkening, relentless bogland. Each field looked the same as another, distinctive only to the locals, who knew which land was owned by whom and which land was common ground. John Joe kept his eyes on the road, and nobody spoke for the hour; the only sound was the crunch of the old horse's hooves on the gravelly road.

John Joe pulled into the boreen that led up to Doherty's Cottage. It was in a remote spot and the path up to it was long. Biddy had been here once or twice as a child, as her parents had had a travelling shop, but young Paddy Doherty had always run down and met them on the road. Biddy was surprised that Aileen's mother had not come to meet her with John Joe and was expecting for her to come to the door to greet them.

When she didn't come out, Biddy got down from the cart and went to the door with Aileen.

John Joe waited. 'I'll drop you back,' he said.

He knew where she lived. Everyone did. She didn't like being beholden to the man, but it would take her a good four hours to walk across the island and she was exhausted already, so she nodded to him.

Aileen was standing at the front door, hugging her coat tight to herself, looking around her vaguely as if she was a stranger to the place. Biddy said a silent prayer that her mother would be fit to comfort her, but she already had a bad feeling about that. She was about to knock on the door when Anne came out. She was not wearing an apron, something that one would expect to see in a woman caught off guard in her own house, and was patting down her dress.

She was clearly not expecting anyone to be with Aileen.

'Thank you,' she said, holding the door closed, 'for bringing her home.' Then giving John Joe the most cursory of waves in thanks, she said, 'Aileen, come inside now.'

Biddy was scandalized, but reminded herself that grief affects people in many different ways.

Aileen stood in the doorway looking at the sky, like her own mother was a stranger.

'Aileen!' Anne called.

Aileen looked at her mother and in the moment that the young woman recognized her, Biddy witnessed the dawning of the sad truth across Aileen's face, which all but broke her own heart: she was home. Without her father and brothers, she was home. A dark cloud swept across the mountain behind her and Aileen suddenly turned to look at it as if she had heard it gathering at her back. Then she turned back and said the first two words she had spoken since they had left the bothy in Scotland.

'Where's Jimmy?'

Chapter Sixteen

Jimmy opened his eyes. They had taken the bandages off while he was sleeping. With the shock of his lids tearing back from each other, a stream of tears escaped and poured down his cheeks. He could feel them stinging as they crept into channels of sensitized skin and ran down to his ears.

He saw the back of his mother's head across the room. She was talking to a man in a white coat whose voice he recognized. His doctor.

Jimmy knew he was in hospital, although he still could not remember how he got there, and for a good while after arriving, he had not been fully aware of the extent of the injuries he had incurred in the fire. However, the longer he lay in the cold, hard bed, the clearer it became: he had come as close to death as any man had the right to come.

He remembered everything in the lead-up to the explosion at the bothy: going to the pictures with Aileen, kissing her, touching her, then buying her chips and coming back with Sean to find the barn on fire. He remembered the adrenaline rush of tearing into the building to save the men, the black smoke; he remembered one minute trying to rouse Paddy Junior from his bed; then, as his father opened the doors, it seemed that a ball of fire came out of nowhere hurtling towards him; there was a loud bang that seemed to reverberate through his very bones, then . . . nothing. Next thing he was lying here, all wrapped up like an Egyptian mummy, unable to move.

'He's lucky to be alive,' he heard somebody say when he first woke up.

He could see or feel nothing of himself except a terrible searing pain all over his body that seemed to be coming from the inside out. He thought he might be in hell and wondered if the words were being spoken by the devil himself.

Then he heard his mother's voice saying, 'He's awake! Thank the Lord he's awake!' His mother was the only person who would have noticed the slight movement he had managed to make with his hand. She must have known his fear because she moved in close to him until he heard her steady voice talk directly into his ear. 'You're in a hospital in Glasgow, pet – don't try to speak.' She gulped heavily and he knew she was trying to hide the fear in her own voice. 'You're very badly burned, son. We've got you covered in bandages now, Jimmy. We'll get you better – don't you fret. Doctor, can we get something for the pain?'

She could not even touch his hand, although he could sense her hovering over him closely, wanting to hold and comfort him but unable to.

For a while after he woke Jimmy's whole body, including his face and head, was bandaged up. He could not speak, even if he had had the inclination to do so, which he did not. Day and night meant nothing to him anymore – beyond the muffled voice of his mother telling him, 'Goodnight,' it was difficult for him to calculate how long he had been there.

With his head covered in bandages, all sounds were muted. Aside from holes to breathe through his nose and one big enough to hold a straw in his mouth for eating, he was completely encased in bandages. Jimmy slept as much as he could. If he moved at all, he would wake with pain, then try to sleep again. People could not see his eyes, and it hurt to move his limbs, so he guessed those around him – his parents, the doctors and nurses – did not know if he was awake or asleep. As a result, they barely spoke to him. He could hear them moving around, discussing him, whispering speculations when they thought they were out of his earshot.

'You must stay positive,' he heard a man say to his mother – an English accent, a doctor. 'He'll pull through if he has the will.'

'We're praying for him,' said another – a priest perhaps.

He wondered sometimes if they thought he was dead already under all the bandages. At times he felt that this was what it might be like to be a ghost. Dead and entombed but remembered. Still a part of people's lives but living on the edge of their consciousness. Central to everything and yet never part of the action.

When they changed his dressings once a day, he knew he was alive because of the pain of physical contact. No matter how gentle and kind the nurses were, there was always pain. They moved him around, this way and that, two of them – nuns, he imagined, as he could not see them – making kind, reassuring noises. They did not intend to hurt him, but certainly for the first while they did. The worst part was when a bandage was removed and the cold air hit the raw wounds. That was when he was reminded that the bandages were there because he had no skin to speak of.

Sometimes the younger nurses forgot that his brain and ears were working. Once, a rough-handed girl said, 'Ew – that looks very nasty,' as she was unwrapping the layer of bandage next to his skin, and the other added, 'Don't know why we're bothering with this one, really. He'd be better off dead.'

They gave him tablets, shoving the bitter pills in through the small hole of his mouth, followed with a straw of cold water. They were supposed to ease the pain, but all Jimmy could do was wonder what the pain would be like without the supposed numbing effect of these strong drugs.

Worse than all of this, though, was the terrible, empty despair. It was like a black hole that was growing inside him. He was grieving for the loss – not of his limbs or his ability to move, to hear properly, to see, but of Aileen.

He did not even try to ask for her. He knew she wasn't there. He could feel it. With the same certainty with which he had loved her, he now knew he had lost her.

One afternoon, a few weeks in, while his father was sitting with him, he managed to ask, 'Aileen?'

'I don't know if you're ready to hear this, Jimmy, but you'll find out sooner or later anyway.'

His father then told him what had happened, to everyone.

The men had died and Aileen had returned with the rest of the women to Illaunmor to bury them. It had not been Jimmy's fault. They had died of smoke inhalation before he had even entered the building.

'It's by God's grace you're alive, son,' his father said. Then his voice broke as he added, 'If I hadn't opened the doors when I had . . . If I'd have known—'

His mother's voice cut in: 'Shh, Sean, don't torture yourself. Our son is alive – that's the main thing.'

But it wasn't the main thing for Jimmy. The main thing was that he had lost Aileen. He had wooed her and won her and now he had lost her. He had tried to save her brothers and father, and in failing to do so, he had let her down. It didn't help that his father told him it would have been impossible. The impossible was what love required of you. When he was with

Aileen, he could do anything; the impossible was what he was all about. He was a boy who could swim oceans, but now he was not even able to raise his arm up off the bed to touch his own face. He was completely dependent on other people – to turn him, to toilet him, to feed him. He could do nothing for himself. The complete loss of independence was a torture in itself, but what made it unendurable was the fact that his one true love was a world apart from him again.

Without Aileen, there was no hope of a future for him. He would get out of here, probably, possibly, but what was the point if Aileen wasn't there to share his life with?

For the first few weeks of his care Jimmy was disillusioned and depressed thinking of all he had lost. Then as the pain began to lessen, which it did by a little every day, and his body began to heal, hope began to creep back in.

'The skin is healing very well,' he heard the doctor tell his mother. 'We'll have you back on these feet in no time,' he said more loudly, gently patting Jimmy's leg.

He was getting better. He was coming back to himself. He would go and get Aileen again. He knew where she was. He would beg her forgiveness, and if she didn't forgive him there and then, why, he would stay right next to her and wait until she did. It did not matter to him if it was five minutes or five years – or fifty. He would do what he did before, which was, quite simply, keep her within his sights, except this time he'd never let her go. He had won her before and he would win her round again.

The bandages on his face were the last to come off entirely. For the longest time he could not open his eyes and there were doubts as to how far the fire had damaged them. There was speculation that perhaps he was blind, but there was no way of knowing until the skin around his eyes had healed.

The nurses called for the doctors and there was great fuss and excitement when it was revealed he could see. His mother came and held his hands and cried, and while it was wonderful, there was only one person whom Jimmy really wanted to see. It came upon him then that he preferred to have his eyes closed, because then he could imagine Aileen's beautiful face. He could visualize her swimming up to him off the steps in Aghabeg, her red hair like crimson seaweed snaking down her back, or coming in close to kiss him. He replayed their embrace in the cinema over and over and over again, and listened for the soft timbre of her voice, and the whimpering of her passion as he had taken her into his arms. When he remembered, his whole body ached with such intensity that he could not tell if it was the burns or his heart breaking in his chest with the fear of never holding her again.

As each day passed, Jimmy's resolve to recover and get Aileen back strengthened. He watched as the blisters abated and the skin grew back on his limbs. His arms and legs were revealed to him again. There was scarring in places – that was to be expected – but the doctors told him that seawater had miraculous healing qualities and that they had heard he was a fine swimmer. He was to go swimming in the healthy saltwater around the island each day and his scars would soon soften. His face was the part of him still to be uncovered completely. In the days leading up to the unveiling, the dressings were loosened so that his skin could become accustomed to the air. As they took the bandages off, he studied the faces of the nurses for clues as to how he looked. Their calm features were unmoved, which he took to mean he looked all right.

The week leading up to this had been a frenzy of progress and change. He was able to sit up, and although his tongue still felt swollen in his mouth, and his voice therefore sounded somewhat strange to him, he could now speak. His legs were shaky and he would have to learn how to walk on them again after such an extended period in bed, but the doctors were confident that there was no permanent damage and that with practice 'and some fine home cooking', he would be right as rain in a few months.

It was all good news and now that the face bandages were gone entirely, it meant that it would only be a short time before he came back entirely to himself.

He tried to sit up, and as he did, he grunted and his mother came quickly from across the room. She smiled at him, a soft smile full of love, but he thought there was perhaps a slight mixture of pity in her look too. She had been through a lot with him these past few weeks, surely. He was her only child and he felt the pressure of her holding him close to her. He remembered how she had fought his father, not wanting them to go to Scotland. It was as if she had known something bad was going to happen to them. 'A red-haired girl? The thundering wee eejit! Oh well, then – I might have known.' Why had his father told her about Aileen? He knew she'd fuss. Still, she seemed happy now. He was going home. He would get himself in tip-top shape and then he was going to find his girl. Everything was going to be all right.

He tried to smile, but his face felt peculiar. Tight.

'Bring me a mirror,' he said to his mother. 'I want to see myself.'

It was not like Jimmy to bother about how he looked, but he felt that perhaps there was something amiss and, well, he was simply curious. He had been burned after all, so there must be scarring. He thought the scars would be like the ones on his arms, but time and the magical, medicinal powers of the Aghabeg seawater would make them fade.

His mother flinched. He saw her actually flinch, then look at the doctor, who nodded and handed her a round hand-held looking glass. Jimmy had a strange, ominous feeling that there should be such an item so readily to hand. It was as if they were expecting him to ask for it, to want to look at himself, as if there was something wrong.

His mother took the mirror from the doctor and gave it to him without saying a word. Her serious expression and silence gave him some idea of how she thought he might react. She handed the mirror to Jimmy face down, gripping it tight, clearly reluctant to let him take it in his swollen, red hands. Jimmy kept his eyes firmly fixed on his mother's face and saw on it a mixture of apology and fear.

He turned the glass and looked straight into it. A terrifying monster looked back at him.

It seemed that Invincible Jim was not so invincible after all.

Chapter Seventeen

Aileen cried at the funeral. She cried until she thought she would run out of tears, then cried some more. She clutched at her mother's arm as they both sobbed through the Mass, then walked behind the coffin, crying all the way to the graveyard and as they both threw a handful of earth down into the mass grave where all ten men were buried together. When they turned to leave the graveyard, her mother stumbled and then collapsed. As she doubled over from the physical pain of the grief hitting her, she let out such a wail that it resounded all around, bouncing off the stones of the graveyard walls and beyond – it seemed to be begging itself to be a loud enough noise to raise the dead themselves. Anne Doherty's keening for her husband and sons captured the despair and desperation of all the grieving islanders and so the other women joined her in a unified cry. Together they sent a powerful howl of despair up to their God and for days afterwards the wind echoed it around the headlands and beaches and mountains of Illaunmor until it seemed that the women's terrible grief had become a part of the landscape itself. The grey clouds seemed like puffs of poisonous smoke; the ordered waves of the summer sea threw themselves up at each other with the chaotic stirring of a fire, spewing rocks up onto the shoreline and crashing at each other in vast, angry explosions.

Cut bogland resembled shallow graves, and the purple heathery mounds of land between were like sleeping bodies waiting to be buried.

When Aileen and Anne got back to their cottage, their mutual weeping made things easier between them.

There had been a man in the house the day before, when Aileen had arrived home. Biddy dropped her at the door and when Aileen went inside, he was sitting at the kitchen table, although there was no tea in front of him. She had seen this man about the area before. He was neither young nor old, nor rough nor smart – he had jet-black hair and dark yet strangely piercing eyes, and was a visiting tradesman of some kind. Maurice Something, her mother had introduced him as – 'He's a friend of your father's.' She remembered then having seen him with her father once or twice outside the house. She could not recall what her father had said of him, even now with him standing in front of her. Aileen had never had any reason to take heed of this man before and she had no reason to now, except that he was in her house the day before her father's and brothers' funeral.

He had excused himself hastily and left through the back door, but after he had gone, Aileen and her mother had not embraced, as Aileen felt they should have done, but moved around each other somewhat awkwardly, making preparations for the next day's funeral without mentioning the funeral itself. That night and early the next morning, Aileen could almost pretend that they weren't getting ready to go to the church. She could almost believe that things were just as they had been at the end of every summer that had gone before, with the two women busying themselves about the house ready for the men's return from Scotland.

It was perhaps this illusion that things were normal that

caused such a shock in both of them at the funeral itself, leading them both to let go in their despair as they had.

Meals still had to be cooked, chickens fed and fires built. Aileen returned to her tomato plants, which were thriving, and she planted enough lettuces to feed them in the coming months. The seeds that she had sown from the pods that she had found on the beach the day before she had left had started to come up in a line of sturdy little seedlings in the long tray. These seedlings had been the last things she had planted before leaving on the journey that had killed almost everyone she loved; they were still living while her father and brothers were not.

She watered the curious little plants daily but found that she had lost heart for the gardening that she had once so loved. It seemed wrong to be carefully tending things to life with the rawness of death so strongly about her.

Instead, while the weather was still fine, she threw herself into the hard outdoor labour of trimming back the grass in their field with a single scythe. Aileen drew comfort from the physical work. Down on her hands and knees hacking at the strong weeds with the curved blade reminded her of the work in Scotland. The exertion, the pull of the muscles in her arms kept her grounded in the moment; then the rhythm and the earthy smell of the wet grass and foliage carried her back to those happy days in the fields with Jimmy watching over her and working beside her. Then a blanket of dread would fall over her mood as she wondered if he was even alive or dead.

'In the hospital,' was all Biddy could tell her, 'but very badly burned, Aileen. I couldn't tell you if he'll make it out of there is all I know.'

She knew too that she was unlikely to find out now. Aghabeg was a long way away and nobody wanted any news from there after what had happened. Everyone on Illaunmor was keeping their heads down and leaving well alone.

That is what Aileen should have been doing. She knew she had no place dreaming of romance after all that had happened, but still she could not help herself; she wanted to draw some comfort, some light at least from the memory of love to help her forget.

However, as soon as she tried to call Jimmy's face into her mind's eye, all she got were the faces of her father and brothers. She would see them with their eyes closed, their mouths slack and a thread of black smoke creeping out of them, quickly thickening and swallowing their images up in a black cloud of death and she would feel a sickness washing over her. There seemed to be no way of thinking about Jimmy without thinking about her father and brothers. When she thought about her father and Paddy Junior and Martin, a pain as heavy as lead fixed itself in her chest and could only be moved by weeping it out – drop by painful drop. Hour after hour, day after day, she wept for the men, fighting back the pain with the scythe and waving it away as if the grief itself was as thick and lush as the foliage. She kneaded her grief through the soil. As she worked, she recalled a memory from the night before she left for Scotland. She wanted to bring her favourite apron with her, but her father shot down her pleas. As she went upstairs, she heard Anne make a case for the apron. Her mother had sewn a scapular into it, so she was more concerned her daughter bring it as a talisman to keep her safe rather than as a work garment, but her father said, 'You can't send her over to Scotland with a rag like that, Anne, and I hope you've packed her a decent dress so the other girls won't be laughing at her on a Sunday?'

'A decent dress?' her mother started. 'It was far from dresses good, bad or indifferent you were reared, Paddy Doherty,' and before too long they were tearing strips off each other. It was always the same fight – Anne Flannery from Ballina was a snob who thought she was too good for him because her father 'worked in a shop', Paddy said. His wife retorted that her father had 'been *manager* of the biggest draper's in all of Mayo' and that she was too good for him didn't half cover the truth of it. Any fool could clearly see all she had sacrificed to live on this 'godforsaken slab of boggy rock', as she called it. They always fought the night before he went away, but in the morning Aileen would go down and find them wrapped around each other under a sheepskin on the settle bed by the fire. Her mother's face was peaceful as she lay sleeping in her father's heavy naked arms, her legs curled up under her, while Paddy slept with one foot on the floor to steady them both from falling off the narrow seat. Their marriage had been neither arranged nor approved. Anne and Paddy had fallen in love and married despite the ways of their time, and their determination to be together had put the affections of their own families in jeopardy. So in spite of all their fighting, the couple would continue to love each other always for the privilege of the sacrifices they had made to be together.

When Aileen came in from the field and back into the kitchen, Anne would often be sitting at the table with her head in her hands, her shoulders convulsing with grief. Anne had truly fallen apart, and whatever sorrow and discomfort Aileen felt, it was clear to her that the loss had hit her mother harder still. Aileen would put her arms around her mother and comfort her in a way that she could not comfort herself.

'You're all I have left,' Anne said one day, gripping on to her skirts as she wept into her young daughter's chest, although to Aileen, her mother's assertion was more of an accusation than a comfort.

After a while, Aileen decided that the easiest thing was to think about nothing except for the job directly at hand and to manage her mother along the same lines. So daughter became mother. Each morning Aileen pulled her mother from her bed, dressed her and instructed her on her work about the house, while Aileen worked outside. Most of the time she was in the field, but she also whitewashed the walls of their cottage – an attempt to freshen up their house of grief. She only came into the house for meals and to check on her mother's progress. Sometimes she would find her mother sitting down at the table weeping, her hands and face covered in flour, or kneeling at the grate, the brush and pans lying idle in her shaking hands. Then Aileen would bring her mother outside, give her a paintbrush and work alongside her, talking all the time of this and that and of nothing in particular.

They had few visitors in that time immediately after the funeral. Though he was very ambitious, Father Dooley, the parish priest, was at heart a good man, but the women found small comfort in the religious medals and platitudes he offered them. Then there was an official from the mainland who had been appointed to distribute a sum of money that had been raised by the kind people of Cleggan. The female official came in a car, refused tea and, standing at their door, said she had simply come to establish if Anne would like the money given as cash or put straight into a bank account. It was, she said, a considerable sum of money – £200 in total. It would have taken Paddy ten years to earn such an amount. The woman informed them that her bank branch in Westport would be happy to arrange all of the paperwork for them, but Anne asked her to come back with the money in cash at her earliest convenience.

'I did not like the look of that woman,' she said to Aileen

when she was gone. 'Very high and mighty. And that suit she was wearing was meant to be expensive, but it wasn't – I could tell clearly from the cut of it. I know her type, looking down her nose at us island people. Does she not think we have the wherewithal to put the money in the bank ourselves?'

Aileen said nothing but was glad that her mother had seemed to have got a bit of her fight back.

John Joe had called on them once or twice over the weeks and had brought them their messages from the island shop. However, on this day Aileen had planned to go to the store with him, on a bit of an outing. She was nervous about leaving her mother behind, but at the same time was anxious for a change of scenery. Locked up in the house with only each other for company, she was worried that perhaps the two of them were going slightly mad; they certainly needed a break from one another. So Aileen was surprised when, in the morning, Anne got herself up, washed and dressed, and pushed the list into Aileen's hand with the same bossy assertion she had done in the 'ordinary' times before any of this had happened.

'You make sure that Clarke woman gives you the full pound of butter, mind – she's a thief, so check the scales yourself. Oh, and I want the raisins that are sealed in a bag, not the ones in the basin behind the counter. They are more expensive, but the last batch they gave me was pure dry.'

The sun was shining and the bright colours of John Joe's cart were glowing as he came up the drive. He had brought the kids with him, 'for the spin'. Ruari was a lively raven-haired eight-year-old, and his sister, Mary, was ten. A plump child, she was wearing a very old-fashioned white lace bonnet, something like one would expect to see in an old cowboy film.

'I like your hat,' Aileen said, and John Joe got down to open the back of the cart.

'It's from my first Holy Communion outfit,' she said, bursting with pride. 'John Joe made it for me.'

Aileen just managed to suppress a giggle and quickly looked across at her mother, who was smiling. Her heart filled to bursting to see her happy – even if it was just for an instant.

'And a very fine hat it is too, Mary.' Then Anne added, 'Your uncle is a talented seamstress.'

John Joe's face burned bright red as he pretended not to hear the exchange and held out his hand to help Aileen up onto the back of the cart.

'I'll have her back to you by suppertime, Anne.'

'We're having a picnic,' Ruari shouted down. 'Uncle made a special cake!'

'And sandwiches,' said Mary, 'with the crusts cut off of them!'

'And he said we could buy some sweets in the shop.'

'And some fancy biscuits – Uncle John Joe likes the ones with the pink icing!'

'Indeed?' said Anne, and she looked across at Aileen, who thought she might explode altogether.

John Joe closed his eyes in mortification and paused before stepping up to the driver's seat.

'If it stays dry, I told them we'd go down to the big house,' he said, 'for a picnic.'

'Well, have a great day,' Anne said.

As they trundled down the drive, Aileen looked back and saw her mother standing at the gate, still smiling at their neighbour's peculiarly feminine ways. She remembered it was only the two of them now and felt the tears welling up in her. She waved and in return Anne blew her a kiss – and with it her sadness blew away too.

*

As John Joe whipped the horse along the bog roads and eventually onto the main road to Illaunmor village, Aileen remembered that the last time she went along this road her father and brothers were with her. The children sat silently, as they had been taught to do when there were adults present, but Aileen did not want silence, so she chatted to them. She took Mary's hat and admired the stitching.

'Our father died young, and my mother was a seamstress,' John Joe confided in Aileen when she said it was a genuinely good job. 'She taught me to use her machine. There is no shame in it.'

'Of course not,' Aileen said.

'People think it's strange for a man to sew and cook and keep himself tidy,' John Joe said, 'but I think it is strange for a man to do otherwise.'

Aileen thought of her own father and brothers. They could barely butter their own bread. She remembered her father once joking that the first time he went to Scotland, he had to ask Anne how many spoons of sugar he took in his tea, so he could instruct the women who would be looking after him.

'You might write it down,' he had said, joking, 'although there'll surely not be a woman as grand and educated as you in the whole of Scotland. "You'll have to fend for yourself, Doherty" – that's what she said to me. Ah, but your mother can be a cruel woman when she wants,' and he had winked. Paddy brought laughter and light-heartedness into the lives of his 'two girls'. Her mother, serious and in her own way a bit of a snob, and Aileen, who was bookish, tended towards worrying. What would they do without him?

Aileen surprised herself by sharing all these thoughts with John Joe.

'You'll meet a man and get married yourself before too long,' John Joe said.

'I've met the man I want to marry already,' she said, and liked how normal it sounded. Talking about love made her feel brighter, so she carried on, 'A fisherman from Aghabeg. Jimmy Walsh?'

John Joe heard hope in her voice. There was some story here. He shook his head. 'I'm more farmer than fisherman, Aileen – I know very few of the men from the other islands.'

Aileen seemed disappointed about that, but carried on talking about him, full of enthusiasm.

'He's a bit of an eejit, really, and not as handsome as . . . well, some lads, I suppose . . . but, well, we fell for each other anyway. He took me to the pictures and bought me sweets, except . . .'

She stopped and took a deep breath before starting again, determined to tell him about this young man who meant so much to her, to assure him of how special he was. 'He's very brave, though – his nickname was Invincible Jim.' Then she laughed brightly and said, 'Stupid really, but he really was fearless and . . . you know, he went into the barn while it was burning to try and save the others, and . . .' She couldn't go on.

John Joe paused, but he felt she needed to continue, so he asked, 'He got hurt?'

John Joe thought that, judging by the way she was mixing up her words, this could be the first time Aileen had spoken of Jimmy since the fire. She bottled things up, this girl. And John Joe knew something about that. Bottling things up was necessary, but sometimes you had to let go.

'Burned,' she blurted out, then looked away. 'Maybe dead . . .'

She whispered the last part so quietly that John Joe could barely hear the words, but he did. She didn't say 'alive'. Perhaps after what those women had been through, 'life' was too much to hope for. 'Not dead' was the kind of halfway state grief puts you in for a while. He knew that from losing his own beloved mother.

After John Joe's younger brother became widowed, he went to England, leaving his brother as the guardian of his two small children. Seven years had passed and he had still not returned for them; the children were ten and eight now. They wanted for nothing. John Joe had enough money and plenty of good land. He was a hard worker and looked after his brother's bairns with the same tender care as if they had been his own. He felt paternal towards this Doherty child. Her father had been a good neighbour but had found John Joe strange – many men could not imagine a worse fate for a man than looking after small children and keeping a clean house for them, but John Joe was unapologetic in his ways. There was no point, he had long since decided, in being any other way.

'He'll be back maybe – certainly if he has any sense,' he said, trying to lift her a little, 'though by the sounds of him, this Jimmy Walsh lad hasn't much of *that*!'

Aileen laughed, relieved that someone seemed to understand – that someone else knew Jimmy, even if it was only through her few words. But she was weeping too, so John Joe decided she had had enough high emotion for now and continued to chat away himself, sharing abundant details with her about his own life – how his brother was doing well in London in the building trade, although, he confided out of their earshot, he would be happier if he got in touch more often now that the children were getting bigger.

Aileen had never known John Joe to be so verbose before, but he seemed comfortable in her company and she joined in with him and soon they were chatting like old friends. Even so, John Joe continued to sense a deep sadness in her around this

Jimmy boy. There was a sense of loss that could be as great as the death of her father and brothers, although it seemed wrong to even think such a thing. He had never experienced it himself, but he knew that love lost was a hardship, especially for the young, and he vowed to say a novena to the Blessed Virgin that week asking her to send Jimmy Walsh back to claim Aileen.

With all their talk the journey passed quickly and they were soon arriving into the village.

'Biddy!'

As luck would have it, Aileen saw Biddy walking almost directly in front of the cart. She had thought about getting John Joe to take her to call in on her friend. He knew where she lived, having driven her back from her house the day they arrived. Biddy had been so kind and Aileen had not had the chance to thank her, and besides, she might have some news of Jimmy. Also, there was the germ of an idea forming that perhaps Biddy and John Joe might make a romance. They were around the same age, and, well, her father had always said John Joe Morely was badly in need of a wife.

'Biddy! Biddy!'

The older woman walked straight past the cart, ignoring Aileen's call.

'Don't waste your breath,' he said. 'That woman speaks to nobody these days.'

'Nonsense – she didn't hear me. Biddy!' she called again.

Biddy turned her head and gave Aileen a withering look, then cocked her nose in the air and walked on.

Aileen took a sharp breath and John Joe, seeing her upset, put his hand on her arm.

'Don't let her upset you,' he said. 'She has gone very peculiar with all the talk.'

'How do you mean?' Aileen asked.

So John Joe told her. It seemed that as fore graipe for the
bothy, Biddy was 'responsible for building the fire that burned
the place down and killed the men?' He presented it more as a
question than a statement, then added, 'You'd know more about
that than me, Aileen. Anyway, everyone on the island seems
clear that it was her fault. She's not even had the face to show
herself at Sunday Mass since she got back – although I've seen
her there on a weekday morning. Lord knows if it's true – not
that it would matter to people around here. Anyway, there'll be
an official inquiry before too long, so it'll all come out then.'

Aileen said nothing, but as she stepped down from the cart,
she wobbled on her feet so that John Joe had to catch her.

'Are you all right?' he said.

The flue had been her fault and now Biddy was taking the
blame.

She did not know what she should say or do about that, so
for this day at least she would say and do nothing. Things were
already bad enough as they were.

Aileen Doherty found her feet, hooked her basket to her elbow
and went in to collect the messages for her mammy.

Chapter Eighteen

As he was leaving the hospital, the nurses gave Jimmy a mask to cover the burned side of his face. It was not clinically necessary, but the doctor had said it would 'help him adjust' to the outside world. The crude prosthetic was the colour of real flesh with a smooth finish and sat just under the eye, where the lid dragged down, and then ran down and across the side of his face, creating a false cheek. His mother secured it with a strap running behind his ear and under the right side of his chin. Jimmy was sitting, dressed, on the edge of the hospital bed, waiting to leave. He could not stop the tears from pouring down his cheeks at the humiliation of having his mother attach this fake face.

'You have made an excellent recovery,' the doctor said, and his mother thanked him for all they had done for her son.

Jimmy pretended that the tears were simply his eyes watering, smiled and nodded to the surgeon who had removed the hot coal from his face and saved his life, if not his looks. He could not bring himself to thank the doctor verbally, because the truth was, he wished he had been left to die.

For the whole of the journey home Jimmy thought of little else except for how he could throw himself over the side of the ship or under the wheels of the train without causing his parents even more pain than he already had.

On the train from Dublin to Donegal Town, they were joined in their carriage by a mother and two children. As they sat down, the young boy asked, 'What's wrong with the man's face?' and the smaller child began to cry.

'I'm sorry,' said their mother, and Morag responded by recounting in detail the events of the past few weeks. Jimmy and his father stared resolutely out of the window as the two women discussed them. Morag Walsh was not a person who would normally tell her business to strangers, but the two men understood that she was simply relieved to have another woman to talk to about the ordeal. Her need to share was greater than their embarrassment, but nonetheless, in the recounting of his mother's story Jimmy found himself retreating even further into himself. He closed his eyes and slept through much of the rest of the journey.

He and his mother stayed overnight in a boarding house in Donegal, while his father went to collect a boat to bring them back out to Aghabeg. Jimmy went straight to bed in the guest-house, barely looking at the fine meal put in front of them by the landlady. The next day, he boarded his father's boat with no sense of excitement at the journey, staying in a hotel for the first time or travelling back home. He had fallen into a listless state, a pathetic invalid lethargy that his parents feared he might never come out of.

'You'll be back out in the boats with us soon surely,' Jimmy's father would say hopefully every morning, now they were back in Aghabeg. 'You might come down to the steps with me this afternoon for a swim?'

Jimmy had not left the house or seen anyone for almost two weeks. Morag desperately tried to rouse him out of his torpor with food and care and, in the end, strong words.

'There's no sense in feeling sorry for yourself, Jimmy. You might not be as handsome as you were, but you're alive.'

'And sure he was never that great to begin with,' his father joined in, joking, trying to lighten the load.

The two of them were trying to appear brave, but while their hearts were breaking for Jimmy, they were also only too aware that he was alive, unlike the other poor souls from Illaunmor. Morag herself was also conscious that their son's face was a constant reminder to her husband of his part in the fire. Deadly smoke alone had killed the others, and if Sean had not opened the doors when he had and ignited the explosion, Jimmy would have come out with no more than a blackened face and a sad demeanour.

However, their problems with Jimmy were compounded by other worries. Hospital bills in Scotland still had to be paid. Sean's pride, and shame that he and his son had both survived when all the other men had died, meant he had refused to accept any 'charity' from the Scottish firemen and then had given all of their tattie-hoking earnings to the Illaunmor Island Widows and Family Fund. The Walshes had spent all of their meagre savings getting back from Scotland and in hospital fees so far.

Sean was already back out at sea with his fellow Aghabeg fishermen catching and selling fish, but the transition back to work on the island had not been easy. Sean and his strong son had, after all, abandoned their colleagues to raise money for a 'big boat'. Now Sean was back and looking to take his share of what was turning into a difficult 'dry' season. The Aghabeg men were not begrudgers – they looked out for their own, and there was a deep loyalty in them – but they were superstitious and there had been talk of Jimmy's face turning monstrous, though none of them had actually seen him since his return. In addition, there was talk of the Walshes' misfortune having been caused by the boy fraternizing and falling in love, no less, with a red-haired girl. Nothing happened without a reason and for such bad luck to have befallen them on their money-making foray, there must be strange forces at work, and who knew what those strange forces might do next? Young Jimmy had always been seen by the community of fishermen as an extraordinary young man with 'special powers' for luck and good fortune. A talisman, he had defied the sea with his swimming skills, and there was always a good haul when he went out with them. Perhaps his powers were turning against them now – and he had brought a bad sea back with him from Scotland.

Pragmatic Sean would not dignify their nonsense by openly defending his son. The only way to stop the speculation was for Jimmy to get back to work. Sean needed Jimmy with him, not just to man their own currach and make him less physically dependent on the others, but to gain back the confidence of their neighbours that all was well on Aghabeg. Secrecy bred doubt, and doubt was a dangerous thing on a small island. This hiding away in the house was making things worse – for everyone. Jimmy needed to be back at the centre of island life to return things to the way they were before. Not just for his own sake, but to show the other islanders that, despite his injuries, he was the same as always.

Except that Jimmy was not the same.

Jimmy was no longer himself. Not in any part. One look in the mirror reminded him instantly of that. The right side of his face was as it had been before; the left was where the explosion had hit. The centre of his face had been burned off by the flying hot coal so that the rim underneath his eye was pulled down, the cheek was scooped out and that side of his mouth had no lips but descended into a hollow. Face on, he was unrecognizable, because while one side was fine, it contrasted with the horror of the left side, which drew the eye across to its deformity. When he turned to the left and looked at his profile, his face was as it had always been, but there was no comfort in that either, because Jimmy knew, deep inside him, that he was not the same young man as he had been before. He was not the handsome, fearless young rascal Aileen had fallen in love with – that was certain. She would doubtless recoil if she saw him and he knew there was no way he could go and find her now for that reason.

The extreme pain had taken its toll on him and Jimmy felt weakened by it. Jimmy had thought he knew what pain was. He had swum underwater until he thought his lungs would explode, he had brushed his skin on coral and watched it bleed out into the water, every inch of him had been stung by jellyfish, and where grown men would have cried, Invincible Jim had laughed it off.

The burns from the bothy had broken him. Even now, with the pain long gone, sleeping in the comfort of his own bed in the kitchen with the soft woollen blankets on his skin, he would look across at the embers glowing in his mother's grate and his limbs would start to ache and he would suddenly cry out with just the memory of how he had felt lying in that hospital bed.

His mother would come to him and put his head in her lap, as she had done when he was a small boy, and stroked his forehead to soothe him back to sleep. He would close his eyes and pretend, for her sake, to be comforted, but always, always as he found himself falling into an agitated sleep, he would feel nothing more than that he was simply entering a different, quieter corner of the familiar endless black pit of despair. There was nothing inside him anymore. Where he had always felt full – 'full of life', people had said of him – now he felt empty. The fire had burned his skin, but in truth, Jimmy felt as if it had burned him from the inside out. His body was nothing more than a shell. The words he spoke, the food he ate and passing thoughts of weather, warmth, his parents' wishes – they were just ashes fluttering about within.

On his fourteenth day of self-incarceration in the house, Jimmy woke to find his mother standing over him holding out a bucket of steaming water.

'You are going out in the boat with your father today and I will not hear a word from you otherwise,' she said, thrusting a bar of carbolic soap into his limp hand. 'Now get out the back and wash some of that pity off yourself, then come in for your breakfast.'

Jimmy wanted to complain, but he could see that Morag had had enough and that there would be no fighting with her.

He may have been a grown man, but his mother was the type who would take the strap to a person if she was sufficiently roused – it wouldn't matter a damn if they were woman, child, animal or a full-grown hairy man. His father had taught him that it was generally prudent to do his mother's bidding, but there were also times when it was imperative, and this was one of those times.

Jimmy stripped and went out the door, then lathered up the carbolic and spread it along his limbs. The disinfectant smell stung his nostrils, bringing his senses alive, and as he rinsed off the soap with the warm water, he could feel a small bite to the air, making the skin around his scars tingle. He looked around him at the world as if waking from a deep sleep. It was a clear day, the sky a solid blue; the sea was a straight line of sparkling diamonds on the horizon beyond the fields. He felt nothing as strong as happiness, but he had a good feeling that he was home, that he was where he belonged. The gravel felt sharp under the soft skin of his unused feet, and as he looked down and saw the water trickle across them and turn the stones from grey to a dozen shades of brown, he thought perhaps it was time for him to get back to the water after all.

He walked a few steps towards his mother's small flower garden and, without thinking, bent to smell a mature rose. It had such a rich, feminine scent it reminded him immediately of Aileen and the stab he got propelled him quickly back to the house. He was determined that he would hold on to the small thread of sanity his mother had handed him and, for this day at least, put his lost lover to the back of his mind.

Jimmy dressed and headed down to the boats with his father. His mother gave him a box of sandwiches and a bottle of tea. Walking across their fields, Jimmy felt strong. Not as strong as he had before the fire, but nonetheless he could feel his muscles tighten and strain against the effort of movement and it felt good. His father took the bag of food from him so that Jimmy could swing his arms to help steady his legs and pick up speed. He stumbled once or twice on the rough ground until he eventually stopped, bent down and took off the boots his mother had put on him, leaving them where they were to pick up on the way back. As his feet found the soft cushions of moss on the round rocks and the bounce of the heathery bogs underfoot, Jimmy found his Aghabeg feet again, and for the first time since he had woken up in that hospital bed, he was really, truly grateful to be alive.

As they came into sight of the boats, Sean's stride grew steadier and the swing of his arms more narrow and masculine. His manly demeanour invited Jimmy to walk in line with him, and as the two men came to the edge of the field where the rock steps led down to the jetty, the faces of the half-dozen fishermen came into view. They were openly staring at Jimmy. Three of the men crossed themselves, and one fell to his knees in prayer.

Jimmy felt sick and wanted to turn back, but Sean grabbed the arm of his jacket and pulled him along until they had reached their audience.

'Are you counting the stones, John?' Sean said to the kneeling man. 'I never took you for a mathematician.'

John coughed and stood up, but the expressions on all the men's faces were a mixture of incredulous horror and fear. Behind them, the water was as flat and still as a mirror; the small boats bobbed so gently they were like old women swaying in their seats to a ballad.

Jimmy wanted to cry out and run, but before he could, Sean turned to him and said, 'What are you waiting for, boy? Swim out and catch that currach before we lose it to the sea altogether.'

Padraig Feeney had been freeing his family currach when the others called him to look at Jimmy Walsh coming over the field. In his horror, the simple young man had dropped one end of the rope and his father's boat was now drifting gently out into the open sea.

'Mother of God, she's gone,' he wailed, and his father, John, let out a mighty roar and gave him a wallop over the head.

All faces turned to the water as Jimmy dived in fully clothed and went after the boat.

As soon as his body hit the water, Jimmy felt as if he had never been to Scotland, never been away from the sea. His arms and legs ploughed through the water with such speed, such ferocity that he truly felt as if the water itself had infused him with some magical power. He caught the side of the boat easily and, using every bit of strength he had in him, paddled it to the steps.

When he arrived back, Sean and John Feeney leaned down and pulled him out, while Padraig and another grabbed the errant boat and tied it up. The rest of them were smiling down at Jimmy, cheering and clapping.

'Invincible Jim! He's back all right!' somebody said.

Jimmy was so exhausted from his efforts that he lay on the jetty with his eyes closed and breathed slowly, trying to catch his breath. Without the cold water on his skin, all he wanted to do now was sleep – as if a lifetime of energy had been used up in one short exertion.

Jimmy did not want the others to see how much the swim had taken out of him, but as he sat up, he looked out and saw something else bobbing towards the steps.

'What's that?' Padraig Feeney said.

Jimmy stood up next to him and put his hands over his eyes to shield them from the sun. It was much smaller than a boat, but more substantial than a large piece of driftwood or a clump of seaweed. As it came closer, Jimmy could see it was rounded – like a buoy come loose perhaps – except they were usually brightly painted and this was a dark, muddy colour. He took a deep breath, ready to swim out again, even though he did not feel able, but whatever way the tide was travelling, it was almost upon them, so one of the men waded down the steps and threw out a rope with a piece of wood attached to the end which they used to catch unsecured currachs when Jimmy wasn't at hand to save them.

The men followed him down as he dragged the mystery object up to the steps, but he let go of it as quick and turned away retching.

It was the bloated but intact remains of a dead man.

Chapter Nineteen

'Can we go to the big house for our picnic, Uncle John Joe? Can we? Can we?'

'I don't know, now, children. Aileen might be anxious to get home to her mother.'

Aileen wasn't particularly anxious to get home, but at the same time she had no particular desire to go on a picnic. After what John Joe had told her about Biddy being blamed for starting the fire, she had found herself barely able to concentrate on her mother's grocery list. 'A half-pound of raisins, please, in the bag . . . No, not in the bag.' She had tried to put it out of her mind, but the truth kept creeping up on her, like a rat scratching in the corner of a room, distracting her, pulling her back for an honest look. The fire had been her fault. She had heard the flue close, but she had been in a hurry to get out and go to the pictures with Jimmy. As a result, everyone had perished – her father, her brothers . . .

'Let's go to the big house.' She said it loudly and quickly, drowning out the voice in her head. 'I've always wanted to see what it is like up there. Hurry along, now, John Joe – we're hungry for our cake and sandwiches!'

Aileen looked around. The sun was out; it was dry. The blue of the sky made the green of the fields glow brighter, and the form of the trees faded into ghostly spindles with the strong light behind them.

'Count the sheep,' she said to Ruari, 'and, Mary, you count me the cows!' If she kept looking, kept talking, she could keep herself distracted from the sick feeling that was opening inside her like the devil's hand.

'Tell us about the big house, John Joe. Tell me the story of what happened there – I've never heard it.'

John Joe thought this quiet young girl was being very talkative, but the day was good and stretched out ahead of them. There were worse situations a man could find himself in than in the company of three youngsters going on a picnic. Children didn't judge a man. John Joe was not the marrying kind, but when his brother had been widowed young, he found he was happy to mind his niece and nephew while Frank went to London to work. People thought that children were women's work – John Joe knew that – but he loved Ruari and Mary as his own and was not ashamed to show it. When Mary had taken her first Holy Communion the year before, Anne Doherty had offered to take the girl to Westport to find a dress, but John Joe had politely refused her offer and taken her himself. Not only that, he had altered the dress to suit the child's height better and used the leftover fabric to make her a bonnet. He knew such behaviour awakened suspicions in people, as did his starched shirts and groomed appearance, but there was no one could tell him that those children were not as well cared for and in as clean and well ordered a house as any mother in Ireland could provide for them.

On two occasions islanders had conspired to take the children from him. Father Dooley, the parish priest, had offered Ruari a place with the Christian Brothers on the mainland, and the Sisters of Mercy had sent down two nuns to try to persuade

Mary up to a boarding school in Dublin that was attached to a commercial laundry. John Joe gave both sets of religious members high tea served on his mother's china with starched linen napkins and homemade tea brack, then invited them to stay for the full family rosary – bell, book and candle – sparing no novenas. To drive home his point, John Joe had his charges polished, poised and ten minutes early for Mass every Sunday and had not missed one Holy Day of Obligation service since those children were put into his care. Even the Pope couldn't find a reason to take those children from John Joe Morely because he prided himself on being a clean-living Christian. John Joe knew from his own experience as guardian of two more or less orphaned children that what young Aileen Doherty wanted more than anything was her father back. The least he could offer was his friendship and some entertainment to help distract her from her troubles.

So as they drove, the neat older man told Aileen the story of the big house. It had been built in 1860 as a ten-bedroom holiday retreat by Richard Blake, a retired English industrialist who had allegedly had his arthritis cured by the seawaters off White Strand Beach. He lived there for a number of years by himself, as his first wife had died. He provided employment for many of the islanders as house staff and gardeners. 'Including my own mother,' John Joe said proudly, 'who was his house-keeper. Now there was a woman who could bake.' Richard Blake was popular locally, good-humoured and generous, but as a rich man, it was not long before he found himself a second, much younger wife on whom to spend his money. His new wife had no interest in living on a remote Irish island, so she moved him back to London.

'He wrote to my mother and told her to pack up the house for him and send everything back to England. He paid her well for it, and as compensation for losing her job, he gave her some silver and much of his table and bed linen. Most of his tea crockery was stamped with the initials of his first wife, so his new wife didn't want it. My mother sold the silver and rented out and laundered the linens to boarding houses on the Strand. She was a smart woman, my mother. A lady . . .' He paused and his eyes filled with a small light as he remembered her. Aileen wondered at John Joe admiring his mother so much. She didn't admire Anne in that way and felt briefly guilty that she was a bad daughter . . .

'So it was because of an Englishman that my father was able to build up his farm stock and provide us with such a fine two-storey house.'

Aileen cheered at the telling of the story as she realized that relaying this back to her mother would be as much entertainment as the best daughter in the world could give her.

The house fell to rack and ruin, John Joe continued, and although a few of the former staff dropped in on the empty building from time to time to try and keep it secure from the many raids and robberies perpetrated on it over the years, it had remained empty. The Republicans, believing it was owned by a rich English 'imperialist', set fire to the house during the Irish Civil War and now only the shell remained. Richard Blake was presumed dead and no heirs had come to claim it.

'I heard it was an unlucky place,' Aileen said.

'It was lucky for me and my family,' John Joe said, 'and I can't speak for anyone outside of that. People have a bleak way of looking at the world sometimes, Aileen,' he said, turning the carthorse up a tree-lined boreen where the foliage was so old and overgrown that it created a dark blanket above their heads, 'especially around here.'

His words and perhaps the sudden darkness of the overgrown

avenue sent a shiver through Aileen. Mary saw this and pulled the woollen blanket from her shoulder and placed it over the older girl's legs. Aileen had to push back tears at the small act of kindness; if only these people knew what she was really like, what she had done.

As they reached the top of the avenue, the trees separated and the ground cleared. In front of them was a grand, grey stone house. The windows were empty of glass, and the huge front doorway was edged with blackened scraps of burned wood. It seemed like an eerie place for a picnic; the house looked like death itself.

John Joe pulled the cart up to the front and began to unload the picnic things, while the two children leaped out. Ruari ran through an archway in the stone wall to the left of the house. Mary grabbed Aileen's hand and they followed Ruari through a courtyard to a heavy wooden door. Ruari jumped, too short to reach the handle, and Aileen laughed and teased the small boy as she pulled on the cold brass circle.

When they stepped through to the other side, Aileen stood for a moment, paralysed with astonishment. It was the most beautiful garden she had ever seen. While there were no flowers bar the white trumpet flowers of deadly bindweed crawling across walls and hedges, and the scruffy yellow of the dandelions and ragwort that had conquered the lawns and flower beds, the bones of what this garden had once been were perfect. They stood at the front of a path that was lined either side with no less than a dozen stone-edged flower beds. In front of them, set into the ground in its own circle of pebbles, was a three-tiered fountain. She looked around frantically, trying to take it all in: glimpses of statues hidden in overgrown hedging, large stone pots with decorative scalloped edges big enough to grow pota-toes in, and beyond them again, a huge tree with what looked like a marble seat at its base – although it was so grown over with nettles it was barely visible.

Aileen could not put into words why she felt so overwhelmed by the sight of this ruined patch of stone and weeds. Except that when she closed her eyes to blink against the sun, the garden in its glory days, or rather, as she imagined it might have been, appeared in front of her. A bank of swaying poppies and fennel to her left, leaning into an arch of sweet pink clambering roses; neat boxed hedgerows arranged into a small, perfect maze to her right; the fountain spraying diamond sparkles in the sunlight; and on the marble seat under the large tree was an embroidered cushion and a copy of *Wuthering Heights*. When she opened her eyes again, she could clearly see that every inch of the flower beds and path were covered in ferocious weeds, the fountain was long since dry, and it had been so long since this garden had been tended that one could hardly call it a garden at all. Even so, the image was so strong that it endured in lifting her spirits.

'Isn't it beautiful?' Mary said.

Aileen didn't reply. Perhaps Mary could see what she saw when she closed her eyes.

'Don't be annoying Aileen, now,' John Joe said. 'We'll set up in the usual spot,' and he walked towards the tree.

Aileen and the children helped clear away the seat, and they ate and drank in hungry silence. Aileen had barely finished her last slice of Madeira cake when Mary grabbed her arm and dragged her along on another adventure.

'Come and see the greenhouse.'

At a far corner of the garden was another door, which led to what was, in effect, a walled field. To the left of them as they came through was a large glasshouse built up against the old wall, with a long, slanting roof. At first, it was hard even to make out that there was a building there at all because it was so packed inside with foliage that it just seemed to be a solid green clump.

As they came closer, Aileen could see it had been taken over, on the inside if not the outside, with bindweed. Mary could barely get the door open. She was frustrated.

'It's usually empty,' she said. 'I don't know where these white flowers came from. They weren't here the last time and now they're everywhere. They're horrible!'

It was hot and damp inside the greenhouse. Small wonder the bindweed has taken off in here, Aileen thought. Bindweed was a pernicious plant, voracious and snivelling in the way it wound its way round everything. It wasn't strong enough to strangle plants but would shade and compete with them for light, and the weight of an infestation could break the underlying plants. However, it was weak and flimsy to the touch.

'It's nothing – look,' Aileen said to Mary, grabbing a handful of the noxious weed by the door and tugging it, only to find that its leaves were entwined in a shallow terracotta tray on the nearby window ledge, causing it to come crashing towards them. The girls laughed and started to pull at the bindweed all around them, throwing the heart-shaped leaves and their curled, spindly stems in a pile on the ground. Then Aileen noticed the weeds were tugging at something more substantial. She called for Mary to calm her frantic pulling in case she damaged what was underneath, and carefully moving aside the laced string of the bindweed, she revealed the thick trunk of a strangled vine underneath it.

The wood was pure grey.

'It's dead,' Mary said, and Aileen found herself blanching at the reference.

'Not necessarily,' she replied, and carefully freed the upper part of the vine from the suffocation of its creeping attacker.

Once she had started, Aileen felt herself moving down towards the ground to clear all around this dying plant. She knew it wasn't dead; she could hear it calling to her – the faint murmur of sap beneath its dry, grey stem. There was the pulse of a vein running through it – she could feel that.

At its root, she found a single ragwort weed that was sucking the moisture from its roots. Aileen looked at the ugly little yellow flowers and thought, You may have conquered the dry earth, little weed, but you're a pasture weed – you don't belong in here and you know it.

Ragwort weeds were loud bully boys; their muscular roots punched out anything and everything that got in their way. They were not as sly and pervasive as bindweed, Aileen knew, but if you didn't show them who was boss, they'd throw their weight about and take over nonetheless. Since she was a small child of six tending to her vegetable garden at home, Aileen could barely pass a ragwort and not dig it up. Without thinking, she picked up a rusted fork that had been abandoned on the ground and began to scoop earth from the roots of the tenacious weed. As she did so, she noticed something: a small shoot at the very base of the grey trunk. Tiny and thin, but unmistakably green and firm to the touch, with barely the beginnings of a leaf at the end of it.

'It's alive,' she said, almost shouting with excitement and calling Mary over. 'I wonder what it is.'

John Joe had followed them in and, coming over to see what that fuss was about, looked down vaguely and, disinterested, shook his head.

'It's too hot here,' he said. 'We'll maybe stop at the lake on the way back. I'll load the cart . . .'

'Can you leave me that bottle of water, John Joe? I'll be out in a minute.'

Aileen sliced the fork through the ground quickly and pulled up the hefty ragwort weed, fingering the soil left behind to check for any residual roots.

Then she carefully placed some of the fresh soil at the roots of the vine and soaked the ground around it with the full bottle of water.

Aileen carried the uprooted weeds, including the bindweed, out of the greenhouse so they could not re-root, although there seemed little point, as three-quarters of the building were still given over to a jungle of weeds. Closing the door of the strange hot building behind her, she looked across at the single branch of freed vine and said a small prayer that its frail bud would survive until the day when she might come back to this strange place, whenever, *if* ever, that might be.

Chapter Twenty

It was the first body that had washed up on Aghabeg Island in living memory.

This was all the more extraordinary considering that there was a war raging across Europe. Bodies floating in the sea close to Ireland's shores from ships blown up along the coast, or even falling from the skies, were a common occurrence. The black, bloated bodies would be picked up by those working at sea and then carried ashore to be claimed or buried. If the gulls had got to them first, as was often the case, the fishermen would weigh down the remains with whatever rocks and metal they had come to carry on board for that very purpose and bury them at sea. That was how the harsh reality of the World War visited Ireland: in the sickening shock of finding a shattered soldier's torso at the bottom of a day's catch; in the cruel joke of an excited child running down to the beach only to discover that the large mammal beached there was wearing a soldier's uniform.

Miraculously, in the three years since the war had started, the islanders of Aghabeg had never found one single body.

However, in this case, the fishermen had some idea of where the body had come from.

Some months ago, there had been an accident further up the

coast when a mine had exploded a small British Navy engineering vessel that had been sent to retrieve the deadly contraption after it had come loose from its position alongside other mines planted to protect the British coastline from German invasion. The accident had been observed and reported by Irish Coast Watching Service volunteer Dan Murphy. Dan was one of eighty men who sat in tiny concrete huts on the rocky precipices, far-flung tips and craggy edges of Ireland. From these lookout points they recorded the movements of German and British warships and submarines.

Since Germany had taken France in 1940, Ireland was strategically placed between the Nazi forces and Britain. Both sides knew it and the activity just outside Ireland's three-mile neutrality zone had become intense. While the ordinary Irish people's lives remained largely unaffected by the war, the men on its peripheries were watching armed submarines circling their bays and loaded aircraft flying ominously low over their heads. Desperate to get at one another, the Germans and British wandered in and out of Ireland's neutral zone neither fully caring nor believing there was much the Irish could do to curtail them. Churchill hated the Irish anyway and believed they were in cahoots with the Germans. The Germans knew the Irish hated the English and harboured ambitions to use Ireland as a base to get to them. Ireland was stuck in the middle like the child of warring parents, and the only people who were fully aware of how close the war came to Ireland were those who worked the coastline, either as fishermen or as war volunteers.

On a clear day, Dan could see up to thirty miles out to sea from his small outpost on a cliff edge, and he just happened to have his telescope trained on the unidentified boat as the explosion occurred. He got an awful shock, and by the time the vast wave the explosion had caused crashed down on the rocky beach beneath him, Dan already had the local Volunteer Force unit and adept local fishermen out looking for survivors.

The vessel that had blown up had been a small British Navy service boat with just a young naval officer and a bomb-disposal engineer on board. The explosion had obviously been a terrible accident, and Dan had felt that, as one of the Irish coastguards who had reported the mines as a problem, he was somewhat responsible. The engineer survived and was rescued clinging to the remnants of the boat. Dan and his men brought him ashore and started a two-day search to find the other missing man.

Naval engineer Anthony Irvine was relatively unharmed, except for the beginnings of hypothermia from the freezing Atlantic water, but he was very distraught and anxious to find his fellow officer, Jack Hart, whom he maintained was still alive. The two of them had escaped the explosion, he said; he had known that the mine was going to blow and had shouted as much to Jack. The pair of them had jumped ship and swum at the same time: there was no reason why he should be alive and not Jack. Of course, they had been thrown underwater by the explosion and covered in debris, but he was certain his colleague was still out there.

The nearest hospital had treated Irvine for shock, giving him a good dose of morphine to calm him down, then sewed and bandaged up a few small cuts so he was fit to travel home. However, the engineer refused to go back to England until his friend's body was retrieved. He returned to the area and Dan Murphy took the young engineer back to stay in his home for a few days as they searched the coastline for his missing friend. After a week more, it was finally decided that Jack Hart's body had been lost at sea and the brave Irvine returned, heartbroken, to England. Despite his being, in effect, an English soldier, Dan had liked the lad and admired his loyalty to his friend and his persistence in trying to find his body. It turned out that Anthony had Irish blood in him on his mother's side, and although his accent was English, he had an easy, Irish way about him. Armed with this fact, the Coast Watching Service volunteer sent special word out to all the fishermen working that coastline, and the islands around it, that any intact bodies washing up were to be reported to him.

As the Aghabeg fishermen stood around and looked down at the body, they were unified in their thoughts. It was good luck and the Blessed Virgin that had kept the horrors of war from their tiny coastline, and it was ill fortune and Jimmy Walsh that had brought it upon them now. Standing over the soaked mound of rotting flesh, they blessed themselves compulsively, partly to call Holy Mary down to them, but also to keep the poisonous luck of the deformed beast among them at bay.

Sean Walsh could hear his neighbours' superstitious judgements on his son as clearly as if they had said them out loud, but he would not indulge them for a second. Neither would he walk away.

'God rest his soul,' Sean said, as he took off his coat and laid it over the head of the body. Out of respect, of course, but partly to hide the grotesque deterioration time and water had caused. No man should be seen in such a state.

The other men just stood and looked from the body to the Walsh men – mostly Sean, as they were somewhat afraid of Jimmy now. It was clear to them that the Walsh lad had brought this disaster to their shore – as certain as if he had killed the man himself – and they were weighing up how they should react to this affront.

Sean sensed their discontent and took immediate charge. It was the only thing to do in these circumstances: time for the men to reflect would only lead to trouble.

'He must be the poor young engineer Dan Murphy sent word about. Jimmy, you go off now and bring me back a stack of turf and we'll get a big fire lit straight away to let Frank in the lighthouse know that something is amiss. David, Eddie, the tide is with you, and if you head out to there now, you'll be with him in an hour and he can get a message to Dan Murphy. It's early yet – the Coast Watching Service could get a telegram over to England before the day is out and tell the poor boy's family.'

Jimmy stood and began to march straight across the field in long, running strides. He seemed to act on his father's instruction, but in reality Sean and the others knew he was simply going home to hide himself away again.

The men did as they were bid. Sean Walsh was a strong man and this was no time for a mutiny, and what else were they to do?

So as the men of his island went about getting a fire going in the highest point of the field and preparing the currach for the five-mile journey along coastal waters to the nearest light-house, Jimmy ran into his house, past his mother and into the bedroom.

Morag followed him in and started badgering him. 'What's going on? Why is there a fire lit in the field? Why are you back?'

Jimmy felt an enormous rage rise up in him. He wanted to be left alone. Why must his parents persist in trying to force him to live in a world he was not fit for?

He roared across at his mother, 'Leave me alone, woman!'

Under normal circumstances, his mother would have roared back and perhaps even picked up the broom handle to wallop some manners into him.

On this occasion, she did not; she simply backed out of the room and closed the door.

Jimmy realized then that his face was so ugly, so deformed that he could even frighten his own mother.

He did not leave the house for several days after that, and Sean, disheartened by his thwarted attempt to bring his son back into the fishing fold, left him alone. Jimmy helped his mother about the house, dug out some onions and hung them out to dry, then began to fix up the drystone wall on the far side of their field – a boring, laborious jigsaw of a job that neither his father nor himself had had the inclination to do before, but Jimmy now found the repetitive work distracting and comforting.

Five days after they had found the body of the soldier, Jimmy saw his father come over the hill towards the drystone wall where he was working. He knew by the cut of his father's walk, straight back and long, manly stride, that he had somebody with him. Jimmy groaned. It was pointless trying to hide; it must be the case that his father was bringing this person specifically to see him. His only escape would be across the neighbouring fields, which he did consider for a moment.

As they grew closer, Jimmy could see that the person following a respectful distance behind Sean was a man wearing smart clothes, a suit jacket and a shirt and tie. Jimmy was curious – he must be a foreigner, not from the island at all.

The sun moved behind them and Jimmy saw the shadow of his father wave at him, frantically, excitedly, holding him in his spot. Jimmy put down the rock he was fixing in place and wiped his hands down the front of his working trousers.

'This is Anthony Irvine.'

Jimmy held out his hand, and as he did, the man's face came into view.

'Good to meet you, Jimmy,' he said. 'I believe you are the man I have to thank for finding my friend Jack.'

His accent was English, and he was a good deal older than

Jimmy – thirty or more, anyway – but the most striking thing about him was the deep, mauve scar that ran down his face like a jagged railway track, pulling the corner of his right eye down towards his mouth and turning the edge of the lip up to meet it in a permanent smile.

'Sean tells me you've been in the wars too?'

'Well, a fire.'

'Went in to save some chaps and got struck down yourself, from what I hear?'

'They were dead already, so I needn't have bothered.'

'You can't have known that,' he said, 'otherwise you'd have been a damn fool going in in the first place, wouldn't you?'

Jimmy smiled despite himself. In less than a minute this man had cheered him up more than the doctors or his parents could ever hope to do. He understood.

'Thing is, I just had the one chap with me and he's dead too . . . Tried to save him but didn't. Not a nice feeling, but then, no point in feeling bad about it, eh? Compared with them, we got off scot-free.'

Jimmy had a pang of guilt. There were days he envied the Cleggan dead.

'Now, Sean,' he said, clapping his father on the back, 'I was promised tea. I heard there was a Scottish woman on this island makes the best soda bread west of the Shannon.'

'That's my Morag,' said Sean. He was glowing with delight. It was as if he had manifested, through his own will, not just his legendary wife but this guest with his good humour and his brave hero-talk.

On the way back to the house, the two men gave Jimmy the news of what had happened in the days since the body had washed ashore. Jack's body had been transported to the local undertaker for safekeeping. Anthony had been alerted and travelled immediately from his home in London to take charge of formalities. The remains themselves were beyond identification, but like all naval officers, in the event of such a tragedy happening, Jack had a number of effects on his person, a ring and an unusual pendant, that Anthony was able to use to ID him, and which he took back with him as mementos for Jack's infirm father, his only surviving relative, who was too sick to travel. Given that fact, Jack's father had signed the body over into Anthony's care and was content for his son to be buried at sea by the fishermen who had found him. And there would be a proper military service for him back in England too.

'What about you?' Sean said, as they reached the house. 'That's a nasty injury you must have got.'

Anthony stuck his thumb deep into his scar and drew down the length of it with such vigour Jimmy was afraid he might draw blood. 'Oh, this. No, Sean, I got this a while ago. I'm a regular hero, me,' and he gave them a conspiratorial wink that left both men unsure whether he was joking or not – but certain that there was some amusing story to be told!

Morag got into a terrible state when her two men arrived back with a guest. Not just a guest, but a stranger! Entertaining such a visitor would require enormous preparations for any island woman, let alone a house-proud Scot like Jimmy's mother. She ran into the kitchen to put some bread on before Sean had the chance to introduce her properly to their guest, and came back a few minutes later having taken her apron off and patted down her hair. Jimmy also noticed that she was wearing some lipstick. 'The Lipstick' was rarely used but sat permanently on the windowsill above the sink in the back scullery in front of a small shard of mirror. As a child, Jimmy had always believed that the gold tube was a kind of magic talisman – like the miraculous medals he had pinned to his vest or the holy water font by their back door. He was astonished when he discovered it contained a 'pink crayon' and coveted it for much of his childhood. For a moment he smiled to himself, remembering how he had once been such an innocent. He was a man of the world now and in the company of this English officer who called him a 'fellow' and wore the scars of his own bad luck with such pride Jimmy felt like even more of a man.

Morag served them all tea in the good willow-pattern china, and warm soda bread with butter and jam. Anthony stayed for the best part of the afternoon. He told them stories about his life in London, about his late Irish mother and about how 'London is full of us Irish now – we'd be lost without you fellows coming over and doing the work us war chaps are leaving behind.'

Jimmy thought it was funny the way Anthony spoke about being Irish with his London accent, using words like 'chaps' and 'fellows' like the actor David Niven, but it made him feel important nonetheless that this debonair officer saw himself as one of them.

He was most fascinated, though, when Anthony talked about the surgeon in England who had worked on his face.

'It was pretty straightforward, just a few stitches really, but there's no doubting this Archibald McIndoe fellow is a genius. He can more or less fix up any chap's face to be as good as new. Puts them together more or less from scratch, I've heard – some of them come out from him better-looking than before they got blown up!'

Sean and Jimmy flinched before forcing a laugh. The explosion was still too close to home, although both men were thinking the same thing. Morag knew what they were thinking too and, as a diversion, started to grill their guest about his war experiences. Had he been to France? Where else had he been in Europe? When was he expected to go back into active service?

It turned out that Anthony Irvine was a proper war hero. As an engineer with the Royal Navy, he had both built and disarmed mines. He had sustained his injury from a bomb that had been found near a beach on the coast of England where he had been visiting on leave from his job with a bomb-disposal unit. The unexploded bomb was found by children buried under the sand. Anthony volunteered himself and got the local defence force to clear the area of people, including themselves, while he carried the bomb to a safer place, in a deep cave further down the beach. The idea was that they would cordon off that area until Anthony could return properly equipped and organize a controlled explosion. However, while he was walking back along the beach, the bomb went off. Anthony was flung forward and a flying shard of rock cut through his cheek.

'Can't complain,' he said. 'They stitched me up and it was back out again with me. Lots of chaps plenty worse off than me. Lucky to be alive.'

They had given him a medal, although Anthony didn't tell them that. Dan, the watchman, had told Sean. When Sean mentioned this, Anthony reacted in an odd way, saying, 'They give those bloody things to everyone. Means nothing.'

The man's face darkened. Either he had experienced too much anguish or felt awkward talking about subjects of battle in front of Irishmen, given their own history of conflict was so recent. Either way, Morag came to his rescue.

'Anthony doesn't want to talk about the war, my love – we must respect a soldier's diversions . . .'

He left shortly afterwards with Sean, who was taking him back to his digs on the mainland while there was still some light.

As soon as they were out the door, Jimmy said, 'Did you hear what he said about the surgeon?'

Despite having done all he could to flatter and charm his

hostess, Morag had not warmed to the visitor. Now she liked him even less.

She picked up the crockery and on the way out to the scullery said quietly and firmly, 'You are not going to England.'

Jimmy followed her. He stood at the open arch that separated the main room from the five-foot-square kitchen scullery where his mother prepared all their food and did most of her washing chores. Raging, he turned the 'bad' side of his face to her and said, 'Look at me, Mam.'

She turned her face away and he held up his fist in frustration.

'Look at me!' His hands reached out as if he were going to grab her face in his hands and force it in his direction. Then he threw his hands down again by his sides and said, 'Even my own mother is afraid to look at me.'

Morag fixed her eyes on the window and said in a solid, uncompromising voice, 'You're a stupid boy, Jimmy Walsh – go outside and fetch me in some fuel and get the fire lit before your father gets back and brains you for giving me cheek.'

When he left, Morag Walsh rested her hands on the side of the butler sink and let her chest collapse for a moment.

It was not looking upon her son's disfigured face that had frightened her; it was the look of despair in his eyes.

Chapter Twenty-One

As they were coming back from their picnic, the same man Aileen had seen on their return from Cleggan passed them out on the road leading up to the house.

He raised his cap and smiled. Aileen waved back at him out of politeness, but John Joe didn't greet him in return.

'He's a friend of my mother's,' Aileen said.

John Joe just grunted in reply.

Aileen added, 'I can't remember his name. Do you know him?' but John Joe ignored her again.

When they came up to the house, John Joe got down from the cart and, passing Aileen her box of messages from the back, said, 'You bring those in and send your mother out to me like a good girl. Ruari, Mary, you go inside and help Aileen unpack.'

Anne was stony-faced when Aileen told her John Joe wanted to talk to her and marched, more than walked out to him. Aileen could sense there was something badly wrong. She put on her apron and busied herself by telling the two children to go and play together in the garden, which, sensing her altered manner, they did without question. Aileen could hear from the strained tone of her mother's and John Joe's voices that they were arguing. It could only be about her, about something she had done or said. Perhaps John Joe had guessed from her manner when they saw Biddy that it was *she* who had caused the fire. Perhaps he was urging her mother to have her confess to the police. Aileen felt certain that's what it was. What else could it be? She felt a sick dread rise up in her and her hand sought out the scapular that was sewn into the pocket of her apron. Perhaps if she had taken the apron anyway, against her father's wishes, hidden it in her bag, she might have better observed the rules of the Sacred Heart hidden within it and would not be being punished now for letting Jimmy Walsh touch her in the way that he had. For a moment Aileen entertained the terrible idea that perhaps God had punished her whole family because of her romantic transgression. Then her mother came back in and she heard John Joe whip and 'hup' his horse back down the boreen.

For the next few days mother and daughter resumed the choreography of their simple domestic life, moving around each other quietly as they cooked, set fires, scrubbed tables, swept floors and fed chickens. Aileen sensed that her mother was troubled, that there was something dark on her mind – something darker still than the death of her husband and sons. She was not despairing like before, but cold and thoughtful, which Aileen found even more troubling. She said nothing, but kept her mood even and continued with her chores.

On the fourth day, her mother sent Aileen running down to meet the postman on the road, where she was to give him two letters. One for Anne's sister and the other for an office address in Dublin that Aileen did not recognize but presumed was to do with the Cleggan compensation fund.

On the fifth day, Anne slaughtered, gutted and plucked all of their six hens and left them in the cold cupboard in the scullery.

On the sixth day, she took their one remaining suitcase and filled it with her and Aileen's clothes.

'We are leaving,' she said when Aileen finally asked what she was doing. 'We are going to stay with your aunt Eileen in Ballina. It's for the best.'

Aileen did not ask for how long; she had never met her aunt Eileen or been to Ballina, her mother's hometown, but she did not argue.

It was her godlessness and selfish stupidity that had caused all this. Living with strangers on the mainland was better than prison – although perhaps prison was what she deserved. In truth, Aileen did not care where she lived or with whom anymore. She had caused the death of her family. Her life was over.

John Joe collected them. Anne loaded the six dead chickens and the rest of their perishable food into the back of his wagon, and he gave her cursory thanks and said he would distribute the chickens among their neighbours before they turned. Beyond that, John Joe and Anne did not speak for the rest of the journey, despite sitting next to each other at the front of the cart. Anne's head was held high and her back stiff and unmoving. John Joe was, in truth, their only friend on the island and it sickened Aileen to think she had drawn such a wedge between him and her family in this way. Aileen chatted busily to Mary and Ruari, talking about going on her 'great adventure to the mainland' and assuring them she would be back before long. It was a total pretence, and the naturalness with which she was able to maintain the lie to these two gullible children made Aileen all the more certain that she was a thoroughly bad person.

'But *why* are you going, Aileen?' Mary pleaded.

'Because I have a rich, important aunt living in great style in the big town and I want to see how it is to live like a grand lady for a while!'

Aileen wished for her mother to turn round and smile at her version of events so that her mother's approval might make it true, but she did not. Both Anne and John Joe sat looking ahead at the mountain and the bogs and the flat sea beyond, unmoving and silent against the lines and undulations of the landscape ahead – estranged from each other yet united in their stoicism.

The car Anne's sister, Eileen, had sent for them was waiting on the mainland side of the bridge. Anne and Aileen had to walk across, as John Joe's old nag would not cross the bridge. The animal had become island-bound; it happened to humans and animals alike – a kind of inbuilt instinct that something bad would happen if they crossed water.

As John Joe took down the case from the back of the cart and she and Anne stood at the mouth of the bridge, Aileen found herself saying, 'I'm not going.'

Her mother turned to her. 'Don't be silly, Aileen – hurry on. John Joe has to get back. Look –' she pointed across to a dark brown vehicle parked on the other side '– Eileen's car is waiting.'

Aileen was not certain what had come over her, except that her feet were locked to the ground. As she tried to move forward, she felt a terrible dread holding her back; it was as if she were on the edge of a cliff and her mother was urging her to step off it into a crevice so deep she could not see the bottom.

'Come on, Aileen,' her mother said. 'What's come over you at all?'

John Joe took her arm and tried to walk her forward, but she threw it off sharply.

'I'm not coming with you.'

The words came out with a clarity that shocked even Aileen herself. She was not sure that she even meant to say them, but once she had, she knew they were true. 'I am staying here.'

Aileen's head was telling her to follow her mother, yet there was another, higher instinct holding her back. Some physical force inside had her paralysed.

Anne was raging and came back and grabbed her arm.

'You are coming with me, young woman, and that is that. For God's sake, what will Eileen think?'

Aileen looked at Anne. Her mother looked tired and worn; the two of them should be back in the cottage trying to rebuild their lives together after the terrible thing that had happened. Aileen knew that she had caused her mother all this worry and distress, and it wasn't fair, all this upheaval.

'Stay, Mam – let's stay here. We can face this together.'

Anne's face contorted with horror and shock when she said that, but Aileen felt relieved that her terrible truth was almost out. 'I know this has been all my fault, Mam, but I'll make it right – I promise I will. Let's stay in our own home. I don't care what anyone says about me, Mam – I don't want to leave the island, and you're only doing this for me.'

'I can't,' her mother said, and she grabbed the case and ran towards the car without another word.

Aileen was speechless. What was going on? Was Anne expecting her to chase after her? Did her mother assume that in running, Aileen would surely be behind her?

Aileen looked across the bridge, stunned, as her mother bundled herself and the suitcase into the back of the car. The car started, turned and drove off along the mainland road without her mother giving her as much as a backward glance.

John Joe put his arm around her shoulder and squeezed it with his large hand in a gesture of comfort.

Her mother had abandoned her? Surely not.

Aileen shook her head in disbelief. She did not understand what was happening. Why would her mother run away like this? She knew what she had done was terrible, but her own mother leave her behind? After all they had been through?

'Grief is a terrible thing,' John Joe said, answering her unspoken question. 'It makes people do things they would never dream of doing otherwise.'

John Joe walked her back to the cart and Aileen sat up front, as stiff as her mother had been. She was numb, too confounded and hurt by her mother's actions to cry or even fully take them in.

She looked around the island and all about her she noticed that the world was growing and beautiful. Weeping fuchsia flowers reached out from the sides of the road, their pretty buds yielding to the slightest breeze. There was a crowd of delicate wild roses clambering across the wall of an otherwise unremarkable cottage, and a bank of lavender whose scent was so strong it followed them down the road. The sun was shining, and the island all around was glowing with life. Inside, Aileen felt dead.

As they reached the turning for their house, John Joe suddenly roared at the horse to hurry, and when the poor animal wouldn't pick up speed, he cursed the 'bastard nag'. John Joe never swore and the occurrence pinched the children into a kind of terrified silence. He then pulled the horse to a halt, and barely calling for them all to stay where they were, the older man leaped down from the cart and took off running up the drive at remarkable speed.

It was only when Aileen heard John Joe roar something that sounded like 'Come back till I bate you!' and saw her parents' friend Maurice coming out from the back of their cottage that she realized John Joe must have thought him an intruder. John Joe had seen him before – did he not know he was a friend of her mother's? What on earth was he doing? Aileen had some vague idea that John Joe didn't like the man, but to assume he was robbing their house?

She jumped down from the cart herself and ran after him; she was nearly at the house when she saw the argument between them turn into a fight; Maurice poked John Joe in the chest and the solid farmer landed him such a punch that the slimmer man fell to the ground. She managed to catch John Joe just as the man was getting up and the sturdy farmer was standing over him, fists raised, as if planning to put him down again.

'Go back to the cart, Aileen. Let me handle this.'

'She's gone,' the man wailed, looking up at John Joe. 'Where has she gone? Merciful hour of God, man, will you not tell me?'

He was drunk, either from alcohol or the punch – it was hard to tell – and his words were slurred slightly as he noticed Aileen and said, 'Oh, may the Lord be good. Girl . . . You're her girl, right? Oh Jesus, but she can't be gone after all. Girl, where's your mammy now? Where is she?'

'Another word out of your mouth and I'll bang your teeth clean into your neck,' John Joe spat at the man. 'Have some respect and leave this family alone if you have anything decent left in you. Get out of here now and we'll say no more about this.'

'I'm not leaving until the girl tells me where her mammy is.'

John Joe picked him up by the collar of his shirt and Aileen was afraid herself for the mixture of fear and rage that emanated from him. This Maurice must have done something terrible altogether to him to elicit such anger from mild-mannered John Joe.

Suddenly, the man, Maurice, reached over and, grabbing her arm, held her eye and blurted out, 'I am in love with your mother.'

Aileen saw his dark eyes move from flashing fear to tenderness and she knew he was speaking the truth. The facts hit her hard, in three cruel slaps, like a teacher cracking her ruler down on a wooden desk: the man had been in the house on the day they got back; he was the first person her mother had ever introduced to her as a 'friend'; when John Joe had 'found her out', her mother's shame had been so deep she had run away.

Everything fell into place: her mother fleeing and John Joe's anger as he tried to protect them both.

She felt like she wanted to be sick.

Had her mother been courting this man all the time they were away in Scotland or just since her father had died, in some terrible surge of madness brought about by her grief?

She looked at John Joe and, in some part of her, tried to blame him for all this, but their farmer neighbour's face was so dishevelled with hurt and anger that she knew in her heart and soul he had done all he could to protect Aileen and her mother from this horrible reality, as well as, doubtless, to protect the memory of her father and brothers.

John Joe waved the man away and seeming to know the fight was over, he scuttled off across the bog. The older man put his arm around Aileen and led her back to the cart.

He lifted her up into the back with the children, and even though it was a warm day, he placed a blanket over her shoulders, then said to Mary, 'You lean in there to Aileen like a good girl and give her some comfort, Mary. She's coming back to stay in our house for a while.'

'Why didn't you go in the car, Aileen?' Ruari asked as soon as John Joe pulled down the drive. 'On the bridge – why didn't you run after your mammy?'

Being motherless himself, the young boy was still reeling from the fact that Aileen had not chased after her mother, although he was equally mystified as to how she had turned down a ride in such a fine vehicle as Eileen's brown car.

Aileen didn't reply. Her spirits were drowned in the tidal wave of truth she had just learned and she was flooded with black hurt. There was something in what the boy said that nagged at her. Something from before the fullness of this drama had revealed itself: the mystery of her own mule-like refusal to leave the island.

Chapter Twenty-Two

After two days' travelling, Jimmy arrived in Camden Town.

He had found the journey to London much more gruelling than the journey to Scotland had been. Most of the passengers on the boat were male, and every one of them was going to England in search of work.

While he himself was comfortable travelling on the rough sea, within twenty minutes of the ship sailing out of Dublin Port everyone around him was vomiting wildly. An hour into the ten-hour boat journey and the upstairs deck was swimming in sick.

While the inside of the boat was worse again, the makeshift bar was the worst of all. The few seats were permanently occupied by the more seasoned passengers, who had drunk themselves into a stupefied state before getting on board, while the rest of the space was filled with men in the midst of a drinking and vomiting cycle as they drank more and more to try and ease the discomfort of their swaying insides.

It was savagery the likes of which Jimmy had never seen before and hoped he would never see again. It seemed that while the shipping company was happy to sell drink to their Paddy passengers, they felt less obliged to provide them with proper seating or toilet facilities. Indeed, as Jimmy noted to himself while wandering through the boat looking for somewhere to settle himself for an hour, even a few carefully placed buckets would have achieved a lot.

He was glad to get off the boat and onto the train at Holyhead, and although it was packed to its lid with everyone from the boat, most of the passengers used this leg of the journey to sleep off the excesses of the boat.

Jimmy lay down on a corridor floor and slept using his small knapsack as a pillow. He had brought very little with him. On his last journey to Scotland, his mother had packed his bag. This time, she had not even come to the door.

'She's stricken with grief,' Sean had said to him, handing him his knapksack and ten pounds. 'She doesn't want you to go.'

Jimmy was not happy that his father had borrowed the ten pounds he needed, but he had no choice, so he took it.

'I'll send back as soon as I can, Da,' he said.

'Never mind that – just come back soon and in one piece.'

'In one piece.' He'd been in one piece when he left the last time, but the fire in Scotland had claimed a part of his face and now he was going to get it back. Jimmy had a little hope in his heart again. He would earn a fortune working as a navvy on the buildings, and this doctor Anthony had told him about would fix up his face. Then he would come home good as new. Better even than he had been before, because now he'd be a man of the world: strong, mature and rich – ready to go and claim his own true love.

'You do know England's not all it's cracked up to be?' Sean had said.

'You mean the streets aren't really paved with gold?' Jimmy joked.

'Be careful, son.'

Somewhere in the bottom of his heart, Jimmy believed that, for him at least, they might just be.

Jimmy had been in London for less than an hour and he liked it already. It was early morning when they disembarked from the train at Victoria Station and there were hundreds of people rushing past each other in straight lines, determinedly going about their business. Jimmy had never experienced anything like this before. This was not the shuffling, murmuring crowd of a boat queue, where everyone looked the same and was going to the same place, for the same reason. Here, each person was different from the next: a man in a pinstripe suit with a bowler hat and a briefcase; a woman in a smart dress, the likes of which you might see only on a doctor's wife in Mass once a year; ordinary girls in plain dresses; men, like himself, in working clothes; a lady selling flowers; a cockney man waving papers in his hand and doing transactions with passing customers while scarcely acknowledging them and with them scarcely missing a step. He saw a man with skin as black as coal; then within a minute he saw another – two black men in the same place in as many minutes and nobody paying them one bit of heed, as if such a sight was a commonplace thing. He stood for a moment and watched the scene in front of him. All these people rushing hither and thither, all in a mad rush to get somewhere yet nobody talking, or touching or stopping to notice each other at all. Everyone here was minding their own business.

On the boat, he had been plagued with men asking about his face, and one drunkard had tried to take the mask off him. Although some others had stepped in to defuse the situation, Jimmy had felt violated by their questions and gawking. Irish people wanted to know everything about you. That was just the way his countrymen were, and that was fine as long as you were Invincible Jim – the dandy man – ahead of the crew. Now he found their questions intrusive and upsetting.

Suddenly, standing on the concourse at Victoria Station, all that was gone. He was just a man in a mask, nobody paying him any heed at all. This was a great place altogether. This was a place where a man could get on with things and not be bothered.

He had at first thought that he should stop somebody and ask directions to Camden Town, but now he decided that if all these people could work out where they were going, it couldn't be that hard. Sure enough, across the concourse, he spotted what looked like a map jutting up on a pillar out of the ground. Negotiating his way across the flitting bodies, he found it was not an ordinary map but some class of a diagram for the 'London Underground Railway'. Various coloured lines mapped out train lines and Jimmy quickly found Camden Town among them. Now all he had to do was find the train. He stood for a moment, then simply allowed himself to be swept along by the crowd around him, streaming down a wide stairwell, at the bottom of which he joined the queue at a booth selling tickets. Within seconds he was in front of a man behind a window.

'Camden Town,' he said, passing over a shilling and hoping for the best. The man gave him back his change without even looking up at him. This was surely the best place in the world – but there was more to come.

After showing his ticket to another uniformed guard, Jimmy was astonished to see that the crowd in front of him seemed to be disappearing in a strange, smooth downward movement into the bowels of the earth. His stomach churned with a mixture of excitement and dread as he followed them, stepping onto a shaking slat of wood and metal, part of a moving stairwell that descended in a mechanical motion down into a tiled cavern below. He stood, part of the silent crowd in a curved well-lit cave, and looked across to the straight-line diagram in front of him – the colour of the Blessed Virgin's cloak – with the names of the stations: Victoria, Green Park, Oxford Circus, Holborn, Russell Square – but no Camden Town.

He turned to the person next to him, a woman in a plain grey wool coat, and said, 'Can you tell me the way to Camden Town, please?'

For a moment he saw a flash of alarm pass across her eyes and he remembered how strange he looked. 'Change at King's Cross,' she said, just as the train whooshed into the station like an angry snake. Its doors flew back as if by magic. They both stepped in through its open jaws and the woman disappeared into the throng. Jimmy knew he would never see her – or, in all likelihood, any of these people with whom he was crammed at such close quarters – again. With that knowledge, Jimmy felt such a rush of freedom that when he alighted at King's Cross as he had been told, he found himself almost skipping as he searched cave after cave, through cavernous, snaking corridors and up and down sets of endless moving stairs, for a line that said, 'Camden Town'.

He must have walked for an hour, but Jimmy didn't mind being lost. He was enjoying the feeling of being invisible, moving easily in and out of the crowds unnoticed.

Eventually, he got on another train and, after a short ride, found himself in Camden Town, where he followed signs for the exit and hopped on the escalator as if he had been travelling them all his life. As he reached the top of the tunnel, Jimmy felt the sting of fresh air hit the good side of his face. He looked out and saw London spread out either side of him and for the first time since he had left Aghabeg Jimmy felt slightly afraid.

Down on his left, sitting against the exit wall on a pile of abandoned newspapers, was a vagrant man nursing a bottle of wine.

He looked up at Jimmy and in a Mayo accent as broad as the shivering Atlantic asked, 'What happened to your face?'

Chapter Twenty-Three

Life goes on. Somebody had said that to Aileen's mother at her father's and brothers' month's mind Mass. They were standing outside the church, slightly back from the rest of the widowed families, and Nelly French, a rather large, talkative woman who lived near the church, came over to Anne and said, 'You must be terribly lonely, Anne. Still, you have this lovely young woman for comfort –' she squeezed Aileen's arm '– and life must go on, eh?'

Anne had bristled and responded to the mourner with nothing more than an icy smile. It was among the many things Aileen had heard people say, outside Mass, in the shop – stupid, awkward things said for the want of offering some solace in the face of terrible misfortune. *They're in heaven now with God. They're at peace.* Pointless words that didn't help and only served to make you feel worse. 'Life goes on' was a popular one and particularly pointless, Aileen felt. Of course life goes on: it was obvious we were still alive, yet this expression was supposed to mean 'normal' life after someone had died. It was nothing more than a myth, people wanting to believe that everything would go back to how it was before. What made that expression all the more irritating for Aileen was that in some part of her she had hoped it would be true. Even though her father and brothers were dead, somehow she had hoped that life might go back to how it had been before they had died. That was what Aileen had been trying to make happen: recreating her world as it had been before she had brought this bad luck on them by travelling to Scotland. Clearing the garden, painting the cottage, trying to make things 'normal' again. Then her mother had run away on her and changed everything.

Aileen decided that the only way she could approach this dramatic change in her circumstances was to change everything around her. She felt dead inside. That would never change – not now. Her family were either dead or had abandoned her. Jimmy was a memory too painful to accommodate. The dark, anxious feeling she had now was who she was; there was a permanence about it; the fire, its destruction and death had branded her. Her only hope for survival now was to change everything about her life and never go back. She would never be happy again, not deep down, not how she had been when playing on the beach with her brothers as a child or kissing Jimmy as a young woman. But Aileen could, she found, at least pretend to be happy when she was around John Joe and the children, and for all that it was a lie, it was better than the black despair she knew she would fall into if she went back home alone.

So Aileen did not go back to her cottage; she stayed living with the farmer and his niece and nephew. She joined in their simple, ordered life as if she had always been there: cleaning the house and preparing the meals while he worked on the farm, sitting in front of the fire reading to the children in the evenings and sharing a bed with Mary, who was particularly thrilled to have her there, although Ruari and John Joe were equally welcoming.

A week after she moved in, John Joe offered to take her back to the cottage to get some more clothes. Aileen told him that her mother had taken all of her clothes with her in the case. He went to the wardrobe in his room and took out a large trunk, opened it and began pulling out piles upon piles of women's clothing – dresses, skirts and blouses, even a woman's coat.

'They belonged to my late sister-in-law,' he said. 'She won't be needing them now. I knew they'd come in handy one day!'

He held up one enormous coat; Aileen could have fitted into it three times over!

'Maisie was a substantial woman,' he said, and they both laughed. 'She couldn't find clothes big enough to fit her in the shops, and she was too embarrassed to go to the dressmaker, so she made most of these herself, which meant –' with great aplomb John Joe whipped a woollen blanket from a corner table and revealed a shiny black and gold Singer '– she had a sewing machine, complete with a double foot-pedal. As complex and brilliant a piece of machinery as any you'll find on the farm. We could do some alterations? Make you a dress?' He said it with such an air of keen hopefulness, as if it were she doing him a favour instead of the other way round, that Aileen laughed again.

Over the coming days, after the chores on the farm were done and the supper things were put away, John Joe fashioned Aileen a whole new wardrobe out of poor dead Maisie's clothes. The fabric was of varying quality, but it seemed that John Joe was something of a genius on the machine. One Sunday morning, she got up early and found a tweed skirt, fashioned to the middle of her calf, and a matching jacket with a perfectly fitted nipped-in waist laid out on a chair at the end of the bed, along with a yellow blouse that from the soft feel of it had been made of silk.

'You'll be good for Mass now,' John Joe said, when she put it on and twirled round the kitchen.

Aileen said nothing, then felt bad when he quickly took his words back, saying, 'Of course – when you're ready.'

Three Sundays had passed since her mother had run away and Aileen had not joined John Joe and the children at church. She could not face the whispers and the concerned looks. Even though the island was wild, with large tracts of uninhabited land between them and their nearest neighbours, islanders seemed to know every detail of each other's lives. It was as if news travelled on the wind and landed itself directly into the ears of interested parties as they sat in their kitchens. However, the majority of news was discussed in the church grounds on a Sunday morning after Mass, and since the tragedy the widowed families of the Cleggan Ten were under the constant scrutiny of their neighbours. Most people meant well, and several of their neighbours had called to the cottage with food parcels and to help after she had come home. The immediate aftermath of death had now passed and given way to often arch speculation about the compensation fund. Money coming onto the island was always big news.

'*They'll be glad of the few bob.*'

'*They've been through a lot surely.*'

'*They're saying there was thousands raised – more than any family could spend.*'

'*Perhaps they'll make a donation to the church fund . . .*'

'*Perhaps . . .*'

People never said what they meant and Aileen was her mother's daughter insofar as she preferred to keep her business to herself.

She knew that tongues would be wagging about her mother's disappearance and about her having moved in with John Joe. It was beyond naive to think that the whole island did not know she was living in his house, and it looked very bad on him, his going to Mass without her. Now that Aileen understood that such things were possible after her own mother's transgression, she could barely bring herself to speculate about what they might be saying.

Aileen did not care so much what they thought of her, but she did not want to hurt John Joe. He had acted in the way of a father to her and he deserved the best of respect for his kindness towards not just her, but his brother's children. When the truth came out about what she had done, when she finally came clean, which she would have to do – soon – she would face whatever punishment, but John Joe was a good man and should have no part of it.

Aileen knew life would be made easier for John Joe if she were to at least be seen out with him and the children as the normal, rosary-saying, God-fearing family they were. But when she thought about walking up the aisle of the church and everyone looking at her, Aileen's blood ran cold. She had a vague recollection of getting off the boat in Dublin and being watched by a million eyes as they walked after the coffins down the quays, although the experience seemed so distant – more like a dream than a memory.

'Why don't you take the children to school,' John Joe said, 'in the cart? They are due back tomorrow and it'll be a way of you seeing people without . . .' He faltered, not wanting to offend her. Not for the first time Aileen felt a stab of something like the love she had felt for her father.

'Being *seen*?' she said.

He nodded, still unsure.

'That's a splendid idea!' Mary said.

Aileen laughed. She had been reading Enid Blyton to the children and they were both starting to talk like the English children in her books.

'Spiffing!' John Joe said, and it was agreed.

*

Aileen drove the children across the island to the schoolhouse. The novelty of driving alone without John Joe made the three of them so giddy that the old horse seemed to join in and go at twice his usually plodding speed. Aileen wore the smart Sunday suit and blouse John Joe had left out the day before and called, 'Good morning!' cheerily at the three or four carts they passed on the road. That would be enough to quieten tongues, she thought. Far from hiding herself away, Aileen was out driving the children to school, so despite what may have happened with her mother, there couldn't be anything untoward going on. The experience passed with such ease she thought she might even make it to Mass the following Sunday.

The children hopped down from the cart and ran towards their teacher, a Miss Nolan, of whom they seemed very fond. Aileen had heard all about her; she was a spinster of not yet forty. She waved, but as the teacher walked towards the cart to talk to her, Aileen panicked and, pretending she hadn't seen her, drove straight off. She had meant to turn the cart in the clearing outside the school, but decided to travel along for a while in the wrong direction until she was certain classes had begun so she would not be accosted again.

'It's a fine day,' she said aloud, realizing that this was the first time in quite a while that she was entirely by herself and she felt happy about that. The horse plodded along the narrow road with little guidance, while Aileen looked ahead for a clearing where she might turn him round. She saw what looked like an opening up ahead, and as they grew closer, she realized they were at the gates of the big house. She had not been there since the picnic and turned up the drive with a vague curiosity.

As they reached the front of the empty house, instead of following Aileen's instruction to turn, the horse stopped and began to munch grass from an overgrown but rather grand, elaborate urn near the burnt-out doorway. Aileen looked at the watch John Joe had given her so she could calculate getting the children to school on time. She had a few hours before the farmer would be in for his dinner and she had left out a cold meat salad and some boxty for him anyway, so there was no need to rush back. In fact, John Joe had suggested she take the cart down to the bridge and call into the church on her way back.

'Have a day out for yourself, Aileen,' he had said. 'If I don't see you until you're back with the children after school, there's no harm. You might call into the shop and get yourself some sweets?' Then he had insisted on her taking sixpence, even though she had no intention of risking seeing anyone.

She got down from the cart and loosened the bit on the horse so he could wander around. He was old and would not go far. He snorted gratefully and then continued pottering to feast on the rich, swaying grass of what must once have been a lawn.

Aileen walked through the courtyard into the garden. It had been a few weeks since they had picnicked here and it was markedly more overgrown than before, but she did not stop to consider that and headed straight for the second door, yanking down the brass handle and heading into the second walled field. So much had happened in the intervening time that Aileen had not thought about this place at all since that day, but now that she was here, she found herself compelled towards the old greenhouse. She could see that the bindweed was thriving inside, but she was nonetheless curious to see what had happened to the stem she had cleared. As she tugged open the door, she saw it straight away, standing bare, just as she had left it, defiant in the face of the creeping, chaotic weeds. More than that, the plant had miraculously sprouted soft green leaves and they opened towards her like stretched hands. Moving closer, she could see that little fruit buds were forming – of what she did not know – but as she leaned in to smell the flowers, she could hear the source of the stem whispering three words to her, the same three words over and over in the pulse of the sap being sucked through the veins of the leaves: *Life goes on. Life goes on. Life goes on* . . .

As if propelled by its rhythm, Aileen threw off her coat and immediately, ferociously set about clearing the overgrown greenhouse.

Chapter Twenty-Four

Jimmy could not find his digs. The address he had on a piece of paper from his father's friend in Donegal had seemed straightforward enough: 5 Carroll Street, Camden Town, London. However, Camden Town, he discovered, was a very big place with a lot of streets in it. Many of them seemed to be the full length of the island he grew up on. He tried to stop one or two people, but they kept walking past him and he knew it was because they were afraid of his face, which put Jimmy's nerves on edge. While the Underground had seemed to him a place where he could hide among people, up here on the residential streets he felt exposed. The one or two people he had managed to ask had no idea where he was talking about, and he had no map to help guide him. He had thought that if he walked around for a while, he was sure to just fall upon the right road, but after two hours, he was starting to despair. As he took yet another turn onto another seemingly endless street, he saw that he was right back where he had started, directly opposite Camden Town Tube Station. There were men outside on scaffolding. The building had been bombed – he remembered now hearing two veteran navvies on the boat talking about it.

'Two years ago and they're still clearing up the mess.'

'Only four killed, but it took the side of the station clean off. The Underground was fine, though, and the trains kept running.'

'I don't like those tunnels at all. I'll take the bus anytime.'

'Nasty business this aul' war, but then, somebody has to put London back together for them lads – am I right?'

A group of navvies were now coming off the scaffolding and heading to a pub across the road, the Mother Redcap. Jimmy hesitated. He did not want to ask for their help. He had got as far as Camden Town by himself and he could make his own way. However, he knew that, in reality, he could not. There were six of them crowded round the bar. Jimmy took a deep breath and walked across to them. There were pint glasses filled with milk on the bar in front of them with the biggest pile of sandwiches Jimmy had ever seen. He suddenly felt starving and wondered how much it would cost to get his own pint of milk and a sandwich.

'What happened to your face?'

'Leave the lad alone – sure he's only off the boat.'

The men were bawdy but friendly and helpful – in their own way. Two of them were from Donegal, and when he showed them his address, it turned out that they were staying in the same digs as him.

Celebrations all round.

'Buy that man his inaugural London pint!'

'There's no drinking during the day once you're a working man, Jim, so take the lunchtime pint while you can.'

'Then you'll have to be saving it up for the Friday skite like the rest of us.'

Jimmy had never drunk alcohol before. His father was a pioneer and he had taken the vow at his own confirmation and had never seen any reason to break it.

But he had already had to explain about his face and his fate, and he wanted to fit in, or rather, he needed to fit in.

The beer tasted vile, bitter, like the worst kind of medicine. However, after a few sips, he got used to it and before the men went back to work, they left three more up at the bar for him and said they would be back at four to take him to the digs.

All the sandwiches were gone.

Jimmy did not remember anything after that until he was woken up by a large foot pushing into his cheek. The stench and the strength of it were evidence that he was sharing a bed, head to toe, with another man. A narrow bed, because as he turned to escape further attack from the hairy toes, Jimmy fell face first onto a filthy brown carpet.

His head was pounding with more pressure than pain, as if there was a rodent in there banging to be let out.

He eased himself up onto his elbow, but found there was barely room to sit up as there was another bed directly next to the one he'd just fallen out of. He stood up and saw that the room he was in contained five single beds – four in a line and one across the width of the room, which was barely twelve foot square. In each bed were two men, sleeping head to toe. What followed was a miraculous choreography of twelve big, largely naked Irishmen dressing themselves in an extremely limited space: tucking elbows in a way to keep them safe from nearby chests, crossing their legs to avoid unnecessary precarious dangling, passing pants and socks and trousers to one another across an assault course of wobbling beds and other big Irishmen. They did this with extraordinary speed – as if they were in a tremendous hurry.

'What time is it?' Jimmy asked.

'Five,' one of the men said, and another added, 'The site opens at six. The foreman says he'll try you for the day.'

Jimmy, who was still dressed from the day before, grabbed his bag, which he had spotted under the bed, and followed them out of the room as the men pounded down the stairs of the small suburban house in the dark and into a small scullery kitchen, where they all squashed in and stood around in silence so as not to wake the family whose bedroom they were renting. After a few minutes, the landlady came in and passed each one a mug of sweet, milky tea, which they drank standing; a few minutes after that, she came back and handed them all a hunk of white bread with two sausages rolled into it. It was the first food Jimmy had eaten in two days and he devoured it in one go. He looked pitifully at the woman, but she glowered at him sharply to make it clear that was his lot.

'You were in some state last night, lad – I'll be expecting a deposit from you before I give you your tea tonight.'

'I'm Sean Walsh's son, from Aghabeg.'

'I don't give a damn that you are,' she said. 'You're all "Paddy" to me.'

'Dolores is not as bad as she seems,' one of the men, Brian, said to him as they left. 'She's a good Donegal woman.'

'She's a greedy bitch,' said another. 'You're lucky we weren't three to the bed last night – she's tried that before.'

'When there's a big room next door to ours with only three small children in it?'

'Don't be looking in the other rooms, Aiden, or you'll get us all thrown out.'

On the way up to the site, the lads explained that Dolores ran the cheapest house in London, which meant they could send money home every week, 'and still have the few bob for a good skite of pints on Friday'.

As they talked, they walked through the dark streets of London towards Camden Town Station. Jimmy had no recollection of making this walk the night before and vowed never to drink again. Despite his sore head, he thought that perhaps things were going to turn out all right. The digs were pretty grim, but the lads seemed nice, and if he saved all his money, instead of spending it on drink, he'd have a fortune saved in no time.

However, Jimmy's career as a navvy was to be short-lived.

An hour after he was on site, Jimmy dropped a load of bricks from a hod he was carrying clean down onto the ground from the first floor of the scaffold. Jimmy had not realized how much his peripheral vision was impaired. With the hod up on his shoulder, one side was completely invisible to him and it affected his balance.

The English foreman was very nice about it, considering.

He could see that Jimmy needed the work, as did all the young Irishmen who came to him, and he had a particular compassion because he knew things would be hard for him given the state of his face. He kept him on for the rest of the day, sweeping the dust from one place to another on the ground floor. Jimmy knew it was over, but he stuck it out for the one-day wage of two pounds.

It was a Friday, but he left the other men to the Mother Redcap and headed for the Tube station.

Jimmy had one more card to play – an address that Anthony Irvine had pressed into his hand that day as he left the island. When he took out the crumpled sheet of paper, he saw it said, 'Turn left out of Piccadilly Circus Station,' after the address and instructions on how to get there.

This was a man who knew what he was doing.

Chapter Twenty-Five

Aileen looked around the old glasshouse. With the weeds all gone, she was amazed by this unusual, airy building. It seemed similar in size to her own house, except laid out as one long room. The floors were tiled, and the walls were red brick to waist height. The rest of the building comprised long glass windows – even the sloping roof. Glass was expensive and they only had three small windows in the whole of the cottage she grew up in; two of them were simply glazed gaps in the wall to allow some light in, and the third 'proper' window they were never allowed to open for fear of breaking the catch. Even on the brightest summer's day, their house was dark, but this place of about the same length and breadth was so bright that Aileen's eyes hurt. It was as if the Englishman had found a way of catching the sunlight on the island and had gathered it all into this one place for his own personal use. Aileen could almost hear her father's voice saying, 'That's the bastard English for you – they take the best of everything.'

At one end of the room were tables whose tops were cluttered with pots and plates of various sizes. Running along the edge of the walls was a series of thick rusted pipes. On top of these were shallow trays, like semicircles of the pipes themselves built into the top of them – some mysterious piece of engineering at work. As she cleared the bindweed, Aileen could see how the weed had been able to take over the space so thoroughly. Running at head height across the room was a series of horizontal metal bars, and along those bars were wound the fat trunks of fruit vines similar to the one she had cleared. There were eight of them in all – grey and dead, but still solidly clinging to their metal anchor. Aileen followed them down to their roots and saw that their trunks had been trained through cave-like holes cut into the bricks at the bottom edge of the outside wall. They were planted outside.

Clearly, the crazy bindweed had followed one of the vines through one of these holes, and despite the ferocity of its growth, Aileen discovered that the chaos was all coming from one plant. In the absence of anything to curtail it, the single bindweed had run riot and made itself look like far more than it was. Aileen wondered at the ability of one small thing to create so much chaos and shuddered for a moment as she thought that was what the Cleggan fire had been: one small oversight. She shivered, then shrugged the thought aside and went over to the trays and pots on the tables. Many of the larger pots still had earth in them, although it was as dry as gravel. As her fingers lifted the dead, dry soil, she remembered the barn after the fire and put her hands into the pocket of her coat to feel if the burned soil she had carried from Scotland was still there. She felt a slight lift in her stomach when her fingers touched the earthy ash, and for no reason she began to mix it with the soil in the pots.

'Water,' she said aloud.

There had to be a well or something in the vicinity – as she was walking out, she almost tripped over another of the pipes which was running along the centre of the room under the vines. The answer to their peculiar shape came to her in such a flash she could only imagine that she must have read about it somewhere in a book: steam. The closed pipes heated the trays on top, which were filled with water and made steam. If they made steam, there must be water nearby. The thought had barely occurred to her before she was drawn to a thicket of nettles behind the back end of the building, and pushing them aside, there was a water pump. She found the handle of the pump and pulled it upwards. It was stiff and took some strength, but Aileen found she had it, and more besides! She pumped the stiff handle up and down until she thought it would yield nothing, but then, after a few minutes, a splatter of rusted liquid ran out of its tap. She speeded up her pumping and before she knew it there was clean water spraying down onto the ground in front of her. Aileen's boots and skirt got soaked and she screamed, then, laughing out loud, ran back to the greenhouse to fetch the dusty pots with the Scottish soil.

She watered each of the pots and laid them down next to the pump. Aileen was astonished how the soil seemed to come back to life as she made a cup of her hand and spooned the water into each one. Seeing how springy and new the nettles were in that area, Aileen intuited that the ground underneath them must be especially fertile, so she clawed with her fingers around the pump and supplemented the pots with some of the rich black soil she found there.

As she picked up two of the bigger pots to carry back into the glasshouse, Aileen stood for a moment and got an overwhelming feeling of excitement in the pit of her stomach. Greater than when she had heard her father was bringing her to Scotland, greater than the anticipation of her travelling on a train or a boat. There was no reason for it that she could think of except for the notion that entered her head, which was, the greenhouse, the pump. If she cleared some of these weeds outside as well, goodness knows what treasures she might find.

Without caution for her nice clothes or her bare arms, Aileen tore around the garden. In the overgrowth round the back of the glasshouse and the pump Aileen quickly found a spade, a rake, an old wheelbarrow and a rusted long-handled scythe. Armed with these weapons, she began to battle the overgrowth and discover the garden underneath. Every swipe of the scythe seemed to reveal something new: a bunch of fledgling holly-hocks cowering behind a bank of swaying scutch grass; the stone wall of what was once a flower bed with giant sweet peas, their delicate purple and blue flowers clambering heroically among the weedy litter of spent dandelions and dead scrubs. One undulating stretch of ground had such regular little hillocks that Aileen knew it could only have been used for potato ridges, and next to it was another, raised bed, which she guessed would have been ideal for lettuces. Across from them was a huge lump of foliage almost as tall as a tree. After some investigation, Aileen discovered it was wrapped round a triangular metal structure that had probably been used for climbing peas.

At the very back of the field, there was a small stone cottage with a pretty scalloped door frame. Aileen stepped inside reluctantly. It had been empty for years and was eerie and damp. Aileen got a peculiar fright when she saw signs of human life – a few broken plates, a rotting chair – and having neither the desire nor the curiosity to explore the remnants of somebody else's existence, she left immediately. There was so much more to be found: flowering apple trees; a bank of gooseberry bushes in fruit, their plump, sour balls already rotting underfoot; a sea of rhubarb as fat and red and juicy as she had ever seen. There were tall balls of purple flowers that smelt of onions, clambering roses that led her to another gate at the back wall, which, as far as she could tell, led out into the island itself. It seemed to Aileen that this garden was a kind of island in itself. At the moment, Illaunmor was bleak and boggy with an emotional thunderous sky. In this garden, there were flowers and fruits and things to distract her.

Aileen was so busy adventuring through this magical place that when she remembered to look at John Joe's watch to see if it was time to collect the children, she could barely read its face because it had grown so dark. It was 9 p.m. Could it be that late? Oh my goodness, the children! John Joe would be out of his mind with worry! Aileen ran through the door, past the ornamental garden and to the front of the house. The cart was there, but the horse was gone. Aileen thought she should have tied him up, but then she had become so absorbed in the garden she had forgotten about the poor animal – small wonder he had abandoned her. He was an old horse and knew his way around the island with little to no guidance from a driver, so she hoped that he had wandered home to John Joe and alerted him to collect the children, who were, in all likelihood, with the nice teacher, who would surely not have left them at the side of the road.

As she began to calm herself down, Aileen felt a strange ease come over her that she could not recall having felt for a long time. Certainly not since she was a small child, perhaps, snoozing in the arms of her father on a warm day on the beach to the whisper of the shore, although this felt like a different kind of peace. There was an indefinable quiet here in this garden; it was as if God was with her, even though it felt as if He had long since abandoned her. Even that thought could not deter the deep feeling of peace that had begun to take her over. Aileen climbed up into the back of the cart, and pulling the blanket over her, she lay down on the painted wooden slats and looked up at the night sky. The island was far west of mainland Ireland and at this time of year the sky itself held some light until almost midnight. The clouds moved across her eyeline like kindly, fat ghosts, and before long she had fallen into a deep, empty, dreamless sleep.

'Aileen. Aileen.'

John Joe was calling her. It was dawn and she drew back with a shiver in the damp air as her bones caught up with the idea that she was cold.

'I'm here,' she said.

He had the horse with him. The animal had led him here; the two of them must have walked across the island to get her. They might have been walking all night.

'I'm sorry, John Joe,' she said.

The older man surely had questions: how could she have forgotten to collect the children from school? What had she been doing here all night? However, he did not ask them and she offered nothing to him.

Instead, he tethered the tired old horse to the cart and the two of them travelled back across the island to the burgeoning of the day in comfortable silence.

Chapter Twenty-Six

'Ah, my friend!'

When Anthony opened the door, Jimmy felt an overwhelming sense of relief wash over him – he was in the right place!

Soho was indeed a strange place. With its short, narrow streets, it wasn't nearly as confusing or intimidating as Camden Town, and there were so many distinctive landmarks you couldn't get lost. It had the feel of a village, with little shops, but all different. There was a butcher's right next to a shop selling ladies' underclothes. Then a shop with strange meats hanging in the windows and another shop selling ladies' underclothes, then a little cinema and a bakery with cakes in the window, then a fishmonger, a dress shop, a hair salon, a bookshop and then *another* shop selling ladies' underclothes.

Anthony's flat was above a shop that sold magazines and posters. Well, the window was all blacked out, and there was a big sign on the front of it that said, 'Magazines and posters for sale.' Jimmy looked in and was surprised to see no magazines or posters, just a man behind a counter who looked Asian and nodded at the door, saying, 'Anthony is upstairs.'

It didn't really matter, though; Jimmy was just delighted that Anthony remembered him. Jimmy was aware that he was smiling too broadly, but he could not help himself. That was the kind of man Anthony was, the way he made people feel. Special.

'Remember me? Jimmy?' he said.

'Of course I do, Jimbo! And how could I forget a face like that? How *are* you, old man?'

He ushered Jimmy in the door. The apartment was like nothing Jimmy had ever seen before. Well, perhaps once, in one of the two Hollywood movies he had been to see with his mother as a child.

The walls were covered in ornate flocked paper, and there was a cream carpet on the floor so thick that it would nearly cover your shoes. There were no hard chairs that he could see, just two settees that seemed too deep and soft and luxurious to do anything but sleep on. On each one was lounging a girl so beautiful and glamorous that Jimmy could barely look at them, but at the same time felt compelled to look from one to the other as if asserting to himself that they were really there. One had red hair like Aileen's, but of a more vivid hue, pale white skin and red, red lips. The other had hair as black as coal and eyes that were a glossy chocolate colour – like a movie star. Both were wearing long silky dressing gowns and underneath them was – he could gather even from this distance – very little else.

'Jimmy, this is Mandy,' Anthony said, waving his hand across to the dark-haired girl, 'and this is Lily.' As he said her name, the redhead walked across to Jimmy and held out her hand.

'Pleased to meet you,' she said, before gently brushing her fingers across his damaged cheek. Jimmy felt a sudden thrill move across his whole body. His eyelids fluttered and he looked straight ahead at the wall. He had glimpsed that the girl was bare-breasted. Her small white breasts were peeping out from the edge of her gown, which was undone and gaping to the waist. He hadn't dared look any further down than that, because that would have finished him off altogether. It was clear that the girl was deliberately provoking him and Anthony was watching his face intently, as if looking for signs of desire. Obviously, this Lily was his friend's girl – maybe even his wife – and was deliberately teasing him. He knew the English had a reputation for amorality, but this carry-on took the biscuit altogether. Jimmy smiled benignly at the wall behind the girl's head, giving nothing away, although, truthfully, every inch of his body was burning up in trying to push his desire to one side. Jimmy panicked, not wanting to cause upset or awkwardness, and he coughed, which broke the appalling awkwardness of the moment.

'Leave my friend alone now, Lily,' Anthony said. 'He's not interested.' Her seductive mood disappeared as suddenly and as shockingly as it had come on him and she wrapped her robe round her and left the room. 'You too,' he said, somewhat harshly, to Mandy, then, as if remembering they had a guest, said, 'I want some time to talk to my good friend Jim here.'

Mandy grabbed an apple from a bowl on the table in front of her and sank her teeth into it. Then giving them both an ironic smile, she followed her friend.

'So, what have you been up to?'

Jimmy told Anthony about his experiences, coming over on the boat, losing his job as a navvy after one day. It was a short story, but Anthony listened as if it was the most fascinating tale he had ever heard.

'I want to earn enough money to get my face fixed,' Jimmy finished, 'with that surgeon you were telling me about. That's why I am here.'

Anthony said nothing about the surgeon but got up to make tea.

'So you'll need a job,' he said. 'I think I can help you with that.'

Jimmy's job was as a courier. Part of Anthony's business involved delivering packages to various individuals around different parts of London. Obviously, being a businessman, he was too busy to deliver the packages himself, and Jimmy, being a bright, intelligent, agile young man, was perfect for the job. Anthony assured him he was far better equipped to navigate the London Underground and ensure that these packages were delivered on time. The packages were generally small – never bigger than his coat pocket – and Anthony advised him to keep the parcels tucked away to avoid being the target of robbery. Jimmy asked what was in the packages, but Anthony said the envelopes contained items that were too delicate for the postal system and that the contents would be too complicated to explain. Jimmy thought that was a bit silly and was slightly put out that Anthony did not feel he was smart enough to be taken into his confidence, but then, as his new boss told him, he was 'new to this game' and only just off the boat from Ireland, so he didn't push it. The important thing was that he had a job that paid him good money and that he enjoyed.

Anthony gave him a hardback book called *The A–Z of London* that had maps of every street in this vast city. It was to use simply as a guide to find the places he was going to, but Jimmy devoured its contents and within days had learned the relationship of hundreds of streets in Westminster, and the names and relationships of many of the suburbs: Hampstead, Richmond, Hendon, Finchley, Orpington, Willesden. He spent his days whizzing around in the dark anonymity of the Underground and then emerging into the daylight, where he would head briskly for his destination, whose route he would have already worked out in a series of left and right turns. Occasionally, if he was going out into the wilds of the country – to, say, Chigwell or Dagenham – he would take a bus, but he found that there were few places on his list of deliveries that were not within less than an hour's walk if you picked the right station. Once at his destination, he never engaged in conversation, just handed over the package to whoever answered the door – mostly men of the age, build and demeanour of returned soldiers. Jimmy would be gone before they had scarcely registered his presence, walking fast past the hundreds of faceless houses and shops that comprised this unimaginably huge place and down into the bowels of London, where he felt safe and invisible and in control of a destiny that, for that day, consisted of nothing more than getting from one place to another and back again.

Most evenings he sat in the small room that Anthony had rented to him above the shop and read his *A–Z*. There was an excellent working man's cafe run by an Italian family directly across the road and Jimmy found that, between the travel expenses and generous courier salary that Anthony paid him, he could easily afford to start his day there with a full fried breakfast and end it with an excellent portion of 'Marco Manzini's famous fish and chips'. In terms of food and shelter, London gave Jimmy everything that he could ever have dreamed of and more. He ate like a king and had his own bed in his own room and there was no drunken navvy sticking his feet in his face as he slept. If he wanted company, he would seek out Anthony. He avoided going into Anthony's flat as much as possible. He did not know what Anthony's relationship was with the two girls and he did not ask. All he knew was that he felt uncomfortable in their company and Anthony, he knew, sensed his discomfort, so they would wander around instead to a tiny, narrow Irish pub called the Tipperary on Fleet Street. Jimmy stayed true to his vow and drank lemonade, while Anthony rarely had more than one, or perhaps two, gin and tonics. He was a temperate man, Jimmy could see, and a good friend. Jimmy wrote to his father and told him as such.

Anthony is looking after me very well. He has left the army now and has gone into business for himself. He has sorted me out with my own digs in a place called Soho and I am working as a courier for his business, delivering packages all around London, which is as vast and as busy a place as you could possibly imagine. I am managing fine as I have a map, which is more of a book, truth be told, and is called The A-Z of London. Anthony says you need brains for the work I am doing and I am glad I came and found him and didn't stay in Camden. In any case, this job pays better than being a navvy, so I'll have the money saved for an operation on my face and be back home with you all again soon enough. The place in Camden Town was a hovel, so tell Padraig not to be sending any more lads over there from Donegal again – it's pure bad.

P.S. Tell Mammy that I am eating well because I know how she worries. I have found a cheap place to eat with an Italian man and woman.

Sean wrote back himself, but his letter was brief because he was not a 'great man for the pen'.

WE ARE ALL FINE HERE. THE LORD WILL PROTECT YOU FROM THE BOMBS. WHAT KIND OF BUSINESS IS HE IN? FIND OUT

WHAT IS IN THEM PACKAGES. DON'T BE EATING FOREIGN FOOD –
IT WILL DAMAGE YOUR BOWELS.
  REGARDS.
  P.S. TELL ANTHONY WE APPRISCHATE SAID THANKS FOR
LOOKING AFTER YOU.

Writing was his mother's forte, so Jimmy knew Morag was still annoyed with him when she didn't write herself. He also knew that the content of the letter was hers entirely.

'What is in the packages?' Jimmy asked Anthony one night as they were settling into a booth in Manzini's.

'Those bloody girls are driving me stone mad, to be honest with you, Jimbo. They're pretty, but they never bloody eat. Cook a dinner? Sometimes I wish I'd hooked up with a proper woman – like gorgeous Juliana here,' he said to the proprietress, a substantial woman in her late fifties, who had come to take their order. Anthony grabbed her around the waist and pulled her to him jokingly.

'Heeey, you – hans off my missis,' Marco called from behind the counter.

'You're a lucky man, Marco. You better watch out, though – she's some firecracker. Two lasagnes. Ever had it, Jim? Delicious. Trust me – you'll love it. I've had every dish cooked by this woman and I've never been disappointed yet,' and he gave the middle-aged lady such a slap on the bottom he thought it would surely draw her husband from behind the counter, but instead he roared with laughter and his wife toddled off rubbing her rump with a big smile on her face. Everybody loved Anthony.

'I wouldn't ask, only that . . . in case something happens, if I drop or lose one or if somebody stops and asks?'

Suddenly he had his boss's attention.

'Has anyone asked? Have you lost one?'

'No, no,' he reassured him. 'I would just like to know, that's all.'

Jimmy held Anthony's eye. His mother had asked him to find out what was in the packages and that was what he was going to do. He would not allow Morag to cast a shadow over his new life. He had been right to come here; he would get his face fixed and go home and show her, then go and get . . . He did not even dare think of Aileen. Not yet . . . not here . . . not until . . .

'Can I trust you, Jim?'

Jimmy did not reply. Anthony looked out of the window and then seemed to make up his mind.

'The thing is, Jim, I *am* going to trust you. I am going to tell you the truth. The truth about my war.'

There were tears in his eyes as Anthony told Jimmy the most extraordinary story he had ever heard.

Jimmy heard about bombs and deaths and terrible, terrible tragedies. He heard about injuries incurred falling from planes, and limbs torn to shreds from clambering through forests, and muscles seized from hiding in ditches. He heard about sweethearts abandoned in villages in France, and crawling for days without food and water, and about how it felt to hold the head of a dying friend in your lap. But there was something about the way Anthony told the story that Jimmy didn't believe. He could almost hear the Scottish snap of his mother's voice saying, 'What a load of cock and bull.'

'. . . and so, Jimmy,' Anthony finished, his face full of anguish, 'in answer to your question, those packages contain medicine. Medicine, my friend, to soothe the body and, yes, the spirits of those poor souls who, like me, fought for this country and lost.'

Jimmy did not ask what type of medicine it was and why Anthony was administering it instead of a doctor, or indeed why he was delivering it in uniform brown parcels. He was getting paid, his life was just fine, and he was on the road to his own recovery. Jimmy did not ask any more questions after that. He did not want to know.

Chapter Twenty-Seven

On their way back, Aileen asked John Joe to stop by her parents' cottage, where she went straight across to the raised bed and pulled out the half-dozen tomato plants, squeezing their roots into tight balls of soil to protect them, and called John Joe over to help her carry them to the cart. As an afterthought, she looked at the tray of beach seeds that she had all but forgotten about, and seeing that they were still pushing through the shallow tray, she brought them with her too.

When they got back to John Joe's house that morning, Aileen did not settle for one moment. She went straight into the house and changed into her working apron and old working boots, then gathered a number of small tools from the shed and was waiting in the cart with the children by the time John Joe came out to take them to school.

There was no question that John Joe had to take Aileen straight back to the garden. Neither of them even felt the need to properly discuss the matter; it was an unspoken understanding.

John Joe left Aileen at the garden and she continued with her work, scything back the weeds, discovering small stone boundary walls for flower beds. Although it was nothing she could explain, she felt relieved to be there. In this garden she felt safe, as if the boundaries of her very life could be contained happily within its walls. All she had to do was to work, sow, grow and every-thing outside of that – the shock of death, the grief, the drama of her mother leaving – became suspended by some mysterious decree of nature by sheer fact of her being there. She could not work on restoring this garden and be sad. The earth would not allow it.

Aileen found and began to restore an old grass-cutter; she uncovered an aged lawn-roller from behind a shed. There was so much work to be done she forgot to eat the sandwich that John Joe had packed so that it was still where she had left it on the glasshouse sill when he returned with the children after school. John Joe must have known she would not come back with them that night because when she said, 'I am staying the night here. I don't want to leave,' he went straight to the cart and took out an old horsehair mattress and a pile of blankets – along with a small stove and kettle. Even as Aileen had said the words 'I am staying the night here' she knew they sounded strange and yet they felt right.

'I don't know what you are at,' John Joe said, 'but if you are going to do this, you may as well be comfortable and you may as well do it right.'

Visibly excited that she had his blessing without having to explain herself, which she would have felt entirely unable to do, Aileen gave John Joe a list of things she needed him to bring to her the next day. Some oil for the grass-cutter, some tools to sharpen the scythe, a hammer, nails and a sharp saw – the one here had fallen apart with rust – horse manure, although on second thoughts the horse manure could wait, she said. The ground would have to be prepared properly before she fertil-ized it and in just saying that she began to hop from foot to foot, anxious that she was wasting time, that John Joe and the children should leave now and let her get back to her garden.

This *was* her garden. Aileen felt that and in the following days she was absorbed so thoroughly in its restoration that she lost all sense of time, space or herself. She rose with the light and slept when it was dark or when exhaustion enveloped her, whichever came first. She cleared and she dug. She waded into the stagnant pond and pulled out armfuls of weeds and sludge, and threw them in a pile with the comfrey she had gathered to make compost. Only then did she think she should have stripped off before going in, and she cursed the time she had to waste rinsing out her muddy clothes. She went back into the pond naked and waded across the slimy stones and dug through the congealed banks looking for plants worth saving. She dressed again when she felt the chill reaching her bones and heard the clip of John Joe's horse and cart on the cobbles in the yard, cursing him for causing this interruption in her work. Only for the diligent farmer coming twice a day with the children and forcing her to eat, Aileen might have collapsed and died in the mud and the plants and flowers grown up around her. If she had not been so intent on her work, Aileen might have entertained such an idea as romantic and let it happen out of her love for this peculiar patch of land.

Aileen measured time by the activity she had completed. She did not set goals or stop to consider her achievements – she simply moved on to the next area that needed clearing, the next bush that needed cutting, the next bed that needed digging, the next trellis that needed repairing. And gradually the garden was cleared. There was nothing to stand back and admire. The flower beds were scrappy, with huge gaps where the weeds had been; the pond was a puddle of plain brown mud; the vegetable boxes had no vegetables in them whatsoever; but the garden was now ready for the business of gardening. She had the blank canvas of a garden structure ready for planting and Aileen was excited.

All the time that she had been clearing, Aileen had been taking cuttings from healthy plants, rescuing seedlings and struggling plants from the undergrowth and sifting through patches of soil looking for bulbs and seeds that she could bring on. All of these things she cultivated and cared for in the glasshouse, potting and planting the seeds directly into the shallow trays on the table and everything else into pots.

She put her tomato plants into a long trench and planted the seedlings from the beach pods into the fifteen pots she had sprinkled with the Scottish ash. There was no reason for this except that she had a silly feeling of sentiment around them as they were the first pots she had planted here.

She had got the hothouse steam system working, and although the weather was still warm, she nonetheless filled the shallow pipes and put the stove on once a day. She stuffed it with scraps of wood and debris from her garden-clearing – stuff that could not be composted. Aileen had put all of the weeds in a concreted corner of the backyard and said a silly curse over them – 'Sally rod beat, sally rod beat, bear down cross and bear down stone' – to kill them off and make sure they did not re-root. She had been saying this curse over uprooted weeds for years and it rarely worked, but here it did.

Aileen was in the greenhouse assessing the health of her various plants and making early decisions about what she should put where when she heard the clatter of John Joe coming through the wall door. He was talking, so he had somebody with him. Surely the children could not be finished school yet? What the hell was he doing here so early? She turned her back to the door, foolishly imagining that he might go away of his own volition if she pretended not to see him – or rather, hoped that if he saw how absorbed she was, he might wander off and leave her alone with her plants for a bit longer.

But he did not.

'Look who I have with me!'

Aileen turned round and saw John Joe, who, while he was smiling, had a look of transparent nervousness on his face that was almost comical. Standing squarely beside him, her unsmiling face shadowed with an uncertainty as to why she was there at all, was Biddy. The two of them were standing in front of the door and virtually took up the width of the glasshouse, otherwise Aileen might have fled.

'John Joe says you've not been eating – you have him worried out of his mind.'

Aileen might have told the pair of them to go to hell, except that John Joe was shuffling, and while Biddy's words were tough, there was a shake in her voice.

Aileen felt pressure build up inside her. This was what she didn't want. This was, she realized in this terrible moment, what she had been avoiding: the truth.

'It was me,' she said suddenly. 'I cleaned the fireplace and the flue came down and I knew it, but I left it because I wanted to go to the pictures. I killed all those men.'

She blurted it out and – there – it was said. Biddy could do what she liked now. The old woman could shout at her, beat her and call the police. John Joe could banish her from his home; she might spend the rest of her days languishing in prison or, perhaps, probably she'd be hanged. Whatever the case, although she could not say she felt better, it was a relief to speak out.

Biddy's complexion reddened and she walked across to Aileen and slapped her squarely across the face. Shocked, Aileen put her hand up to her stinging cheek. The old lady packed some punch – she thought her head might come clean off.

John Joe moved forward and muttered, 'Here now . . .' like he was afraid himself.

'Do not ever, *ever* – do you hear me, Aileen Doherty? – say anything like that again. Do you hear me?'

Aileen didn't understand.

'But it was me, Biddy. It was—'

'It was *not*. *I* was in charge. The fire is the fore graipe's responsibility. The blame rests firmly at my door.' Then she grabbed Aileen by both her forearms, squeezed them together and said, 'Promise me now that you will never breathe words like that about yourself in your own mind and never, *ever* to another living soul.'

Aileen started to cry. She could not help herself.

'But you're taking the blame for everything, Biddy . . .'

Biddy's voice hardened again. 'That is the proper order, child. The Lord is good that He spared us our lives; any carrying the blame of others is a small penance to endure. The shame I carry in my heart is my crucifixion surely, but it is *my* cross, Aileen, not yours. Now,' she said suddenly, 'we'll have no more about that,' and turning to John Joe, finished, 'I thought you said you had food in that bag, man? Well, get it out before we half starve.'

They ate, and for the first time Aileen felt her anxiety at getting back to her work ease up. They chatted about this and that, Biddy and John Joe flirting back and forth like they were old friends.

'I saw this one wandering down the road as I was coming out of Mass this morning,' John Joe started, 'and I said to myself, There's a woman who knows how to wear a hat.'

Biddy blushed. 'You are some charmer, John Joe Morely – and truth be told? You always were.'

Aileen quizzed them and they told her they had known each other as youngsters. Aileen teased them about romance and they both got a bit cross, but not in a bad way.

John Joe looked seriously offended and Biddy got a bit giddy.

Aileen found the pair of them so amusing that she was almost sorry when John Joe got up to leave.

Biddy stayed and Aileen heard her say something to John Joe at the door along the lines of 'Don't worry – I'll look after her.'

They had been plotting, but surprising herself, Aileen was glad when Biddy turned to her and said, 'Now, let's have a look and see what needs to be done.'

As Aileen walked Biddy around the garden, through the cleared paths of the flower beds, the naked pond, the hedged but empty ornamental maze, the scrubbed but dry fountain and finally the black crumbly soil of the vegetable patch – rich with manure and waiting for its first planting – the older woman held her hand to her mouth to keep herself from letting out small sobs of shocked amazement.

'How long did it take you?' she asked, letting the words out through a gap in her hands, then closing them off again to prepare herself for the answer, 'to get it ready like this?'

'Oh, I don't know,' said Aileen, shaking her head, genuinely confused, 'just . . .' and she trailed off. If she tried hard, she might have thought back and counted off the number of times John Joe had been out, but even then she could not remember.

Biddy knew it had been a week. John Joe had told her as much, when he was relaying his fears about the young woman's health and his own inability to keep up with his work on the farm and look after her at this distance. That aside, he was concerned about this obsession of hers and asked Biddy if she might come and take a look – calm her down a bit perhaps. Seeing the work she had done in just a few days, on her own, Biddy now understood his concern. Everybody knew that this garden had been derelict for decades. This young woman had taken on the job of clearing an overgrown jungle, but aside from the insanity of her motivation was the fact that she had succeeded.

What kind of powerful force was at work when a slip of a girl like this could complete such a gargantuan task single-handed, in such a short space of time? Biddy remembered the tattie-hoking and the speed with which Aileen had worked. Even so, this work here required physical strength as well as dexterity and determination.

Biddy followed Aileen around as she relayed her plans to her friend with great enthusiasm and, the older woman observed, the added manic tone of the religious zealot.

'I want those big blue flowers there, the bell-shaped ones – I don't know what they are called . . .'

'Delphiniums?'

'I want them there,' Aileen said, sweeping her hand across a wide bank. 'And in front of them the little – what are they called? – like different colours, white and purple and blue and—'

'Pansies?'

'No, *no*. I know what *pansies* are. Smaller than that but like tiny bells . . .'

'Campanula?'

Aileen looked at her blankly, then carried on. 'Maybe. *Anyway*, I want them coming down over the stones and covering the path across here, and then I want the roses to start here –' she pointed down to the beginning of the arbour '– and then climb up all over here in like a big . . .'

Biddy had taken her hand away from her mouth and it was slack open, punctuating an expression of total incredulity. Aileen trailed off, aware that perhaps she was overestimating her gardening knowledge.

'Well,' she said, 'I know I don't know the names of every-thing, but . . .'

Quite suddenly Aileen felt a dark cloud descend over her as

surely as if it had been a real cloud raining a dark mist down onto her head. That word 'but' – and it was a very big 'but'. She couldn't do this. Bring this garden to life? Plant it all, with what? She didn't even know the names of the flowers, for goodness' sake. Her, restore a stately Englishman's garden? What on earth had she been thinking? What on earth was she—

'Not a problem,' Biddy said, her hands on her hips. 'You tell me what you want and we'll find it. I have a book my father gave me at home with the name of every plant under the sun.'

'Really?' The cloud lifted somewhat.

'Oh yes,' Biddy assured her, 'and pictures too. Beautiful colour illustrations to leave no doubt in your mind as to what is what.'

'I saw a book like that once in the travelling library,' said Aileen. 'I wish I had paid more attention to it now. Do you think it would be of use?'

'Certainly,' Biddy said.

'And do you think if I had a book like that and knew the names of things, that I might be able to order some plants from somewhere? Do they cost much money, do you think? I am wondering now . . . how . . . '

She did not finish the sentence. Part of Aileen knew that restoring this garden was no longer merely an improbable idea but had grown, in actual fact, into an impossible undertaking. However, if she gave that part of her a hearing, she would have to walk out of the garden that moment and away from all she had done so far. If she did that, Aileen feared that a part of her would die. There was not so much of her spirit left that she could afford to lose any more of it.

Whenever Aileen allowed herself to hope that she might transform this garden into something magnificent, despite herself, Jimmy came flooding into her mind.

He was always filled with hope and possibility.

'I'll buy you a ring with a diamond the size of a boulder; then I'll buy a boat as big as a house.'

'You're a dreamer and a fool, Jimmy Walsh,' she'd say.

'We'll sail round the world . . .'

'Where do you get these silly ideas from at all?'

'. . . and we'll go on our honeymoon to Paris.'

'A dafter eejit never walked this earth!'

All the time she'd be laughing and thinking that if any man could make such dreams come true, it was the invincible Jimmy Walsh.

She did not ask Biddy if she knew whether Jimmy was alive or dead because the older woman would volunteer the information if she knew but also because Aileen didn't want to know. As long as she was uncertain Aileen could dream. Every night, as she lay in her greenhouse bed, after she had listed off the names of plants she had fed and watered, and listed off the jobs that had been done for the day, Aileen allowed herself to dream of Jimmy and the wild future of boats and diamonds and world travel he had planned out for them. With her body exhausted and her mind too tired to fully reason, Aileen could allow her heart to open and wonder about her lover. Perhaps he was alive and well and simply waiting to take delivery of his crazy big boat? Perhaps she would be on the beach one day and see an enormous ship ploughing through the water; then it would stop in the bay, with the whole island out looking at it; then a wiry figure would emerge from the sea, dripping wet and laughing – her crazy, impulsive Jimmy come to claim her. Where would they go then? What would they do? How would she feel when he looked at her again? And she'd melt into the soft night half believing he lay beside her.

Other times her mind was not tired enough to go straight from sweet thoughts to sleep and her rational mind would hijack her heart. Aileen would remember that Jimmy's injuries were serious enough that they might have killed him. Even if they had not, her dreams of his romantic return were wrong in themselves because they would make her feel happy and it wasn't right for her to feel happy after all that had happened. Then Aileen would realize it was dangerous to allow her mind to wander into such territory, that the best thing she could do was to put all thoughts of Jimmy Walsh to one side.

Aileen's life now was this garden. Here she had found a way of living that made her feel safe and useful and, if not fully alive, then at least connected to life itself.

This was a huge job, she knew that. Would Biddy be able to help her? Was she crazy even to be thinking of attempting this restoration?

Biddy shook her head and waved her hands in front of her face in a gesture of definite assurances, as if to contradict her would be a pointless, fruitless, laughable exercise.

'My dear girl, you can buy any plants you like and even the most exotic seeds from all over the world for a halfpenny through my relations in the mainland shop. Really. Not a problem. Goodness me, as easy as . . . making bread. Now, are you planning to grow vegetables at all?'

Aileen came back to herself and all but ran through to the vegetable garden and stated her plans.

Biddy had tomatoes and lettuce seeds and onion bulbs and any number of good ordinary Irish vegetable plants she could bring up the following day.

What Biddy did *not* have was a relationship with anyone who could get their hands on exotic flowers at any stage of their existence, or indeed an encyclopedia of plants given to her by her father or otherwise.

Biddy knew what she needed was a miracle, but as she watched the red-haired girl down on her knees, her white hands lifting the soft crumb of the soil she had created as if it were sand running through her fingers, she thought perhaps she had already found one.

Chapter Twenty-Eight

When Jimmy had first arrived in London, he was determined that his time here would be merely a means to an end. Like every Irishman in London during wartime, he was here for one reason only – to earn money. He had planned to save every penny for an operation on his face, after which he was determined to return immediately to Ireland to claim his true love, Aileen, like he had promised. Like he wanted more than anything. Getting the girl was his clear goal, his mission, his obsession.

However, the longer the young fisherman stayed in London, the more it started to feel like home. Not the home he had in Aghabeg, where things were so familiar that he didn't notice them: his mother's plain cooking or the faces of the island fishermen he had known from birth, the curves of their warm brown faces as familiar and everyday to him as the simple wooden furniture in his parents' cottage. In London, as soon as things become recognizable, they could change. He had just got to know the man in the booth selling tickets in Leicester Square Station when he was replaced by somebody else. The shows playing the theatres along Shaftesbury Avenue seemed to change names with the flash of a light; the photographs of the actors with their made-up faces caught mid-expression would be torn down and a new set of people in the midst of great passion or amusement put up in their place. Walking down the main streets around Piccadilly Circus or Leicester Square, Jimmy rarely noticed the same face twice.

On top of all this, it was 1942 and there was a war on. The bombing of London and the air raids had stopped, but there was still a sense of uncertainty in the smashed buildings and the decimated streets Jimmy passed on his rounds every day.

The backstreets of Soho, where Jimmy lived himself, were different in that things there seemed to remain more the same – the shop windows with their opulent mixture of cured meats and clothes and books; the Manzinis never altered their menu and that gave Jimmy a feeling of home.

In a few weeks Jimmy could not believe how his life had become so different. In Aghabeg, taking a swim out to sea was the biggest adventure a day might contain, and if you had a good haul of mackerel on top of that, you'd be finished off with excitement altogether. Your mother might get a bit of bacon once a week, and at the end of the month, she'd be doling out the last of the shop-bought jam like it was a precious elixir. In contrast, even with the war rationing, London seemed to Jimmy to be a land of plenty: plenty of food, plenty of entertainment – all the jam you could eat. His father had warned him that the streets weren't paved with gold, but for Jimmy they might as well have been. He had always craved excitement, ploughing his wiry arms through the dangerous water of the sea, while others stood on the shore and called out for him to be careful. Now he was in a place where everything was different and it felt as if anything could happen every day. He wasn't swimming alone anymore. Within weeks of arriving in London he felt like a different person to the one who had arrived, wet behind the ears, straight off the boat. He looked back at the boy who had never eaten a lasagne or drunk coffee made from proper grounds or travelled on the London Underground and he could not believe he had ever been that innocent.

Manzini's cafe became his regular haunt. Rationing seemed to make little odds to the food here, as the Italian mamma had the gift for thrift as well as flavour and produced mountainous plates of pasta flavoured with spices and cured meats. As a result, the cafe was always bustling with a regular crowd. At breakfast time, each booth was occupied with single men, like himself, eating a proper meal to set them up for their working day. He had got a few looks in his first few days, but Jimmy quickly came to believe that his initial discomfort was unjustified. Nobody really paid heed to your appearance here and Jimmy grew to think that their curiosity was more to do with the fact that they had not seen him before. Why, after a week, he was a regular and had started studying the faces of newcomers himself! The evening crowd was more mixed. A few Italian families coming in for a cheap plate of pasta, the odd tourist and couples mooching over a bottle of wine before the theatre. When Jimmy wasn't eating with Anthony, Juliana 'Mamma' Manzini put her best customer in a corner booth and brought him across a copy of *The Times of London* – as if he were a fine gentleman.

One evening while he was eating with Anthony, his English employer announced, 'I want to buy you a suit.'

Jimmy let out a small laugh. Anthony was a natty dresser himself, and while Jimmy thought the offer rather strange, he then looked down at his own hand-knitted and now rather tatty jumper and the good wool jacket that his father had got married in and had given him for this trip and realized, for the first time, just how badly he was dressed compared with Anthony and the other smart men around town. 'Straight off the boat' was an expression he had heard used in relation to his countrymen. That was how he was dressed and he didn't like it.

'Sure I'll buy a suit myself,' Jimmy had said. There were plenty of men's clothes shops in London. He had passed them and looked in the windows with a vague curiosity but had never ventured into one because he had never thought of it before. To be honest, his overall appearance was the last thing Jimmy liked to think about – given what had happened to him. However, now that Anthony had put the idea into his head, Jimmy was all for it. There was no harm in being well dressed and he wondered why he had not thought of it before. He had money for new clothes after all. An inkling flashed through his head that perhaps the occasional disgusted looks people had given him had not been them judging his disfigured face but his scruffy clothes.

Anthony was insistent: 'You are representing my company, Jimmy,' he said, 'so it is my responsibility to make sure you look smart when you are going to see my clients.'

Jimmy never did anything more than swap packages with any of them. Mostly they just opened the door a sliver and pushed an envelope of money back out at him.

Jimmy never asked Anthony too much about work because the Englishman did not like talking about his business. As far as Jimmy could gather, his office seemed to be the home he shared with Mandy and Lily. Jimmy's bedsit had a large chest in the corner of it where Anthony kept his supply of medicine under lock and key. He trusted Jimmy more than the girls, he told him. He could see that Jimmy was an intelligent and trustworthy person who cared about the plight of the veterans he was helping and wouldn't dream of stealing their medicine. Jimmy had no interest in the medicine one way or the other. He had had enough of them in hospital to last a lifetime, he told Anthony. Anthony smiled and said he was of the same mind, but some people . . . and he punctuated his sentence with one of his mysterious smiles.

'In any case, there might be some other work coming up for you, Jimmy – other than the courier deliveries. How you look will be important.'

Anthony said that without any pause to consider Jimmy's face. Perhaps because of his own scar, even though it was much less severe than his, Anthony genuinely seemed not to notice or care about Jimmy's dropped, gnarled features. That was how Jimmy knew that for all his eccentric secrecy, Anthony was a good friend and a kind man whom he could trust: it was in what he did not say.

So, although Jimmy was intrigued about the possible change in his work, he didn't push for more information.

'Nonetheless I can buy my own clothes, Anthony. I'm not a child.'

Anthony looked shocked at the very suggestion.

'Goodness me but I know that, Jimmy! This is a business. Let me get this suit for you,' and he raised his hands as Jimmy tried to object, 'as a gift. You can buy the next one.'

The *next* one? For a man to have one suit was something – for funerals and to get married in and now, it seemed, for just mooching about town in – but *two* suits? He had never known such extravagance, yet here he was in a place where an ordinary man such as himself might own more than one smart outfit.

They went to Marks & Spencer in Marble Arch. 'I was going to take you down to Piccadilly to my tailor,' Anthony said grandly, as they walked up Oxford Street, 'but then a fine-figured slip of a lad like you, Jimbo, can buy off the peg and we'll get it altered if need be.'

All his mother's and father's smart clothes were made by a tailor in Donegal town, aside from the ones his mother was able to knit or sew herself. Jimmy was therefore much more impressed by the idea of going into a city department store. Marks & Spencer did not disappoint. When they walked in, they were faced with an enormous room with racks and racks of clothes behind wooden counters manned only by girls – each one prettier than the next. Even the menswear department was staffed by girls: all the men were away fighting. Anthony marched them straight down to a section of the store where the walls were lined with men's clothes. There was an artificial torso of a man sitting atop the wooden counter, smiling from under a slicked-back hairdo and pencil-thin moustache, and wearing a shirt, tie and slim-fitting knitted woollen vest in a shade of yellow as bright as summer sunshine. Jimmy instinctively reached out to touch the fabric, and as he did, a young woman popped up and said, 'I see you've met Errol? After Errol Flynn. Well, we had to call him something considering there are no men around here anymore.'

'Well, we're here to keep up the numbers,' Anthony said. 'As you can see, we've already been through the war, so we need to make sure we're not letting the side down any further with shabby clobber.'

The girl's eyes filled with a mixture of intense pride and pity. Jimmy felt guilty at the lie and looked down.

Anthony nudged him to not be such a sap and checked the girl's name pin.

'So, Daisy, meet my friend Jimbo – as you can see, he is in rather dire need of some of your finest men's clothing.'

'Hello, Jim,' she said, giving him a wink that he could not quite identify but thought could be flirtatious. 'Now, what are you after?'

'A suit,' Jimmy said. He wished he could have thought of some witty way of putting it. He had always found some round-about clever way of saying things with Aileen, but that was different. Aileen lit him up and made him charming, but that was before his face . . .

'Grey, blue, brown?' The girl had already walked over to a rail and was pulling things off and holding them up to him. Jimmy looked around for Anthony, but he had wandered off. Jimmy shrugged. He felt so stupid. So gormless! Daisy put a wide selection into a changing booth and said, 'Let's try them all on, then.'

She pulled the door closed and Jimmy started to strip off. In the changing-room mirror he looked at his reflection; deep scars ran down his arms and his torso under his vest. When he was out and about enjoying London, eating lasagne, drinking coffee, seeing the sights, hopping on and off trains, Jimmy forgot. The girl had been chatting him up, flirting with him like there was nothing wrong, but there was something wrong: his grotesque appearance. A suit wouldn't cure this.

'Are you ready yet?' the shop girl called in. 'Come along – don't be shy . . .'

Jimmy wanted to hide in there forever.

He walked out and the girl said, 'I'm not sure brown is your colour, sir. Try the grey pinstripe, and this . . .'

She handed him a fresh shirt and the primrose-yellow vest he had seen on the way in.

Anthony came along just as he was coming out again.

'Oh, very smart,' he said. 'Daisy, you're a genius!'

As she was packing up the clothes, Jimmy had a moment where he thought he might ask her to go for a coffee. She was pretty enough, and although not beautiful like Aileen, she reminded him a little of her. She seemed kind and had bright, intelligent eyes. Would there be any harm, he wondered, in being friends with such a girl? He imagined the two of them in Lyon's Corner House, him in his new yellow vest, saying, 'Have whatever you like – it's my treat,' and her blushing sweetly and ordering a fancy cream cake, and him joking, 'I'll be Mother,' and pouring the tea for her. He noticed that her hair was pulled up at the back and her neck was creamy and white. What noise would she make if he leaned in and kissed it? The pleasure might overwhelm her before she had the chance to object. Then he remembered Aileen's low groan and he knew he had better stop imagining.

Anthony paid, but she passed the bag to Jimmy.

As she handed him the bag, he carefully watched her face and instead of light flirtation he read polite pity and perhaps a shred of fear. Jimmy wanted to cry.

This girl, a stranger whose job it was to smile and hide such things, could not fully conceal her pity for him.

He and his boss walked back out into the vast, anonymous flow of Oxford Street and Jimmy's resolve hardened. He could have no life with a face like this and he wanted to get home to claim back his dreams. He was a proud and passionate Irishman and not about to compromise his love for Aileen to settle for some pretty London shop girl, however kind she seemed.

Jimmy Walsh was going to see the surgeon that very week and get his face restored.

Chapter Twenty-Nine

Biddy felt terrible, but she explained to Aileen that she had mislaid her father's gardening book. However, by some divine providence John Joe found two that had once belonged to his mother hidden in a box with some of her precious things. The first was called *The Ladies' Companion to the Flower Garden*, which John Joe saw was inscribed by the wife of the head gardener in the big house. She must have given it to his mother when they moved back to England. The inscription said, 'Going to a flat in Orpington, so won't need this anymore!'

Aileen had never heard of Orpington, but it was surely close to heaven itself because this book was a godsend.

While Aileen was skilled at growing simple vegetables, *The Ladies' Companion* contained everything she could possibly want to know about growing any kind of plant. The typography was so tiny she had to hold the book right up to her face to read it, so much so that John Joe gave her his magnifying glass on permanent loan. Although it was a slim volume, it contained more information than she could possibly absorb in a lifetime. On its well-worn, yellowing pages were detailed, meticulously configured black-and-white drawings of every kind of garden structure, from square boxes for propagation to instructions to give 'one's gardener' on how to build a wire trellis or a climbing tower or a frame for a fledgling tree. These included three side-ways diagrams detailing the working of 'Greenhouses and Vinery', illustrating the exact placement of the bricks and heating pipes as well as the machinations of their plumbing. Aileen got very excited because she recognized the buildings and imagined the glasshouse in her garden might have been built to this very specification from this very book.

The section on glasshouses contained details on how to propagate and force all sorts of strange and wonderful foods that Aileen had barely even heard of. She listed them: pineapples, peaches, cherries, oranges, avocados and grapes, which she felt certain she was already growing on the vine that had come to life. She determined that one day, when she could afford to buy seeds or plants, she would begin growing these exoticisms, but in the meantime she concentrated on the other volume that John Joe had given her.

The Observer's Book of British Wild Flowers was another revelation. Aileen had been looking at the names of flowers in her *Ladies' Companion* but had been barely able to discern one from the other with all their unintelligible Latin names. They all sounded exactly the same and she had become overwhelmed with the mere idea of trying to select plants for her flower beds. *The Observer* featured only wild flowers, which could be found on any hillside or growing at will in any garden. With beautiful colour illustrations the artist had made even the common clover look like a beautiful flower. The pages detailed the English names, with the Latin equivalent underneath alongside pretty, clear pictures – some in colour and followed with short descriptions.

HAREBELL
Campanula rotundifolia
On heaths, hilly pastures and roadsides the harebell will be found in abundance.

That was the very plant she had asked Biddy to name for her. She recognized almost every flower in the book, even if she was not familiar with their names. Foxglove, toadflax, a fat, deadly lad called viper's bugloss, pimpernel – the pretty flower that told you rain was coming by closing its leaves – wild strawberry, lady's mantle, parsley, primrose . . . These were all plants that Aileen already knew, and many of them were growing in some measure in the garden itself, while those that weren't could be found in abundance elsewhere on the island.

Aileen was decided. She would build a wild-flower garden, using only plants that she could take from cuttings or seeds herself, and save her money for exoticisms in the greenhouse.

Once the idea was set, she had John Joe driven demented driving around the island with her while she foraged in fields and at the side of the road for cuttings and rooted plants: iris, orchid, periwinkle and dozens of calor lily bulbs. She did not stop until she had found all the plants she wanted. When she felt she had enough to keep her busy, John Joe would deposit her back at the greenhouse. Here, she sorted and seeded, nursed and nurtured them into strong, healthy plants, ready to take up a place in their new, organized, elegant home, away from the wild fields where they were born, where they might be trampled by a sheep or eaten by cattle. Here, they would be kept safe, part of the cosseted destiny Aileen was creating for them. A higher calling of beauty than the one they had been born to.

Aileen kept both books permanently in her apron pocket, along with the magnifying glass, which she also used for studying the leaves on wild seedlings to help identify ones too small for the naked eye.

In the meantime, Biddy also moved into the garden. She could not leave Aileen sleeping in the greenhouse by herself, but equally she could see that the girl was not for moving. So Biddy put her bothy-management background to good use and made a home out of where they were. It still being summer, the first thing she built was an outdoor kitchen in the yard in front of the glasshouse. 'Bring me bread, sausages and a few rashers of bacon,' she said to John Joe on the first morning. By the time he came back with the children after school, Biddy had found an old pan and scrubbed it clean, and one of her makeshift brick stoves was built and fired up. That night, she rigged herself up a bed in the old gardener's cottage, and by the end of that first week she had the place looking as if the house had never been unoccupied. She tried to persuade Aileen to join her, but the girl remained insistent on sleeping outdoors in the greenhouse. That being the case, Biddy made sure that at least she was comfortable. Poor John Joe had his horse run ragged between collecting blankets and kitchen accoutrements for Biddy, seeds and additional gardening things for Aileen and taking the children to and from school.

Aileen was a gifted gardener and her plants grew more quickly than one would have expected. Lettuces shot up; tomatoes seemed to flower and then fruit at a rate that was bordering on miraculous.

Aileen was excited about being at the stage where she could plant out the vegetables she had been propagating. As soon as small threads of roots had appeared at the base of her cuttings, she had to hold herself back from planting them straight away. Those early days with Biddy there to help her were exciting, and after a couple of weeks, things settled into a routine. Or rather, as much of a routine as Aileen could allow.

For the first while after Biddy stayed, Aileen enjoyed the luxury of being cooked for and the noise of somebody else being close by. Biddy brought her battery-operated radio up from the house and they played music on it. With Biddy watching her, Aileen's work took on a slower pace, and while she enjoyed sitting down to eat a hot meal and stopping throughout the day for tea, she was becoming more anxious as each day passed. She was concerned that the garden was not happening at the pace she hoped. She had planted as much as any one woman could possibly plant and yet the beds were still mostly bare, the pond was still empty of plants, and while the vegetables were growing well, it did not feel like it was . . . enough.

'Sure what are you rushing around for, child?' Biddy asked her. 'Let nature take its course. What are you trying to achieve with all this worry?'

Aileen smiled and said nothing in reply, because there was nothing to say. Inside, though, she was burning with anxiety to get the garden . . . not finished, because she knew that in nature nothing is ever finished, but flourishing: alive.

She also knew that, as much as Biddy was a strong, hard-working woman, and that she herself had what they called green fingers, between them it would take a long time to get this place the way she had envisioned it could be.

Aileen needed that vision of her garden to come true. She felt that, somehow, her own future was utterly entwined in bringing the garden back to life.

On this day, Aileen got up very early to go out to the green-house. The night before, there had been a full moon and a high summer storm blowing. Biddy had lit a fire and cooked a stew and insisted that Aileen stay in the cottage with her and 'leave the wretched plants alone for one night – sure what do you think will happen to them?'

She was starting to get on Aileen's nerves already. Sleeping by the plants was important. Aileen didn't know why, and certainly wouldn't attempt to put words to it because it would surely sound foolish, but nonetheless it was what she *did* and now Biddy was messing it all up for her.

It was not much past dawn and the ground outside was misting with dew and still bore the residue of last night's relentless rain.

Aileen clicked open the greenhouse door and as soon as she stepped inside she sensed that something was different. She felt the pit of her stomach recede. Curse Biddy for keeping her away from her charges for the night. Something was up: she could hear a whispering, a conspiracy among the plants.

Then she saw it. Over in the corner: a flurry of green that had not been there the night before.

The pots with the Scottish soil that she had planted with the beach seeds had shot up – although, strangely, not all of them had grown. The ones that had come to life were all the same – sprouting tufts of soft, fine grass, green and vigorous. They had flourished overnight.

Sick with excitement, Aileen ran the palm of her hand across the grass and felt a tingling, as if life itself were emanating through its leaves. She counted the live pots and there were ten of them. Why? Why had ten pots grown and the others not? Aileen had an idea, stranger still than the tingling in her hands, stranger than any compulsion she had experienced to date – stranger than sleeping with plants or clearing an old, derelict garden. There were ten pots – one for each of the men who had died in the Cleggan fire.

That afternoon, Aileen put the ten live plants in a sunny, heated corner. She looked at the tall, slender leaves through her glass and checked these against her book. She could not find a match.

So she watered the plants and waited. In the following days

she noticed no peculiar growth. The grass may have sprouted suddenly overnight, but it did not continue to grow at the same rate. She measured the plants before she went to bed and then tried sleeping in the cottage with Biddy again. She had a sneaking suspicion that her presence at night might have been inhibiting their growth. The next day, the plants were exactly the same. As she was emptying the pots that had not grown, she found herself vigorously checking the roots and realized that she was searching for one more to show signs of life. Ten men had died, but what about Jimmy? Was there not a plant growing for him? If not, what did that mean?

Aileen tried to put her silly notions aside and carry on with her work, but the strange phenomenon was nagging at her, as if there was something she should do, although she could not say what that might be.

The answer came when John Joe told her that there was a service being held for the Cleggan women the following Sunday.

'I don't know that Biddy will want to come,' he said, 'given the way things are.'

Biddy, for all her huffing and puffing about being 'imprisoned' in the garden, had been less and less keen to leave it. She had not attended any Sunday Mass since she got here, and John Joe had not forced the issue. He himself could feel the tension rising on the island about 'who was responsible' for the fire. There had been talk of an inquiry being held. Experts coming down from Dublin – it was a terrible business.

'She'll get her comeuppance yet.'

'Not shown her face around here for a while in any case.'

'Proper order – she has no place in God's house.'

John Joe did not know if Biddy knew the full extent of the bad feeling towards her, but while she was telling herself she was staying in the garden to mind Aileen, in reality it was a relief to be hidden away from the whispering accusations and the cold faces.

Biddy was nervous when she heard about the service and said she would stay behind and prepare a nice dinner for them all. John Joe would come back with the children and they would have a meal together and say a decade of the rosary themselves for the dead men.

'The Lord knows where I am,' she said, 'and that is good enough for me. Let Him strike me down at any time if that's His will.'

It was such an awful thing to say, Aileen thought. God had given her a second chance and He would do the same for Biddy – she was sure of it.

Aileen got dressed in the tidiest clothes she had to hand – a navy wool dress and her good boots. In case she was in any doubt as to what to wear, John Joe had taken the precaution of altering an old coat of his mother's for her. Sewing snazzy black beaded buttons across the collar, he really was 'the giddy limit', as Biddy said.

While John Joe and Biddy were occupied with one another, Aileen quickly loaded the ten grassy pots in the back of John Joe's cart and covered them in a blanket. She did not want her guardians to know what she had planned, because they might try and put a stop to it, although she was doing nothing wrong.

They arrived early at the church, as she had known they would. Aileen let John Joe get out first, and while he was talking to Father Dooley, the priest, and the gathering congregation, she quietly and quickly transferred the ten pots from the cart to the back door of the church. The women would be seated in the front two pews, as was the traditional seating arrangement for the bereaved, and she had half hidden the ten pots underneath the statue of Our Lady next to the altar, where they were concealed by a large floral arrangement. The church was already set, the candles were lit, and there would be nobody in to move them before the service began. Aileen sat at the outer edge of the second pew back and waited for the other women to come in.

They filed in and Aileen stood to let them sit and watched each one carefully, assessing who belonged to each of the deceased men. Claire Murphy came in first with her mother, Fatima, and three younger siblings. They had lost Claire's twin brother, Iggy. Then Attracta Collins came in. Like Aileen, she had lost a father and two brothers; she had her mother, Nuala Collins, with her, another woman, who might have been her mother's sister, and two children, doubtless siblings. Behind them was Noreen Flaherty. She was with her long-time widowed mother, Monica, and they were both feeling bereft after losing James, who had been the man of the house. Last in was Carmel Kelly. Aileen almost did not recognize her. She looked older. She had never been an especially pretty girl; nonetheless the defiant light had disappeared from her eyes and she seemed lifeless. She did not acknowledge Aileen as she walked past her to the front pew with her mother and two younger siblings. It was not a delib-erate affront, as Aileen might have expected from their past rela-tionship. Carmel, she sensed, more than any of the others, having held off her grief for the journey home, had now lost herself entirely to it. Last time Aileen encountered Carmel, she was half mad, dancing around behaving like nothing had happened. Now, in her deadened demeanour, she had lost her very soul to the truth of her grief.

Without fully thinking, Aileen reached out and touched Carmel's arm as she sat directly in front of her. Carmel turned briefly as if knowing she should respond, but then looked through Aileen without a shred of curiosity or recognition. Her expression, the way her shoulders were hunched with her arms hanging so carelessly from them, was cold and lifeless. Aileen felt slightly afraid of her as the girl turned round again, withering Aileen's small smile to dust.

The Mass began and Aileen's nerves started to fizz. She imagined the eyes of the congregation were all on her; they had surely noted that she had not been to Mass since her mother had disappeared. Did they all know about the man Maurice? Was the word on the island that her mother was a whore? Did they think she was the same and having untoward relations with John Joe? Was John Joe standing at the back, as he always did? If she ran now, would he follow her, and could they head off on the cart together and back to the safety of her garden? Aileen felt panic rise up in her, almost moving her limbs to flee. She looked down at the ten pots, peeping out from behind the Blessed Virgin's feet. Ten pots. Ten men. She had this to do – this was what was intended for her. Then it would be over. Then she could disappear again.

Father Dooley went through the motions of an ordinary Mass; then, when it came time to read his sermon, he started to read out the names of the Cleggan dead: 'We pray for Patrick Doherty, forty-seven . . .' Before he could continue with her brothers' names, Aileen came out from her pew, took a few steps down towards the pulpit, then walked over to the pots and carried the one bearing her father's name and laid it on the front step of the altar. The priest was dumbfounded at this girl suddenly standing in front of him with an ordinary terracotta plant pot filled with what seemed to be grass. He paused while she laid the pot at his feet and then stood looking at it as he continued, '. . . his elder son, Patrick Junior, aged just . . .' As he said her brother's name, Aileen moved across and brought over the other pot and laid it beside the first. The priest looked out at the congregation, who were, in themselves, starting to shuffle in discomfort with the peculiar interruption to the traditional memorial service. Was this the priest's doing – this coming and going with pots? Father Dooley didn't quite know what to do. He could not confront the girl – the last thing you wanted in Mass was a scene – so he just went with it, pausing while the girl laid down the second pot before continuing, '. . . twenty-two . . . and Martin Doherty, aged just nineteen . . .' Sure enough Aileen Doherty went and collected a third pot and laid it down. He had it now. A pot for each dead man in her family. Goodness but this child was strange. He was certain that was that, but as he named the next person – '. . . Mick Kelly, foreman of the group, aged fifty . . .' – the Doherty girl went over and chose another pot from her seemingly endless stash. With this the priest saw her walk across to Mick Kelly's daughter, the one who had gone stone mad, who was sitting in the front row. The priest felt very uncomfortable, but nonetheless paused over Mick Kelly's name; what else could he do? The whole congregation looked on, breathless as to what would happen next.

Aileen stood in front of Carmel and held the pot out for her to take. Carmel looked straight through her again. People started to shift in their seats, except for the grieving women and children. Each one of them had their eyes fixed on poor Carmel's face. Aileen pushed the pot forward to touch Carmel's chest, but the girl did not respond. So Aileen balanced the pot on the pew in front of her, then reached down and took both of Carmel's cool, limp hands in the warmth of her own and arranged them in a cup round the pot of grass. With her own hand then she traced the letters that spelled out Mick Kelly's name in her own, simple handwriting on the front of the pot in pencil. Carmel stroked the letters with the thumb of her left hand, then turned it towards her slightly and checked the lead mark on her skin.

She looked at Aileen, then her thumb and then the pot, and began to cry. As Carmel cried, her face came to life, as if she was waking from a terrible dream. Aileen put her arms around the other girl and walked her up to the altar, where she knelt holding the pot.

Aileen went and began to fetch the other pots and the priest followed her lead: '. . . and his son, Michael Kelly, aged twenty . . .' Carmel's mother was already there, reaching out to take the pot and then carrying it across and kneeling down next to her daughter. The other women followed, each taking a pot and kneeling at the feet of the priest, who managed to bumble his way through a wholly improvised blessing with holy water that convinced the impressed parishioners that this piece of religious theatre was intended all along.

The women went back to their seats, leaving the pots where they were, sitting squarely like ten squat soldiers in front of the altar.

During the silence after the communion rite, while the priest and his servers were going through the ceremony of wiping the chalice and putting things back in place, the organist at the front of the church started playing. As she did, a shaft of sunlight burst through the stained-glass windows behind her, sending coloured shafts of light flickering wildly across the front of the altar over the plants. The pretty lights seemed to be dancing in time to the music. It looked, to some of the people in the church, like a miracle was occurring, but to others it was just the trickery of sunlight during a particularly moving Mass. However, when the light faded back to grey and the priest began his final prayer, Aileen and some of the women saw the grass glow a ghostly green. Privately, Aileen thought it seemed that, even from this distance, the grass had grown another half-inch since the service began.

Chapter Thirty

Aside from the discomfort in the London heat, Jimmy's cheap hospital mask was also becoming discoloured and scruffy, but he had no idea where he might get a new one and in any case was reluctant to make investigations as his real aim was that he should be able to dispense with the mask altogether.

Archibald McIndoe, the doctor whom he had earmarked to restore his disfigured face, was in the newspapers every other day and Jimmy became convinced that he was the man to help him. From what he read, it seemed that the ground-breaking surgeon was doing great work on burn victims from all over the world in his hospital in a rather ugly-sounding place called East Grinstead. The men in his care called themselves the Guinea Pig Club and their courage in undergoing endless operations and the genius of the New Zealand consultant was a story that featured in the paper almost constantly, presumably because it gave people hope in the midst of war.

While he continued with his courier runs during the day, in the evenings he and Anthony had started to go 'out and about', as his boss and mentor called it.

'You spend too much time mooning over this sweetheart of yours, Jimbo.'

'You'd want to meet her, Anthony – she is something special. You'll meet her one day. I'll bring her over.'

'Of course you will, and I'd *love* to meet her, but in the meantime we need to get you out and about, young chap – turn you into a man about town, eh?'

So, after eating their dinner early in Manzini's, as had become their habit, Anthony started to take Jimmy out to a club in Piccadilly.

Often they would go over to the apartment first, then the girls, who were often only getting up at that time, would get all dressed up in satin dresses and roll their hair into fat curls like Hollywood film stars. Sometimes Jimmy wondered if those girls ever left the apartment at all. While he felt uncomfortable at their seemingly constant state of undress, he was getting used to it and was always careful to avert his eyes from them to spare their blushes, although most of the time he was aware it wasn't them blushing but him.

Aside from Mandy and Lily, Anthony kept mostly male company.

The club he went to almost every night was called Percy's. Although there was no name on the door and it was on a rather insalubrious, poorly lit backstreet, once you got in the door and down the steps into the basement room, the place was pure luxury. There were velvet booth seats and candles on every table. Everyone was so friendly and they all loved Anthony. It was a relaxed, happy place with everyone always on the best of form. The girls, even though they were in a roomful of men, seemed more at ease here than they did in their own home and that Jimmy took to be testament to the hospitality of Percy himself, whom they met on their first night in.

'Who's "the Face"?'

He asked it straight out, addressing Anthony but nodding at

Jimmy. Percy was dressed impeccably, in a tailored suit, as were all the men in his club.

He moved like a cat, which made Jimmy feel uncomfortable, although he was not sure why.

'This,' Anthony said with a flourish, 'is my friend Jimmy from Ireland.'

'I'd be careful making friends with this one, Paddy,' Percy said straight off. 'You don't know *what* mischief he'll have you getting up to . . .'

Anthony laughed and Jimmy laughed, but Percy didn't. That was the way Percy carried on: always making jokes that other people found hilarious but never cracking any more than a small sardonic smile himself.

Jimmy decided, very quickly, that he liked Percy after all and before long had got into the swing of the way Anthony and his friends bantered back and forth with each other.

They called him 'the Face' and he didn't mind. It was like he was one of the gang.

One night, Jimmy confided to the small group that he intended to go and get his face fixed and Percy said, 'Oh, nobody minds a few scars these days, dear. There's a war on, in case you hadn't noticed.'

'We hadn't!' one of the others said, and another shouted, 'Thank goodness!' and they all laughed again. Jimmy wondered if they were all veterans, like Anthony, but didn't like to ask.

They drank alcohol but in moderation. A G&T was a favourite among the group, but unlike his bawdy countrymen in Camden Town, they didn't put him under any pressure to join them. So Jimmy stuck to his coffee or lemonade. He listened to the jazz, and the girls taught him to dance a little.

In Percy's, some of the men danced together, which Jimmy thought was a little strange. In fact, Percy's was a strange place overall in that it seemed sometimes that there were more men in this basement than he had seen anywhere in one place at one time. There were no girls, except for Mandy and Lily, to either distract or reject him, so he could converse with other men in peace.

In any case, Jimmy felt safe there, among his new friends. So much so that he took to calling in there on his own in the early evenings sometimes, if Anthony wasn't free. Percy would give him coffee and a sandwich if he was hungry, and in return Jimmy would pick up a brush and sweep the place out for the evening shift or give the tables a wipe-down. Despite his sometimes harsh humour and the flourishing way he had of speaking, Jimmy trusted the proprietor. He sensed that he was kind and, in a strange way, Percy reminded him of his mother, Morag, because he was full of practical advice and homespun warnings.

Buoyed up with the sense of sophistication his new life was bringing, one early evening over coffee Jimmy confided in Percy that he intended to present himself at McIndoe's East Grinstead clinic for treatment.

Percy sucked in his teeth with cautious scepticism.

'Be careful, Paddy,' he said. 'All those war heroes and machismo? Plus it's in the *Home Counties*. Men like us don't do well outside London, dear . . .'

Jimmy wasn't sure what Percy meant by 'men like us' and he was starting to feel strange about being called 'dear' all the time. However, he was glad that Percy saw him as one of them. They were, after all, men of the world and made up the small number of men left who, for their own reasons, were still here in London and not away fighting the Germans.

'McIndoe helps men from all over the world, Percy. In any case, I have money.'

Percy said, 'Hmm. I wonder about that, and besides, money

isn't everything, Paddy dear.' Then he wiped down the table, and gathering their cups deftly in one hand, he walked off towards the kitchen. Jimmy smiled after him, thinking really how strangely very much like his mother Percy was in both temperament and manner.

Jimmy had saved fifty pounds. A fortune. Almost every penny he had earned. Anthony surely was the most generous boss in the world. It would have taken him a year, maybe even two, to save such a sum working the buildings and paying rent to some grubby landlady. Jimmy also had an idea that McIndoe would not charge vast sums of money. After all, most of his patients were just ordinary soldiers. What qualified them for his revolutionary plastic surgery treatment was not their background but rather their need, and if there was one thing that Jimmy knew that he had, it was a great need of restorative surgery. You only had to look at his face to know that.

He took the London Underground to Victoria. He hoped they would give him some notice about an operation so that he could give Anthony a warning that he'd not be able to work for a while. However, if they wanted to take him in straight away on that day, he could hardly refuse.

From Victoria the train took about an hour and for that whole time every nerve in Jimmy's body was fizzing with excitement. This was it. He could hardly believe he was so close to achieving what he had come here for.

The closer the train came, the more excited he got, and as they pulled into the station, he was in such a rush to get off that he tripped and accidentally knocked an old lady to one side and she dropped her bag.

'I'm terribly sorry,' he said, but he could see the fear in her eyes as she was faced with his masked face.

'Let me help you with that,' offered a man who had stopped to help them. Jimmy could see that he had been burned even more badly than himself. Half of his face seemed to be missing altogether, and he had a huge tube of skin, like a stuffed sausage, where his nose should have been that ran down under his shirt collar.

'Ooh, thank you, Charles,' said the old lady, as if she saw a face like his every day, and she gave Jimmy a withering look. 'If you weren't wearing that stupid mask, you'd be able to see,' she said, as she walked off.

Jimmy remembered reading how McIndoe's job was partly to rehabilitate his men back into society despite their disfigurements. Clearly, it was working.

'Yes, the tube is a bit shocking,' the man, Charles, said when he saw Jimmy gazing at it, open-mouthed. 'Part of the treatment. It's just a means to an end. At least, that's what the maestro says, although it does look pretty wacky, I must admit. What about you? You must be in a shocking state altogether if you need to wear a mask? McIndoe doesn't go in for them. "Hold your heads, men," is what he says. "Let them see what you did for king and country – no sense in hiding yourself away." What squad were you in?'

Jimmy ignored his question and just said, 'Yes, I'm new.' Then in his best English accent, 'First time here, so looking for where to go.'

'Matter of fact, I'm off there now. Only a short walk and the exercise will do us good, or so Archie says. So what's your story? Air or ground? I got shot down over France. Broke a leg and had to crawl out with my hair on fire. Bloody hot. Don't remember a thing till I woke up in the hospital.'

'Me too,' Jimmy said, although he was starting to feel uncomfortable with the war talk.

'Bloody lucky to be alive, though, that's what I say. All the other chaps say it as well, although not lost too many of my lads yet, but it's still early days. Look at the last time – the Great War. Nasty business, although we'd have got out of it a lot quicker if it wasn't for the bloody Irish kicking up all that fuss over there.'

Jimmy felt a bit sick. He nodded and tried to stop his heart from flying out of his chest.

'Now the country is crawling with dirty sods building the roads, working the farms all over the place. Cleaning up, they are. Round them up, I say, or make them work for nothing. Like the blacks. What do you say, eh? Didn't catch your name?' Charles asked.

'Percy,' Jimmy said. 'Percy Smith.'

It was the first thing that popped into his head, and enough, in any case, for Charles to continue to assume that he was 'fellow RAF'. While the disfigured man ranted about 'evil Germans' and 'bloody foreigners', reserving a particular dislike of the 'bloody Irish', Jimmy's dream moved further and further away from him. He invented a story in his head that he hoped might get him in there. He had been shot down over Germany and all his papers and ID had been lost. He had amnesia and could not remember anything that had happened before the fire. In which case, how did he know he was RAF? They would ask. They weren't stupid, the English. There were some Irish soldiers fighting this war for them, but he wasn't one of them. When they found out he was Irish, they'd look for even more paperwork. They'd find out he was just some simple lad who, through his own stupidity – rather than any act of bravery – had been caught out in a fire while tattie-hoking with his father in Scotland. He had been trying to impress a girl and it had backfired: he should have died. He deserved to have died. These men had been fighting to save a country; they were heroes, and McIndoe helped war heroes. Not ordinary Paddies like him. Not for fifty pounds – not for anything.

By the time they reached the door of the hospital, Jimmy had ruled out all the stories and lies he had begun to concoct. He was humiliated enough with the mask and the stupid circumstances of his injuries and the simple fact of his being Irish in an Englishman's country, avoiding an Englishman's war.

As Charles opened the door for him, he said, 'I'm just going to have a quick smoke and a walk on the grounds before I go in, gather my thoughts.'

Charles gave a small salute and said, 'See you shortly, old chap.'

Then Jimmy walked quickly back to East Grinstead and took the train to Victoria.

Later that night, alone in his bedsit, Jimmy took off his mask and held a mirror to his face. This was who he was, this monstrous vision. Ugly, deformed, unlovable. McIndoe's men would get better, and even if they didn't, they would get sweethearts or keep wives they already had, because they were heroes.

He wasn't a hero. Not to himself and certainly not to Aileen. He had tried to save Aileen's father and brothers and he had failed. Now he looked like this and she would never, could never love him again.

Jimmy had thought that going to see the surgeon would make him better, but in actual fact it had made him worse, because not only could he now see what his future looked like, but the stupidity and pointless recklessness of a past that had led him to look like this was now laid out in front of him.

When Anthony called to take him to Percy's, he found his young charge weeping.

'What's the matter, Jim?' he asked, and while Jimmy explained, Anthony could only guess at the true level of his despair. He took out his keys, went over to his locked cabinet, took something out and locked it again.

'What you need,' he said, 'is some of my medicine.'

'But I'm not in pain,' Jimmy said, though even as he said it, he realized that this was just a different sort of pain than the one he was used to.

'Oh, but you are,' Anthony said, and his voice was soft and warm and Jimmy knew that he was telling the truth, 'and *this*,' he said, holding out a phial of white powder, 'will make it go away.'

Chapter Thirty-One

Aileen's mother wrote to her from the mainland.

She was in the greenhouse with Biddy, John Joe and the children when she opened the thick white envelope. Her mother had spent money on expensive stationery. Was she already returning to her genteel roots?

Maurice had followed her across to the mainland and the two of them had got married. It was a small affair, 'given the circumstances'. Anne's sister and her husband had been witnesses, and there had been no celebration, as such. She and her new husband had taken a small house in Ballina and his first cousin had got him some work in the local flour mill. It was the Ballina connection that had first brought them together. They were very happy, Anne assured her, and she hoped that Aileen would come and visit them soon.

She enclosed a money order, which Aileen threw to one side, on top of the seed catalogues she had sent for from England. These were the only things she was interested in spending her money on.

'P.S.,' her mother wrote, 'you are to have another brother or sister, as we are already expecting our first child.'

'First child,' said Aileen. 'How could she have moved on so quickly?' Aileen was still not used to the fact that her family had all gone and now it seemed that her mother was rebuilding another one without her.

'Humph. Pregnant *already*,' Biddy said after Aileen silently passed her the letter.

'I know,' said Aileen. 'They've only been married a matter of weeks.'

Biddy was about to say something, but John Joe gave her a mutinous look.

He had just told them that he was planning to leave for London the following week on business and was hoping Biddy and Aileen would look after the children for him.

Aileen did not know what business John Joe could possibly have in London, except perhaps making arrangements with his brother about the children, but as she was about to question him, Biddy butted in, reminding her that 'a man's business is nobody else's business', so Aileen left well alone.

It wasn't just her mother's situation that had changed; her own life seemed to be moving along too.

Biddy had moved in things from her own house so that the deserted gardener's cottage in the abandoned garden was now fixed up as a full home. The older woman had insisted that Aileen sleep in a bed in the house 'like a normal person', although most mornings she went out and found her young charge already working through the dawn. However, while John Joe was in London, the two children would be able to sleep in the cottage with Biddy, and Aileen settled back into the idea that she'd spend her nights sleeping in the greenhouse again, alone with the plants, where she felt she most belonged.

So Biddy had moved from her home into the garden cottage, John Joe was going over to London, and her mother was settled in Ballina. Everyone around Aileen was moving themselves to different places. Aileen just wanted to stay where she was. She had found a place where she felt happy and could not ever envisage leaving it. In any case, there was too much to be done yet. While her garden was well under way, it was not complete. She would move on when she felt the garden was fully created to her satisfaction, when it was finished. Although Aileen knew that, in truth, a garden was never finished. It just grew and died and came back to life in a never-ending cycle.

The day the women came to her garden, Aileen was in the thick of it.

She had woken that morning to find her vegetable patch all but disappeared. The lettuces looked like a plague of locusts had been at them.

'Slugs,' she said, 'curse and damn you,' as she saw that the grass all around was covered in their silvery trails. Of course, there was not a slug in sight. She came out sometimes at night to check and had picked the odd unwise slug who was feeding off the thin end of a rhubarb leaf, but she had never experienced anything like this before. At home, certainly, but not here. Being surrounded by a high wall on all sides meant that Aileen's garden was never subject to the strong winds coming in off the Atlantic and appeared to remain a few degrees warmer than elsewhere on the island. 'Creating a microclimate' was how the *Ladies' Companion* described the purpose of walled gardens like these.

It had been Carmel's mother's idea. Mary Kelly had wanted somewhere nice to plant out Mick's and Michael's pots and had heard that the young Doherty girl was spending a lot of her time down in the Englishman's garden.

On an island this size, watching other people coming and going passed for entertainment. The movements of John Joe's cart and the visitors in and out of the gates of the big house had been duly logged and had created a certain level of interest and speculation among the islanders. Smoke had been seen rising in the sky above it; 'the witch', as she had come to be known, Biddy had been seen going in one day by a neighbouring farmer and was never seen coming out again. John Joe was a respectable churchgoer and a good man, but surely there was something *just not right* about him. What kind of witchcraft or strange shenanigans could be going on in there? Since Aileen's perform-ance in the church curiosity levels had been raised even higher.

The memorial service had affected all of the mourning women deeply and each had taken their pot home with them. The women were generally at a loss as to what to do with these peculiar gifts, yet they held enough significance to not be simply tossed aside.

When Monica Flaherty suggested to Mary they go as a group to see Aileen, the women all agreed it was the right thing to do, not least because they were curious anyway to see what was going on behind those high stone walls. Nobody would walk up the drive of a house like that. Even with it being derelict and the proprietor long gone, it just would not seem right, so they met on the road behind the house and walked across Timmy Harrington's field, which ran adjacent to the back garden wall, where Timmy showed them there was a door leading into the garden itself.

'I've not been in there since I was a young lad stealing apples,' he said, 'although the fruit trees are all gone now, I'd say.'

The women didn't announce themselves; they just walked in, the whole lot of them, through the back door of the garden in a line.

Aileen happened to be in the greenhouse and saw them look around briefly, then walk down the path towards her carrying their pots.

Aileen did not know what to do.

Especially when she saw Biddy coming out of her cottage to see what the noise was, and then retreat like a snail. As the old lady backed in, Aileen caught a look of blind terror on her face and started to panic herself. Why were they here? Had they come to chastise her, or were they on a witch hunt for Biddy? It was enough that there were unexpected, uninvited guests in her sanctuary.

Aileen stepped outside and met them at the door of the green-house. Claire Murphy spoke first: 'We've come to thank you for the . . .,' they had not quite decided what to call the strange pots, '. . . gifts and we were hoping you might find us a suit-able place to . . .,' again she faltered, unprepared for quite what she meant, '. . . put them?'

Aileen was relieved. As soon as she realized they wanted to plant the pots, the only thought in her mind was, Where? With the challenge of finding a place to put these special plants all other thoughts disappeared. Biddy, the fact that there was a gaggle of women in her garden, none of it mattered above where – *where* should she put these plants? Aileen all but snatched the pot from Claire Murphy's hand and began walking around the garden holding it out from her chest at arm's length. It was always like this. She might try to plan, to think things through, decide where this and that might go, but ultimately Aileen ended up just walking around holding the plant out and waiting for the ground to call out to her.

All Aileen could see were the scrappy gaps between plants and the empty corners and the patches that were bare of flowers, but the women following her were open-mouthed in amazement. The garden was the most extraordinary place any of them had ever seen. Roses clambering over their heads on a delicate trellis, banks of lavender, flower beds with a cacophony of pretty wild flowers, a freshwater pond with white lilies floating across it, paths with tidy gravel that crunched underfoot and little, trimmed circular hedges that looked like they might be the measured borders of fairy houses. How long had Aileen been working on this garden? How was all this growth possible? They had been told this place was derelict, but it seemed as though it was in full bloom. She must have had help. There were still patches of exposed earth here and there, and some of the hedging was bare and twiggy, but overall it was a beautiful place. Nobody said a word while Aileen fussed about in front of them trying to find a spot for the unusual grasses, but the women, who believed they had witnessed an actual miracle in the church, could already feel that this was a magical place.

'What about here?'

Aileen had not found anywhere in the flower garden where the plants would fit to her satisfaction and decided it was because the garden would not talk to her when there was this much company around. Even though the women were following respectfully behind her in a silent procession and there were spaces in her bed that she had been longing to fill, Aileen could get no sense of where these plants belonged. She decided to simply put them back in the greenhouse and wait until the women had gone before deciding what to do with them. She felt somewhat irritated then that she had gone to all this trouble in giving them away and now they were placing the responsibility for them on her again. However, as they crossed through back into the vegetable garden, Aileen saw that Carmel had run ahead and was standing at the edge of the decimated lettuce bed.

'I think this would be a good place.'

It occurred to Aileen that these were the first words Carmel had spoken to her since the Cleggan fire and, probably, certainly, the only civil ones ever.

Aileen went and placed the pot down on the earth and nodded for the other women to do the same. Once all the pots were arranged at intervals along the beds, the women knelt and, pushing aside the earth with their bare hands, planted out the grassy pots. As they tipped out the rooted bulbs, each one of the women felt a shiver run through them, like a current of life coming from the plant.

'Would you look at that,' Monica, Noreen Flaherty's mother, said, standing up after her planting.

All of the women looked across to the gardener's cottage, where Biddy was standing at the doorway, wiping her hands on her apron, although to Aileen it looked more like she was nervously wringing her hands. The women saw her stern features set in a look of defiance, but Aileen recognized immediately that this was an act of courage: to face her detractors.

Aileen's own three pots were sitting outside on a bench near the greenhouse. She picked up one of them, then walked across to Biddy and gave it to her, putting her hands on her arm so the other women could see they were friends and signalling the nervous Biddy to follow her lead. Then she walked back and picked up the remaining two pots and the two women got down on their knees in the black earth and planted them out. As they finished, Biddy closed her eyes and grabbed Aileen's hand; then holding her down in her kneeling position, she took a pair of rosary beads out of her apron pocket with her other hand.

'Hail, Holy Queen . . .' she began and said a decade of the rosary, while the other women, now standing at the sides of the bed, joined in.

The whole time they were praying, the older woman held Aileen's hand in a tight grip so that she knew that this was an act of contrition: Biddy and Aileen begging the Virgin Mary's forgiveness for setting the fire badly that night – prostrating themselves at the feet of the women whose loved ones had perished due to their fecklessness.

As the women prayed, their tears fell and watered the ground.

When the decade was over, Biddy lit a fire outside and cooked sausages and bread and tea for them all, as she had done in the bothy in Scotland, asking that each woman sit as she served them.

When the meal was over, it seemed that, without a word having been said, her penance was complete.

The women stayed on that afternoon and insisted on working in the garden with Aileen, watering and planting and weeding and potting.

'You've moss on the lawn,' Nuala Collins said to Aileen. 'That means your ground's too wet – it needs draining.' She took Aileen over to the wall of the flower garden. 'Those trenches there are called culverts,' she said. 'They're blocked with weeds and leaves, look – they need clearing or your ground will be pure sod and you'll never grow a thing.'

The following day, she returned with all of the women again, each carrying a shovel.

They set about digging around the edges of the walls, clearing out the drainage channels that had become blocked, making the earth claggy and damp and overrunning the grand lawns with moss.

The next day, they brought their brushes and scrubbed down the flagstones and the outside of the greenhouse.

The next day, they whitewashed the gardener's cottage and replanted the vegetable garden with new seedlings.

The more work the women did, the more work they found.

With the women's labour, the whole garden sprang to life in a way that Aileen knew it would never have done with her alone. From being reluctant about their company, she started to thrive on being surrounded by others, and the more she thrived, the more her garden grew.

It grew and grew at a rate that was, by anyone's standards, unusual.

Underneath the arbour was a permanent carpet of plump pink rose petals that never seemed to wither or wilt into a mush, but renewed itself daily so it remained fresh and satin-like under-foot. The grass lost its mossy patches and became vigorous and a soft, solid green, but the wild-flower beds were the most beau-tiful of all: a symphony of colour and movement, they attracted swarms of brightly painted butterflies that shimmered above them constantly in moving clouds of crimson and blue. The garden was peaceful, but if you closed your eyes and listened, the noise was almost deafening: the buzz of bees and hum of hoverflies competing with the twittering of small birds, loudly objecting to the human presence from their safe perches high up in the trees.

Aileen saw how beautiful the garden was, but while she was proud of it and at times even in awe of its beauty, she could not allow herself to enjoy it fully. That would mean her work was finished, and when her work was finished, well, what would she do next?

Deep in her heart there was a nagging. For the men she had lost to the fire. Her father and brothers and Jimmy. Invincible Jim. For those few weeks they had been in love he had been her hope, her future. He had meant a life away from the island, although that dream had ended almost as soon as it had begun. Aileen was back on dreary Illaunmor; the place she had been longing to get away from, but as long as she had this garden to escape to, she felt safe. Safe, Aileen decided, was all she needed now. This was her domain, her paradise. There was no reason to leave it. Ever.

Chapter Thirty-Two

John Joe had been to London a number of times over the years, although it was more difficult since he had been minding the children.

Once the Lord had sent him the gift of being their guardian, John Joe had devoted himself to them as entirely as he was able to. But in truth there were times when he felt as if the calling to the church he had experienced as a young man was coming back to him. He knew he could not follow through on the priesthood at this late stage of his life, especially as it would mean having to give up the children, but at the same time John Joe wondered what message the good Lord was trying to send him with this attraction towards men that he seemed, despite his best efforts, unable to escape.

Such desires did not happen to men of God, and if he had joined the priesthood when Jesus had first called him, God would surely have made these feelings go away. As it was, he had to live with them, and as long as that was the case John Joe had to manage them as best he could.

There were other men like him in London: Englishmen, foreign men and even the occasional Irishman. These men gathered together outside of the realms of ordinary, respectable Christian society and formed their own secret groups. There was a place

John Joe frequented and just to be there with other men like himself was a tremendous relief for the isolated farmer. A contact at the club arranged introductions for shy men like himself, so he was spared any awkwardness, and as for the physical side of things, the sin of consummating his base desires, he had done that too in the past and had no doubt that if the opportunity presented itself to him in the future, it would happen again. However, it was the lie of pretending he was someone he was not that ate away at John Joe more than his physical needs. While he was in his London club, he *felt* normal and that made living the falsehood of his life somewhat easier for a while at least.

With the women looking after the children, John Joe had given himself ten days in London and a day at either end for travelling, so almost a fortnight in all. Biddy and Aileen could easily manage the horse and cart to bring Ruari and Mary to and from school, and he had packed plenty of clothes, all ironed and starched, as he wouldn't have Biddy thinking he was falling behind. Had he packed their prayer books? Yes. Had he remembered to tell Biddy about Ruari's loose tooth? Yes. Although, perhaps he shouldn't be going away when Ruari had a tooth coming out. Suppose the tooth got infected? That was very common. In fact, Mary had to have an infected tooth removed just last year by the dentist in Westport. Would there be enough money left for a trip to the dentist? Would Biddy know what to do? Would Ruari complain to her or just suffer in silence? Did he put oil of cloves in the bag? Did he remember to pack their toothbrushes? On and on the questions went – all the way to Dublin, across in the boat and until John Joe reached the boarding house in Soho where he always stayed on his visits here. Once he arrived in London itself and knew there was no turning back, John Joe the anxious Illaunmor farmer disappeared and he became simply 'JJ from Ireland'.

The boarding house on Old Compton Street was above a dry-cleaning business. Unlike some of the places around Soho, it was a very respectable establishment and run by a middle-aged man who he sensed was like himself, as he was quiet in his manner and, more importantly, liked to keep things orderly and clean. John Joe had no interest in paying good money for a bed unless it was as immaculate as the Blessed Virgin's robes.

'Single men only,' it clearly stated on a sign above the desk. If you wanted company, there were other rooms in other establishments that could be rented by the hour. John Joe knew where these were too, but he liked the feeling of being respectable that this place gave him.

'Nice to see you again, Mr Morely,' said the man at the desk.

'Nice to see you again, Mr Neville,' John Joe replied.

Mr Neville was wearing an impeccable mustard-coloured sleeveless jersey set off with a sky-blue shirt and maroon tie that John Joe found very fetching.

'I like your jersey,' John Joe said.

'Why, thank you very much,' Mr Neville said.

At home in Ireland, such a comment would draw suspicion, John Joe thought. Not indeed, he realized, that he had ever seen another man wear anything on Illaunmor that would cause him to admire them.

'I bought it in Marks & Spencer on Oxford Street,' Mr Neville added, and seeing the shy Irishman blush at his revelation, said, 'A very inexpensive shop for the everyman, Mr Morely. Certainly worth a visit while you are in town. I can draw you a map if you like?'

'That would be lovely – thanks,' said John Joe, and he smiled a little thinking of what they might make of him back home if he turned up to Mass in a brightly coloured sweater instead of his usual brown suit!

Mr Neville handed him his key and said, 'Will you be eating out tonight, or would you like me to make you a sandwich?'

'I ate on the train,' John Joe said.

'Very sensible.'

For a moment he wondered if he should ask this man to join him that evening, directly ask for his company. However, there were no words for such a request. Just considering asking seemed ludicrous, even though he had travelled for a full day and half a night to seek out male company.

John Joe went up to his room and got changed out of his travelling clothes and into his smart navy suit, which he pressed in the electric trouser press. John Joe loved the convenience of electricity when he was on holiday, although he remained suspicious of it and could not imagine living with it all the time. Then, as it was late, he headed straight over to Percy's.

The basement bar was packed. As soon as John Joe walked into the smoky lounge he felt relaxed and started looking around for his contact. Although it was late and he had been travelling for almost twenty-four hours, his pleasant exchange with Mr Neville had put him in the mood for some company.

John Joe had only met Anthony Irvine once, on a previous trip, when Percy had recommended him as a 'fixer-upper'. The arrangement was simple: Irvine introduced him to a man in a social setting. If they got on and one thing led to another, John Joe left a 'gift' for him behind the bar. It was all very discreet and he had had two encounters under this arrangement, both of which had proved to be 'satisfactory' in their own way, although neither had led to the lasting friendship that John Joe had been secretly hoping for. Although this Irvine fellow was perfectly affable, there was something about him that did not sit right with John Joe. He would have preferred to deal with Percy himself, but the proprietor did not arrange introductions.

There was no way that John Joe could approach anybody on his own, and it seemed unlikely to him that anybody would approach a shy Irish farmer in a place like this off their own bat.

'Paddy!'

John Joe hated when English people called him that, but then, there were worse things they could be calling him and Percy was so . . . ebullient he could get away with saying almost anything.

'Lovely to see you again, JJ. I have a booth right here waiting for you. I do know how you "old" boys like to sit down.'

John Joe laughed and blushed and wished he could think of something smart to say back. Percy always made him feel like a bit of an eejit, but he was impossible to dislike and there wasn't an ounce of harm in the man.

'Too early for whisky, too late for tea – what can I get you?'

'I'll have a beer, please, Percy. Is Anthony about?'

The look of disdain that passed across Percy's face was so slight it was virtually imperceptible. A less sensitive person would not have noticed it, but in any case Anthony popped up behind him as if on cue. He had somebody with him; John Joe kept himself from even looking at the other person until he was formally introduced. His stomach was churning with excitement.

'Aha – Mr Morely, welcome back to London town. Although I'm afraid you've been knocked off the spot as my favourite Irishman by another Paddy!'

Anthony pushed forward a young man. John Joe could tell he was young – too young. The lad was wearing a mask over half his face: there was something else wrong with him too.

'John Joe, meet Jimmy Walsh.'

The name was familiar, although there were a lot of Walshes about the place – he could be anyone.

'Otherwise known as Invincible Jim.' Anthony patted the lad on the shoulder, pushing him down into a booth seat, and then said to John Joe in an audible aside, 'Jimmy has had a difficult time, as you can see. I thought as a fellow Irishman you might offer him some comfort.'

John Joe felt sick.

He was pretty sure he knew who this lad was, but he needed to be sure and he needed to get his bearings himself.

'What happened to your face?'

Jimmy threw him a weary look. More weary than he had the right to be at his age. He could not be more than twenty, twenty-three at the very most. A boy of that age had no business doing this – whatever 'this' was exactly.

'It got burned.'

'In a fire?'

Jimmy looked back at him dryly.

'Sorry – of course it was a fire.' John Joe took a deep breath. This was Aileen's lad, he was sure of it, but what should he do? Well, of course he knew he *should* simply walk away from this potentially frightening situation, but there was Aileen to consider. By some miraculous, if awful coincidence, God had put this lad in his path and he could not simply run away.

John Joe smiled and the boy did not smile back. His some-what off-putting appearance was not being helped one iota by his surly, actually downright unpleasant demeanour. Maybe some men were into that type of thing, but John Joe most certainly wasn't and he was beginning to think this lad had no idea why he was here. A 'brave eejit' was how Aileen had described him. John Joe decided that either this guy was the meanest, most deranged character he had ever laid eyes on, in which case poor Aileen had been horribly duped and thank goodness she was over there and he was over here, *or* the lad was an innocent eejit who had no idea he was being pimped out.

John Joe decided to take a chance, for Aileen's sake, and he might as well go for the truth as there was nothing else he could do in this terrible circumstance.

'Would you be an island lad by any chance?'

Jimmy's face hardened. 'What's it to you?'

'I'm from Illaunmor – a lot of our people were lost in the Cleggan fire and a young friend of mine Aileen . . .'

'You know Aileen?'

Jimmy's face lit up as soon as John Joe said her name.

'How is she?' The young man's difficult manner was transformed. 'Is she still as beautiful as ever?'

'She is that,' said John Joe, smiling. 'A beautiful young woman surely. She lives with me now,' he added. 'Since her mother left for the mainland, she moved into the house with me and my two children.'

Jimmy looked shocked, then crestfallen.

'Not like *that*, for goodness' sake. What sort of a man do you think I am? I am looking after her in place of her mother and father!'

The boy leaned across the booth towards him. 'Does she ask after me? Jimmy Walsh from Aghabeg. Has she ever mentioned me by name?'

There was an innocent urgency in the way he spoke that made John Joe's heart ache. Goodness knows what horror lay under the mask. The boy had been through a lot, so what on earth was he doing here in London, of all places? And in this haunt? John Joe knew that this was the Aghabeg beau he had heard Aileen talk about so often, but in that moment he realized two other things. Firstly, Jimmy had lost his heart utterly and completely to his young friend Aileen, in which case he did not belong in a place like this. If Jimmy did not 'belong' here, then he probably had no idea what John Joe was really here for. John Joe could see that this young, disfigured man was an innocent. However, if he stayed here mixing with the likes of Anthony Irvine, he would not stay innocent for very long.

'Of course – she talks about you all the time. In fact, that's why I'm here,' John Joe said, having a sudden epiphany around his 'story', 'to send you a message from Aileen. She wants you to come and see her on Illaunmor. She needs you, Jimmy. She is lost without you.'

As the words came out of his mouth, the most extraordinary thing happened to John Joe as he realized that it was true. Although Aileen was reluctant to talk about Jimmy to him, Aileen *was* lost and John Joe knew that the damaged young man sitting in front of him was a large part of the reason for that. It was peculiar, the way she was hiding herself away in that garden. John Joe and Biddy were the only company she had and they had forced themselves upon her along with the children. She was gifted with the plants, that was certain, but she only seemed content when tending them, and that in itself was not the right way for a young woman to be. She was grieving – of course she was – but that aside, she needed to be with other people of her own age with similar interests. When Aileen had mentioned Jimmy to John Joe, she had spoken about him as if he were dead. There was as much heaviness and sadness in her voice as when she spoke about her father and brothers.

'He might as well be dead,' she had said to John Joe when he asked about him, 'for all that it matters now.'

He had not asked any more, but it was clear to him that poor Aileen had given up on all idea of love. If John Joe could get this Jimmy lad to come back with him to Illaunmor, the farmer realized he might be able to save them both, and if he could

save these two young people, that might offset some of the
penance he would surely be due to serve for the colossal sin he
had been planning to commit that very evening. Jimmy being
sent to him in this way was doubtless a sign that he had put
the good Lord into a very punishing mood indeed!

'How did you know where to find me?' Jimmy asked him.

'Oh,' he said, 'your friend Anthony is very well connected,'
he lied, 'and I was told I would find you here.' Then before he
could be quizzed any further, he got straight to the point. 'Well?
What do you say? Will you come back with me? Your fare and
everything paid for?'

Jimmy looked at him intently, seeming to consider first if the
offer was genuine, then the offer itself. Then his good eye filled
with tears. He looked away, and when he looked back, there
was a look of abject misery that John Joe had never seen before
in his life. The boy reached up slowly and took off his mask.

'Would she love me still,' Jimmy said gently, 'looking like
this?'

John Joe instinctively turned his face slightly to one side; he
could not hide his shocked disgust, and by the time he tried, it
was too late.

'She would surely,' the older man said, but even knowing the
sort of soft woman his young friend was, he did not sound
convinced, even to himself.

'I thought not,' Jimmy said.

He clipped his mask back on, then stood up and shook John
Joe's hand like a gentleman.

'Thank you for trying to find me,' he said, 'and remember
me to Aileen.'

As he walked across the bar, John Joe thought of chasing
after him and trying to persuade him further, but he could not
be certain Aileen would thank him. In the end, she and this

young man had their own destinies of love to fulfil – just as he had his, and there was no way of knowing what they would be.

Although John Joe knew that, for certain, his was not going to be found in Percy's club that night.

Chapter Thirty-Three

At first the grass in the ten pots had never bloomed beyond the golden balls of feathery foliage she had carried to the church. Even when planted out, they had grown to a certain size, then stopped. This was all the more peculiar because every plant they shared a bed with seemed to grow at an extraordinary rate – almost out of Aileen's control. The vegetables in the plot where Carmel had chosen to initially plant them had gone altogether berserk. Lettuce seeds were reaching a full head in the blink of an eye, tomatoes were crawling out onto the paths overnight, and brassicas like broccoli and cauliflower were blossoming to the size of a human head.

The seeds that Aileen had ordered from her London catalogues were thriving and already she had trays of exotic plants and flowers peeking through that she was hopeful would be ready for planting out the following year, if she could keep the glasshouse pipes warm throughout the winter. The grapevines that she had first discovered were already more than earning their keep. In addition to watering and feeding them, Aileen had set up a complicated arrangement of mirrored glass around the place to reflect as much sunlight as possible back onto them. Nurtured with her kind and determined hand, the vines had rewarded her by bearing fruit in an abundance that surprised and delighted everyone. So much so that she was wrapping bundles of them in tissue paper and boxing them once, sometimes twice a week to send to Findlaters food merchants in Dublin.

The women came to the garden every day now. The ten of them who formed the core group had found that working on Aileen's garden was a way of not just supporting one another but creating something beautiful. As their garden grew, the women grew closer to each other. They seldom discussed what had happened in Cleggan, each understanding the boundaries of their pain better than outsiders could. Despite the length of their journey back to Ireland, and the Masses and the memorials to each of their dead, the women still felt the burden of their loss as an immediate shock. They were united in their grief. It seemed also that the more time they spent together in Aileen's garden, tilling the same soil and bringing things to life, the closer they felt to one another. This was evident mostly as a synergy among them as they worked in silent meditation, a choreographed intimacy. Aside from the beauty of the garden itself, it was this obvious phenomenon of female bonding that visitors to the garden found most fascinating. The women knelt in the vegetable patch pressing soft undulations in the black, crumbling soil, passing tools and seedlings to each other wordlessly; as one woman discarded messy weeds at the edge of a flower bed, another would pass by with a wheelbarrow and clear them without invitation. They moved around the different parts of the garden doing what needed to be done – watering, feeding, weeding, planting, trimming, tending – with no rota or discussion needed. Each knew there was some greater instinct at play, but nobody questioned it. If it was magic, the spirit of their dead moving through them, well, then to speak of such a thing out loud might break the spell. Otherwise they were simply keeping themselves occupied so that they had no time to think of their troubles or losses. They were escaping to a different world where there was work to be done, but where the air fluttered and hummed with the sound of bees and butterflies, and smelt of lilac and roses.

There were tears sometimes, but the jagged, disbelieving anger of the young and the endless, wailing keening from the older women eased as the garden became more fruitful and abundant.

After the women planted the grass and started working in the garden, they noticed a strange thing happening: it seemed that as they got better in themselves, the plants started to change.

Even though autumn was approaching, the weather in the garden was always a few degrees warmer and that bit more clement than outside it, as the high, thick walls protected it from the worst of the winds and island chills. As a result, things seemed to keep growing with the same voracity as in high summer.

The first plant to break through was Carmel's.

The women had taken to going together to Mass on a Sunday morning. They gathered at the gates of the gardener's cottage with two horses and two carts, including John Joe's, who had come back after just under two weeks away. Aileen found that she could leave the confines of the garden in this way; flanked and surrounded by the other women, she felt safe, as if she were taking her garden with her. She was careful always to stay at the centre of the group as they filed into the church and sat in the middle of the pew between John Joe and Biddy. She did not pray but simply watched the light from the windows play across the altar and allowed herself to fall into a kind of trance.

Of all the women, Aileen could see that Carmel had blossomed the most. Her spoilt nature had been tamed somewhat since the death of her father and brother, but she was as outspoken as ever. So when Kevin Kerrigan approached her after Mass one morning and asked if she would step out with him, she snapped back, 'And me still grieving? Whatever would make you ask such a cold-hearted thing?' then turned away, although all the women could see that her face was beaming with such joy, her eyes glittering with pride and pleasure, it was as if her veins had been injected with the elixir of life itself.

The following morning, back in the garden, Carmel called Aileen over to her plant. Growing through the centre of the grass was a thick stem, half an inch deep and a good two inches tall already. It was clear then that this was not grass at all but merely the leaves of an exotic flower.

Everyone gathered round to look at what had happened to Carmel's plant, but over the coming days all of the grasses grew flower stems. There was nothing so unusual in that except that the women could attribute their growth to each other's well-being. The better the women felt in themselves, the healthier and stronger the plants became.

Biddy fed everyone. Every morning when the women trooped through the back gate past the door of the gardener's cottage, Biddy would remember why she was here. Her part in these women's pain was certain: it had been her carelessness in not checking Aileen's fire that had led to the deaths of their men, ten of them, each and every one. The damage was done. Feeling sorry for herself would achieve nothing, so she would close her eyes and pray and ask God to guide her in a way of making good on her terrible act. Every morning He sent her the same message: cook for them.

So Biddy cooked. She cooked as if her life depended on it. Each day's recipes were carefully planned. Like most of the island women, given the distance and cost of doctors, Biddy knew about the healing properties of herbs. However, she had never thought about using them in her cooking before. Feeding tattie-hokers had always involved heartiness before health – bread, meat and potatoes were the staple foods – and time had always been a factor too. Working in the fields, she never had more than an hour to prepare food for twenty people. Now, Biddy rose at dawn and began to plan and prepare their meals for the day. Using fresh produce from the garden, she infused every meal with healing herbs – even cakes. She added finely chopped dandelion leaves to salads to aid digestion and clear their bodies of impurities; plenty of garlic and onions in every stew to keep the blood thin and fight infections; rosemary in her soda cakes for concentration and memory to keep the women alert; lavender jelly to calm their moods and spirits; and nettles as a base for her soups, to help breathing – so they could better experience the life they were creating all around them.

Aileen and the women had been hopeful that they could feed themselves on the fruits of their labour, but within weeks it seemed that their ambitions were vastly underrated.

News spread of their endeavours and now they were feeding half the island. Biddy ran the garden shop, bartering food for food with farmers and taking money from the wealthier people who were coming over from the mainland in cars from as far away as Westport to buy their weekly fruit and vegetables. Many of them arrived hungry, so with some of the money the women clubbed together and bought some items from a house-sale dealer – twenty wooden kitchen chairs, five small tables of various heights and purposes, and two full tea services – and opened an outdoor cafe of sorts. Biddy cooked on her open fire and visitors to the garden lapped up her hearty bothy food – hot home-cured sausages on slices of thick crumbly brown bread served with piping-hot sweet tea boiled and made in her very own enormous black kettle.

As it became known that Findlaters in Dublin were buying

grapes grown in Ireland, customer curiosity led the reputation of Aileen's garden to travel right across the country. Already a somewhat popular holiday location, Illaunmor had had a boom summer as news of Aileen's magnificent garden filtered through to gardening enthusiasts, amateur botanists and curious holiday-makers keen to come and look at how these grieving island women had carved such beauty out of their, by now well-documented, pain.

Aileen's contact with the world increased as her garden grew. There was the everyday hubbub of dealing with plant and vegetable customers, and Biddy's cooking attracted crowds of buyers and hungry gawkers. People bought from them, but many just came to experience the extraordinary beauty of the place. When the skies above Illaunmor were grey, the colours of the wild-flower beds seemed to glow even brighter, and the drizzling rain never dampened the silky rose-petal carpet. People said the garden was miraculous, that it was impossible that such things could be happening in Ireland, at this time of year. Some whispered that Aileen must be a witch of some kind. Others said it was God giving these grieving women a helping hand with clement weather and good soil.

Aileen found that now she was not expected to leave the garden, she could easily deal with the grocers who came from as far as Dublin to inspect and buy her produce. As the garden grew more like Paradise, and her confidence grew alongside its beauty, so did her reluctance to leave. Her fear of the world became so severe that she found herself nervous about stepping outside the walls of the garden itself. As far as the top of the drive to the big house felt like a separate universe to her. Aileen's world was inside the tall stone boundaries, and 'outside' was the courtyard that led to the front of the house. Beyond that was a wider world that, for no reason she could decipher, had begun to feel foreign and dangerous to her. It was like stepping off the edge of the world itself and into the black unknown. Her only trek each week was to the church, but that felt safe when she was surrounded by the other women. The cottage she grew up in and John Joe's house, places where she had previously felt secure, had become as terrifying as the bottomless expanse of water that lay beyond them. Her ultimate fear was the sea and the idea of having to cross it. Where once she had stood on the beach and looked across the water dreaming of what joy and adventure lay on the other side, she now felt the ocean was a path to pain. Across the water was Scotland, the place that had killed her father and brothers; across the water was the mainland, where her mother had disappeared to and left her here alone.

When she was inland, in her garden, Aileen didn't need to worry about such things. She could be herself and she felt like there was no reason for her to ever venture beyond the walls.

The only question Aileen ever had about leaving her garden was the possibility of seeing Jimmy again.

When John Joe returned from London, her question was answered.

'I bumped into a friend of yours,' he told her. He said it casually, but she noticed he had waited until the end of the day, when the glasshouse was cleared of people and they were unlikely to be interrupted, before telling her. Aileen did not have any friends in London, none that she knew of, although there were one or two seed suppliers there to whom she had been writing. 'Jimmy Walsh . . .'

The knees went from under her. She leaned back on the vine for support and reached up her hand, grabbing a branch to steady herself.

John Joe tried to keep his voice even, but he could see she

was shaken and immediately regretted having said anything at all.

'. . . from Aghabeg.'

He went over and led her to a bench to sit down.

Aileen stayed silent for a moment and John Joe was not sure if that was a good or a bad thing, so he just talked. They met in a pub, he lied, in Camden Town. There were a lot of Irish there, he said, and they were introduced by a fellow Irishman. It was some coincidence, he continued. Aileen still said nothing, just looked at the ground in front of her. Listening intently. She was shocked, he could see that, so he just said, 'Nice lad,' and when she realized he wasn't going to continue beyond that, she put her hand on his arm and asked, 'How is he?'

Aileen herself hoped she had said it lightly so that John Joe would not know that it was the most important question she had ever asked of anyone, that his answer could change everything for her.

'Oh, he seems in fine form. Working . . . doing well . . . you know?'

'I heard he was injured in the fire?'

'Oh yes, well, he got burned all right. His face . . . well, it's terrible to tell the truth. Disfigured . . . but he wears a mask . . .' The well-meaning bachelor got flustered then, not wanting to sound bad against the lad. 'Although, he has a good job, well-paid work he gave me to believe, lots of friends.' That sounded perhaps like the lad was careless. 'Seems to be settling down nicely . . .'

In any case, he could see that what he was saying wasn't helping his young friend and he was right. Once Aileen realized that he was not going to say what she wanted to hear – 'Jimmy still loves you. He is coming back for you' – all other news of Jimmy were slaps of rejection.

John Joe was only tying himself up in knots, so he finished up: 'He said to say he was asking after you.'

Even to his own ears it sounded like pathetically small comfort.

To Aileen it was the end. Jimmy had a new life in London, without her. The final flicker of hope from her past had been stamped underfoot and extinguished like a discarded cigarette.

John Joe left and Aileen took a deep breath, then exhaled in one, heavy sob. She would not cry, not now – not for what might have been when she had cried enough for the deaths and what had been already. As she sat gathering herself, her eye was caught by the line of barren pots she had left under the counter on the day the ten pots had first sprouted. She had left them there hoping that one might sprout up for Jimmy, not fully understanding that the plants had grown from the spirits of the dead men, although now she wondered if that was true. The strange plants were flourishing as the women healed themselves and as they tended the ground the plants grew in. It was the women's love that was making the grasses grow – not the spirits of the dead men themselves. She knelt down and touched the dry soil in the dead pots. Jimmy was alive and happy living a new life far away. Her love was not enough to bring him back. Her love for him was not strong enough to breathe life into this dead soil.

She left the pots where they were in their dry corner of the greenhouse and resolved to leave the bit of her heart that loved Jimmy Walsh there with them until it too crumbled into dust.

Aileen had no other choice but to resign herself to life in her garden. Jimmy was gone to her now. Without him, there was no need for her ever to leave this place. In any case, she told herself, what need had she to see the outside world when the world was coming to see her?

She took another breath and allowed it to propel her out into the sunlight towards the bed where the crazy magic plants were thriving. Aileen knelt down and drank in the smell of the warm earth until she felt safe again. Then reaching into her apron for a pair of scissors, she snipped off a cutting from one of her own plants, then wrapped it in a small piece of tissue. She would send it off in tomorrow's post to the Botanic Gardens in Dublin and get a name for this mysterious grass that somehow seemed to be telling her the story of her life.

Chapter Thirty-Four

Dr François DuPont wiped the mist from the glasshouse window with his handkerchief and looked out on another dreary Dublin morning. In front of him was one of the ornate sweeping flower beds of the Botanic Gardens. The showy shape and colour of what was surely one of the most magnificent gardens in Europe did nothing for the young botanist. For him, the beauty was all in the detail. What could be seen under a microscope, the complex patterns of mites and plant cells was infinitely more interesting to him than a man-made flower bed. Science made a mockery of man's attempts to create almost anything. It was an opinion that did not make him popular, but François cared nothing about his own popularity. He was much more interested in plants.

He moved away from the window and vaguely checked the growth of a hybrid orchid he had planted less than three days ago, finding it had already pushed through the soil of his carefully named and numbered tray. Professor DuPont tried to drum up a feeling of satisfaction at his own achievement in encouraging such rapid growth, but he could not.

DuPont had been here working in Dublin's Botanic Gardens for almost six years. He had been offered a place at Kew in London, but had chosen Dublin because his mother was 'Catholique' and he preferred the temperament of the Irish people.

He had thought it would be fun. He had been wrong. Two things were playing on François's mind that morning.

The first was the war back home – as it was every morning. When the possibility of his leaving Paris to research and catalogue the wild flowers of Ireland had first been mooted, the invasion of France by Germany was little more than a threat. Nobody ever imagined it would actually happen. Yet the unimaginable *did* happen. Paris was under the control of the Nazis and his parents were living under the rule of the German Army. It was the first thing François thought of when he woke every morning: his brother and sister were fighting in the French Resistance, while their middle sibling was here, in dreary, rain-soaked Dublin inspecting the new stem of an *Alstroemeria pulchra* with a pair of tweezers. He had tried to leave his position of visiting research librarian on a number of occasions, but each time he had been persuaded to stay. At just thirty, he was the youngest academic of his stature in Europe and he had an obligation to finish his research. The older botanists, many of them very eminent world-class scientists, argued, what was the point of going back to a war when there was such essential research work to be done into the healing properties of wild flowers occurring in nature? In isolating the healing compounds of plants in order to mimic them in conventional medicine – what could be more important than that?

In any case, his mother would not let him return under any circumstances. She said she would have him arrested at the dock herself if he as much as set foot off Irish soil. 'It's safe there.' François could not make her understand that his own safety meant nothing to him as long as his country was at war. Although believing that did not negate the fact that his plant research *was* of enormous historical and international significance. There was little doubt, even to himself if he was honest, that Dr François

DuPont, with his horn-rimmed spectacles and his slight, bookish physique, was a far better academic than he would ever be a soldier.

'Study flowers – win prizes,' his father's words rang in his head when he finally managed to get him on the telephone after Paris had been taken. 'Let your brother and sister play with their guns and you stay there and get on with your important work.'

His father made light, but in reality François knew his parents were terrified for his siblings, Vivette and Jerome. While nobody would argue that his work was more important than fighting a war, the best thing François could do from here was assure his parents that they would come out of this war with at least one child still alive.

The second thing that was bothering François was a long, slim leaf that was sitting on a sheet of white paper on the desk to his left. He had received the sample five days ago from a woman on one of the remote islands off the west coast – a place whose flora he had yet to investigate, at least partly because he had not thought its climate and landscape sufficiently dissimilar to the nearby mainland areas for them to warrant a visit. The Burren, with its unique limestone geology, was where all the rare stuff was, so he thought there was no point in moving further west. He was, it seemed, wrong about that. If there was one thing François DuPont hated, it was being wrong about his work.

He had spent two full days checking and rechecking the leaf against every book and periodical in their extensive library and had come up with nothing. What made it particularly frustrating was that this seemed to be such an ordinary plant. To the untrained eye, this looked like a common-or-garden blade of grass. But it wasn't. Through the centre of the narrow leaf ran a thread of gold, barely visible to the naked eye, but under his microscope the minuscule line shone with a clarity that suggested it was metal, which, when he tested it, he found it was. François was flabbergasted. While some plants did contain metallic elements, it was not in such a way that they could constitute an actual structure – like the adornment of a gold thread. Such an idea was preposterous. Yet here under his microscope was a plant that appeared to be doing just that.

More annoying yet was that this common gardener person, this woman who had sent him the leaf, seemed aware of the thread's existence. She could see it, and as she said in her letter, 'I have looked in all of my collection of books but cannot find a note of it anywhere. Also, I know this may appear strange, but sometimes it seems to glow like gold.'

She had checked in her book collection, and if she had seen the gold itself, she must have studied the leaf under a microscope. All of this could only mean one thing – that he had inadvertently come into contact with a plant enthusiast and there was nothing that upset the sensibilities of an academic botanist more than the semi-informed opinion of an amateur.

Nonetheless, baffled and curious and in the interest of science, Dr François DuPont had no choice but to journey out to the island of Illaunmor to find out more about this strange plant and the person who was no doubt going to try and 'claim' it as their own if he failed to identify it.

Irritated, he picked up the frustrating leaf from his desk, placed it into a tissue sample envelope and took it straight over to the director's office, who, having listened to the young Frenchman's rant, relieved him of all his lecturing and touring duties for the coming days so that he could investigate this strange anomaly.

By mid-morning the Westport train was pulling out of Kingsbridge Station and the eminent young botanist was gazing out from his warm compartment at the autumn drizzle. It rained in France, but not like this. Not all the time, every season. People said it was good for the plants, but it didn't make any difference. Plants would evolve and adapt to their surroundings. If only people could just understand that. François missed the sun; he missed the feel of it on his face, the way it bronzed and weathered his skin. The summer was gone now in any case. Dreary autumn in Ireland was well and truly under way and he was another year away from his family. He couldn't think about that now, so he took his heavy encyclopedia out of his small knapsack – it was almost the only thing in there aside from a packed tent and a change of clothes – and began to check it against the leaf again.

It was late afternoon before he could get a car to take him from Westport Station to the far reaches of the island where this woman had stated her address to be. He supposed he should have written in advance of his coming, but then again, if she was a keen amateur botanist, he thought cynically, she would be thrilled to have alerted the attention of somebody from the Botanic Gardens, although he supposed she might think she knew better than him.

His fears were alerted further when he gave the swarthy taxi driver the woman's name and address and he said, in a barely discernible brogue, 'Isn't that yer wan with the famous garden? I'm going there myself, as it happens.'

The sun was setting as they drew up to the front gate of the old, derelict house. As soon as they pulled in, François's worst fears about some keen gardener looking to make a name for herself seemed confirmed. In the front courtyard of the house were brightly coloured traditional Irish horse carts filled with potted plants and a big 'Garden Flowers for Sale' sign in front of them.

The taxi pulled up, and after François had paid, the driver grabbed a dead chicken from under his seat, then followed him out of the car.

'The wife told me to get some vegetables. They've all kinds of fruits out the back – you wouldn't believe. She was selling grapes last week! I wouldn't have believed it if I hadn't seen it with my own eyes! Anyway, the wife is gone stone mad for the food here and I'm sent up every night to see what she has.' He held up the chicken. 'I'll put the chicken in and they'll give a bag of fruit and vegetables back. You'd want to see the size of the tomatoes coming out of there! The size of a cat's head, some of them! Fair trade and they take money too if you're interested.'

Even though it was late in the day, there were still plenty of people milling about. As François followed a woman in an apron through a door in the high stone wall, he entered the formal garden he was expecting. There was the rose-covered arbour, the miniature maze, the formally planted beds, a monkey puzzle with a marble seat, a fountain and all the usual bourgeois garden accoutrements rich people across the world used to create their own version of Versailles to try and impress.

However, the botanist heard it as soon as he walked in. The *thrum* of sap rising, the crinkle of things growing: the sound of science happening. He turned round and there it was: every wild flower he could possibly imagine in a huge flower bed, dancing alongside each other. The rare, the mundane, the ordinary and the beautiful all living impossibly, miraculously in equal measure, in harmony, in one place. There was a small patch of ground elder with a spray of pretty poppies pushing through it – undeterred. Dandelions were arranged in a solid lump of showy yellow as if somebody had actually planted the weed and not one of them had strayed onto the paths or other beds. Lilies and cornflowers, daisies and ragwort and lady's mantle in an ordered symphony existing in a controlled way, yet there was nothing contrived here, nothing unnatural. There was just every plant that was interesting to him here in one place. François dropped to his haunches to check the temperature and texture of the soil. As he did, the Frenchman felt a ray of glorious sunshine, a heated glow, hit the side of his face. When he turned and looked up, he saw there was a young woman standing over him. Her hair was a tumble of fiery red, and in her hands she appeared to be holding a pot of gold leaves.

Chapter Thirty-Five

The meeting with John Joe was a turning point, of sorts, for Jimmy. When he took off his mask and saw the look of horror on the man's face, he finally realized that it was pointless dwelling on dreams.

Aileen was in his past; the love they had, the love he had felt for her was part of who he had been before the fire. Things were different now. He looked different and he felt different. Anthony introduced him to people as Invincible Jim, but Jimmy realized that it was simply a joke. He went along with Anthony's hard-man humour, shrugging and laughing at his disfigurement so that people wouldn't see he cared. If they knew he was hurt, then they might see the truth – that he had once thought himself invincible – and that would be the biggest joke of all.

Jimmy's ambition in coming to London had been to restore himself and return to the man he had been. When he realized that surgery was not an option, part of him had still harboured a small notion that he might return to Ireland anyway to claim Aileen. He could not go home without some significant change in his appearance in any case: that would be a failure. He had come to London a penniless monster to make his fortune and fix his face. He could not stand before his parents again without having achieved those things. His parents aside, he still loved

Aileen, but he could not put himself in front of her looking as he did. He had thought of other options besides the surgery. Someone in Percy's had told him about his father who had lost half his face in the First World War. There was an artist called Francis Wood who made the man an extraordinarily lifelike mask that was 'so realistic you could barely tell he was wearing it'. 'Oh, he's long dead,' the man had said unhelpfully when Jimmy had asked where the man worked, but Jimmy felt certain there must be another such person working in London who might help him.

However, his encounter with John Joe had quashed even his ambition for a modest fake solution. A mask was a mask – Aileen would know the man underneath. It was never going to happen. Jimmy was never going home.

This was where his life was now; this was who he was.

Perhaps it was not so bad after all, he decided. There were girls in London who would go with him looking the way he did. In fact, he knew now that there were girls in London who would go with *any* man if he had a few bob in his pocket. Mandy and Lily were those types of women. It had taken a while for it to sink in, but since his odd encounter with John Joe, Jimmy had opened himself up to seeing what was happening in the world around him. He knew everything now.

Even about Percy's. The night after his encounter with John Joe, Anthony had insisted he come to Percy's with him again and had introduced him to another man – a man from the north of England whose father was Irish.

'You'll get on,' Anthony had said.

Jimmy was sick of meeting his boss's friends. They kept wanting to take him off out for dinner, or to their hotels nearby for drinks instead of staying where they were. Jimmy had had a long day and was tired. He hadn't eaten and said he wasn't in the mood for meeting new people, so Anthony gave him some Benzedrine. Without being told directly, Jimmy had gradually realized that, actually, Anthony wasn't selling his clients proper medicine at all but was selling them phials of powder that would either wake them up – Benzedrine – or put them to sleep – morphine. Jimmy guessed he was breaking the law, but did not ask questions. He was working and earning money and that was good enough for him. It had to be good enough for him: he had no other choice. Besides, Anthony had been good to him: he was his friend. When he came back from East Grinstead that day, Jimmy had never felt so desperate in his life. He felt completely hollow inside, like somebody had scooped the bit of hope he had built up since the fire and cast it aside. Anthony had given him a phial of morphine and it had made him forget everything. He felt as happy and free as he had been as a small child swimming off the rocks in Aghabeg. Then he fell into a deep sleep. Jimmy had only taken the morphine once or twice since then and he preferred it to the other stuff. The Benzedrine wound him up like a clock spring and made him talk too much and grind his teeth. After taking it at night, Jimmy would be so exhausted at work the following day he would need to take some more just to keep himself going.

Anthony told him he could have as much of the Benzedrine 'medicine' as he liked, but the morphine was too expensive to waste. Jimmy was told that he must always ask his boss to administer it and never take it directly himself from the client's supplies. Jimmy was shocked that Anthony would ever think he might steal from him in such a way, but then there had been a number of occasions when he had fallen asleep on the Tube and been tempted to open an envelope, although he could never be sure which powder he should be taking as the phials were unmarked and all looked the same.

On this particular evening, he had been talking, and talking, and talking at rather than to this man – paying very little attention to him beyond the fact that he was a few years older than himself, had a beard and seemed a little drunk.

Quite suddenly the man shouted over the music in a slurred drawl, 'You talk too much,' then leaned across the table, roughly grabbed Jimmy by the back of his head and pulled him across and tried to kiss him. Jimmy got a terrible fright and the beery buffoon's tongue reached inside his mouth before he was able to land the drunkard a hard enough wallop to extricate himself from the man's grip. The burly northerner stormed off, embarrassed more than angry, but while a few people looked over to see what had happened, Jimmy noticed that nobody seemed surprised at the extraordinary nature of the attack or rushed to help him.

Jimmy was shaken, his mask askew, and as he adjusted it, Percy came over and helped settle him. 'There, there, now, sweetheart. I'll get you some hot sweet tea.' Jimmy knew, when he said that, that Percy was a homosexual man: a man who lay down with other men. The veil fell from his eyes immediately and Jimmy realized that he must have known all along but denied it because he enjoyed their company. Even though what they were doing was against the law, even though what they were doing was against God and was morally very, very wrong, Jimmy had not flinched from their unnaturally feminine company. Jimmy knew he was not like them, but at the same time he knew in his head, if not his heart, that it must be wrong of him to be here mixing with men like these. As Percy was fetching his tea and the other men were looking across to see if the fuss had died down, Jimmy noticed that Anthony was nowhere to be seen. Another veil fell as he realized now why he had been left with this man, why the man had tried to kiss him. Anthony had set him up. Anthony must have told this man he would lay down with him. How many other men had he said this to? John Joe? No, John Joe was different; he had come to find him with a message from home. Jimmy was enraged and then almost as soon as the fear rose, it diminished again. He had no choice: there was no other kind of work he could do, no other life he could lead. He could not go home, and he could not stay in London without Anthony's help. This situation he found himself in was entirely his own fault. He had been gullible and stupid, but, Jimmy told himself in that moment, he wasn't going to be the innocent island boy anymore.

Over the coming weeks Invincible Jim reinvented himself. He asked around Percy's thespian friends and found that a friend who worked in the theatre knew somebody who worked at Madame Tussauds. This man came round to Jimmy's bedsit and took a cast of his face, then sculpted him a thick rubber mask that was an excellent replica of his face. Jimmy was excited when he first placed the prosthetic over his damaged face, but quickly realized that without movement it was simply a more colourful version of the medical mask he had had before. The lifeless disguise seemed to match how Jimmy felt inside, and he found that if he kept the exposed part of his face inert and his expressive eye deadened, people on the Underground would look at him with puzzlement and fear rather than the pity he had become so used to. Jimmy found he preferred being feared than pitied.

He told Anthony, in no uncertain terms, that he was not a homosexual and if there were any more set-ups, he would have no hesitation in thrashing the living daylights out of him or one of his clients. Far from being upset by his threats, Anthony apologized for 'misinterpreting' his 'sexual preferences', gave him a pay rise and said that indeed if any of his clients stepped out of line or refused to pay, Jimmy was welcome to thrash the living daylights out of them, although, frankly, the ruthless pimp believed that his lackey's ominous new 'look' made it unlikely anyone would cross either of them ever again. Jimmy began to take Benzedrine daily. He found that it kept not just the physical tiredness at bay, but closed off the hollow where his heart had been so that he could forget it was there. Jimmy had no use for a heart anymore; it just made him sad and vulnerable, and there was no place for that in London, in his new life.

Thanks to the Benzedrine, he was able to work more or less round the clock, stopping only for one square meal a day. He spent some of his money on clothes from Anthony's tailor in Jermyn Street and started to dress his thinning frame in pinstripes until he looked like a regular spiv. He bought Lily's company; even though she said he could have it for free, he insisted, knowing that no woman could be expected to love a man like him without getting paid for it. The rest of his wages he sent home to his parents, even though his father had assured him they had no great need for the money. Sean's letters always ended with 'Your mother asks when you are coming home.' Lily went with him to a photography studio in Piccadilly Circus and they had their picture taken. He wore his pinstripe three-piece suit, and she wore her respectable coat. With the new mask he looked, to all intents and purposes in the specially toned picture, as if there was nothing wrong with him at all. He sent it to his mother, saying, 'I got me a girl, Ma, so I'm staying in London for a while,' then waited for his mother's response, congratulating him on his transformed appearance. It never came.

He slept every other night, stealing carefully siphoned shots of morphine from Anthony's locked cabinet, but only when he felt he needed it. Jimmy slept best in the short burst of exhaustion after he had emptied himself into Lily.

The day he lost his virginity to the pretty redhead, there had been no seduction on either side and very few words. Knowing that this was something that had to be done, partly through a build-up of physical need and partly to help him forget Aileen, the young Irishman simply presented himself to Lily at the apartment one afternoon and they undressed and went through the motions. She was kind and effective and it was a relief to get it over and done with. When they had finished, Jimmy twisted his face into the white skin of her neck and buried himself in her auburn hair, recalling his true love, Aileen. He could no longer see her delicate, beautiful face when he closed his eyes, although as his deaf ear pressed against the other woman's flesh, it replicated the thunder of the sea and he remembered the sight of her as a red flame on the beach. Lily let him lie there for an hour that afternoon and it was the happiest he had felt since he had arrived in London. His body wrapped in human embrace and the memory of Aileen playing on his mind, he began to remember how it felt to be loved. Then Lily gave him a little dig in the shoulder and said, 'Best get up now – my next one is due in fifteen minutes.' The pain of knowing she wasn't Aileen and that he wasn't 'himself' startled him. He shot up from the bed and got dressed, then straightened his mask and reminded himself who he was: Invincible Jim, Anthony Irvine's Irish hard man.

Chapter Thirty-Six

Aileen got an awful fright when she realized that somebody had actually come down to see her all the way from the Botanic Gardens in Dublin. She had sent them the sample out of genuine curiosity, but had not imagined in a million years that they would follow it up.

The day François arrived, Aileen was so unnerved by the fact that he had travelled all this way to see her that she was quite rude.

The first time Aileen saw him, Professor DuPont was crouched down at the foot of one of her flower beds. While Aileen was still somewhat wary of strangers from the mainland generally, she had become used to visitors to the garden. However, this one was not merely admiring her handiwork but appeared to be interfering with it. She had never known anyone, aside from herself, to study soil in such a close-up, interested way, and she was quite put out about it.

She was replanting the pot that represented her brother Paddy in the wild-flower bed. The vegetable plot was so overwhelmed with growth and she was hoping things might calm down if she removed one of the manically fertilizing grasses from it. The wild-flower garden, the very place that should have been wild and unkempt, seemed moderate in its growth by comparison.

It appeared to be that Aileen only had to will patterns of growth and they seemed to happen for her, although, in reality, she knew that she worked at it too.

I'd love if the dandelions all stayed in the one spot on a sort of solid yellow circle, she had thought to herself when designing the wild-flower plot. She knew that dandelions grew in chaos when their seeds blew in the wind and so she meticulously gathered the seeds from the flowering plants and then did the unheard of by actually planting dandelions – and it worked. It seemed that whatever she imagined for this garden came true and the fact that she worked for it was immaterial to her because she loved it so much. All she knew was that what she saw in her mind's eye had happened in reality, and that was all that most people, most people who were not like François, saw. People had said it was extraordinary – like a miracle. She didn't pay too much heed to talk like that; in fact, she found it slightly offensive. She read her books and planted her seeds and this was what happened: nature taking its course. She was simply a green-fingered girl. If Aileen found the rate of growth puzzling herself, she did not welcome other people suggesting that there was something odd happening in her garden. Now, here was somebody rooting about in the soil, her soil, with the implication that there was something amiss.

'You'll find nothing down there except worms,' she said to the crouched figure, 'and you'll get your fancy pants mucky.'

As he looked up at her, the sun caught his glasses and made them glare so she couldn't see his eyes. She nonetheless noticed that he was quite handsome, young, with a strong nose and a broad chin and high cheekbones, and the fact that she noticed annoyed her even more.

'I don't care about my trousers,' he said. 'I just want to know who trained these wild flowers to sit together like this:

there must be some special property in the soil preventing their growth.'

'That would be me, and I can assure you there are no tricks in there, just potato skins and comfrey juice – I mulched it myself.'

'Aha – comfrey is a fertilizer, and wild flowers need low fertility. That is how the weeds are contained. Without it, the ragwort would have taken over by now.'

Aileen blushed with a spark of indignant fury. 'I *know* what comfrey is, and what makes you such an expert?'

'I am Dr François DuPont from the Botanic Gardens in Dublin,' he said, standing up to his full height, which was a foot taller than Aileen, 'and I know a great deal about wild flowers.'

Aileen gasped inwardly, but decided that this was *her* garden after all and she wasn't going to have this pompous man telling her what was what, no matter how important (or tall and handsome) he was.

'Do you know how I got those dandelions to grow all at the same rate in a perfect circle?'

He looked taken back. Let him put that in his pipe and smoke it. Although, in truth, Aileen herself was not entirely certain how she had done it.

'No. In fact, I was just—'

'Well then, you don't know everything, do you?'

'I did not say I knew *everything*; that would be inaccurate, and in fact impossible given the size and breadth of the botanic world. However, there are certainly always anomalies worth exploring and I feel certain that your "dandelion circle" – shall we say? – is one of them and we shall find some perfectly logical explanation behind it.'

'"We shall find"? What does that mean? Who is this "we"?

There will be nobody rooting around in these beds except me . . .'

'And yet you are so clever you sent me leaves from a plant that, despite your cleverness, you cannot identify?' he said, tapping playfully on the pot she was still holding. He was clearly enjoying badgering her in this playful way, and truthfully Aileen found that, despite herself, she was enjoying it too.

'So,' Aileen challenged him, 'did you find out what it was?'

He grimaced in reply, she pouted, and they smiled at each other, unsure quite what was happening.

Once Aileen and François started talking, they didn't stop. They walked through the garden discussing the flowers and plants. He knew everything by its Latin name and she ran to get her book so she could test him. The Frenchman strutted around effortlessly reciting the name of every plant she pointed to, delighted with himself. Aileen held her own then as she took him through her potting and feeding routine with the exotic fruits and flowers in the glasshouse. He nodded as if he felt he agreed with everything she was saying – as if all of her actions met with his expert approval. She could tell from the questions he was asking that he was deeply impressed by her and she liked that.

Later that evening, Biddy, who eyed the newcomer with deep suspicion, cooked them both a hearty stew. François devoured it and called Biddy a *'chef superbe'*, which, once it was translated, seemed to sate her irritation at being landed with an unexpected visitor. It was obvious to Biddy that Aileen felt immediately comfortable in François's company. They were talking as if she had known him all her life.

'Can you really not identify my plant?' she said.

He finally admitted defeat, shaking his head and pouting his lips as he did when he was thinking hard.

'It is very rare, and very beautiful. I have never known anything like it before.'

Then he looked across at her and Aileen knew he was talking about her too. She smiled and he smiled back and she thought he was sweet and handsome and for a moment she wondered.

'So it could be . . . a new plant?' Aileen said. 'A completely new discovery?'

'It happens,' he said, 'and when it does, it is a spectacular thing.'

'But how?' Aileen said. 'I mean, how is it possible for something to be . . . completely new?'

He laughed at her innocence.

'Evolution,' he said. 'Weather and cross-pollination can make almost anything happen. Nature is a powerful force.' When he said that last part, he looked intently at her and Aileen felt something pass between them.

'So what happens next?'

He shrugged and smiled flirtatiously, and Aileen looked at the handsome chin of a man who was undoubtedly brilliant and she thought perhaps he liked her. She thought then of Jimmy. Cursed Jimmy! He was gone – away living the good life in London. He wasn't in her life anymore. Would she ever be able to look at another man in that way again? Would his memory stand between her and falling in love again?

'Well, next,' he said, 'my colleagues in Dublin will look at a sample, and once they are satisfied there is no record of it anywhere, they will send it off to Kew in London, who will do the same. In a matter of time, if it is not identified, it will be declared a new discovery and there will be a great deal of fuss.'

'Oh,' said Aileen. She could not imagine what 'fuss' meant, but she had already asked a lot of stupid questions and François was reaching for more brown bread to mop up the last of his stew.

'You'd think you'd never eaten a scrap of food before in your life!' Biddy said.

François didn't seem to hear her but just kept eating.

'French!' Biddy said under her breath, and left the room. Aileen wasn't sure if it was an insult or an excuse, but she was glad he hadn't seemed to hear her. François was, she could see, very like herself. Not fully here: caught up in the world of plants and flowers. Jimmy had quipped with Biddy, chatted and flirted and sung around her. Jimmy had made the noise and allowed her to be quiet in the world. Aileen's love for Jimmy had been certain, but she had thought that his promises had been certain too and yet he had not followed through.

Now here was a man who was as quiet as her, a friend. Certainly a friend, if nothing more.

Chapter Thirty-Seven

The man at 7 Winchester Close, Wood Green did not pay for his package. He was a regular customer, not a notably friendly man, but he always paid. However, when Jimmy called on this particular day, he opened the door an inch with the security chain on, then stuck his hand out and grabbed the envelope from Jimmy's hand before mumbling, 'I'll pay next time. Tell Anthony I'm good for it,' then closing the door in his face.

Jimmy didn't know what to do, so he simply went back that evening as usual to give Anthony his day's takings and told him that the man in Wood Green hadn't paid.

His boss reacted with weary resignation more than anger. He shook his head and said, 'It's important that he pays, Jimmy.' Then, more ominously, 'You'll have to get the money out of him, Jimbo – this stuff is expensive. I can't be giving it away for nothing to every Tom, Dick and Harry who wants it.'

Jimmy reddened. Perhaps Anthony thought this was his fault.

'I'm sorry, Anthony – he had a chain on the door and he just grabbed the envelope and . . .'

The scarred ex-soldier looked at him and smiled.

'Jimmy, I know this isn't your fault, old chap. I am just pointing out that he *has* to pay, and as the chap on the frontline of all this, I'm afraid you're the one who is going to have to make him do it.'

Jimmy almost stopped himself short of saying, 'But how?' because he knew the answer, but it came out anyway. Anthony laughed.

'You'll find a way, Jimbo – I know you will. You're a bright boy – you'll work something out.'

The following day, Jimmy went back to Wood Green. His heart was pumping ten to the dozen as he walked down the High Road and across and over the suburban streets to the short cul-de-sac where this man lived and knocked on the door of number 7. Jimmy knew Anthony's customers only by their addresses; they were nameless people to him. He banged and banged on the door, then realizing that he would not be expected, he thought that perhaps the man was not in. He was turning away, almost relieved, when the door opened, again by an inch with the chain on. He wasted no time in jamming his foot in the door.

'What do you want?' the man said.

'I want Mr Irvine's money.'

'I told you he could have it next week.'

'Next week isn't good enough – he wants it today.'

'Who the hell do you think you are?' the man said, and he pushed the door into Jimmy's ankle. It hurt like hell and Jimmy felt anger rising up in him at the attack. He hadn't felt angry like this since the early days of discovering how he looked after the fire. The days before the deep sadness had set in.

Jimmy reached up his free hand and peeled off his mask to reveal the full horror of his face to the man.

'I am the man who has nothing to lose,' he said. 'Now go and get me Anthony Irvine's money before I break this door down.'

Jimmy had neither the intention nor indeed the physical where-withal to break down a door, but he was hoping his face would frighten the man into doing something.

The man took a good look at Jimmy's face and deep into his eyes, searching for some sign of real menace. Clearly he found none because he banged the door in two short sharp bursts on his assailant's ankle until Jimmy, yelping with pain, withdrew his possibly broken foot.

'Now piss off,' the man shouted through the letterbox, 'and come back next week, like I said.'

Jimmy was enraged and his ankle was swelling fast. He saw a gate at the side of the house and hopped over to it. It was open. He managed to put weight back on his bad foot and leaned over to a half-open window. Still clutching his mask, he started banging on the glass before peering in to see a woman, lying on a bed directly in front of him, looking at him, pointing and screaming. He realized that he had terrified the poor woman who, when she didn't get up out of the bed and flee, he realized must be sick. He began waving at her and shouting, 'It's all right. It's all right,' but the more he waved, the more hysterical she became, until the man he knew only as '7 Winchester Close' – her husband in all likelihood – came in and, giving only a pitiful, cursory glance at Jimmy, tried to calm her down. Jimmy saw him produce a white phial from his pocket as if he were about to administer it. Morphine. The cure for fear – as well as other things. Jimmy was shaken by what he had done and went back and stood at the front door hoping that the man would come out and confront him so he could apologize.

The man did come, and he handed Jimmy an envelope.

'I'm sorry,' Jimmy said. 'I didn't mean to frighten your wife like that.'

'There's her gold bracelet in there,' the man said. 'I'll have the full money in cash next week with interest and I'll be expecting the chain back.'

'There's no need,' Jimmy said. He had already decided he would pay the man's money himself to Anthony and pretend he had successfully collected it.

The man's face was set. 'Take it,' he said, 'and you can tell your boss you did your job and I won't be late paying again.'

'I'm sorry,' Jimmy said again. 'I didn't mean to frighten your wife—' but the man had already closed the door on his face.

All through his rounds that afternoon Jimmy felt sick at what he had done. Everyone else paid; as usual nobody looked him in the eye.

At seven o'clock, he returned to his bedsit and, still feeling impossibly sad at his behaviour that morning, took a shot of morphine. Not a full phial, but just enough to bring him up and calm the nervous fluttering in his stomach. Then he changed and, realizing that he had forgotten to eat for several hours, walked across to Manzini's.

Juliana brought him over a menu. 'You all right, my love?' she asked him. 'You look a bit tired. I'll bring you paper and nice plate of spaghetti, all right?'

Jimmy smiled at her. The morphine had properly kicked in and he was pleased to note that he had taken the perfect amount: he felt warm and happy inside and yet was still alert enough to read and enjoy the paper.

The first two pages of the paper always detailed the latest on the war, which Jimmy had no interest in whatsoever, so he flicked to page five, where they put something light-hearted to cheer up readers after the doom and gloom.

NEW SPECIES OF PLANT DISCOVERED IN IRELAND

A completely new species of plant has been discovered on a small island off the west coast of Ireland. The unusually hardy grass is not of a type that has been seen before anywhere in the world. It contains a seemingly unique metallic compound that causes it to glow gold under certain weather conditions. The locals have nicknamed the plant 'gold grass' and it was initially discovered by a young Irish woman who found it growing in the gardens of an abandoned house near where she lives. It was subsequently sent to Frenchman Dr François DuPont of the Botanic Gardens in Dublin to be researched. When its provenance was established, it was then sent to our own world-class botanists in London's Kew Gardens to have its 'new species' status verified. The new plant will be named 'Illaunmor gold' after the remote outpost of its origin.

The article itself was short, but even at that Jimmy's eyes barely skimmed the words; they were transfixed on the large photograph, almost a quarter-page of the broadsheet. Aileen was standing holding up a plant, and next to her there was a man who was tall and handsome and certainly not a monster like him. Aileen was smiling broadly. Even in the murky black-and-white he could see that her eyes were shining with joy. She looked hearty and happy, a million miles away from the pale beauty he had fallen in love with and yet . . . it was still her. She was still the woman he loved – it was just that life and time had passed, and he could clearly see from this picture that she had filled out and grown content. She had grown into the woman he knew she would and he was glad to see her happy. Except that here she was, thriving in the company of another man.

Jimmy knew Aileen would not wait for him, not after he had failed to rescue her family, not when he had survived and they had not. He had known too that she could not love him looking the way he did. His meeting with John Joe had, after all, clarified that for him.

Yet . . . and he reached up and held his hand to his heart and gripped that side of his chest in case it should burst clean out through his skin. Oh, and yet he still loved her and that love had kept some kernel of hope alive in the centre of his heart. Now that kernel had exploded and his heart was breaking.

It hurt and it hurt until Jimmy struggled to his feet and stumbled out of Manzini's and across the road to his bedsit.

He didn't bother picking the lock on Anthony's chest, but simply wrenched it open and took out a handful of morphine phials.

He took three, maybe four, maybe five – he didn't count or care what happened to him. He just wanted the pain to go away.

Chapter Thirty-Eight

'"Remote outpost"?' Biddy exclaimed. 'How dare they? The bloody English think they're the centre of the universe! That's why the world is in the state it's in – the English thinking they should be in charge of everyone.'

Biddy harboured the belief that, along with every ill in the world, this war was entirely the fault of the English. Neither her fellow islanders nor the amused Frenchman bothered disabusing her of the notion.

'Still,' John Joe said, 'isn't it great all the same, Illaunmor making it into the great *Times of London*?'

'Pfft!' It was François's turn for cynicism. 'Not such a great paper when they clearly care nothing about accuracy! 'World-class botanists in London's Kew Gardens'! They make it sound like they verified the whole thing. They did not! They heard we found something and asked for information, which, purely as a matter of some politeness to fellow academics, I sent to them. Then they tell *The Times* that the whole thing was their discovery. *Then . . .*' He was getting so worked up that Aileen tried to interrupt him, although she knew better than to try to placate him on his two Achilles heels – the irrational fear he had not yet earned the title 'World's Most Renowned Botanist' before reaching thirty and, of course, common – or in this case garden

– male pride. He held his hand up to stop her interrupting and continued on his rant.

'. . . "Frenchman," they say! "*Frenchman* Dr François DuPont", as if I am a Frenchman first and a botanist second – as if it is nothing. They say their "world-class botanists" are the most important. Well, let me tell you something about botany, the great *Times of London* . . .'

François went off into a rant that nobody understood, because, in his anger, his French accent took over until his English became more and more obtuse. It was almost amusing, except that Aileen knew about the worry that lay behind his babbling. As when the newspaper referred to his nationality, it highlighted to him the fact that while his countrymen were at war, he was here, in Ireland.

Aileen had come to grow fond of the Frenchman. Their love of plants and nature was undoubtedly unique. 'Ah – can you hear the crickets?' he would ask, and the two of them seemed like the only people to hear the precise chirruping sound. He taught her a huge amount about the plants she was tending and yet acknowledged her gardening and growing skills were greater than his own. The other women commented on how similar the two of them were: both given to long bouts of silence and eccentric outbursts. Aileen believed, from the way that he looked at her sometimes, across the room with a kind of quiet longing, that he might be falling in love with her. She was flattered by that; after all, François was an educated, handsome young man, a catch in many women's eyes, yet Aileen did not feel disappointed that he had not tried to kiss her. He was still weighing up how to approach her, and for her part, Aileen kept his advances at bay. She liked him, a lot, but he did not touch the tender part of her heart in the way that Jimmy had. Where a look or a soft word from him might snap her across the room and into his arms in an instant. Her feelings for François were those of kinship, respect, admiration and a cautious kind of love that was perhaps friendship, perhaps more. Only a kiss would give her the answer, and the fact that she was not anxious to kiss him was, perhaps, an answer in itself.

Sometimes, their working silence started to cloy and she felt he might lean in and approach her, so she would start asking him about himself. He talked about his family in France a lot, and the war. He had been confiding in her his worries about his sister, Vivette, fighting for the Resistance, saying that his brother was an idiot and could not look after her properly. 'Vivette is reckless,' he said, 'like you.'

'Do you not want to go back,' Aileen asked him once, 'and be with your parents?'

It was only after it had been said that Aileen understood how indiscreet it was of her to say such a thing and realized she had asked the question then to deflect attention away from her somewhat.

However, his answer hadn't provided the distraction she had hoped for.

'Of course I would like to go home to France,' he said. 'But I can't. My work, my research is here in Ireland and now I have . . .' He trailed off, but she knew what he wanted to say, even if he was afraid to say it.

At first Aileen was annoyed that François might use his feelings for her as an excuse for not going back to France, but at the same time she was secretly flattered for almost exactly the same reason. She must mean something to him – more, in any case, than she meant in this moment to Jimmy Walsh. Aileen had put aside her memories of him as best she could, but still in a hidden corner of her heart there was an ache for her first love.

Since François had come to her garden, Aileen's life had changed and so, in some ways, had she herself.

Aileen had been delighted and not entirely surprised to discover that her strange grass was an entirely new species of plant. François had taken the whole thing very seriously indeed, and when his fellow academics at Kew had verified the plant's status and *The Times of London* had sent somebody all the way out to the island to photograph them, Aileen had, despite herself, and to everyone else's surprise, been quite thrilled. The paper had asked for her to travel to Dublin, but Aileen explained to François that she could not leave the garden. Being a man who was obsessed with his own work, he saw no reason why Aileen's passion for hers should be interrupted when, if the paper wanted to photograph the plant, they could make their way across – as he had made his way here from Dublin. In any case, François hoped to interest the journalist in the magnificent display of wild flowers that Aileen had created and perhaps explain something of his own research to them during their trip. In the end, to nobody's surprise but François's, the young English reporter had no interest in botany and rushed straight back to his hotel with the photographer after asking the most cursory of questions. This foreign assignment was already peculiar enough given that there was a war on, without spending any more time in the company of this odd Frenchman, and there was plenty of black beer in the hotel bar before they left early the next morning for the ferry back.

François had left the island only once himself since the day he had set eyes on Aileen: to bring a sample up to Dublin and deliver a progress report to his fellow academics. By this time the thick stems that had appeared at the centre of each flower had simultaneously produced a bud. It was bulbous and grew to be the size of a large lotus bud in a matter of days. François noted that it was less a tightly wrapped bundle of leaves that one might expect to flower, but rather pod-like in shape and clamped shut. Although nature would surely open it in time, the mere sight of the huge pod ignited such curiosity in him that there were times when he was tempted to prize it open and set about it with his tweezers and microscope. If it weren't for Aileen and this ridiculous, romantic assumption that she, and her fellow superstitious islanders, had made that the plants were somehow connected to the spirits of their dead men, he might have done just that. Although such notions were an insult to science, the Frenchman had a higher level of empathy with the grieving women than he might have done in the past. After all, with his country at war, François was now under the constant shadow of receiving bad news from home. All the same, he thought it was a shame that an intelligent and talented person like Aileen should be so caught up in these silly ideas and notions about plants holding the spirits of people. It was the foundation of her Celtic island heritage, he knew that, but at the same time part of him wished she could share some of the more sophisticated ideas of his atheist academic background.

François spent four days in Dublin, then brought the plant back to Aileen and did not leave her side again. Being apart from this girl had brought about a kind of a sickness in him that François had not experienced before: a yearning in his stomach like his insides were being stretched and pulled. Then, when he saw her again, in the glasshouse, her fine white hands tucking soil in around the edges of some fledgling plant, the stretching stopped and all returned to normal and he felt like himself again.

François understood this feeling to be love, and while there were moments when he thought he might walk across and take her in his arms and kiss her – just like that – like a proper

Frenchman would do, there always seemed to be something to stop him. She would ask him a question, or it was suddenly lunchtime, or an interesting thing would have happened that she needed to show him.

He knew that Aileen's heart had been broken before – Biddy had told him about some fool in Scotland – but that was in the past. François was here now, he had means, he was educated, and the mere fact he was French was certainly more than enough to render him more desirable than the most dashing of Irishmen.

When you loved somebody, especially somebody as innocent and beautiful as Aileen was, you asked them to marry you before anything else – and so that is what he did.

François did not fully think through whether Aileen loved him back or not. She had given him no indication one way or the other, in truth. However, he was, in the end, a pragmatist and supposed that would be made clear in her answer to his proposal, which he made, quite out of the blue, in front of Biddy and a few of the women after they had had their midday meal.

'Well, Biddy, I must say,' said Fatima Murphy, 'I think this is the best bread I ever tasted.'

Mary Kelly studied her slice. 'Have you some class of herb in there?'

'Feverfew,' said Biddy. 'I don't know why but it peps me up.'

'Well, it's delicious – Carmel, be a good girl and hand me out another slice of it there.'

On top of this mundane talk Aileen smiled across at François, for no discernible reason, as she was wont to do, and he got a sudden burst of courage and blurted out, 'Will you marry me, Aileen?'

Aileen laughed. François was in love with her – of that there was no doubt. That they had never kissed meant very little to her. She liked François, very much. She knew that other people found him pedantic and thought his personality a little pompous, but despite that, she knew he had a sweet and thoughtful side. Perhaps the fact that she saw that in him was a kind of love. She had known true passion with Jimmy and she knew in her heart that she would never love like that again. He was her 'first love', as people called it, and although her heart believed that he was her only love, her head told her that François was a good man who loved her and that he would look after her, so she said, 'Yes.'

He smiled so broadly and for so long that for a moment each of the women got a glimpse of the handsome charmer they imagined all French men should be.

'Well, go and kiss her, then!' Attracta Collins said, and then the women started clapping and chanting, '*Ceád míle Pógues! Ceád míle Pógues!*'

'What does it mean?' François said, smiling, his day's work done in the proposal.

'"A hundred thousand kisses", you fool,' said Biddy, poking him in the shoulder.

He came across and kissed Aileen. He drew her into his arms in a flourish, then bent her across and kissed her long and hard on the lips. It was a masterful kiss, and not without tenderness or feeling, and when he was done, the delighted Frenchman turned to accept the cheers of the other women, bowing slightly, as if he had just earned some great accolade. He was bursting with joy.

Aileen swallowed her disappointment. As he was kissing her, Aileen was only reminded that this was not how things were meant to be. In the confidence of François's marriage proposal and her acceptance of it, she knew, for sure, forever, that Jimmy was lost to her now. He was never coming to claim her: he was gone and so was the certainty of knowing true love. The love that you didn't have to question, the love that was so certain from the start it felt as inevitable as breathing. Such love happened only once in a lifetime and Aileen knew she was lucky to have been given a second chance. François was no Jimmy, but nonetheless he had been sent into her life for a reason. A man who shared her interest in plants suddenly turning up in her hidden corner of the world was so unlikely there must have been some destiny at play. Perhaps her father and brothers were sending her a message of sorts. François had come here, after all, as a direct result of wanting to know more about 'their' plant.

Once Aileen agreed to marry François, things began to change very quickly. Within days François was talking about leaving and going back to Dublin. They would get married in the city, of course, a small church ceremony; he did not want any fuss. Aileen agreed insofar as she did not want any fuss either: she did not feel ready for a huge celebration after losing her family, but then, neither did she feel ready to leave the garden, let alone the island itself.

She told her fears to François, but he shrugged them off.

He told her that she was suffering from a mental condition called agoraphobia. 'It's a fear of open spaces,' he said, and she explained that she was not simply afraid of 'open spaces' per se but of leaving her garden. When he asked why she was afraid of stepping outside the boundaries of her self-created world, Aileen could not express why but remained adamant that her fear was so great she could not leave. The young Frenchman sent away to Dublin for a book called *The Psychopathology of Everyday Life* by the German psychiatrist Sigmund Freud. Aileen read the whole thing cover to cover and thoroughly enjoyed it. Regardless of the book's contents, which explained considerably more about François's obsessive behaviours and inability to relate warmly to people than it did her own fears, Aileen felt that merely the act of reading itself was doing her some good. For the first time since she had discovered this garden, she found herself able to sit for an hour, sometimes more, absorbed in the book while the other women worked around her.

'It's good to see you sitting down,' Biddy said. Privately she thought that perhaps this François character who was trying to take their lovely Aileen off the island and away from them all wasn't such a bad character after all. Aileen seemed more content, more settled since his arrival, and both she and John Joe only wanted what was best for their young charge.

'Perhaps you can call in to see your mother in Ballina,' Biddy said, within François's earshot, 'on your way to Dublin?'

'That would be an excellent idea, Biddy,' François said. 'It would be a good thing to get her "blessing", yes?'

Aileen knew her mother would be delighted to see her land on the doorstep with a betrothed. Biddy, John Joe and François all felt this was the best thing for her, and although she was not certain of her feelings for him, she also knew that she had to move on with her life. Aileen could not stay dreaming of Jimmy forever; she had to get on with her life and in order to do that she had to leave the garden and the island. It was the only way to expiate the demons of her father's and brothers' deaths. The only way was to keep moving forward.

As Dr Freud explained in his book, the only thing that was stopping her was the irrational fears of her own mind.

If only she could believe that this agoraphobia was all that it was, and that there wasn't something more powerful at play.

Chapter Thirty-Nine

Jimmy opened his eyes and his head was filled with a blinding light. Was he dead? Was this heaven? If it was, it hurt like hell.

As his eyes adjusted and the familiar institutional green of a cotton curtain came into view, he realized he was in a hospital. Was he still recovering from the burns? No – he remembered the pain from before, and if he remembered it, that meant it wasn't still there, which meant this must be a different hospital and a different time. The effort of working it out made him close his eyes again, but the light from the bulb above his head seared through his closed lids. Goodness but his head hurt. He felt nauseous and tried to sit up, but his limbs hurt too. Not in the sharp way from before, but a dull muscle ache. He felt his stomach heave, but there was nothing inside to come up, just a vague, empty stabbing feeling. He remembered he hadn't eaten for days: he had ordered spaghetti in Manzini's, but he had seen the picture of Aileen in the paper before it arrived.

Aileen – he had lost her and he felt the pain of that drench his spirits like a wave of acid. He remembered then how he had gone back to his room and taken two, three, how many phials of morphine? He had not been thinking about killing himself –

he had just wanted to kill the pain – but by God, he wished he was dead now.

'Hello, old man.'

Anthony was here. He remembered everything now: how he had upset that man's sick wife, that he had stolen drugs from his boss. He did not want to see Anthony. He did not want to see anyone. He wanted to get up and run away, but it was too late now. Why hadn't he done the job right and killed himself? Whatever was ahead of him now, he could not face it. He could not take any more disappointment or pain. Jimmy Walsh realized that was all that his life had amounted to these past few months: a series of false hopes followed by disappointments and pain. There was no doubt in his mind that he was better off dead, and as soon as Anthony Irvine had said what had to be said, and done to him whatever he was going to do, he was going to go off and do the job right. He would find the highest spot in London, maybe St Paul's Cathedral, and throw himself off the top of it and be done.

When Anthony Irvine had called round to Jimmy's to collect his money that night, he had not expected to find the scene before him. His young charge was stretched out on the floor; his mouth was stretched open in a grimace that highlighted his already macabre appearance, five emptied phials of morphine – enough to kill a horse – on the floor beside him. Anthony thought the boy was dead. His initial reaction was one of panic – the drugs! The chest! But then the boy's burned and disfigured face drew him back.

Anthony had earned his scar; there was no doubting that: when the bomb had exploded on the beach and he had fallen on the sharp rock, slashing his face, it had certainly hurt like hell. However, the physical pain he had experienced, even though it was in an act of heroism in which he had saved hundreds of lives and for which he had been publically rewarded, was nothing like the carnage that had been wreaked on this lad's face in his brave pursuit to save ten men who were already dead.

When they gave Anthony his medal, he couldn't wait to get back out there and prove himself again. Everyone thought he was a great man and he wanted more of it. Anthony was a born hero: saving people's lives was what he did. They brought him to McIndoe, but he said he didn't need any reconstruction – everything would grow back fine, which it did. Within four weeks Anthony Irvine looked battered but more or less back together and insisted on going straight back out into the field. His wound was barely healed by the time he was sent out on his next mission, but then he was a hero – what did people expect? An army psychologist examined him and felt that, given the severity of the explosion he had experienced, it was too early to put Irvine out directly into a warzone: his nerves might crack. Anthony assured his commanding officer that he was fine – stronger than ever. So when a promising young naval officer, Jack Hart, was taking a vessel out along the Irish Sea to disarm some errant mines that the Paddies were complaining they could see floating about their coastline willy-nilly, Irvine's bosses decided this would be a good introduction back into the field for him. Nothing too exciting, a soft intro back into the war. After all, disarming British mines was something he could do with his hands tied behind his back.

The two officers headed off in the boat and got on well enough, although Anthony felt this was a bit of a comedown for him and he resented somewhat being sent out on what felt like a baby-minding mission with a novice.

They sailed out, found the first mine and pulled it gently up to the back of the boat. While Jack went to check the engine, Anthony found himself staring at the rusted sphere: petrified. His hands shook as he forced himself to open the thing, and when he opened the mine and saw the wires and tried to fathom what went where, it was like a switch in his brain flicked.

Anthony knew he had lost his nerve, but he told nobody.

Only he knew about the nights when his body jerked awake with the memory of his pain on the beach as the shard of stone had seared through his cheek. Only he could remember the thunder of a large explosion reverberating through every vein, every muscle, every nerve in his body, snapping the very core of him in half so that he could never be fully repaired. The person he had become, the fearful shadow version of himself, could be disguised, painted over, but no matter how much he lied to himself about it, he would never be the same man again.

He pretended he was fine because he hoped that, once he got back out there, the hero magic would kick in. Only Anthony knew that it was *his* faltering hand, *his* fear in handling the explosives, in doing his ordinary job of disarming a mine – the thing he was trained to do and had done a thousand times before – that had caused the young naval officer Jack Hart's death. It had been *his* voice that had refused to make a sound when he opened his mouth to call out the warning to the young officer. With seconds to spare, Anthony had panicked: he jumped and swam and left the young officer to be blown to smithereens.

When he himself was found and rescued by the Irish coast-guard, clinging to the wreckage of their blown boat, Anthony knew Jack Hart was dead, but he could not admit what he had done – even to himself.

He told the Irish coastal guard Dan Murphy that he was certain Jack was still alive.

He made them search and search, and when the body did

finally turn up, he was not shocked that Jack was dead – only that his body was still in one piece. The power of the blast must have thrown him whole in the air. Perhaps he jumped after Anthony but had not got as far.

Anthony took his pension after that. Even a hero could only do so much active service. He told them the mine was faulty and that it had been shoddy workmanship that had killed his friend. Somebody was bound to ask how he had escaped the blast when his friend hadn't, so he went with the story that they had both jumped at the same time.

Anthony set about turning the army pay-off into more money. He was, after all, a war hero now – he had a medal. Aside from being a hero, making money was the only thing Anthony could think of to make himself feel better, to help him forget. Anthony could charm everyone but himself, so that's what he did. He found a couple of girls willing to work for him in exchange for generous salaries and protection. He inveigled himself into the lucrative underground homosexual scene in Percy's; he dabbled with drugs. Jimmy had been a real godsend because he'd been getting fed up with the delivery rounds and dealing with the customers. So Anthony Irvine became an arch spiv and lived out his seamy fantasies without giving much thought as to how he had come to be doing what he was doing until he found himself confronted with the possibly dead body of a young, disfigured Irishman who, like young Jack Hart, had fallen into his charge.

When he saw the twisted figure, the shattered cheek resting in a puddle of bile, what struck Anthony Irvine was not the pitiful sight in front of him but the cruelty in his own grotesque nature that had allowed this situation to happen – perhaps even encouraged it.

After all, Anthony had been invincible himself once: fear had turned him cowardly, and that cowardice had turned into bitterness and greed. He fed the bitterness and greed to keep it alive so he wouldn't see what was underneath it.

What was underneath it was the body of Jimmy Walsh: a brave young man, broken.

One part of Anthony Irvine – the drug-dealing pimp part, the man who had jumped ship and left a man to die – thought of clearing any trail of evidence leading the young Irishman to him from the room and walking away.

Then there was the other part of him, the man who had cleared a beach and carried a German bomb on his shoulder to save the lives of complete strangers. The man who had given little thought to his own well-being in the service of others until the unthinkable happened and he had discovered that he was as human and vulnerable as those people he was serving to protect.

Establishing that Jimmy was alive, he dragged him out of the small room and into the hallway, closing the door on the drugs. He called for an ambulance on the phone in the hall and then walked his young friend round on his dead limp legs until they came, to try and get him to regain consciousness.

He then went to the hospital with him and waited. He told the hospital staff that he was a neighbour of the young man and that he had called to find him in this state. He planted a couple of phials in his pockets so they would have enough evidence to know what was wrong with him – then he went back to Jimmy's bedsit and cleared out the rest of the drugs.

It was two days before Jimmy came round from his morphine coma and Anthony was there, waiting, when he woke up.

'Why did you do it, mate?' he said.

'I'm sorry about the morphine, Anthony. I'll pay you back. Every penny.'

Anthony waved his apologies aside.

'Why did you take all those phials? What were you thinking of? Be honest with me, Jimmy . . .'

Anthony had to ask, even though he was somewhat afraid of the answer the lad might give. If Jimmy told him the truth – about how he had been so miserably corrupted and addicted as a result of Anthony's vile exploitation of his innocence – it could be the truth that might save him from himself. Perhaps it might even turn him back into a hero. Hell, he'd saved the boy's life in the past two days – he was halfway there already!

Jimmy took a deep breath and said, 'It's my girl, in Ireland . . .'

Anthony almost laughed out loud – partly from relief. All this drama for a girl? God, the Irish were a romantic bunch.

'She's met somebody else.'

'Has she married him?'

'No . . . Maybe . . . I don't know.'

'Well, then you must go to her at once and find out, and if she hasn't married him yet, you must claim her. And if he *has* married her, then you must take her anyway!'

'I-I can't,' Jimmy stammered. He was confused that Anthony had not brought up the stealing. 'My job, the money – I can't go back.'

'Ah yes,' Anthony said, 'I forgot to say – you're fired, so here's your passage back to Ireland and some back pay.'

Anthony handed him an envelope. There was a lot of money in there. Jimmy knew by the thickness of the envelopes Anthony traded in. Anthony was right to sack him, but there was no need to pay him off.

The older man placed the white wedge on the bed and nodded at it. 'Once the doctors told me you'd be back on your feet, I took the liberty of booking you a ticket home. The train leaves Victoria tomorrow.'

Jimmy did not question being sent home. Some part of him, perhaps, knew it was the right thing.

'She wouldn't have me anyway – I'm so ugly.'

'You'll get uglier if you stay here,' Anthony said. 'Well, goodbye, old chap.'

He took up his hat and was about to put it on to say his final goodbye and leave when he paused.

'Let me tell you something, Jimbo,' he said, pointing his hat at the young man's face, and then before he spoke, he closed his eyes, paused again as if changing his mind, then eventually blurted out, 'It takes more courage for a man to face who he is than anything else. Medals, bombs, trying to save men from a burning building – all those acts of bravery don't mean anything if a man can't be who he is.

'You might be an ugly bastard, Jim, but be a man – go and face her anyway.' Then as he turned and headed out the door, Jimmy heard him say, more to himself than him, 'You'll be more of a man than I'll ever be,' before he headed back to his girls and his drugs in Soho.

Chapter Forty

'Is that all you're bringing?'

The women were all in the gardener's cottage saying goodbye to Aileen the night before her big move to Dublin. Biddy had had an awful job getting rid of François for the night: that young man seemed to have no understanding whatsoever of social etiquette. Women sometimes liked to gather on their own and it was the same with men. Maybe it was because he was French, but he was always hanging around Aileen's skirt tails. In the end, Biddy forced him on John Joe, who bluntly informed him they were going drinking in the hotel, even though neither man drank – although François was such awkward company John Joe seriously thought about taking it up for the evening.

As the women trooped in, Aileen's small case was already sitting by the door. She had packed only a few changes of clothes and her two gardening books. She would wear the dress and jacket John Joe had made for her on the journey, as François had arranged for them to get married on the evening they arrived in Dublin in a church near Kingsbridge Station. 'In this way we can go straight back to my lodgings and save booking into separate rooms.' It made sense.

Carmel gave the case a disparaging poke with her foot on her way in.

'That's not much of a trousseau!'

Aileen had come to realize that Carmel did not mean any nastiness with her harsh tone: it was simply the way that she was. In the same way that she herself could be withdrawn and, at times, sharp, Carmel was blunt in her manner. Everyone was different. Aileen had learned to look behind the facade. People were a lot like plants, she thought – plain, pretty, spiky or smooth. What you saw on the surface seemed to be everything and yet each living thing, even something as small and simple as a daisy, had a complex and miraculous life force pushing through it. Younger plants, like people, were tender and needed more care; older ones grew tougher skins and, sometimes, very sharp thorns. In the end, none of it mattered. No matter what people thought or felt, in the end we were all just vessels for the frenetic activity humming within us – life itself. A blade of grass and a woman, both could have the life crushed out of them. One by the simple stamping of a foot, the other by the cruel turns of life itself.

Aileen felt she had lost everyone she loved in her life and that was how she had come to love plants more than people. François was the only other person who seemed to understand that. She and he had a good friendship, so even if her heart was not entirely in tune with her head, she kept telling herself she would grow to love him as time went on.

'Carmel, watch your tongue!' her mother said then, with the other women gathered behind her. She came over and presented Aileen with a box. 'A wedding gift,' she said, 'from all of us.'

She peeled back the newspaper and inside the box was a piece of tapestry depicting the flowers from her garden, including the fat, rather ugly pod of their new discovery.

'We all did one,' Carmel said, '*even* Attracta – and she's got two left hands.'

'I don't know what to say,' Aileen said, and she didn't. Nobody had ever given her a gift like this before.

'I think "thank you" is what you are looking for,' said Biddy, afraid she'd fall out with them all – again.

Aileen was speechless and just looked at each of them and smiled. She was beyond sad to be leaving, not just her garden, she realized, but all of them. The garden had become her lifeblood, and these women, and their nurturing and their work and their soft company, had become a part of her too.

They ate heartily that evening. After the women left, Aileen went to her glasshouse to spend her last night there, her last night alone. She was dreading the next day. She had no idea how she was going to get out of the garden, never mind across the island and over the bridge. François had assured her that her fears were irrational, that although her terror felt real, it was all in her mind and that he would be with her every step of the way. François promised he would catch her and put her back together if she fell apart – which in her heart she knew she certainly would.

Aileen lay on the horsehair mattress and looked up at the navy sky and the dark grey shadows of the clouds moving across it: the world turning. She fell asleep listening to the crinkle of the vine leaves as they stretched and curled in the cooling of the day and the murmur of growth coursing through their stems: the sounds nobody else could hear.

Jimmy did not know if it was the wrong thing or the right thing to follow Anthony's advice, but he did know that he did not have a great deal of choice in the matter. He briefly toyed with the idea of going back up to Camden Town and taking his chances on the buildings again, or even throwing himself at Percy and seeing if the homosexual club owner might fix him up with some work, but in his heart of hearts, Jimmy knew that he had to get on that boat back home.

'Do you love her?' Anthony had said.

Jimmy loved Aileen; he knew that more than ever now. But he also knew that he had all but lost her. Like he had said to Mr 7 Winchester Close, he was a man with nothing to lose. He may as well go back and face Aileen and finally know where he stood. He would show Aileen his face and have her reject him or pity him or put whatever other heartbreak was coming his way in front of him, because until she did, Jimmy would still hold on to the tiniest shred of hope that she might still love him. Having hope, he had come to think, was the cruellest thing of all. Without hope, there was no pain. Without hope, he could be the shambling failure he was and live out his days hiding himself away in his parents' house on their small island. He could let loneliness fill his pockets with stones and drag him down to the seabed for all he cared.

Jimmy got off the boat in Dublin Port, then walked to Kingsbridge and boarded the next train to Westport. From there, in his London suit and with money in his pocket, he had no problem getting a taxi as far as Illaunmor.

'Where do you want to go on the island, son?' the driver asked.

Jimmy didn't know.

They were at the bridge, and as the driver pulled up, Jimmy began to shake with fear. Aileen was somewhere on this island. He had been driven here by some strange despondent longing placed in him by Anthony. Jimmy had come for the want of anything else to do, anywhere else to go. It felt like this was the end of the line. If Aileen rejected him, his worst fears for himself would be realized, and she would, surely, reject him.

'Is there someone in particular you're looking for, son?' the driver asked again. 'If you give me a name, I'll probably know where to find them.'

'No,' Jimmy said quickly, 'nobody in particular. You can just let me out here.'

Agoraphobia is a very serious condition, a kind of madness, and the behaviour of people suffering with this could be very extreme. François knew that and yet he had not bargained for Aileen's reaction when he took her out of her garden.

Although he was happy to pay for a car to come and take them from the garden all the way to Westport, John Joe and Biddy had insisted on taking the horse and cart as far as the bridge. François had conceded, even though he felt that the less they had to get in and out of vehicles, the easier it would be for Aileen, but it seemed these island people were full of all sorts of superstitions and customs that he was expected to go along with, even if it was just for Aileen's sake. In truth, he had started to find them a little annoying. Very annoying, actually. The quicker he got his wife-to-be away from this backward place and into the civilized world of culture and academia and the everyday machinations of city life, the better.

When Aileen reached the wall of the garden, it was as if her body was being filled with the black toxic smoke of the fire that had destroyed her life, that the despair had filtered into her very organs from her soul and was poisoning her from the inside out. Her mind kept telling her it was all right, move, move, move forward, but the rest of her did not believe it. As had been the case on the day her mother left and she had been unable to cross the bridge, every fibre of her being seemed to be hauling her back into the safe confines of her garden. To the others, she simply turned into stone. Short of tugging her or lifting her – neither of which he wanted to do for the sake of their dignity and his pride (was he forcing her to leave after all?) – François had the idea of asking her to shut her eyes. 'Trust me,' he said. 'Nothing bad is going to happen.' Gently her fiancé led her as far as the cart, where John Joe lifted her in.

As they drove through the island, Aileen became more and more distressed, moaning and rocking and digging her long fingers into François's arm so hard that he feared her nails might cut through the fabric of his wool jacket. 'Breathe deeply,' he kept saying. 'It's all in your mind, Aileen. There is no danger. Your fear is irrational – it is not real.' His reassurances didn't seem to be working, and by the time they were within sight of the bridge, François was beginning to get seriously concerned about whether he was doing the right thing. Firstly in taking Aileen off the island – perhaps she was more entrenched in these naive tribal customs than he had thought – but also her behaviour was making him wonder if he wanted to marry somebody who was quite possibly more unstable than he had realized. Aileen was beautiful and she had an innate understanding of botany and was undoubtedly gifted with a talent for plants, but really, he was beginning to think that the girl did not have a rational bone in her body. He had supposed he loved her because he had never experienced the feelings of warmth or companionship with anyone else, and Aileen was mesmerizingly beautiful – like the most exotic flower. However, this, this *carry-on*, as he had heard Irish people describe indescribable behaviour, was not something he had bargained for when he had asked her to marry him.

'I can't do it, François. I can't. I can't cross the bridge,' and she threw her head onto his shoulder, afraid to look up.

'You'll be fine – really. Everything will be fine, Aileen.'

Biddy looked back and gave him such a look, like this was all his fault, which, in a manner of speaking, it was. John Joe pulled the cart over to the side of the road. These two people cared for Aileen a great deal and François could see that they loved her. He thought about his own parents and how they worried about him.

'I'll be good to her,' he said to John Joe. 'She'll be happy with me. I promise you I will make her happy. She'll be fine once we get onto the train. I am sure of it.'

He was sure of no such thing.

Aileen's body beside him had gone from tense and stiff to shaking and limp, almost as if she was too exhausted to fight anymore, as if the fear had won. François led her from the seat to John Joe, who gingerly lifted her body down like a child and put her standing on the ground by the bridge. François took her arm and readied himself to walk her across, but as he did, Aileen lifted her face and he saw a change move across her. She cocked her head to one side and seemed to be looking intently at something on the other side of the bridge.

As François followed her stare, he saw a figure, some thirty feet away at the end of the slatted path, making strange movements around his head. Aileen was momentarily mesmerized and calm. Curious himself, François let go of her and quickly slipped on his strong glasses. As he looked across, he saw there was a man who was peeling a mask from his face. Before he could fully comprehend the grotesque disfigurement of the man's face beneath the mask, François's senses were overwhelmed with a scent so powerful, so sweet that he thought he might fall to the ground in a dead faint.

This was the first day that the women had been in the garden without Biddy or Aileen. Each of them was determined to keep things ticking along as normally as possible. Attracta Collins had taken charge of the kitchen and was lighting the outdoor fire ready to put on the stew that Biddy had prepared for them, while Noreen swept the cobbles. Even though Biddy had left everything perfect for them, the women were determined that she would come back from her ordeal of saying goodbye to Aileen and find the place . . . well, even more perfect than when she had left it. All the other women were in the vegetable garden, picking and preparing their produce for the day.

'Shh,' Attracta said. 'Do you hear that?'

'What?' said Noreen.

'I don't know,' she said, confused herself. 'A sort of . . . nothing?'

The silence was eerie. The sounds of nature – bees buzzing, birds tweeting and leaves rustling – had entirely stopped. The almost indiscernible symphonies of nature that we feel more than hear – sap rising, the fluttering chatter of flowers, woodlice scrabbling, worms burrowing – had also ground to a halt.

Into the unnatural silence came a noise from the vegetable garden: a low moan from the women calling out together. Noreen and Attracta rushed towards the others, but as they reached the edge of the low-walled beds, they hit a wall of perfume so strong and sweet that it stopped them in their tracks. Their mothers and sisters were kneeling on the ground, gazing in awe at the sight in front of them.

The pods of all ten plants had flowered simultaneously and their open leaves were sending a fragrance out across the entire island so sublime that afterwards there was only one description that any of the islanders who were there that day could put to it: pure love.

Aileen immediately realized the figure was Jimmy. Her legs, which had been so obstinate, were suddenly filled with flight as she ran towards him. She ran with the lightness and speed of wind in a summer storm. The bridge, the sea and her fear all crumbled to ash in the backdraught of her urgency to be with him.

Without words she threw herself into his arms and he gathered her up as if she were as light and as beautiful as an armful of forest bluebells.

'Jimmy, Jimmy, Jimmy . . .' She said it over and over again until each word caught the tail of the last and sent a thread of tunes skywards to catch the very sun.

'I'm back,' he said. 'I told you I'd come back,' but he was crying so hard that he just held her until he was able to gather himself.

When his grip finally loosened, Aileen drew back and looked at him. Somewhat confused, she put her hand up to his face.

'I heard you were badly burned,' she said. 'You look fine to me.'

For a terrible moment he thought she was being cruel, but then he looked into her eyes and could see from their soft humour that she was serious. She could not see his disfigurement, only the Jimmy she had known from before. So that when she touched his damaged cheek, Jimmy actually felt that his face had been restored: his skin was smooth, his eye fully sighted and his mouth plump with one side a perfect match for the other. Nobody else saw what Aileen saw: to the world, he was a severely disfigured young man with tragedy written across his face. In actual fact, Jimmy's disfigurement was always there. Nonetheless when they saw each other again, in that moment, it was as if the fire had never happened, as if the intervening time and pain and life-changing events they had both experienced since first meeting one another had simply melted away. There was only the miracle of love: that was all that existed between them.

*

While the scent of the mysteriously opened flowers seemed to pass Aileen and Jimmy by, it precipitated a series of events for everyone else on the island.

When the perfume hit François, for the first time in his life the Frenchman found himself contemplating the nature of love. He could see from the way that Aileen fled across the bridge towards Jimmy that this was the thing they called love in action. His overriding thought was not that he had lost the woman he was about to marry, neither was it a curiosity about the overwhelming and unmistakably exotic floral scent that had all but knocked him to his knees. François found that his first thought when Aileen fled to Jimmy was of his country and how it had been lost to Germany – then for his family and how he wished only to be with them in France.

Aileen and he exchanged goodbyes, while the boy with the disfigured face stood behind her.

'I'm so sorry,' she said. 'I feel I have let you down.'

'Not at all,' he said. 'I can see . . .' and he trailed off because he was not entirely sure what he could see.

'We'll stay in touch,' she said.

'Ah yes,' he agreed, 'certainly,' although in his heart he knew this would be the last time he would see the first girl he had learned to adore.

Epilogue: The Miracle

François returned to Dublin on the next train, resigned his position and returned to his homeland, where he fought with his siblings in the Resistance. Professor DuPont fought more bravely than was expected of him by everyone else. Aileen and François kept in contact by letters sent a few times a year. She was glad that he survived the war, and his entire family stayed intact too, which was a miracle. François did not return to Ireland after that, but took up a professorship at the Sorbonne and married a plain young Catholic girl called Marie. Marie adored him and bore him no less than six children. François, despite retaining a somewhat distant and analytical disposition, was a good husband and father.

Biddy remained in the gardener's cottage, and the Cleggan women continued to work together on the garden. Together they ran the shop and cafe. The garden became a popular tourist attraction, especially Illaunmor gold, with its single mysterious, exotic pod that never opened since the day Jimmy Walsh came to claim his love on the bridge. Nonetheless, the story spread into legend and visitors came from all over Ireland hoping to be the lucky ones loving enough to make the plant open.

The mysterious flowers on Aileen's 'gold grass' had closed again by the time they all returned to the garden that day and looked just as Aileen had left them that morning. Some people said that the women had hallucinated that day, that grief had heightened the imaginations of the already superstitious islanders and made them think the plants had opened and sent a scent out that healed everything. Grief is powerful and it makes people do strange things, they said.

Aileen was as astonished as everyone else by the women's claims, but in truth, the opening of the flowers, their provenance, their alleged scent meant little to her because now she had her beautiful Jimmy back and that was all that mattered.

However, whatever anybody said, Biddy *knew* that what she had experienced that day was a miracle, and the biggest miracle of all was how the miracles just kept coming.

The first was that she was exonerated from any wrongdoing in a court in Dublin over the Cleggan tragedy. There was a crack in the chimneybreast through which the smoke was seen to have escaped and the courts decided that it had been the landlord's responsibility to ensure that the fireplace was either in proper working order or closed off. When the fireplace had been checked immediately after the accident, the flue had been recorded as open – as it should have been. Biddy vaguely remembered checking it after Aileen had left for the pictures that night, but in the fuss after the fire, she must have doubted her actions.

John Joe travelled with Biddy to Dublin and stood by her in court for the day. He was a great friend, and that was *another* miracle, that she had a nice man in her life with whom she could be friends but who didn't bother her looking for any of that 'other nonsense' that she had never had any interest in pursuing. Afterwards, they had celebrated with tea in Bewley's on Westmoreland Street before collecting a friend of John Joe's who had travelled over from London on the boat. A very nice man called Mr Neville who had written to say he would like to come and spend his fortnight's holiday on Illaunmor. His visit precipitated the greatest miracle of all in Biddy's eyes. Mr Neville never went back home to London but 'fell in love with the island' and stayed right there in the house with John Joe. As a result, the three of them became the best of friends and Biddy found herself living out her years with not just the support of one nice man, which was more than any woman could ever hope for, but two good male friends flanking her in church each Sunday. God was surely good – they all agreed.

After the day they found each other again, Aileen and Jimmy never parted. They were married within the week, and the wedding breakfast was in her garden.

Even though autumn was under way, the garden seemed to have more colour and life in it than when it was in the heyday of voracious summer blooming. The hedges and pathways were a tapestry of red and gold, and on the ground was a carpet of soft, damp leaves. Aileen, Biddy and each of the ten women carried posies picked from the wild-flower beds and tied with silk ribbons by two of the younger girls.

John Joe went into overdrive transforming one of his late mother's nightgowns into a magnificent dress for Aileen *and* he gave her away in church. 'A man of many talents,' all the women had agreed, wishing their own husbands could be as versatile and useful. Jimmy had his suit from London with him, but he chose instead to wear a plain brown wool jacket that had belonged to Aileen's brother Martin. It had been John Joe's idea and he had altered it so that it was a perfect fit.

Sean and Morag came from Aghabeg – both in a state of shock and delight that their son had returned. Although Morag was smarting that he had not returned sooner and to her house first, and that he was wearing a jacket not chosen by her, she waded in with Biddy and John Joe and made sure her presence was felt.

Biddy had her work cut out cooking on the stove, even with all the women helping.

'It's like the loaves and the fishes,' she exclaimed.

'Except with sausages and soda cake,' Morag added, as the two women flew around the place handing out food to the hordes of hungry guests.

The whole island came, at least partly to witness the miraculous flowers, which had closed again into their tight pods as suddenly as they had opened for the moment when Jimmy and Aileen had met on the bridge.

During the service Jimmy had a moment of wondering if this was really happening to him.

'I do,' Aileen said. '. . . In sickness and in health, till death us do part.'

He had been so certain, since the first day that he saw her on the beach. Now, after all that had happened, despite his disfigured face, she was certain too. Life was strange and unpredictable and he knew he was no longer invincible. Except in the eyes of the woman he loved, and, it seemed, that was all that mattered after all.

The autumn colours in her garden that day signalled to Aileen that her story there had come to an end. As the two of them drove off together in John Joe's cart, she turned to wave and thought she saw, through the courtyard, the desolate, empty space the garden had been the day she first saw it.

As she looked back, for a moment she felt as if she was looking into her past and she knew it had been her lost hope that had built that garden. She had found her hope again and knew also that, while she would never forget the garden and the events that had led her there, there was no going back.

Aileen did not return to live or work in the garden after that. She had neither the desire nor the need to be there anymore. Whatever she had grown in her glasshouse, whatever journey she had taken, was now complete. Instead, she moved back into the home she grew up in with her new husband and began to restore the cottage, the garden there and her life. Aileen recovered a friendship of sorts with her mother, and when she met her new baby brother, she realized how much she wanted her own child, a new life with Jimmy.

Jimmy fished the shoreline along Illaunmor and returned to his strong, confident self. He dived straight and fearless off the rocks into the deep salt pools, and when he was underwater swimming, the shoals of mackerel flicking across his damaged skin, he felt fully alive again. His disfigured face became of less importance to him until it was of no importance at all; eventually he himself failed to see anything when he looked into the glass except for the determined shining blue of his own eyes that indicated to him that he was maybe not invincible, but as good and as strong as a man needed to be.

With the Cleggan compensation money, the young couple bought a fishing boat, and not long after that the children came: three of them in quick succession. Once a year Jimmy would go and collect his parents from Aghabeg and bring them back to his home on the 'big island'.

As they drew past the beach, Jimmy would take his children up to the front of the boat and say, 'Can you see your mammy?'

Then there she was just as he remembered from the first time: Aileen, her long red hair flickering like a fire on the beach.

And all he would feel was the miracle of loving her.

Author's Note

This book was inspired by a tragedy that happened in Kirkintilloch, Scotland, in 1937, when ten Achill Island tattie-hokers were tragically killed in a bothy fire. The story was so moving that I found myself researching it further and it became the inspiration for what went on to become *The Lost Garden*.

Out of the greatest respect to the families and descendants of the Kirkintilloch Ten and the people of Achill, I have taken great pains to ensure that this book is entirely a work of fiction – set at a different time and with no reference whatsoever to the actual people involved. Therefore any similarity to any characters alive or dead is entirely coincidental.

What I hope I have captured, in the broadest sense possible, is something of the resilience, humour, generosity, intelligence and unique beauty inherent in the people who live and have lived on the islands off the west coast of Ireland.

The men who died in the bothy fire included three sets of brothers: John McLoughlin (twenty-three) and Martin McLoughlin (sixteen) from Saula; Thomas Kilbane (sixteen) and Patrick Kilbane (fourteen) of the Points, Achill Sound; and John Mangan (seventeen), Thomas Mangan (fifteen) and Michael

Mangan (thirteen) from Pollagh. The other victims were Thomas Cattigan (nineteen), Achill Sound, Owen Kilbane (sixteen), Shraheens, and Patrick McNeela (fifteen), also of Shraheens.

May their souls rest in peace.

Glossary

Alp – a big, lumbering idiot
Amadaun – an idiot
Boreen – a narrow, frequently unpaved, rural road in Ireland
Boxty – a traditional Irish potato pancake most popular in Mayo, Sligo and Donegal
Currach – a type of Irish boat with a wooden frame covered by animal skin
Fore graipe – a person in charge of the welfare of the tattie-hokers, including their nourishment and the upkeep of their lodgings
Geansaí – a sweater
Jackeen – derogatory term for a Dubliner
Month's mind – a requiem Mass celebrated one month after a person's death
Pampooties – shoes made of rawhide, commonly made and worn in the Aran Islands, Ireland
Praties – potatoes
Sandspit – a point of sandy deposit built up into a landform that projects into a body of water
Scut – cheeky lad
Shoal – a sandy elevation at the bottom of a body of water, constituting a hazard to navigation
Skite – a large quantity
Tea brack – a traditional Irish tea loaf

Acknowledgements

Special thanks to Joe Lavelle and his beautiful Dughort Campsite in Achill for his hospitality and to fellow writer Grainne Dargatz for her help in sourcing Brian Coughlan's excellent document/book *Achill Island tattie-hokers in Scotland and the Kirkintilloch Tragedy, 1937.*

Thanks also to Killala friends and neighbours Jimmy Gallagher and Marie Sweeney for their insights into island life.

My friend Aideen Ryan, gifted gardener, botanist and Irish heritage buff, was a constant source of inspiration, ideas and refreshments! Thank you, Aideen.

Thanks to my wonderful editors, Natasha Harding and Trish Jackson, and all at UK Pan Macmillan: Katie James and the talented PR and marketing teams, publicists, cover designers and proofreaders, who always put so much effort into my books – thanks to you all.

Agents Marianne Gunn O'Connor, Pat Lynch and Vicki Satlow for their constant input and support.

Alan, Enda, Diane, Anne-Marie and all the staff at Dillon McCarron Accountants, Ballina, for their patience and kindness towards me as their office squatter.

My wonderful mother, Moira, for her ear and her encouragement as always.

Niall, my other half, for his endless support, and his mother, Renee, for all her practical help.

The staff and board of the Tyrone Guthrie Centre, Annamakerrig, and the Heinrich Boll Cottage for providing wonderful places in which to write.

Lastly to Danielle Kerins, my incredible assistant and all-round Girl Friday – for research, proofreading, editing, hand-holding, promoting, administering and overall support the likes of which has never been known before. I feel very fortunate to have 'discovered' you and your input made a real difference to this novel: it is as much your book as it is mine.

Johnny Ferguson

1963–2013

The Irish screenwriter Johnny Ferguson died while I was writing this book and I want to acknowledge the contribution he made to my work in general and this book specifically. As well as a gift for writing, Johnny had the screenwriter's nose for structure and plot and the copywriter's gift for 'snap'. He was generous with his advice and time, and as a writer as well as a dear friend, I will miss him dreadfully.

References

If you are interested in learning about Kate's references and inspirations, you can go to her *The Lost Garden* Pinterest page.

All online links to Kate's social media sites and books are available through her website, www.katekerrigan.ie

ELLIS ISLAND
by
KATE KERRIGAN

ISBN: 978-0-330-50752-3

**She was living the American dream in the 1920s
but her heart was still at home . . .**

Ellie and John are childhood sweethearts. Marrying young, against their families' wishes, the couple barely survive the poverty of rural Ireland. When John is injured in the War of Independence, Ellie emigrates 'for one short year' to earn the money for the operation which will allow him to walk again.

Arriving in Jazz Age New York, Ellie is seduced by the energy and promise of America. When the year is up Ellie chooses to stay, returning to Ireland only when her father dies. A trunk full of treasures helps fuel Ellie's American dream, but as the power of home and blood and old love takes hold she realizes that freedom isn't the gift of another country, it comes from within.

CITY OF HOPE

by

KATE KERRIGAN

ISBN: 978-0-330-51699-0

An uplifting, inspiring and heart-warming story of a woman truly ahead of her time. Of loves lost and found, of courage and determination.

It is the 1930s and when her beloved husband, John, suddenly dies, young Ellie Hogan decides to leave Ireland and return to New York. She hopes that the city's vibrancy will distract her from her grief. But the Depression has rendered the city unrecognizable – gone is the energy and party atmosphere that Ellie once fell in love with, ten years before. And while she is used to rural poverty back home in Ireland, the suffering she sees in New York is an entirely different proposition.

Walking around the neighbourhood, Ellie sees destitute families and hungry children on every street corner. The horror of it all jolts Ellie out of her own private depression. Pushing thoughts of her homeland and her dead husband firmly out of her mind, she plunges headfirst into her new life to try and escape her grief. All her passion and energy are poured into running a home and refuge for the homeless. Until, one day, someone she thought she'd never see again steps through her door. It seems that even the Atlantic isn't big enough to prevent the tragedies of the past catching up with her . . .

LAND OF DREAMS

by

KATE KERRIGAN

ISBN: 978-1-4472-1081-8

**1940s' Hollywood.
A new Life. A new love.**

A mother's love, a woman's ambition and a Hollywood romance in a time of war. *Land of Dreams* is the stunning third novel in the Ellis Island trilogy.

Ellie's idyllic and bohemian family lifestyle on Fire Island is shattered when her eldest son, Leo, runs away to Hollywood to seek his fame and fortune. Ellie is compelled to chase after him, uprooting her youngest son and long-time friend and confidante Bridie as she goes.

Ellie fashions a new home among the celebrities, artists and movie moguls of the day to appease Leo's star-studded dreams. As she carves out a new way of life, Ellie is drawn towards intense new friendships. Talented composer Stan is completely different from any other man she has previously encountered, while kindred spirit Suri opens Ellie's eyes to a whole new set of injustices.

Ellie sees beyond the glitz of 1940s' Hollywood, realizing that the glamorous and exciting world is also a dangerous place overflowing with vanity and greed. It is up to Ellie to protect her precious family from the disappointments such surroundings can bring and also from the more menacing threats radiating from the war raging in Europe.